GAS GIANT GAMBIT

GAS GIANT GAMBIT

A TALL TALE FROM BEYOND THE CYGNUS RIFT

E.S. RAYE

ALEX PARKER

PUBLISHING

WWW.ALEXPARKERPUBLISHING.COM

First edition, 2025

Alex Parker Publishing

16755 Von Karman Ave, Suite 200 Irvine, CA 92606

www.alexparkerpublishing.com

For my wife, Jessie,
around whom all my worlds turn.

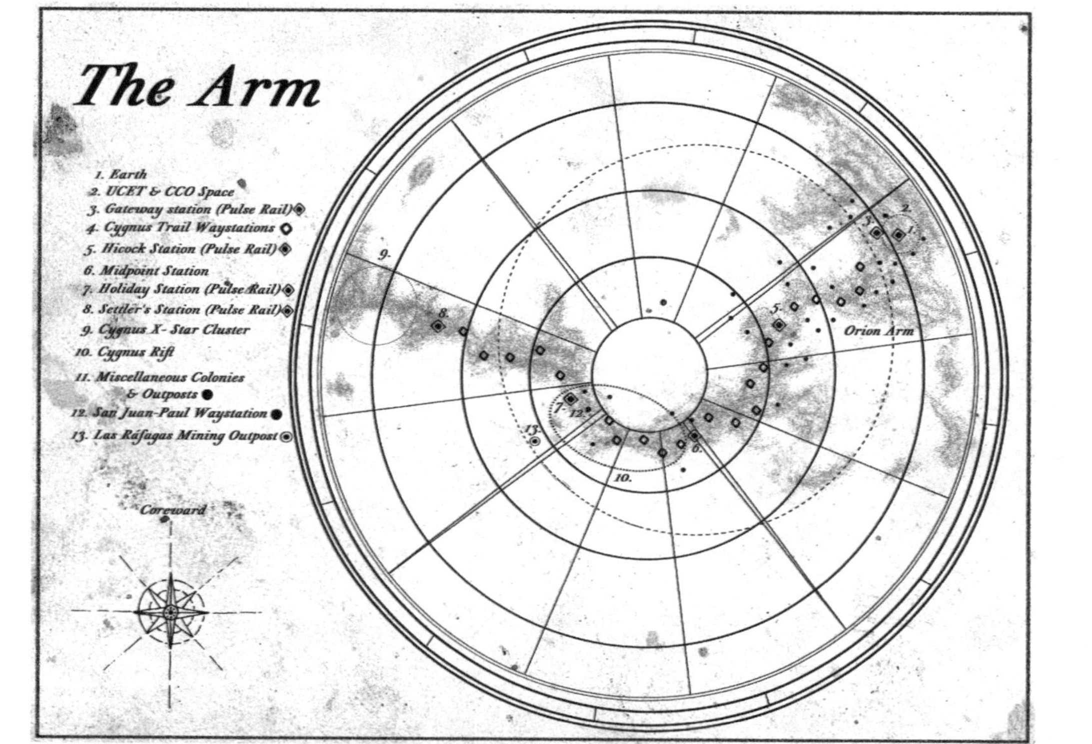

The Arm
1. Earth
2. UCET & CCO Space
3. Gateway station (Pulse Rail)
4. Cygnus Trail Waystations
5. Hicock Station (Pulse Rail)
6. Midpoint Station
7. Holiday Station (Pulse Rail)
8. Settler's Station (Pulse Rail)
9. Cygnus X- Star Cluster
10. Cygnus Rift
11. Miscellaneous Colonies & Outposts
12. San Juan-Paul Waystation
13. Las Ráfagas Mining Outpost
Orion Arm
Coreward

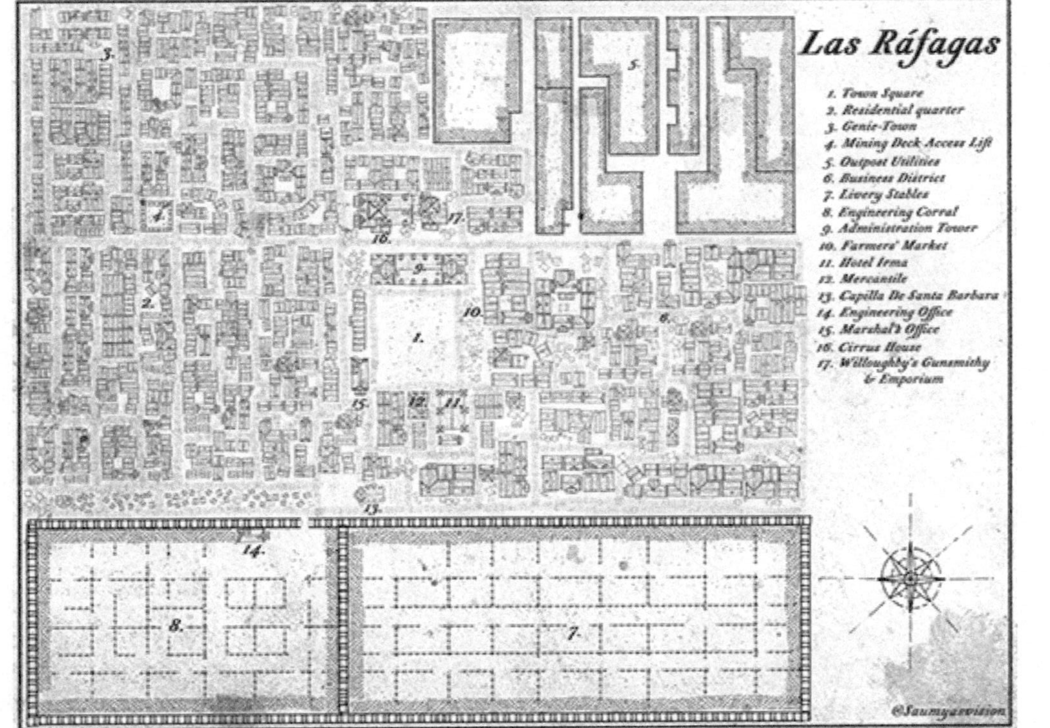

Las Ráfagas
1. Town Square
2. Residential quarter
3. Genie-Town
4. Mining Deck Access Lift
5. Outpost Utilities
6. Business District
7. Livery Stables
8. Engineering Corral
9. Administration Tower
10. Farmers' Market
11. Hotel Irma
12. Mercantile
13. Capilla De Santa Barbara
14. Engineering Office
15. Marshal's Office
16. Cirrus House
17. Willoughby's Gunsmithy & Emporium
@Saumyasvision

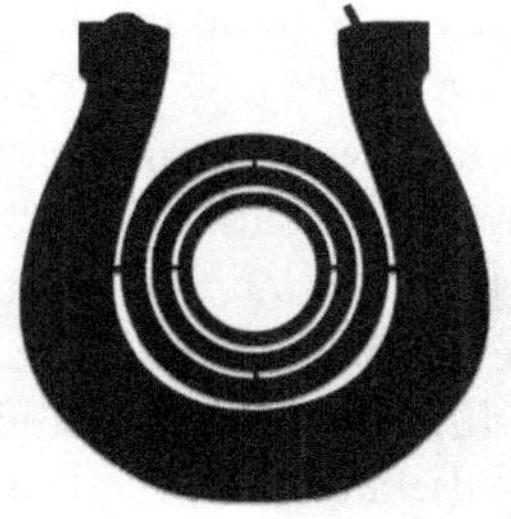

A FISTFUL OF SPOONS

In a flash of white light, *Matilda* dropped from her FTL sprint into a lazy, subluminal canter. Alone in the void between stars, the three rings of her engine gimbal slowed and locked into their flat, standby position. A small pony-mount built for one, she had a long horseshoe-shaped body that wrapped around her engine. Old, beat-up, and with more than a few custom parts, she wasn't much to look at, but she served her master well. Aesthetics didn't count for much to drifters on the Orion Arm.

"Hey, *hermana,* why'd we stop?" Tuco called from the engine room. "We ain't there yet."

The young woman at the yoke's reins leaned back in the saddle and stretched. *I ain't your damn sister.* She worked her gloved fingers deep into her dark curls and massaged light-years of tension from her scalp. Still, it was better than the name she'd left behind—a name she'd never use again. Better to stay the anonymous drifter. Easier to avoid attachments.

Matilda forced air through her ventilation system in a series of dissatisfied grunts. With a roll of her eyes, the drifter sighed and tied her hair back into a bushy ponytail.

"I know, girl. I know," she said as she patted the controls affectionately. "*Tilly* needs a break," she called back to her passenger. "We've been riding her too hard. I don't want to bake 'er." She unhooked her spurred boots from *Tilly's* yaw stirrups and slid from the drive saddle.

The drifter stepped into the engine room without needing to duck under the low hatch. She crossed her arms over the chest of her ancient, patched flight suit and eyed her partner. The dusty pink stains on her left glove stood out against the faded green of her coveralls.

"Alright Tuco, let's have it. Why did you drag me all the way out here? What's at these coordinates?"

Tuco, a small, sweaty, middle-aged man with an unkempt goatee and a mop of greasy black hair, wore his old Cepheid 2248 pistol in a cross-draw holster at his belt buckle. A bandolier of coolant capsules hung across his barrel chest and a long, black, hooded duster covered his overweight frame. The two had worked together before, and while the drifter didn't always like Tuco's methods, he'd never swindled her out of her fair share.

"The Hippotes System," he said. "A red giant with only one world. A gas ball called Aeolus." He stood up from *Tilly's* guest bunk, jammed into the corner of the small engine room.

"Great." She leaned against the bulkhead and pulled a small tin from one of her flight suit's many pockets. "Quit stalling and get to the point. What's out here?" She popped the tin open, and the deep, earthy aroma of ground tobacco filled the recycled air.

"Las Ráfagas Outpost. An old rubidium-87 mining and refinement depot inside the gas giant's atmo. Supplies fuel to all the Cygnus Trail waystations this side o' the Rift."

She nodded and took fresh leaves from the tin and rolled a pair of tight cigars with the confidence of a well-practiced routine. "The San Juan-Paul fuel clerk mentioned it. Said they never got their last shipment from Las Ráfagas and couldn't top me up. *Tilly's* running low. Bounty job?" She lit both cigars with the flick of an old silver lighter and handed one to Tuco.

"*Si,*" he grunted and took the cigar. Tuco shuffled to a window and peered into the void. "Bounty-head's a rob." *Tilly's* environmental control console beeped gently before exhaust fans in the floor and ceiling spun up and whisked the acrid smoke away.

She frowned and took a long drag. "A rob? Don't tell me we're working for the copperheads."

"Hey." Tuco glanced around the messy engine room. "It may not be for me to say, *hermana,* but you're almost down to the blanket 'round here. Ain't that why you took the job? Take the spoons and be glad for it. Besides"—he turned back to the window—"no, it ain't for the CCO. But a family that *lives* in the Orion Colonies did post the bounty, *si.*"

"Any idea what kind of reception we can expect from the locals?"

Tuco sucked on the cigar and coughed hard. "The outpost's privately owned, and my source says the admin's got no love lost for the UCET. Locals are all ranchers and miners. Nothing we can't handle."

"Marshals?"

Tuco laughed. "Since when do you care about that? It ain't nothin' but a backwater. One marshal, no deputies. We'll be in an' out before anyone notices we're there. Easy."

Tuco shuffled his feet and hunched his shoulders. Her eyes narrowed as she handed him a cracked ceramic bowl littered with old butts. "What aren't you telling me, Tuco?"

He stared out into the expanse. "*Nada, hermana.* Besides, you know the deal."

She sighed and nodded at the back of his head.

Of course. They had a simple arrangement, each with their role to play. Tuco showed up with a job and she provided the transport. That way there could be no double cross. The details he had already given her were more than she usually got. And she *did* need the money. Credit spoons meant fuel for *Tilly*, and a full fuel cell meant freedom for her. Everything else not helping her stay alive—and stay free—might as well be dust in the void.

A rob from the CCO. It couldn't just be a runaway—no one paid this big a bounty for that. The damn thing must have killed someone when it ran. The United Colonies of Earth and her Territories and the Confederate Colonies of Orion may be at war, but returning wayward property still paid the bills.

Still, Tuco's fidgeting had her hackles up. She'd never call Tuco *calm*, but this ...

Pivoting back to the saddle, the drifter took her own gun belt down from its hook and strapped it on her left hip. A satisfying *click* rang as the pitted U. S. Army buckle latched. When she turned back, Tuco was leering at her. His cigar cherry glowed brightly against the black beyond the window. "That *pistola*—you ready to sell 'er to me yet? Never seen anything like it. It's a collector's dream."

She pulled Delilah from her holster and held it up. The gun resembled something in an Old Earth sci-fi serial, but with more industrial elements—like a row of exhaust ports running along its left side. The colors had faded and chipped over the years, but someone had once painted a shark's grin on the side opposite the exhaust that was still visible.

"Name your price," Tuco said. He'd been obsessed with Delilah since the first time he laid eyes on her.

The drifter turned the heavy gun over in her hands. How many bad jobs had Delilah gotten her out of? How many times should she have died, were it not for the heat of that pink beam? She had no greater ally—save *Tilly*—and the mount hadn't been with her as long. She dropped Delilah back into her holster. "Not a chance, Tuco. There's no price. Call it a family heirloom."

Tuco *harrumphed* and turned back to the window. "One day, I'm going to get that gun," he muttered. "Can we get moving? I want to get this bounty-head and get out o' there as fast as we can."

"Gotta give *Tilly* a little while longer to cool off. Then it's two more sprints to the coordinates—your Las Ráfagas."

"Podríamos hacerlo en uno si no mima su nave," Tuco mumbled.

"Yeah, we probably could do it in one if we pushed hard. But even with a full fuel cell, *Tilly's* gimbal would be too burned out to leave the system, let alone sprint us the kiloparsec back to CCO controlled space. What's your rush?"

He waved his hand dismissively and kept his eyes on the stars.

Her brow furrowed. "Seriously, Tuco, what's wrong with you?"

"Nothing, I—" *Tilly's* proximity alarms cut him off with a squeal.

The drifter's heart leapt into her throat. *"What did you do?"* she shouted as she shoved Tuco out of the way to peer out the window. Flashes of light, like fireworks, went off all around *Tilly.* A dozen mounts sprinted in and more came with every flicker of light. Another flash lit the hide of one and showed off a five-pointed star. *"Tunk,"* she spat. The San Juan-Paul Waystation bulls—law enforcement on the Cygnus Trail. Their ponies were small, smaller even than *Tilly,* and well beyond their usual range. *Damn bulls must have pushed hard to catch up.* No way they could chase if she ran. Especially if she gave them something to do.

She turned on Tuco and grabbed him by his duster. *"What did you do?"*

Tilly's communications array crackled as the bulls hacked in. *"Attention Steeldust Class-A Transport 94517. By the authority of the San Juan-Paul Marshal's Office, you are hereby ordered to cut all engines and prepare to be boarded. You are under arrest for the murder of Abraham Wallis and the robbery of the Cygnus Union Coach. Comply or be fired upon."*

Tuco shrugged. "I couldn't help it," he said with a smirk. "He practically begged me to take it."

"Oh, you impulsive son of a—"

Tuco's hand dipped toward his gun, but she got there first. His smirk deepened as she shoved the barrel of his own gun in his face.

"Where is it? Where's the damn spoon?" She turned over his bunk, careful to keep an eye on him. A mess of dirty clothes and tack fell from the cot. She kicked through it with the toe of her boot until she found it: a small metallic credit spoon marked with the Cygnus Union logo.

"Now, let's not do anything too hasty," Tuco said. "You and I been in worse scrapes than this. We can fight our way out!"

"Not this time, *pendejo. Tilly's* rifle turret is stuck seventeen degrees off-center, we're halfway to the middle of nowhere with low fuel reserves, and I'm not risking my neck because you can't keep this"—she waggled his gun at him—"in your damn pants. Into the pod." She waved the pistol at the escape pod bulging from the wall.

"Come on now, *hermana*. Be reasonable."

"Reasonable? *Reasonable?* Oh, I can be reasonable." She walked him backwards toward the pod and grabbed an empty spoon and transfer pad from a shelf. The spoons clicked into their ports on the pad with magnetic ease. "Thumb. In the spoon."

"*Hermana ...*" Tuco's voice turned menacing.

"Don't think I won't end you with your own beam-shooter. Thumb. *Now.*"

"*Attention Steeldust Class-A Transport 94517,*" the hacked comms squawked. "*Shut down all engines and prepare to be boarded.*"

After a moment's hesitation, Tuco put his thumb in the hollow of the Cygnus Union spoon. A cheerful *ding* sounded and the transfer began. "*Puta,* how much you takin'?" Another *ding,* followed by *transfer complete.* The drifter slammed the heel of her boot into Tuco's chest, hard. With wide eyes and a breathy *oomph,* he fell back into the waiting escape pod. With a shrug, she tossed his gun in after him as the hatch sealed.

"Since you rutted up the deal I agreed to, I've taken half what you stole," she said and pressed the transfer pad against the pod's window for Tuco to see. "I'd say that's only fair, since it's less than half what you promised me for this trip."

"Why *you*—"

"I'm also charging you for parts and labor on the pod. Which, by the way, I bought on the cheap and modified extensively to fit *Tilly.* I'd button up if I were you. I can't promise all the seals'll hold."

Tuco's face fell into naked panic. *"Puta loca,"* he spat and scrambled to seal up his duster. He dropped his burning cigar on his chest but managed to close up the coat and pull its wide hood over his head.

The drifter watched him with something akin to amusement. "Happy trails, Tuco."

His sweaty face twisted with rage as the life support systems woven into his clothes engaged. In the next instant, the pod jettisoned, trailing his curses into the black.

Her traitorous partner seen to, the drifter sprinted back to the saddle room and swung herself into *Tilly's* drive saddle. She clicked her spurs into the yaw stirrups, warmed up *Tilly's* FTL engine, and flipped the comms transmitter on to hail the approaching bulls.

"Hi there. This is Steeldust Class-A Transport 94517," she said with the sweetest voice she could muster. "You'll find the party responsible for the charges you've laid out in the escape pod in my dust. Turn your sensors to the object 0.47 kilometers off my right-rear quarter. That's your man."

"Attention Steeldust Class-A Transport 94517. All parties onboard are under arrest. You have five seconds to shut down your engine or you will be destroyed. I ain't gonna warn ya again, little lady."

"That's right, officers, Tuco Benedicto Ramírez. That's your man. No need for a reward, I'm just happy to do my civic duty. Safe travels!" With one practiced motion, she flipped off the comms and kicked *Tilly* into an FTL sprint.

Tunk!

The drifter slammed her fist down on the saddle horn. Tuco had been an impulsive bastard for as long as she'd known him. *Christ's blood,* they'd met when he tried to steal from *her.* He thought he'd found an easy mark and ended up with a broken wrist for his efforts.

Tuco had approached her with this job back on Gateway Station, fifty parsecs from Earth and on the edge of the Old Colonies of the UCET and CCO. She had hesitated then. Under normal circumstances, the bounty would have been worth the trip, but crossing the Cygnus Rift with Tuco gave her pause. At over a thousand parsecs to the target coordinates, it would take *Tilly* more than a month to get there. Plenty of time for Tuco to do something stupid.

But the money had been too good to pass up. So, she'd convinced herself she could keep Tuco in line long enough to get paid. He'd brought the job, after all; she didn't think he'd want to sabotage it. Taking the job had been a bad idea. Dumping Tuco to the bulls before getting the details was worse. Without more info, she'd never find the right rob—free robs were a dime a dozen on this side of the Rift. Her recklessness had created her nightmare scenario: stuck out in the middle of nowhere, low on rubidium and spoons, with the bulls on her trail and her job prospects gone.

Outside the saddle room canopy, rivers of light flowed past *Tilly* as the engine gimbal warped the fabric of spacetime around her.

She couldn't turn around. If she headed back to San Juan-Paul, she'd be arrested as soon as *Tilly* popped up on their scope. But the bulls' smaller and slower ponies had no chance of catching up if she ran *Tilly* hard. Messages could only travel as fast as the mount carrying them, so the bigger the head start she got, the longer she could stay ahead of the law.

As far as she could see, that left her with two options.

She could turn back toward the Cygnus Trail and try to double back across the Rift by sprinting past San Juan-Paul Station—doubtful, given *Tilly's* low rubidium stores. Or she could head on to Las Ráfagas and try to refuel at the mining depot. If she pushed *Tilly* to the point of exhaustion, she could make it in one sprint, like Tuco had suggested.

She didn't like her choices. If she pressed on, the bulls would know her destination. There were only so many places to hide out here. But with a full fuel cell she could lose them in the void. Risky, but better than turning around to play Ha Ha Herman with the law.

Air rushed through *Tilly's* environmental system like a complaint. The drifter patted the control panel. "I know, girl. I'm sorry. But we don't have much choice, do we? Hold on for me and I'll get you fixed up and fed. Then we can plan our next move." *That* would likely involve the frontier colonies in the Cygnus X star cluster. Not her preferred place to settle, but laying low on some backwater frontier world for a few months while the heat blew over would be a vacation compared to one of the UCET's "rehabilitation" programs.

She squeezed her spurs to make a minor course correction, then slipped from the saddle and headed for her bunk. The engine would need some babying on the long sprint ahead. Better to get a nap in while *Tilly* was fresh.

Blaring alarms woke her an instant before *Tilly* rocked violently and the drifter was thrown from her bunk.

What the tunk?

Tilly had been sprinting for days and, so far, handled the stress of it well. But her endurance had worn thin. The drifter had expected some resonance vibration and high gimbal axis temperatures, but nothing like this.

A foul vapor was pouring from a broken seal on a coolant pipe in the engine room. Coughing through the caustic gas, she threw her weight against the system's shut off valve. The hissing leak slowed; the fans in the floor and ceiling spun up to gale force, venting the gas into space. She held her breath until *Tilly* scrubbed the air. With fresh oxygen filling her lungs, she ran a system diagnostic. *Tunk.* Something had been weakened when she launched Tuco's pod and ruptured under the strain of the prolonged FTL sprint.

She dropped into the saddle and wiped sweat from her brow. *Too close.* Running *Tilly* this hard would create enough problems with the engine; she didn't need to lose any more coolant, too. She rested her head against the control console and sighed.

As if on cue, the pony rocked and threw her from the saddle. "What now?" she spat and scrambled back into the seat.

They were coming up on Las Ráfagas's coordinates, but the center ring of the engine gimbal had seized and locked into position. It was going to be a rough reentry.

The bubble of light cocooning *Tilly* through her FTL sprint burst, exploding white brilliance throughout the sector as she tumbled—uncontrolled, powerless, and blind—back across the light barrier. Even through the savage tailspin, the drifter couldn't help but notice Aeolus. The gas giant's bands of yellow, red, and rust orange dominated the view through the canopy.

By the light of the planet, she flipped open an access panel behind the main control console and tried to hotwire the backup power. Sparks flew, but the lights came back on, and with them, a whole new set of proximity alarms—*Tilly* awoke unhappy to find herself about to burn up over Aeolus.

The drifter climbed back into the saddle and fought to reclaim control as they screamed through the planet's upper atmosphere. Turbulence shook *Tilly* again and another warning light blinked in angry scarlet. *Hide breach.*

Reaching for an old, dirty-gray poncho hanging from a pressure valve, she draped it over her shoulders and pulled the hood up.

"Dangerous atmospheric change detected," a cheerful voice said into her ear. "Enacting emergency protocols. Prepare for pressurization and life support initialization." She braced as her flight suit inflated and an energy field came down across the front of her hood.

Her hands flew across the controls, flipping switches, slamming buttons, and rerouting power. Finally, *Tilly's* atmospheric thrusters kicked in, but by then they were falling too fast and too steep to pull out of the dive. *Always knew I'd die alone. At least* Tilly's *with me.*

In spite of the thought, she dug her spurs in, pulled back on the yoke's reins with all her might, and prayed.

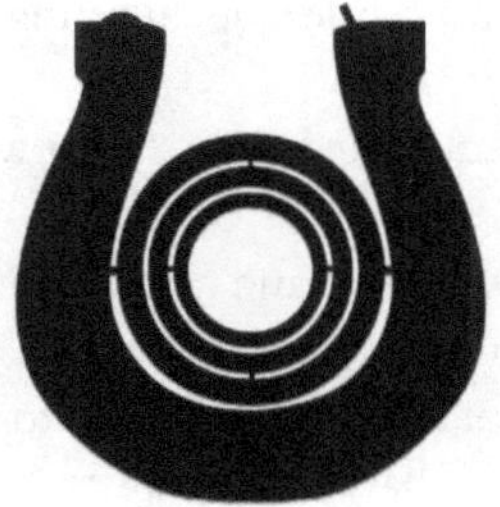

ONCE UPON A TIME IN THE CLOUDS

The drifter managed to pull *Tilly's* nose up, but they were falling too fast for the thrusters to regain control. Burning atmosphere obscured the canopy in shifting streams of red and yellow. The light played across the controls like a campfire as she fought the planet's gravity well.

"Come on, come on," she pleaded as she yanked uselessly on the reins.

A shadow passed over the canopy, so briefly she thought it was a trick of the light. But it returned, matching *Tilly's* speed as she tumbled through the clouds. It was enormous, dwarfing them in its shade. It orbited the falling pony, like a cat circling an injured mouse. And, like a cat, it vanished as suddenly as it had arrived.

A new shadow, this one much smaller—smaller than even *Tilly*—and moving with more purpose, replaced it. A distant voice fought to be heard over the static on the open comm array. "H-y Gu-! -an you -ear -e? If you -an, cut y-u- thr-ster- on th- count -f ..."

She slammed her fist down on the transmitter and screamed into the intercom. "Unidentified vessel, this is Steeldust Transport *Matilda* requesting immediate assistance! Please repeat your last!"

The speakers crackled. *"Three! N-w, -us! Cut your thru-ter- now!"*

Cut thrusters? What was this fool going on about?

Before she could decide if her would-be rescuer was crazy or just plain stupid, coiled steel netting draped over her canopy. *That's it, he* is *crazy.* She shut down *Tilly's* atmospheric thrusters before they could burn through the net. *The crazy bastard is gonna drag us* both *down.*

Immense blue lights flared in the murky clouds above—her rescuer's atmo-thrusters. *Tilly's* were feeble by comparison. The pony's descent slowed until they came to a gentle stop, hovering among the clouds.

Maybe not so crazy after all.

"Wow!" The comms squawked again. "Th-t w-s a clo— one! You alrigh- -own there, Gus?"

Gus? "Yeah, just a few bumps and bruises. Nothing a drink won't fix. Thanks for the save, friend."

"Happ- to be of ser-ice! I'm reading d-mage to your fl-ght systems. How 'bout a tow? The chief an- I have a cho— to attend to, but then –'re heading back -ome for some break–st. You're welcome – join us."

Tilly's gauges indicated minor hide breaches and secondary systems down across the board, but the worst damage was reserved for the engine gimbal. The innermost ring had seized, the bearings were warped, the coolant system had a leak the size of her fist, and the FTL fuel cell was nearly dry. Thruster fuel, more efficient than rubidium, remained at 67 percent, but she'd burned the thrusters themselves so hot on reentry, their housings were melted and useless.

She slammed her fist against the console. *"Tunk!"* Repairs like this would take time and would be more spoons than she could afford. *Tilly* nickered and the drifter's fist softened.

"Yeah, I know." She laid her hand flat on the controls. "Got no choice. Besides, frontier town like this has got to have a crack engineer, right?" Air blew through *Tilly's* vents. "Right," she said with a sigh.

"C-me agai-? -idn't -atch that," spoke the voice over the comms.

"Yes, thank you. Can you take me to Las Ráfagas?" She didn't like being in people's debt, but she'd be happy to repay this favor.

"May-e you should co-e -ack to the homestead first," her savior said after a short pause. "Come on up. You'll be more co-forta-le with us."

Grumbling, the drifter took a few moments to hunt for her rarely used boots' EVA booster attachments. After shimmying out the spent escape pod hatch and using the boosters to reach the hovering mount above, she met her rescuer face-to-face.

To her surprise, she found a rob at the reins. She'd seen his kind be-fore—an early android model, mostly human sized and shaped. He stooped to get through the saddle room hatch.

"Name's Maurice," he said, extending a long, elegantly crafted hand, "but my friends call me Moe! Put 'er there." His silvery fingers were scratched and corroded. Soft cloth, stained the color of oatmeal with time and who knows what, concealed the rough edges of the joints and servos at his shoulders and chest. It gave the impression he wore a snug, well-tailored vest.

She pulled her hood down, shook his hand, and craned her neck to look up into Moe's eyes. A screen on the front of his head displayed the image of a calm, sun-cracked middle-aged man's face. He smiled and his simulated crow's feet and laugh lines became deep canyons around his eyes.

Experience told her that countless synthetic neurons fired across a nine-lobed multiquark IPU behind that screen. Probably an older model—tetra, by her reckoning. The multiquark artificial brains far outperformed the older positronic models, but they had a bad habit of developing emotions after a few years. Those emotions often led to robs *reevaluating* some of their core Asimovian programming. Sometimes they turned into violent psychopaths. Most of the time, they just got a taste of free will and did something unexpected, like shipping out to the frontier to earn a wage as a farmhand. Either way, it was only a problem if they came from the CCO, where they were still nothing more than property.

Thus, the war.

"Thanks for the save back there. Thought I'd be chewing gravel for sure."

"Always happy to lend a helping hand, Gus!" Moe's simulated smile deepened as he released her hand.

"Gus?"

Moe adjusted a scuffed bowler cap and tugged on his trousers in a remarkable recreation of nervous embarrassment. "I, er—ah, that is to say—"

"Moe had a bad crash a few years ago," a little boy piped up as he stepped out from behind the rob. He was maybe eight or ten. "Some of his wires are a little crossed, that's all. Whenever he tries to say anybody's name but his own it always comes out 'Gus.'"

The rob sighed, blushing slightly. "It's a name-specific form of aphasia, and an embarrassing side effect of the treatment I received after my ... *accident*. Besides, all you doppels look the same, anyway!" he said with a wink. "This is Gus Gus, the son of my employer."

The little boy stepped forward and offered his own hand. "Hector Vega."

An aphasic rob and his little boy sidekick. And she thought she'd seen all the Arm had to offer. She took Hector's hand. "Doppels?"

"It's what the robs and genies here call regular people," Hector said and rolled his eyes.

The drifter snorted. *Doppel. As in, doppelganger.*

"Can't say I've heard that one yet. I'll admit, you had me worried for a second there with that rescue," she said to Moe. "But only someone with all their nuts tightly screwed could have pulled that off. I thank you." Moe blushed again.

Gus. The drifter tried the name on for size, mulling it over and rolling it around her mind. It fit like the stiff leather of a new holster. It needed time to break in, time she didn't have. Best start thinking of herself as Gus as soon as she was able.

"As for the name," she said, "'Gus' will do fine."

The drifter—*Gus*—took in the cramped quarters of their mount. Far smaller and even more spartan than her own pony, it featured a saddle room, a ring-shaped engine room wrapped around an FTL gimbal a quarter the size of *Tilly's,* and those oversized atmo-thrusters. A farm mule—small, powerful, specifically designed for the gas giant's gravity and atmosphere—and probably mostly used for chores around the Vega homestead.

Greasy handprints caking the gimbal axis cover suggested the old mule's tiny FTL engine hadn't been operational in a while. Someone had used the coolant system control panel as a workbench as they tinkered with the engine. Maybe repairs were ongoing.

"You're lucky we spotted you. We don't usually come out this way, but we're chasing a wayward greenbottle jelly calf lost in the hydrogen flats," Moe said as he climbed into the mule's saddle. "We've got to get this babe home before she's burdle food. We can talk with the boss about getting you and your pony to Las Ráfagas once she's safe with her brood-sisters."

Great. Every moment passed like a falling domino. "Any way I can convince you to take me straight to town? I can pay," she lied. A longshot to be sure—these agro-types get pretty attached to their livestock—but free robs could be unpredictable.

Moe's face lit up with a smile. "Sure thing! If it's that important, we can get you there—"

"Moe," Hector interrupted, *"Papi* said..."

"Uh—" The rob's face flickered. "Sorry, ma'am. I'm not only responsible for corralling our lost calf, I'm also answerable to this boy's parents when it comes to his well-being. They'll want him home lickety-split. If it's all the same to you …?"

Tunk. She waved him off. If it weren't for the boy, it might have worked. Going hand to hand against Moe wouldn't do the job, either. She'd tussled with robs like him before and knew there was little to no chance she'd overpower him. Even if she did, then what? She leaned against the bulkhead and gazed out the window. Maybe helping would make the task go faster.

"So, what's a greenbottle jelly?" she asked.

"That," Hector said, pointing through the window to a fluorescent green dot in the hazy orange-brown clouds that looked like debris.

That's alive? They closed in on it fast, and Gus got an eyeful. The creature floated under a sail-shaped air sac at least ten feet tall. Beneath the green balloon-sail hung a relatively small, bulbous body and dozens—if not hundreds—of filament-thin tendrils that flowed in the air currents behind the animal. From the top of its sail to the tip of its tendrils, the thing stretched well over a hundred feet.

That's a calf?

"Hey, Gussy," Moe cooed tenderly to the monstrosity outside. He pulled up alongside it and shifted the mule into a parking hover. "You've got to learn to stay close to your brood-sisters when the wind picks up, girl." He turned to Hector. "Ready, chief?" The boy nodded enthusiastically with a bright grin. Moe slid out of the saddle and Hector climbed in. "Now"—the lines in Moe's face deepened as he smiled at the boy—"remember to be gentle with the yoke's reins. Wait until I've got the lariat on her securely. This isn't like when we caught her with the net last week. If you pull too hard, it'll tear—"

"*I knoooow,* Moe," Hector whined.

"Alright, but watch out for—"

"Come *on,* Moe!"

"Alright, alright." Moe chuckled. He pointed to the gun at Gus's hip. "Are you any good with that?"

She nodded slowly. "Good enough." An odd question. What could she possibly need Delilah for out here?

"I could use your help. If you don't mind." He shuffled past her toward the rear of the mule. "We usually use that net for wrangling lost jellies, not rescuing core-bound ponies in distress. I gotta get up top and do this the old-fashioned way, and I could use a lookout."

Atop one of the small mule's platforms, Gus readjusted her hood against the gusting wind, the magnets in her boots clinging to its steel hide. Her HUD struggled to make heads or tails of the swirling gases. Moe stood on another a few feet away, nearly invisible in the soupy clouds. From her vantage, Gus couldn't see *Tilly*, dangling like salvaged scrap beneath the mule, but she could hear the overbuilt atmo-thrusters roaring as they fought to keep both mounts in a stable hover.

"I'm gonna rope Gussy," Moe called out over the din of the engines. "You keep an eye out for—" A violent rush of wind swallowed his last word. Her hand instinctively dropped to her hip.

Moe opened a panel in the mule's hide and pulled coil after coil of braided steel rope from the hidden compartment. He tied it into a loop, and with one hand holding his bowler cap in place, swung the lasso over his head in a wide arc and tossed it smoothly at the giant green calf. As the lariat landed neatly around Gussy's sail, a dark shadow moved through the gas and caught the attention of Gus's HUD. She stared into the clouds, but nothing materialized.

"Okay, chief, let's reel her in. Easy now, Gussy," Moe shouted over the thrum of the thrusters and blowing wind. Hector kept the mule perfectly steady as the big animal bucked and rolled while a winch hidden inside the mule pulled her in.

Another shadow slid through the clouds. Gus squinted in the gloom. The atmosphere's particle density was too high for her HUD to identify it. *Another jelly? Maybe not.* The size and shape were wrong, and it moved against the wind.

She slid Delilah out of her holster as yet another shadow circled. "Ah, Moe?" A third and fourth shadow glided through the gas. As the latest shadow passed near the mule, Gus caught a glimpse of strange, faint flashes of colorful light within it. *Definitely not a greenbottle jelly.*

They were surrounded. Each shadow silently blinked intricate patterns of light into the clouds. Finally, one of the shades approached, cutting through the thick gas like a plow. Instinctively, Gus raised Delilah.

"It's alright!" The rob appeared at her side, laying one hand on her shoulder and the other on the big gun. While he could rip her arm from its socket if the fancy struck him, his eyes remained calm and reassuring, his touch gentle and almost comforting. Wary of both Moe and this new threat, Gus holstered Delilah but kept her guard up. "You might want to look away for this next part."

"I'll be fine. I've been in plenty of fights."

Moe's smile somehow deepened. "That's not exactly what I meant." Then his face-screen went completely blank, like a light burning out.

The rob faced the approaching shadow, and his screen exploded with flashes of brilliant color. The incredible display of colors from across the spectrum—some Gus had never seen before—was so bright, every wisp of cloud stood out in minute detail. Instantly, the HUD dropped its solar filter to protect her eyes.

The approaching shadow replied with flickers of its own. Finally, a skiff, built for gliding and hovering through thick atmospheres, burst from the clouds. It was perhaps fifteen feet long and about three or four feet wide, with four pairs of nearly silent helicopter rotors running from stem to stern, and a single, gigantic harpoon at the bow. Six creatures stood inside the open dinghy. The flashes of light came from what Gus supposed could be considered their heads.

"Sorry about the fireworks. I had to let them know who we were as quickly as I could," Moe explained as his face continued to blast out flashes of color. "The Deiopeans don't like it when folks from Las Ráfagas drop in unannounced." Gus's hand again drifted to her hip. And again, Moe's hand gripped her shoulder. "It's alright." The skiff sidled up to the mule and three Deiopeans hopped aboard.

Gus's skin crawled.

When humanity expanded out from the cradle of Earth, it brought all sorts of critters onto the Arm. Many of those animals were brought on purpose—pets, livestock, beasts of burden. Many more were brought by accident—the creepy-crawlies that found their way into everything humans do and make. These always gave Gus the willies. Few things sent a cold shiver down her spine quite like opening a shipping crate to see a fat spider run out to take up residence in *Tilly's* nooks and crannies.

Besides, spiders were bad for the hive.

When child-sized, bipedal spiders scurried over the mule's back, Gus's blood ran cold and her fingers inched toward Delilah. Moe squeezed her shoulder gently. *Hold,* the squeeze said. *Hold, all is well.*

The Deiopeans' fuzzy hides ranged in color from reddish brown to deep black. They walked upright on their hind-most legs and wore floor-length, hooded robes equipped with two pairs of sleeves. A gust on the breeze shifted their vestments and revealed a third pair of smaller, almost vestigial arms concealed beneath the material. They each carried a long object that Gus couldn't identify at first.

What the tunk is *that?* Her eyes rolled over its cylindrical length, and it dawned on her. *It's a rutting* rifle. *The damn thing's designed with four arms in mind.*

The lead creature stepped forward with its hood down. A distinctive white line ran down the middle of its face to a set of powerful and menacing jaws. The line separated ten pairs of eyes, each set a different size and shape, all with an odd crystalline structure. The eyes flashed brilliant colors in intricate patterns, somehow the source of the light.

As the lead Deiopean conversed by light with Moe, they both gestured vaguely toward Gussy. The jelly bobbed gently next to the mule, securely lassoed, docile as a lamb. The conversation appeared to come to an amiable close as Moe extended his hand. It split between his middle fingers; the part grew until his entire forearm, elbow to palm, divided down the middle. With his two right hands, Moe clasped wrists with the Deiopean. They flashed colors at each other in a clear call-and-response. Finally, the spider-like creature released Moe and directed their companions back to the skiff. Silently, all the shadows turned and drifted back into the clouds.

The wind picked up; the clouds parted and moved westward, fast. Gussy's tendrils steamed behind them. Crisp blue skies above met Gus's eyes, and a vast vista of table-flat clouds slowly swirled in red and orange hurricane-like mesas in the gas layer below. Gus's breath caught in her throat.

Six or seven Deiopean skiffs rapidly disappeared into the distant sunrise.

"What was that? What did he want?" Gus asked as they secured the calf to the mule's flank.

Moe's cheerful cowboy face reappeared. *"They,"* he corrected. "The natives don't have gender the same way doppels do. They come from Aeolus's moon, Deiopea," he said, and hooked a thumb over his shoulder. The moon hung low in the sky, massive and close. "We chased Gussy into the hydrogen flats. We're in their hunting grounds and they wanted to know why. They've been having problems with ... poachers."

The skiffs descended into the lower layer and vanished into a twisting cloud the color of new rust.

"What do they hunt?"

As if to answer her question, an enormous iridescent green and blue geyser burst from the table-like gas layers below and gushed into the sky in the distance. Squinting, she brought her hands to her brow. The HUD zoomed in. It was a flock of some kind, and the Deiopean skiffs chased it—no, they herded it like a pack of wolves stalking buffalo.

As the flock zigged left, a single member zagged right. The Deiopeans were on it, chasing it toward another skiff lying in wait. Gus zoomed in further and strained to get a clearer view of the creature they hunted.

Moe finished tying off the greenbottle jelly and joined her. "There's really no human word for them," he said. "The Deiopeans call them"—Moe's face momentarily changed to a mass of swirling blue and green dots that moved like a flock of birds or school of fish—"but we've mostly taken to calling them *burdles.*" *Sounds like something Hector came up with back in his crib.* As Gus finally managed to center the creature in her field of vision, she had to admit the nickname fit.

Riding the wind on three pairs of shimmering wings with a span of twenty-five feet, the burdle darted to and fro, nimbly changing directions in a display of aerial acrobatics. Blinding glints of cobalt and emerald were thrown with every flick of its reflective, feather-like scales. With no legs or feet to speak of, and a beak the shape of a needle, burdles appeared to be native to the air currents of Aeolus, and almost certainly fed on the greenbottle jellies. A shell-like carapace covered the main bulk of its body and Gus wondered what hunted them other than the Deiopeans. Armor like that suggested something bigger. Something with powerful jaws. She thought of the giant shadow that had tracked *Tilly's* fall. No wonder Moe wanted a lookout.

"Are poachers a problem?" Gus asked. She couldn't take her eyes off the chase. "Looks like there's enough of 'em to go around."

"The Deiopeans value balance and only take what they need," Moe said. "Some folk from town don't share that value. Some feel they can take whatever they want."

Gus zoomed out for a better view of the whole flock. "Yeah," she said, cocking an eyebrow and rolling her shoulders. "I know the type." Moe waved for Gus to follow him back inside. "Now that you've got your lost calf squared away, can we revisit that ride to Las Ráfagas?" she asked.

Moe's face flickered. "I can tell you're in a rush, and I'd love to help you out," he said sheepishly. "But I can't. I've got to get the boy home safely, and our Deiopean friends have given me a disturbing piece of news I need to pass on as soon as I can."

Tunk. Still, the farmers out here often made decent engineers. If she was lucky, maybe she didn't have to look further than the Vega homestead. Hector was waiting for them in the mule's saddle. He beamed at the rob. "Can I drive us home, Moe? *Please?*"

Moe's mechanical shoulders slumped. "Chief, you know your father said you're only supposed to ride with him. He'll have my hide if he finds out."

"*Please?* He won't find out, I promise!" Pouting, he aimed his big eyes toward Moe in a display so pathetic, it would have moved Mother Terra herself. The rob put his hand on his hips, leaned in, and narrowed his eyes at Hector. They stared at each other, one pair of eyes huge and hopeful, the other, digital and piercing.

Moe cracked and a broad grin broke his grim façade. "Oh, I was always going to let you." Only then did the gangly rob seem to remember Gus. "*But* that was before we had to see to this gentlewoman." He winked at Gus slyly. "With her pony in tow, I think it's only fair if we ask her permission first."

Hector practically radiated faux innocence at Gus. "Ma'am, I'm great in the saddle, I promise. Ask anyone. Would you mind if I flew us back home?"

Gus glanced at Moe. The rob nodded slightly. "Sure thing, kid. Have at it."

A little over an hour later, they slipped through the clouds toward the blue glow of a small homestead's anti-grav foundation. The three of them were again crammed into the mule's saddle room, with Hector still at the controls.

Moe tapped his little charge on the shoulder. "Okay, chief, time to slide on down. I wasn't kidding when I said your father wouldn't be happy if he found out." Hector dropped from the saddle with only a hint of disap-pointment on his face. Moe mounted up in an oddly automatic-yet-grace-ful manner and took up the yoke's reins. "Welcome to El Dorado," he said. "Gus Gus's greenbottle jelly ranch and family homestead."

"Oscar Vega's," Hector corrected kindly.

Moe blushed as the mule passed through the homestead's protective energy barrier. Static electricity crackled in the air as they crossed the threshold.

"What kind of fence are you using?" she asked as she shook the tingling from her shoulders. With feedback like that, it had to be an antique.

"Oh, sorry. Should've warned you." Moe said awkwardly. "We had to downgrade to a Type-2 cold plasma fence a few years ago. Anything newer has trouble with the meteorites we get on Aeolus. But we can calibrate the Type-2 more finely, so it lets us in and keeps the meteorites out. Let's get you out to the boss."

About ruttin' time. All I have to do is convince this Vega to lend me his rob for a few more hours. Easy.

The mule floated into an outer building on the anti-grav foundation. Moe gently lowered *Tilly* first, then set the mule down in a soft landing. Hector skipped down the ramp and out of the barn. "We're home!" he announced at the top of his lungs. Once Moe had Gussy free from the mule, he led her across the property to a giant paddock filled with lazily drifting jellies, most three times her size.

With Gussy finally wafting back to her brood-sisters, Moe took a mo-ment to lean against the corral's railing and survey the herd. The adults embraced the juvenile jelly and shuffled her toward the middle of the herd. Gus sighed. She reached for a cigar, flicked open her lighter, and brought it to her lips.

Moe's silver hand shot out with unnerving speed and snuffed out the tiny flame. The fear and anger on his face disappeared so fast, Gus couldn't be sure she'd seen it at all.

"Old habit," he said, in apology. "Fire in an artificial oxygen environ-ment tends to make robs a little twitchy." His self-conscious laugh only did so much to put Gus's nerves to rest. "Melted wiring and burning hydraulic oil are no laughing matter." He smiled crookedly, almost painfully. "Come on inside and meet the boss. Then we can have a closer look at your pony and see about getting you to town in one piece."

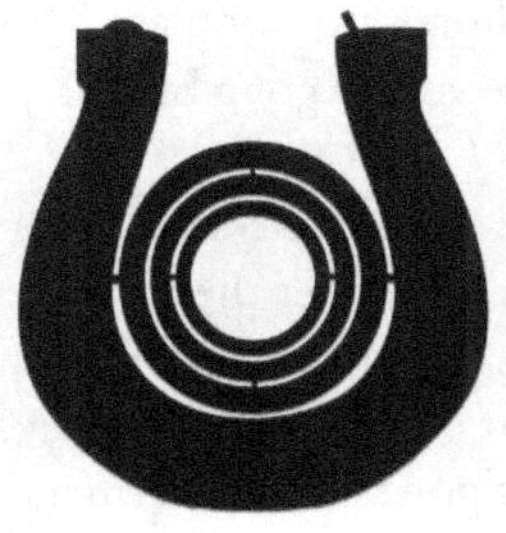

EL DORADO

The farmhouse kitchen glowed in the cozy morning light. The room was shockingly tidy, despite the recent and ongoing baking suggested by the sweet smells wafting from the oven. A short woman with a sugar-caked apron busily moved about the kitchen.

"Come in, come in! Make sure that damned door latches behind you, Moe!" she called over her shoulder without turning her attention from her work.

"Gus, may I present the lady of the house, Mrs.—"

"Bernadette Vega." She put down the bowl she had been whisking, crossed the room, extended a small, pale hand, and saved Moe from another embarrassing misnaming—all in one graceful motion. "And you are?" Her mane of ginger hair framed eyes the color of wild clover.

Gus shook the calloused, flour-dusted hand with her gloved one. "Gus will do fine, ma'am."

Bernadette shot Moe a questioning glance. He returned it with a serene smile. She nodded and resumed her work. "I understand you had a spot of trouble on reentry?"

"Yes, ma'am." A welcoming warmth radiated from the oven and dappled sunlight, filtered through the homespun curtains, and fell across rough but well-loved furniture. Gus hadn't been in a home like this in a long while. "I was hoping I could borrow your, er"—she glanced at Moe—"farmhand and mule for a tow into town."

"Moe is free to do as he pleases when his work is finished," Bernadette said and nodded to the rob. "As for the use of the mule, again, once the day's chores are complete."

"Ma'am, I appreciate you've got a busy day ahead of you, but if it's all the same to you—"

"But it's not all the same," she said. "As much as I'd rather Moe save the occasional aimless drifter then let you take our last ride to the core, the fact is, pulling your ass out of the wind took twice as long as the chore he was sent out for. He was *supposed* to go into town this morning with a haul of goods for the farmers market. But it's too late for that now. Hector's already told me how you helped wrangle our lost calf, so I know you're willing to pitch in to get your way. I think a day's worth of labor ought to be enough to cover our expenses for saving you."

Gus folded her arms across her chest. A day. The clock over Bernadette's shoulder clicked maddeningly. At least another eight or ten hours lost, minimum. Assuming the San Juan-Paul bulls had continued on toward Las Ráfagas after she dumped Tuco, that wouldn't leave her a lot of time to make *Tilly's* repairs. She shifted her weight and rapped her fingertips on the countertop. What choice did she have?

"Alright." She practically spat the word through pursed lips.

Bernadette faced them from across the kitchen. "Very well. If you can continue to show me and my family respect, you are welcome in my home for as long as you need to stay. But the beam-shooter *ain't.*" She nodded toward Delilah. "I ask that you allow Moe to stow it until you're ready to go."

Gus jolted, barely containing a lurch back. It was never a good idea to be more than a few feet from Delilah. She had learned that the hard way. Gus peered up at Moe's digital face. He merely smiled, nodded, and held out his hand. Could she trust these people? Again, what choice did she have? Drooping her shoulders with an exaggerated sigh, she unbuckled the ancient gun belt and handed her most prized possession to Moe.

"Ma'am, I need to speak with the boss right away. I've got a message for him from our"—Moe's eyes darted from Bernadette to Gus and back again—"*neighbors* that he needs to hear."

What had the spiders told Moe that would need passing on? What kind of relationship did they have with those ... *things?*

"Alright then," she said. "You two best meet Oscar out in the barn. He'll have seen your pony by now." Then, to Moe, "You know how he is about those old Steeldust cayuses. Get him workin'."

Moe tipped the brim of his bowler. "Ma'am."

"Moe." She nodded and smiled in reply. When Bernadette's green eyes met hers, Gus's heart fluttered. "Gus."

"Ma'am. Thank you." Their eye contact lingered.

After a breath, Bernadette broke the gaze and returned to her baking with a curt nod.

Gus followed Moe back out into the morning air, Earth-normal and comfortably warm within the fencing. The sunlight glinted off Moe's arms as they crossed the courtyard back to the barn. "The boss'll likely be fawning over your mount by now. He loves early model Steeldust transports. I'll be with you in a moment." The lanky rob strode across the yard to a secure storage locker and placed Delilah inside.

Gus stepped into the cool shade of the barn. The big room was a haphazard mess, with tools lying where they apparently fell. Oscar Vega stood with his hands on his hips, admiring *Tilly*, still caught in the mule's netting.

"Hey, Moe, how'd everything go with Gussy this morning?" he asked without taking his eyes off *Tilly*.

"No problems with Gussy, Boss, but—"

"But I see you brought home another stray." His round face broke into a broad grin as he turned to face them. He grabbed Gus's hand in a fierce but friendly embrace. He stood an inch or two taller than Gus, with broad shoulders and a short crop of thinning, jet-black hair. Like his wife's, his hands were deeply calloused, though splashed with grease instead of flour. "Your pony, *ella es bella*. 2221?"

Gus nodded. "You've got a good eye."

"'Gus,' right? That'll be an easy one to remember, eh, *hombre?*" he said with a wink for Moe, who blushed slightly. "Oscar Vega, glad to meet you." Oscar's attention returned to *Tilly*. He patted the hull tenderly. "I love these old workhorses. They don't build 'em like this anymore. But I guess that's probably for the best, eh, Moe?" He chuckled. Moe smiled nervously. *Tilly* had been built in the years before the UCET recognized artificial sentience, largely using rob labor. "I see you've made some modifications; you can't get away with that on the newer models. They just don't have the same performance."

Gus's back straightened. "You an engineer?" Maybe she wouldn't need to go all the way to town after all.

"*Yo?* No, *retoco un poco*—I tinker—but I'm no engineer." He surveyed the damage to the thrusters and engine gimbal and shook his head. "You'll have to talk to Emmitt over in Las Ráfagas to get the repairs you'll need."

Tunk.

An intercom over the door squawked and Bernadette's voice filled the barn. "Husband, I sent Moe in there to get you moving, not so you could stand around and talk tack. The jellies are getting restless to be put out to pasture. Moe, didn't you say you had an urgent message for Oscar?"

"Yes, dear!" Oscar called up to the intercom. He gave *Tilly's* hide a final gentle stroke. "No rest for the wicked, *mi amigos,*" he said and sighed.

The trio stepped back out into the light. Oscar walked with an oddly labored gait and a grimace to match. "Servos acting up again, boss?" Moe asked as the older man stooped to roll up his pant leg.

"*Si, por supuesto.*" He tightened a few screws behind the kneecap of his travel-worn robotic prosthesis. "It's the damn gas particles, they gum up the works." Oscar stood and tested the knee. "Moe and I have got to see to the herd, but if you're as handy with a wrench as your mount suggests, I'd appreciate it if you'd take a look at the mule's gimbal axes. They seized up last month and I haven't had time to bring her in to Emmitt."

"I'll see what I can do," Gus said.

"*Bueno.* Hector can show you where the tools are, *eh, chico?*" he called back into the barn. Hector popped up from a grate in the floor, grinning ear to ear. "*Hector,*" Oscar scolded, "you know you're not supposed to be playing in the foundation ducts! I'll be getting an earful if *tu madre* finds out you've been mucking about in there again."

Hector's smile faltered. "*Lo siento, Papi.*"

Oscar rolled his eyes comically. "Think you can help Gus here find everything she needs to fix the mule?"

"*Si Papi, de nada!* Come on, Gus!" he shouted and scampered deeper into the barn.

"Alright. Let's see what there is to see," Gus said as she cleared away loose scraps and screws from the mule's dark coolant console. Hector sat in the mule's engine room chair and gently rocked back and forth as he watched her work. She flipped on the main breakers and gave the console a hard smack for good measure. The mechanical guts protested, but the coolant's pump system chugged to life and the readout console illuminated, albeit dimly. "Coolant levels are at seventy-four percent. That should be good enough. Hmm. I'm not reading any clogs in the lines."

"Told ya," Hector sang. "I was there when it happened. *Papi* turned it off right away and dumped the coolant in the lines. I remember because it smelled *really bad!*"

She glared at the console and scanned the display for any sign of a problem with the coolant system. But she already knew what she'd find. Despite the clutter, Oscar kept his tools and machines well maintained. The condition of the mule, though small and cramped—and even older than *Tilly*—proved his competency. He would have spotted and fixed a simple issue before the engine seized. She was going to have to get a little dirty.

"You were onboard when the engine stopped?" she asked.

Hector nodded.

"What happened?"

"Me and *Papi* were going to the market on Holliday Station. You know, the big pulse-rail station? *Papi* had an appointment, but he said we could watch the wagons and the big Campbell four forty pulse-rail trails come in from across the Rift while we ate lunch.

"We got into orbit and *Papi* turned on the engine. Then it made a *horrible* noise! It sounded like when Moe slipped and fell down the foundation steps last spring." He imitated the sound of a metal body tumbling down a flight of stairs.

"Sounds like the main axis gear threw a couple of teeth. Hand me that coil ratchet—no, the thing with the yellow handle—yeah, thanks." She set to removing the axis housing.

"What are you doing?" Hector watched her every move intently.

"Well, ninety-nine times out of a hundred, when a gimbal axis seizes, it's because it's not getting any coolant. That means a clog in the lines. When it's *not* a coolant problem, it means something got caught in the axis gear itself. Usually, it's a broken piece of the assembly, but I don't know—" She pulled back the outer housing, reached into the axis's inner workings, and carefully worked her fingers into the mechanical guts. Gus frowned. Crumbled metal fragments fell into her hands like sawdust, and she pulled fractured cog assemblies from the housing like crumbled cookies from Bernadette's oven. No way a few broken gear teeth caused this. "What the *tunk?*"

She laid her hand on a chunk of twisted metal stuck in the gears. As Hector inched closer, Gus wrapped her hand around it, braced a boot against the axis housing, and yanked with all her might. When it gave way, she tumbled backwards into Hector and sent them both sprawling.

"What is it?" Hector asked as he got to his feet.

Gus opened her hand to find a badly mangled metal tool she didn't recognize.

"I don't know."

But it was clear *Hector* recognized it, even though he clumsily tried to cover his surprise. She spent enough time out on the Arm to know what the boy's expression meant: *sabotage.*

Hector stayed quiet for a while after they discovered what caused the engine trouble, but the job of repairing the damage was both difficult and time consuming. It didn't take long for him to start babbling once again. He watched everything Gus did, asked about each replacement part, and told stories about his misadventures around El Dorado.

Now, with both of them covered in engine grease and coolant vapors, his curiosity turned to her.

"I've never heard your accent before. Where are you from?" he asked. He wiped sweat from his brow, smearing grease across his face.

"The Granum Sector."

"Where's that?"

"It's in the Old Colonies. About twenty-five parsecs from Earth. It was one of the original off-world outposts. Didn't you learn that in school?"

"Don't go to school. *Mamá* teaches me book stuff and *Papi* teaches me about the ranch."

Gus raised an eyebrow. *Imagine being that tied down. That* stuck.

The interrogation continued. "Why'd you come to Aeolus?"

Gus grunted as she tightened a lug nut into place. "I had some work in Las Ráfagas, but it fell through on my way. Didn't see the point in turning around when I was already low on fuel and heading toward a rubidium depot."

"What kind of work? Are you a miner?" Hector's brow furrowed. "I've never seen a miner carry a gun before."

"I'm no miner." Gus slid the axis housing back into place. She flipped a few switches on the coolant control panel and engaged the engine's test mode. The newly repaired axis hub hummed pleasantly. Gus shut it down and wiped her greasy hands on her flight suit.

"You fixed it! *Ace high!*" Hector cheered. "If you're not a miner, you *must* be an engineer! If you don't have a job in town, maybe you can stay with us. We've always got stuff breaking down. *Papi* can't keep up with it all, and *Mamá* says she doesn't like getting the grease under her fingernails."

"Look, kid, your family seems nice and all." Bernadette's green eyes and the curve of her hip beneath her apron flashed across Gus's mind. "But I'm not an engineer, and I don't do ... *this.*"

"What do you mean?"

"Staying in one spot. I'm gonna let you in on something your parents probably can't teach you: the Arm's a rough place. Sitting still for too long ... it can kill you. The only things in this life that matter are the stuff that keeps you riding—that keeps you free. Everything else is dust. And the truth is, your jelly-ranching family ain't got the spoons to keep me here longer than I have to be."

Hector's lip jutted out and trembled. His little hands balled into fists at his sides and his eyes welled up. Before Gus could say another word, the boy fled from the mule with his tears trailing behind him.

Tunk.

"Don't worry about Hector." Oscar appeared in the doorway his son had fled through.

Gus winced. How long had he been there? "I, uh. Sorry 'bout that. I didn't mean to upset him."

"Don't give it a second thought. He's a sensitive boy. Sometimes I worry he's been too sheltered growing up out here. It's good for him to meet people with different views of the Arm. And your ... philosophy ... is new to him. Folk 'round here value their roots. Their community. Not many wander far. But who knows what the future holds, eh, *amiga?*" His eyes were sad, but his smile stayed warm. "How's the work going?"

Gus busied herself with putting Oscar's tools away. "Finished. But I think you may have a bigger problem than a seized engine gimbal." She dropped the warped hunk of steel into his hands.

Oscar's eyes widened. "Interesting." Gus could see the farmer's mind racing behind his gentle eyes. After a moment's consideration, he met her gaze. "Unfortunately, I'm going to need Moe here tonight. I'll ask him to make up the spare room for you. He can tow you to town at first light. Come on inside. It's supper time." Focused on the small hunk of metal in his hands, he left before Gus could protest.

As Gus and Oscar joined a still pouting Hector at the Vega dining table—a small, antique thing, with rusted metal legs and a deeply faded and scuffed red laminate surface—Bernadette laid out the meal. A feast it was not, but there was plenty of food to go around. Gus, however, had lost her appetite.

More time lost. She did the math as the potatoes were passed around and that confounding clock ticked away. If the bulls took Tuco back to San Juan-Paul before coming after her, she might be alright. That would give her a week or more. Plenty of time.

The Vegas talked about the day's work. Oscar said something about trouble with the fencing at the edge of one of their paddocks. Gus tried to pay attention, but her mental calculations dominated her thoughts.

If the bulls retrieved Tuco and tried to follow her right away, she would have substantially less time. Even so, their smaller engines would need a rest, especially after pushing as hard as they had to catch up in the first place. That meant they would probably arrive in thirty-six to forty-eight hours. Depending on the state of the town's engineering corral, that *might* be enough time for repairs. If she was extremely lucky.

But relying on luck had never been her strong suit. She always found it easier to make her own. That took careful planning and a talent for recognizing risky situations—and avoiding them. This situation was riskier than she generally liked. And getting worse all the time.

Bernadette filled Gus's plate with a variety of strange foods, all of which Gus assumed had been produced there on El Dorado. She asked Gus something, and it took the drifter a moment to drag her thoughts back to the meal.

"Hector tells me you're from the Granum Sector. That's quite a long way from here. What brings you to this side of the Rift?" She offered Gus a bottle of pills. Vitamin D. Gus shook her head politely.

Hector slouched down in his chair. His lips stuck out in an exaggerated scowl, and he kept his eyes on his food.

"Work," Gus said. "I had a job in Las Ráfagas go belly-up en route. Thought it better to refuel and be on my way." She took a bite of something that resembled pulled pork but tasted more like fish.

Oscar smiled, but not with the same enthusiasm he had shown that morning. "I guess you're regretting that decision now."

"It's not the only one." She cursed herself for ever taking the job with Tuco in the first place.

"If your opportunity has fallen through, what do you plan on doing next?" Bernadette asked.

An important question—more than Bernadette Vega could know. Gus chose honesty. "Make repairs. Get *Tilly* fed. And then I don't know. Maybe find work in the Cygnus X colonies."

At his mother's beckoning, Hector shoveled food into his mouth and glowered at his plate.

"Have you been there before?" Moe asked. He sat at the table with his hands folded politely in his lap and an empty place setting in front of him.

With her mouth full of some deliciously sweet steak—greenbottle jelly, she assumed—Gus shook her head.

"Bernie's from the colonies," Oscar said around a dinner roll. "Her grandparents were some of the original Cygnus pioneers back in the '20s. This was before the waystations were built, of course. Tell 'er, *mi amor.*"

"The colonies are beautiful. Like how I imagine Earth was an age ago. But if you're in need of work, we may be able to help. Oscar's a decent mechanic," Bernadette said with a smile for her husband, "but the maintenance is piling up. We can't pay much, but we can offer you room and board, maybe even help you make your repairs."

"Bernie ..." Oscar started. Hector suddenly pushed back from the small table and stood.

"Staying too long to help poor jelly-ranchers like us would *kill her!*" Hector shouted and bolted from the room. A stunned silence fell over the table.

"I—" Gus began.

"No need to apologize. He just likes you."

"He doesn't know me," she muttered.

"Maybe not, but this life is all he's ever known. You're something different. A different way," Bernadette said softly.

"My father staked his claim here in the Aeolusian clouds over forty years ago, before the town was even built. I was born here, in that very room." Oscar pointed to the small living area next to the kitchen. "It was my father that tamed the greenbottle jellies and forged relationships with the Deiopeans. The clouds are in his blood. It's natural Hector'd be curious about how other people live. Especially a life like yours, so unlike his own."

"Your father—he still around?" Gus asked.

Oscar stared at the crumbs on his plate. After a moment Moe spoke up, "There was ... an accident."

"It was the same day Oscar lost his leg," Bernadette said in a low tone, as if she didn't want Hector to overhear. Oscar's fists clenched around his utensils.

An "accident?" Like how that tool "accidentally" ended up inside the mule's axis hub? There was a lot more going on out here than a maintenance backlog—and Gus wanted no part of it. She had her own problems to deal with.

After an uncomfortable silence, Gus took a chance. "I appreciate the offer. You seem like fine folk, but I don't belong here. I think it's best for all involved if I just be on my way. How 'bout we take that ride into town now, Moe?"

Oscar shot her a stern glare. "I'm sorry, Gus, but I have a job for both Moe and the mule this evening. He can take you first thing in the morning."

Gus's mind raced. She could try to steal the mule. She could disable Oscar, no problem, but Moe would still be an issue. And fighting them together, without Delilah, on their home soil? Those were long odds. Plus, she had to consider Bernadette and the kid. They didn't deserve to have their home shot up because of the trouble Tuco had gotten her into. Once again, she had no choice.

She chewed on the inside of her cheek and gave in. "In that case, I think I'll bed down now if it's all the same to you."

The spare room was small and sparsely furnished with a cot, a small table, and a dim lamp. Gus opened the room's tiny window to the Aeolusian sunset. The gas giant's atmosphere created some of the most spectacular colors she had ever seen: deep scarlets, blazing oranges, bottomless purples. She reached for her tobacco tin and rolled a cigar. Gus took a long drag and leaned out the window for a better view. As the sun sank beneath the horizon, Deiopea slowly rose toward its apex. The lights of its weblike cities twinkled like firelight.

This day had definitely not gone as planned. Her hands and shoulders ached, and her thoughts trudged slowly, as if through soup. As her cigar burned down to the butt, she watched the mule, presumably driven by Moe, leave the barn and pass through El Dorado's fencing.

Morning couldn't come soon enough.

Gus woke with a start and reached for Delilah. Her heart skipped a beat when she couldn't find the big gun, but the moment passed when she remembered Moe locking it up outside. A blanket of black covered both the small room and world outside the window; Deiopea and its cities' lights had set hours ago. She listened for the sound that had woken her.

Hushed voices—unfamiliar and furtive—drifted from the Vega's kitchen.

What fresh hell was this? Did whoever sabotage the mule come back to finish the job? Unlikely, but the way the flesh on Gus's arms prickled, it felt like trouble all the same.

Quietly, Gus slipped into her flight suit, eased the door open, and cautiously made her way toward the source.

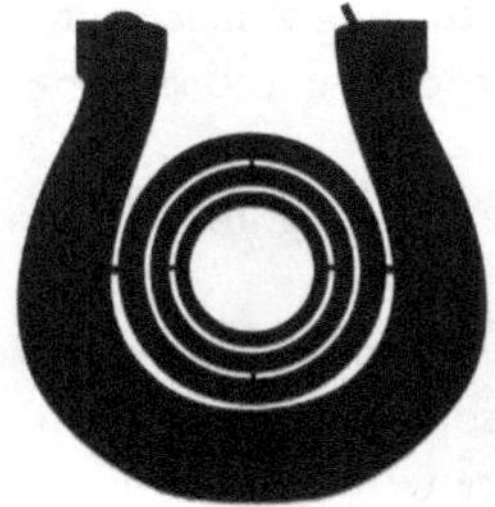

INVITATION TO A BEAMSLINGER

As she approached, Gus could make out a few voices, including Oscar's. A group of people had crammed themselves in the small kitchen along with her host. Agitated opinions, kept low, crisscrossed the room. Oscar's tone was stern but kind.

Gus's heartbeat slowed.

It's a rutting ranchers' union meeting. She rolled her eyes. Nothing to lose sleep over. Gus started back toward her room but hesitated. What harm was there in a little eavesdropping? She might learn something useful. It was unlikely, but maybe she'd even learn something that would help her get off this godforsaken gasball faster. Carefully, she turned her ear back toward the kitchen.

"And what would you have us do, Oscar?" someone hissed, their voice barely contained to a whisper. "The mining rings have been shut down for *weeks. They* say for retrofitting."

"Bah! I don't know what they're doing down there, but it ain't nothing as simple as no retrofit!" a feminine voice scoffed.

"Either way," the first voice continued, "Leconte's offer may be small, but it's the only one on the table. We either take it, or die out here forgotten by the rest of the Arm. What else would you have us do?"

"I would have you fight for what's yours, Wagner!" Oscar fired back. "Your father staked his claim in these clouds just the same as mine. You raised your family here, just like I did. How can you turn over everything you've worked for to Laszlo Leconte?" Voices clamored over one another, the volume rising distinctly as they all tried to be heard.

Gus craned her neck, straining to make out each facet of the argument. She leaned a hair too far and the floorboards creaked beneath her stocking feet.

Someone shushed the gathering like only a mother could. *Bernadette.* "Hector?" she called.

Her cover blown, Gus stepped into the kitchen doorway. Around the small table sat an odd assortment of people. In addition to the Vegas and their rob farmhand, there were six other individuals of varying size and shape.

"Gus. I'm sorry if we woke you," Oscar said.

From the corner of the room, an oddly shaped rob—who Gus initially mistook for farming equipment—spoke up in a light, feminine voice. "Is this the stray pup you saved, Moe? My, she is a pretty piece of calico!"

"What's going on here?" Gus asked.

Oscar sighed. "Come on in. I hoped to spare you from these fools, but now that you're here, I might as well make introductions. This here is Jacob Wagner and Silas Mwangi. They run the nearest small-stake ranches." Two men about Oscar's age, one pale and bald, the other dark skinned with short, dense curls, nodded to her from the table. "This handsome young man is Walter," Oscar said and put a hand on the "shoulder" of one of the most misshapen genies Gus had ever seen. "He runs the mercantile and moonlights as a waiter at Cirrus House."

Genies, descendants of Earth's earliest colonists who used genetic engineering to overcome the harshness of prospecting new worlds, came in all shapes and sizes. Walter had a roughly human-shaped torso, but each shoulder sprouted a number of arms, which Gus had trouble counting thanks to Walter's constant fidgeting. The lower half of his body was mercifully hidden by a floor-length skirt. Walter extended one of his many hands.

"Charmed!" he said through a crooked smile on a face like a melted candle. The deep folds around his eyes and mouth reminded Gus of a bulldog.

"Gretchen has already spoken up." Oscar guided Gus to the big rob hunched in the corner. "She's Walter's wife, and our ear on the mining levels." At nearly eight feet tall, Gretchen's shoulders nearly scratched the ceiling. A ball, roughly two feet across with a small "LRC" stamp on the side, served as her head. This ball sat at about Gus's eye-level, but Gretchen didn't have a face, per se, only four blue, bottle-cap sized eye lenses and a speaker grill, from which her girlish voice flowed.

A lurker. Gus cocked one eyebrow as she took in Gretchen's form. She'd heard about lurkers, but she'd never met one. Built by Legion Robotic Constructs—"Free Robs Built by Free Robs"—they were nothing more than a brain in a box. Lurkers had a modular design, which allowed them to change their bodies the way doppels changed clothes. It made them well suited for whatever lifestyle struck their fancy.

Gretchen was set up for atmospheric mining, with an articulated track-and-wheel base and powerful grasping pincers extending from those tall shoulders. She held out a pincer in an approximation of a handshake.

"It's a pleasure to meet you, dear!" To Gus's surprise, Gretchen took her hand gently.

Finally, Oscar nodded at the last pair of men. "This is Daniel Park, town medic." The older man, in spectacles and a light blue tunic that failed to hide a paunchy body, nodded. "And lastly"—Oscar led her to easily the youngest person in the Vega's kitchen—"Brother Richard." *Is this kid even shaving yet?*

But when he stood—his dark, wooly robes flowing around his small frame—and took her hand in both of his, she recognized a spark of something in his eyes. Something that he shared with Oscar: this boy had cold steel in his spine.

"What's this all about?" Gus asked again. A cold, familiar feeling began to spread through her body. It started in her fingertips and toes and slid with glacial purpose into her chest.

"Vega says you found proof the company bulls tried to kill him," Wagner spoke up.

"*And my son,*" Oscar snarled. Bernadette put a reassuring hand on his knee.

"We found something in the mule's axis hub that shouldn't've been there, but—" Gus began.

"Moe, if you would?" Oscar said.

Moe placed a heavy, linen-wrapped object on the old kitchen table. A collective gasp rose as he unfolded it. Gretchen carefully picked up the tool Gus had removed from the mule's engine and examined it.

"Is that what I think it is?" Daniel asked. He adjusted his glasses.

"Yep," Gretchen said. The blue of her eyes darkened several shades. "It *was* a flanged H-tube key. They aren't supposed to be taken off the mining levels. Oscar, this is a message."

That cold feeling continued to spread. Gus tried to head it off the inevitable. "You guys have clearly got some sort of beef with this Leconte guy, and frankly, I'm just passing through. So, if you don't mind, I'll be heading back upstairs for a few more hours in the sack. Nice meeting you all." She tried to beat a hasty retreat through the kitchen door.

"Please, ma'am. Won't you hear us out?" Brother Richard's quiet, calming voice belied the fire in his eyes. "These people are desperate and afraid."

Tunk. Too late.

Gus folded her arms over her chest and eyed the monk. His face hardened and he planted his sandal-clad feet. Every piece of him dared her to deny him. She might win out in a battle of wills with the clergyman, but it might take all night.

"Fine, let's hear it." She dropped into an empty chair. "But I'm not promising anything."

After a hesitant silence, Oscar spoke.

"For more than twenty-five years, Las Ráfagas prospered. A boomtown. The rubidium-87 mined in these clouds fueled the waystations from the Rift to the Colonies. That all changed when those new Campbell four forty pulse-rail trains went into service with the retrofitting on Holliday Station last year."

"I know about it," Gus said. "When they're done with the midpoint station, it's supposed to only take two weeks to get to the frontier from the Old Colonies."

"Which is why demand for the celerity coaches is dropping off, and demand for Las Ráfagas's rubidium along with it," Gretchen said.

"Since then," Oscar continued, "Las Ráfagas has slowly turned into a ghost town. Most of the town's residential quarter has been abandoned. The mining rings have been shut down for weeks, with the miners locked up in their barracks. Yet no one can get a straight answer about what's going on out of Leconte. He's the town's administrator.

"Instead, he bullies and threatens us with crude means like these." As his voice rose above a whisper, Oscar grabbed the twisted H-tube key and squeezed until his palm bled.

"Oscar, please," Bernadette said softly and eased her husband's hand open.

He sighed and let her take the warped hunk of metal. "He's been forcing our neighbors to sell their land and shares in the outpost for a fraction of what they're worth, even with the town's troubles. And now he's got his sights set on El Dorado and my family."

"There's a simple solution to this," Gus said. "Take the deal."

Bernadette harshly *shushed* the uproar that followed.

"I *told* you!" Wagner spat. "It's not worth dying over!"

"But there's more to it than that, Jacob." Silas Mwangi spoke up with a deep and rough voice. "Tell them what you told me this afternoon, Oscar."

But Oscar turned to Moe instead. "Better you tell it, *amigo.* They gave the message to you."

Gus took out her tobacco tin and started to roll but stopped when she caught Bernadette's disapproving eye. Moe's shoulders drooped and his eyes flitted about the room. He had managed to stay mostly invisible among this crew of misfits and clearly preferred it that way. He fidgeted with his bowler cap but never took it off.

"Well, y—you see, the boss sent me and the little chief out this morning to wrangle Gussy, our youngest greenbottle jelly. Wouldn't you know it? We came across Gus here in all manner of distress." The pain on Moe's face said if he had a throat, he would have swallowed the lump in it. Oscar gave him a small smile and twirled his finger as if to say *get on with it.*

"A—anyway," Moe continued, "we ran into a Deiopean hunting party. It, ah, it seems some of their people have gone missing recently."

Gus sat up straight. "People from the moon are missing?" That *had* to be why the spiders confronted them. *Interesting.* Still, she played it cool. "It's covered in cities. People must go missing all the time."

"Ah, no. People here on Aeolus," Moe clarified.

"Do they have an outpost or something nearby?" Gus asked.

"No one knows." Oscar shrugged. "The cloud density in the lower atmospheric layers where Las Ráfagas is makes proximity scanning impossible. And since Leconte banned trade with the Deiopeans decades ago, they aren't exactly eager to share information."

"They must lose people on hunting trips. Why is this significant?"

Oscar shrugged again and sighed. "It's significant because they've never discussed it with us before. Thanks to my father, we have a ..." He paused, searching for the right word. "... *warm* relationship with the Deiopeans. But they don't exactly drop by to borrow a cup of sugar. The fact that they've come to us with this information at all makes this unique. And troubling."

"So, what?" Gus's brow furrowed. "You think this Leconte is snatching natives, trying to force down the price of your land and shares, and drive you all out of the system?"

They all nodded, some more enthusiastically than others.

"Why?" Gus's question hung in the air like a fog.

Silence filled the room.

"He knows something. Something he's not telling us. Something he plans to use to fill his own pockets, no doubt," Brother Richard said, barely above a whisper.

"Well," Gus leaned back in her chair, "that's not much to risk my neck on."

These would-be revolutionaries fidgeted and traded glances among themselves, but none had the nerve to speak up.

Oscar wrung his hands and glanced across the room at the misshapen genie. "You've been awful quiet, Walter. You've worked for Leconte the longest. The townsfolk talk to you in the general store. I know tongues wag in Cirrus House—"

"In more ways than one!" Gretchen cut in and snickered at her own bad joke.

"What's on your mind, *hombre?*" Oscar asked the genie who sat sulking next to his wife.

Walter took a moment to gather his thoughts before answering. Then he spoke with a surprisingly smooth, powerful timbre. "There's an oddness to the town lately. Energies flow darkly. The company bulls are tense, like a powder keg just waitin' on a spark. Shadows move about. A storm's a-comin'."

Gus gawked openly at him. *Damn genies. The last thing this party needs is that pseudo-mystical gobbledygook. But what can you expect from generations of gene splicing?*

"I don't know what *that's* supposed to mean, but do you people even know what you want to do? Fight? From what I can tell, the only fightin' experience you lot have is from squabbling amongst yourselves. Ain't no way I can do all the fightin' for you, and I ain't got time to train an army of agros. And most importantly"—Gus picked up a fruit that looked like an orange but with a shiny copper skin from a bowl on the table and wiped it off on her flight suit—"how's a bunch of jelly-ranchers, a company-man genie and his gas mining wife, a half-blind medic, and a holy man gonna pay for my services?" The fruit crunched like a fresh apple, but with a tangy, savory flavor she'd never tasted before.

A murmur rippled through the kitchen. *Pay?* Little arguments cropped up around the room with table-neighbors trading barbs. Gus stood and made for the door.

"Where are you going?" Oscar asked.

"Back to bed. Ruttin' agros don't know what you want. I've got my own troubles to deal with. In Las Ráfagas's engineering corral. First thing tomorrow morning."

Oscar's face fell into a frown that wrinkled his brow, but he sighed and nodded.

Gus surveyed the pleading eyes, trembling cheeks, and heavy shoulders around her. "I suggest you people pack up what you can't bear to part with, take the spoons, and start a new life. Elsewheres."

The kitchen erupted into a fresh round of murmured arguments. Gus turned on her heel and headed back to her cot, shaking her head in disbelief.

Ruttin' agros, Gus grumbled to herself as she made her way back to the Vegas' spare room. She'd seen it coming the moment she found the shrapnel inside the mule's engine axis hub, but the request still bothered her. Gus cracked her knuckles and shook her arms, but the feeling wouldn't abate. Back in her room, she dropped onto the mattress hard and glared at the ceiling. She was no hero. She had her own problems to deal with. And with a few hours until dawn, Gus needed a quick smoke before catching a bit more sleep.

When she reached for her tin, she didn't find it in its usual pocket.

Tunk.

She'd left it in the kitchen. As she weighed how badly she wanted a smoke against the idea of going back into that quagmire, Bernadette appeared in the doorway, tobacco tin in hand. When she handed it over, her touch lingered.

"The others may not see you for what you are. But I do." Her green eyes flashed in the darkness.

"And what's that, exactly?"

She turned away before answering and dropped her hand from the tobacco tin.

"A coward. There's a million like you in the colonies. All running, telling yourselves it's toward something when it's really just running away."

"If your goal is to get me to change my mind, you're not gonna do it like that." Gus gave Bernadette a wry smile as she tucked the tin away in its familiar spot.

"You're right—we can't pay you. Not to fix your mount. Not even to fuel her. But whatever it is you're running from? Maybe we can help you come to terms with it." Gus snorted, but Bernadette continued. "These are good people here. Hardworking folk. They don't deserve the lot they've drawn. I've seen your kind before, aye. I've seen 'em run, and I've seen 'em stand. And even them that fall, they fall knowing they've done what's right. When you fall—and make no mistake, eventually your kind always does—will it be the past coming to claim you, or a fight of your own choosing?"

With that, the small woman vanished down the dim hallway.

Two hours later, Gus sat at the small room's window, smoking. A smaller tin she used as an ashtray overflowed with mashed butts. Gus watched the blue-gray smoke rise and dance in the gentle air currents. Hipppotes, Aeolus's sun, had just appeared over the horizon. It painted a stunning palette across the clouds.

She lingered on the revelations of the previous night. Greedy bullies threatening and cheating common folk out of their hard-earned money and hard-worked land. Strange disappearances. A mining outpost that wasn't doing any mining.

Something very odd was going on out here.

She shook her head and tried to clear her mind. Odd or not, it was none of her business, no matter what Bernadette said. *What did little-miss-housewife know anyway? How dare she call me out?* As far as Gus was concerned, Bernadette would be better off sticking to baking and keeping her henpecked husband in line. She knew nothing of what it took to keep going on an Arm that didn't care if you lived or died. Of what you're forced to do to stay ahead of lowlifes that will double-cross you without a second thought. Or corrupt bulls who'll lock you up on a whim then lose the key.

A knock on the door interrupted her thoughts.

Moe.

Finally. Time to go.

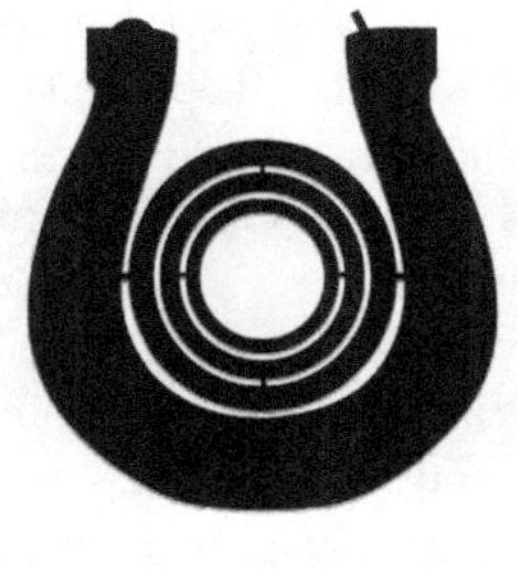

CLOUD TOWN

The trip from El Dorado to Las Ráfagas didn't take long, which Gus counted as a blessing—there wasn't much to see. Aeolus's clouds engulfed the small mount almost as soon as they left the Vega homestead and limited visibility to a few paltry feet.

"How do you ride in this soup?" Gus asked. With one hand on her hip and the other resting on Delilah, she squinted through the canopy at the dim vapors around them. Even the flight sensors were dead.

Moe chuckled. "You get used to riding blind out here. We've got the route to town programmed into the mule's navi-com, so it's mostly done on auto."

"How do you hitch without the proximity sensor?"

"The old-fashioned way." Moe smirked as he flipped on the mule's comms. "This is short-range transport *Burra* to Las Ráfagas Stable Control. I am on approach and requesting two stables in the engineering corral."

"Confirmed, *Burra,*" the intercom squawked. "You are approved for hitching at engineering stables six and seven. I have your approach beacon now. Transmitting hitching signal." There was a pause, and then, "Now."

Suddenly, Moe's dark control panel lit up with data. Their position relative to the outpost had been triangulated and transmitted to them. It was an old system that relied on the incoming mount bouncing a signal off two receivers on either end of the mining facility. Gus had seen it before, but not since her first foal-mount, nearly a lifetime ago.

"Thanks, Stable Control," Moe replied and flipped the intercom off.

They broke through a dense layer of cloud to their first glimpse of the mining outpost. "Welcome to Las Ráfagas Rubidium-87 Mining Outpost and Depot. Constructed, owned, and operated by Leconte Atmo-Mining Solutions," Moe said as the town came fully into view.

"How big is it?" Gus had been on atmo-mining outposts before, but never an operation of this scale.

"From end to end, the outpost is exactly one mile long. She's got twenty mining and refining levels, along with six mining rings: four 2,880-foot diameter primary rings, and a pair of 1,920-foot secondary rings," Moe said. "When operating at peak efficiency, Las Ráfagas can produce one hundred fifty megatons of rubidium-87 superfluid per week." The enormous vertical hoops that extended out from the face of the crescent-shaped outpost sat dark and still. "Above the mining levels, sits the esplanade—the town proper." An old-fashioned glass-like shell encased the town, which sat on top of the facility itself, like a snow globe.

"What's that?" Gus pointed to a huge black tower that rose from the town, and the squat building at its peak, which sat *atop* the town's dome.

"That is the Administration Tower, as well as the Lecontes' private quarters," Moe said. Disdain leaked into his electronic voice.

The mule glided through the clouds, through the outpost's energy fence, and over the dome and Administration Tower, toward the rear of the town and the stables. The main livery stable, a long pier extending into the clouds with hitching posts that provided power and rubidium-87 fuel, was practically empty. Gus tapped Delilah's grip. A town this size, even this far from the Cygnus Trail, should have been bustling, with wagons and carriages coming and going like bees to a hive. But here, only a few rundown and rusted-out wagons waited silently.

Yet, one wagon stood out. Its long, narrow shape reminded Gus of a gold-plated animal skull, maybe a cow or horse. Definitely some sort of pleasure craft, but she had never seen anything quite so *opulent* before. She sneered down at the luxury wagon. *Damn you, Tuco.* There was money to be made here, but thanks to that impulsive *pendejo,* she couldn't risk sticking around to sniff it out.

Moe directed the mule past the livery stable and maneuvered both it and *Tilly* into the engineering corral at the far end of the town.

Las Ráfagas's engineer, an old codger named Emmitt Smith, met them as they stepped off the mule. He scowled and grunted when Gus extended her hand.

"Oscar mentioned you'd be paying me a visit this morning." He squinted at her, sizing her up. "'e said to do what I can for ya." He spat a dark wad to the corral floor.

Gus withdrew her unshaken hand and glared right back at him. "Glad to hear it."

After a tense moment, he grunted again. "A'ight, let's have ourselves a look-see." Emmitt flipped open an access panel on *Tilly's* hitching post and pulled a thick cable from it. Straining under its weight, the old man dragged the cable to *Tilly* and plugged it into a port beneath the saddleroom. "Come on." He led them through the cluttered engineering corral, past wagons missing engine gimbals, burnt-out hides, and huge machines Gus couldn't identify. Before long, they arrived at the old engineer's office, a largish room built against the wall overlooking the entire corral. Its warm, old-fashioned incandescent lights and little kitchenette gave the office a cozy, lived-in atmosphere.

Emmitt slumped down into a well-worn chair behind a cluttered workbench that doubled as a desk. "Let's see what we got," he said. He picked up a tablet, and within moments, the handheld computer's screen filled with scrolling data from *Tilly's* main computer network. "Tsk," the old man said with a click of his tongue. "You've got yourself quite a mess here, don't ya? Half a dozen small hide breaches—one *big* 'un. Atmo-thruster control system's fried. The thrusters're melted. You got a frozen engine gimbal 'n a massive coolant leak. Not to mention ruptured environmental seals in the empty pod shaft. Let's see … is this 'n aftermarket tractor beam? The way you've got it wired is overloadin' your rear power regulator." Emmitt squinted at the readout. He raised an eyebrow and eyed Gus over the tablet. "Pony's a little small for salvage. Whatcha using the hide cutter for?"

"Don't worry about that, old man."

"Uh-huh," he said knowingly. "No wonder you overloaded your engine gimbal. You've got too many modifications pulling too much power. The hide cutter alone is pulling enough wattage to fry your electricals. Ruttin' thing's sucking enough juice to cut through armor plating."

"Forget about the mods. Can you get her void-ready?"

Emmitt rose from his workbench to wash his hands in the kitchenette's oversized sink. "Sure." He shrugged. "But the biggest o' yer problems're in that electrical system. Can't do nothing 'til that's fixed."

Tunk.

Gus's heart sank. It was even worse than she feared. "Alright. What's the damage gonna cost me?" Emmitt tapped his screen a few times, mumbled something about carrying the one, then handed it to Gus. Her eyes nearly bugged out of her head. It was almost everything she had. "You've got to be kidding me!" she roared.

Emmitt kept his baggy eyes locked on hers and didn't budge. "Supplies are scarce out here. Ever since fuel demand dropped, the supply wagons don't come out as often. You don't like it, you can take your business elsewheres."

"Look here, you senile old coot—" Gus waved a finger in the small man's face, but Moe put his hand on her shoulder and tried to calm her.

"She's stuck here without your help. Isn't there something you can do?" he asked in a soothing tone.

Emmitt grunted and gave the rob some serious stink eye. Finally, he swiveled around and poked at his tablet. He turned back, keeping his eyes away from the rob's, and handed Gus the tablet once more. "'ere, 's the best I can do."

He'd brought the cost down some—at least she would have enough for lodgings and some fuel—but—

"Three days?" She waved at the office window and all the empty stables. "Why so long? It ain't like you've got business piling up here!"

"Actually, *girl,*" Emmitt said as he snatched the tablet from her hands, "Leconte's got my crew working double shifts on the outpost's retrofits. Like I said, 's the best I can do."

Gus glared at the old man's creased face, but he stood firm.

"Fine," she seethed. Three days was pushing her luck to the breaking point. By her math, she might have as few as *two* days until the San Juan-Paul bulls caught up with her. And in a town this empty, it would be hard to get lost in the crowd. But what choice did she have? She'd just have to keep her head down and get out as soon as she could. Which left one more matter. "What about rubidium-87? *Tilly* needs to be fed."

"Can't help ya there. Now if you don't mind, I have work to get to," Emmitt said and walked to the door.

"Whoa, hold up a minute," Gus said and grabbed his arm. "What's that supposed to mean?"

Emmitt brushed her hand off. "It means I can't help you. You got grease in your ears? *The rings are shut down.*"

Gus fisted his dirty leather apron and pulled him close. Moe started to step forward, but Gus flashed out a hand to stop him and released Emmitt. She leaned in far enough to smell his singed stubble. Her voice dropped to a growl. "I don't *care* if the rings are shut down. This is a mining town. There's got to be rubidium *somewhere.*"

Emmitt's defiance remained, but as his eyes darted to the door, Gus sensed fear in the old man. But not of her. "There's nothing. Not since before the retrofit started. Nothing in the loading bays, nothing being shipped out. All I've got is my private supply, but I need it to run the corral."

Gus's mind raced. "The corral is an important part of town operations. They must keep your supply topped up to keep your crew working. Where's it come from?"

Emmitt shrugged with a deepening scowl.

A rubidium-87 mining depot without any rubidium. Las Ráfagas literally floated in a soup of the stuff. Even with mining operations shut down, it ought to be spilling out of the outpost's seams. *What the tunk is going on out here?*

"Fix my pony," Gus said and pushed past the old engineer. "We can talk about you selling me your fuel when that's done. Don't worry, I'll make it worth your while. Let's go, Moe. You can show me where a lady can get a room in this godforsaken backwater."

"Welcome to Las Ráfagas," Moe said as Gus followed him out of the engineering corral and into the town proper. "It ain't much, but it's home. Come on this way. I'll take you to the inn."

Just outside the engineering corral office sat the large residential area that took up a large percentage of the land under the town's dome. Gus had spent many nights camped out in old ghost towns, surrounded by long-abandoned buildings falling to ruin and empty lots heavy with dust and debris. Although it wasn't there yet, something about Las Ráfagas reminded her of the deep sadness that radiated from those old towns that littered the Trail. Only a small group of children chasing a yelping dog down the street broke the ghostly illusion.

Gus's heart sank. Under normal circumstances, the empty spaces and absence of prying eyes might have been the perfect place to lay low. But with the law hot on her trail, she needed ample cover that couldn't be found in Las Ráfagas. Worse still, her options for making the spoons she needed for fuel looked *extremely* limited.

Outside the dome, the sky had cleared. Hippotes hung high above the gas giant and bathed the town in an unforgiving light that revealed all its blemishes. A layer of cream-colored dust covered the decades-old outpost—residue buildup from the planet's atmosphere, no doubt. Spider-web cracks dotted the dome protecting the town from the elements. Nothing too serious, but Las Ráfagas had clearly seen a few meteorite impacts over the years.

As Moe led Gus away from the engineering corral, her mind lingered on *Tilly.*

First things first: lodging—cheap *lodging. After that, I'll have three days to come up with something—while keeping an eye out for the bulls.* She already knew one thing: something very strange was going on in this town. And while she didn't care what it was, she knew she couldn't take Emmitt's fuel, by force *or* coercion. That left one option: paying Emmitt for it. How the hell could she lay low *and* make money in this forgotten town?

They crossed a small square and headed toward a little chapel tucked between an empty lot and the corral wall. A sign identified it as the *Capilla de Santa Bárbara.* Its rough stone walls were ancient, even compared to the dilapidated state of the rest of town. Brother Richard stood out front and fiddled with a huge ring of keys.

Next to him stood an older man nearly the opposite of the brother in every way. Where Richard was beggar thin, this man had the waistline of those wealthy enough to ignore beggars. He wore a suit as white as his handlebar mustache, and a flat-crowned gambler hat to match. A bolo tie with a silver burdle skull hung around his fat neck, and a pair of pearl-handled pistols hung from his hips. He urged the flustered Brother Richard to hurry.

"Good morning!" Moe called out to the older man and tipped his hat in a friendly greeting.

The man glowered and strode briskly past, giving Moe a wide berth. "Out of my way, filthy rob!" he spat while appraising Gus with a hunger that made her skin crawl.

With the older man's unnerving stare on Gus, Brother Richard found the proper key, locked the chapel, and descended the steps to meet them. He took each of their hands in a short but friendly shake.

"Moe. Gus. It's lovely to see you again on this blessed morning. I would love to stay and chat, but we've got another burial this afternoon. I need to see to the family right away."

"Oh no!" Moe cried. "Was it...?"

"Mrs. Santiago. I'm afraid so. Mr. Willoughby's mother-in-law," he gestured to the impatient man in white. "Her heart finally gave out. She passed in her sleep late last night."

"*Richard!*" Willoughby's voice cut through the still morning air like a jackhammer. "Let's ruttin' go!"

Brother Richard didn't respond to Willoughby, but his jaw clenched hard, and his head cocked almost imperceptibly. "I am sorry, my friends, but I have to run. May the blood of the world flow through you." He took each of their hands briefly and raced down the street after Willoughby.

Moe watched them disappear into the residential areas before turning back to Gus with a sullen expression.

"What was that all about?" Gus asked.

"Mrs.—" Moe paused.

"Santiago," Gus finished for him.

The rob smiled his thanks and continued. "She's been a staple in Las Ráfagas since its founding. Nearly thirty years ago now, back in '38." Moe said. He led Gus past the chapel and across an empty lot between a row of townhouses and a stubby building with bars over its windows. The Marshal's Office. "She was a leader in the community," Moe continued. "And kept her son-in-law there in check for years. Even stood up to the administrators from time to time. Her death can only be a bad omen."

They stepped into the corner of Las Ráfagas's town square. The façade of the small Marshal's Office squatted on their left with Daniel Park's med-lab and apothecary next to it. Across from them stood the enormous Administration Tower, which threw a dark shadow across the heart of Las Ráfagas. Like everything Gus had seen so far, the square was deserted. *There is nothing in this rat hole town. I need to get the tunk out of here as fast as I can. But how?*

But Willoughby's fine suit and finer sidearms confirmed there was money here. Somewhere. "Moe? What do people do for spoons around here?"

Moe chuckled. "I was wondering how long it would take you to get to that." Gus followed him along the square toward the mercantile and the inn beyond. "Our friend in the white suit is one of the few businessmen left. He owns the Gunsmithy and Emporium on the other side of the Tower, next to Cirrus House. He's not hiring. Shop's been closed up for almost as long as the mining rings."

"What's he waiting around town for?"

Gus shrugged. "Who knows. He's close with the administrators. He can usually be found at the Cirrus House's razz tables—or one of the rooms upstairs—if you care to ask him yourself. Your best bet is probably odd jobs and the like, I reckon. Only problem is there ain't many folks left looking for a helping hand." A few people milled about in the closed farmers market at the far end of the square, and an old woman sat in a rocking chair with a spittoon in her lap in front of the inn, but there were no other signs of life. "Well, let's check in at the mercantile. If anyone's looking for some help, they'll know."

The pair ducked into the shade of the mercantile and found a small but well-organized general store. Walter seemed to sell everything, from chewing tobacco and a little booze, to groceries, clothing, and spare mechanical parts— even a small selection of refraction pistols tucked away in the corner. All of it stamped with the Leconte Atmo-Mining Solutions logo, a smiling little storm cloud wearing an old-fashioned lamped miner's helmet.

An old, boxy, merchant-rob near the door stared off into space while trying to restock a shelf already overflowing with cans of protein paste. She wore a faded nametag labeling her "Maria." Gus nudged Moe with her elbow. "What's up with this one?"

"Poor thing was lo-bot hacked," Moe said. The sympathy in his voice bordered on sorrow.

Of course. Gus had only come across a few lo-bot hacked robs on the Arm. Essentially a computer virus, it effectively lobotomized any rob it infected. It left them passive, submissive, and emotionless; in a word, robotic. Some of the newer models manufactured in the CCO left the factory floor *pre*-lo-bot hacked to prevent that pesky free will from developing in the first place.

"Can't Emmitt do anything for her?"

Moe adjusted his bowler cap, sorrow on his face. "Reversing a lo-bot hack is tricky. The hack itself is all software, but the fix needs a hardware patch. It's delicate work, and he doesn't have the tools. Or, I'm sorry to say, the skills." He placed a gentle hand on Maria's shoulder as they passed. "Keep up the good work!"

An aisle over, Walter took inventory, counting products on the shelves. With his many hands, it was a sight to behold. "Morning, Boss," Moe greeted the shopkeeper.

"Ayup, morning to ya both. Anything I can help you with, Moe? Oscar didn't mention you'd be dropping in. Everything alright? Did Gussy get out again?"

"Oh, no, no, nothing like that," Moe reassured him. "I'm just showing Gus here around town on our way to Hotel Irma. She's looking to make a few extra spoons. Know of anybody needing a hired hand in town?"

Walter considered the question for a moment. His various hands tapped on surfaces and fidgeted with his products. "Now that you mention it, I haven't gotten any handyman requests in a few weeks. Mrs. Santiago's grandson needed someone to take a look at her ventilator, but I suppose you heard that's not really a problem anymore." Walter hung his head and wrung several pairs of hands. "You could always try your luck at Cirrus House," he suggested and shrugged his crowded shoulders.

Fire rose in Gus's belly. "If you're suggesting I become some mining baron's painted whore for a handful of spoons—"

Walter, in an amazing impression of a leafless tree in winter, raised all of his hands defensively. "Oh no! Cirrus House is a brothel, no doubt, but there are many games of chance as well! A void-drifter like you should have no problem getting in a game of razz or Follow-Stanley-Home."

Gus's fire extinguished as quickly as it had ignited and she rocked back on her heels. A casino? Now *there* was an opportunity. "Where's this Cirrus House?"

"Across the square, other side o' the Admin Tower," Moe said. "But I don't think—"

Gus cut him off. "What else am I going to do? Besides, I've played a few hands of razz in my day. I'll be fine."

Gus had already lit a cigar and hidden her lighter away by the time Moe joined her on the boardwalk outside the mercantile. He eyed the smoldering cherry warily but didn't bring it up. "This way."

Hotel Irma squatted next to the mercantile at the corner of the square. The crumbling tavern and guesthouse's roof sagged with age, its windows so caked with grime, a dozen waystation bulls could have hidden inside and Gus never would have known.

She followed Moe through the swinging doors and stepped onto the dusty saloon floor. It could have been any of a dozen frontier inns she'd had the pleasure of visiting. The tavern had a few battered tables and chairs, but, of course, a full complement of stools at the bar.

The rooms for rent would be upstairs, and if they were as finely furnished as the tavern, "Hotel Irma" was too grand a name for such meager lodgings. In all honesty, she was pleasantly surprised. She could haggle the innkeeper down to a reasonable price for three nights. *He'll be needing the business.*

Moe tapped the small bell on the clerk's desk and a moving mountain of a man appeared from the inn's office. He must have been nearly seven feet tall and four hundred pounds. With the palest alabaster skin and one arm in a gigantic cast, Gus couldn't take her eyes off him.

"Good morning, sir. How's the arm?" Moe asked the innkeeper as he settled in behind the clerk's desk. A small nameplate identified him as the establishment's proprietor, Stefano Russo.

Russo grunted and barely acknowledged Moe. Instead, he stared at Gus greedily. His eyes snagged on the lit cigar dangling from the corner of her mouth for the briefest of moments before they moved downward to the more obvious parts of her anatomy. "Well, hello there, little lady. How can I help you on this fine morn'?"

As his eyes washed down her body, a shudder ran down her spine. "I need a room."

"And how long will you be staying with us here at Hotel Irma?" He managed to tear his gaze away from her long enough to flip through a visitor book.

"Three days."

"Fine, fine," he said. "Room thirteen is available. Three days will be ..." He slid a credit transfer pad across the desk toward her.

"You're joking, right?" she scoffed. He was asking for more than she had left. *Tunk*, more than she would have paid for three nights back in the Old Colonies.

"Ma'am, as you can plainly see," he pushed the messy ledger toward her, "we've few vacancies—"

Gus sat on the edge of the desk and let Russo take in the shape of her hip and thigh. His eyes widened with delight. She leaned in toward the big man and beckoned him closer with the roll of a finger. Like a lamb to the slaughter, he happily did as bidden.

With a provocative smirk on her lips, Gus lifted Delilah from her left hip and placed the big gun on the desk.

"Oof, that thing is *heavy,*" she said, and gave her leg an exaggerated rub. "Now, look here. Mr. Russo, is it? I don't want to be here, but I'm stuck until my pony's repaired." She tapped ash from the end of her cigar into a coffee mug on the desk. "And I'm not exactly happy about it, understand? So, instead of selling me this line of *grunk snot,* give me the room for a fair price and be happy to have what might be your last boarder."

Russo's eyes darted from her to the big gun and back again. He snatched the transfer pad back and made some adjustments with his fat fingers.

"Ah, yes, of course. My mistake. I see we got a few last-minute cancellations my assistant forgot to tell me about. I'm sure this will be a bit more to your liking?" He slid the pad back. Even though he'd reduced the price substantially, it accounted for almost all the spoons she had left.

She paid Russo and took her room key. Grumbling, the giant retreated back into his office.

Gus shook Moe's hand. "Thanks. Will I see you around town before I push on?"

Moe tipped his bowler cap and nodded. "The farmers market opens tomorrow morning. The boss and I'll be here first thing."

"Maybe I'll drop by to thank Oscar one last time."

As the gangly rob left the inn, Gus headed for her overpriced room. She smiled despite the absurd expense, buzzed at the thought of a few hands of razz and making a little extra bank as soon as she could.

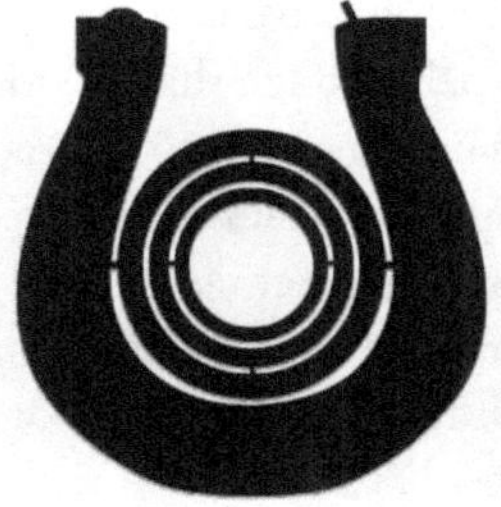

YOUNG GUNS OF AEOLUS

As dusk settled over the Aeolusian clouds, Gus found herself standing outside the batwing doors of Cirrus House. A bulky personal vehicle of some kind, parked haphazardly out front, blocked the empty road. But no one seemed to mind; the street stayed quiet and still.

The casino, by contrast, proved an oasis of noise and activity. Gus pushed through the swinging doors and a thick, tangy aroma—a mix of tobacco and cannabis smoke, spilled liquor, and hot, unwashed bodies—assaulted her sinuses. She breathed deep and relished the familiar scent.

The casino featured a broad, dimly lit gaming floor. Tables with all manner of games of chance littered the space. Compared to the main lobby and tavern of Hotel Irma, the Cirrus House gaming floor was a palace. Reds and golds festooned the walls, with fringes and tassels as far as the eye could see. Gaudy crystal chandeliers bathed the gamers in a sickly yellow glow. A few robs and genies milled about, but they all appeared to be waitstaff of one variety or another. Gus watched a woman with tentacles lead a drunk and horny patron up the stairs and into one of the private rooms.

Gus smirked and rocked on her hip. Vice was always successful, no matter the financial forecast. She sidled up to the bar—an old-fashioned thing with an actual brass foot rail—and caught her own eye in the mirror. Dark bags hung under her eyes and greasy, frizzy hair stuck up at odd angles. *Oh, good. At least I look as good as I feel.*

After ordering a shot of whiskey and a bowl of water, Gus surveyed the room. The razz tables occupied the back corner. She hated games of pure chance—only suckers expected to win playing against the house—but razz was a game of skill and cunning. She smiled. If she played her cards right, in three days, she could have enough winnings to pay Emmitt a handsome price for his fuel. Enough that he wouldn't be able to refuse.

And there might be a little left over for herself, to boot.

When the rob tending bar wordlessly delivered her water and whiskey, she shot one back and splashed her face with the other. She rubbed her eyes, tried to remove at least some of the grime from her cheeks, and ran wet fingers through her tight curls to comb out the worst of the tangles. She ordered another round and tied her hair back while the 'tender poured. After tossing the second shot back, she traded the whiskey grimace for the doe eyes of girlish innocence and headed for the razz tables.

It only took the time to cross the hazy room for Gus to pick out the high-stakes game. The whales stuck out in a place like this with their finely tailored suits, rings with gems so big they glinted regardless of the gloom, and a certain glow to their complexion that only Sol-simulation lamps could provide. Even the gaudy table stood out from the wooden card tables littering the gaming floor with its chrome-steel back, lush green felt, and ornate bas-relief sculptures along its edges.

Three men sat at the table, plus an antique rob card dealer. Willoughby, the oldest card sharp, still wore the same white hat and suit combo as that morning. The other two men were younger, and based on their strong resemblance, brothers by Gus's reckoning.

"How is it that you're always here, but no one ever sees you coming or going?" the youngest asked Willoughby after the former won a sizable pot.

"That's for me to know, and you to go right on wondering," Willoughby said with a scowl as Gus stepped up to the table.

"Evenin', gents," she said and flashed a bright smile she hoped reached her eyes. "What's a girl gotta do to join a game around here?"

Talk at the table came to an abrupt halt and every eye in the game turned toward her.

The older brother's dark, slicked back hair and the way his eyes darted around the room suspiciously reminded Gus of a weasel. He sported a dark blue suit with an elaborate burdle pin on his lapel. The younger brother had short, blonde hair, framing a mousy face with a jovial expression. His clothes were lighter and more casual, yet no less expertly tailored.

"Sorry," the older brother said threateningly. "This is a closed game."

"Now hold on a minute," the younger brother interjected. He beamed at Gus. "Let's see what the lady has to say."

"Aaron," the first brother warned.

Neither Aaron nor Willoughby seemed to hear him. "That's an interesting piece you've got there, ma'am. What's its story?" the gunsmith asked.

Gus gently patted Delilah but didn't draw the gun from her holster. "She's heavy, temperamental, and cap greedy. But she does right by me."

"Sounds like my ex-wife," Willoughby snorted. Laughter rippled around the table. "That said," he continued, "I must say, I've never seen anything quite like it."

"Me, neither!" Aaron chimed in. His eyes widened with an unsettling hunger.

The older brother glared at Aaron but spoke to Gus. "The buy-in for this table is quite high, Miss...?"

"Call me Gus," she smiled and shook Aaron's hand gently.

"I see you've met the Vegas and their cross-wired rob," the older brother scoffed. He threw back a glass half full of some amber liquor and grimaced.

"No need to be rude, Junior," Aaron chided as he continued to hold Gus's hand.

"Oh, that's alright," Gus giggled as she choked on bile. "As a matter of fact, I don't have many spoons to spare, so I was hoping to barter my buy-in." She batted her eyelashes at Aaron.

"What did you have in mind?" Willoughby said. He eyed her holster. Gus had rarely seen a man so impatient to lose his money.

"I can see you've got an eye for sidearms. Is my Delilah here enough to cover my way?" This time, she did unholster the big gun, removed the coolant capsule from the grip, and placed it on the felt table.

Junior began to reject her offer out of hand when Aaron cut him off with a glance. He picked up the ancient gun and examined it closely. "This is really something special," he said and handed Delilah to the gunsmith to inspect. "But as my brother here doesn't share our appreciation for unique weaponry, I'll have to ask you to sweeten the pot a little."

And now to seal the deal.

"You're clearly gambling men. How 'bout a little wager?" Gus offered.

"What kind of wager?" Aaron asked, eyes sparkling. Junior threw his hands in the air in defeat.

Gus pulled an old gold coin from a pocket and flipped it into the air. It tumbled through the haze and twinkled in the low light. "Heads, you keep my Delilah and my lucky 24-karat gold coin for the trouble of my company, and I move on." Junior's eyes widened. "Tails, you give me the chance to win them back," she finished and snatched the coin out of the air.

The three men glanced around the table at each other before Aaron agreed on their behalf. "Deal, but no funny business," he said and pointed a finger at her with a wry smile.

"No funny business," she agreed and flashed her own forced grin. With her right hand hung casually from her gun belt for the table to see, she flipped the coin with her left. It tumbled high into the hazy air and fell back to the table below.

A few hours—and several hands—later, Gus pushed back from the table with a sigh of satisfaction. She holstered Delilah and tucked her lucky coin back into a pocket. She stood, stretched, and collected her winnings.

"'Scuse me, gents, but I think I need to wet my whistle." None of the men at the table would meet her eye, except Aaron, who watched her with an expression close to awe. She did her best to ignore his stare and made her way to the bar.

Another whiskey or two would hit the spot. It had been a profitable evening; she'd won enough to put her mind at ease. A couple of nights like this and she could buy *all* of Emmitt's rubidium-87 at a handsome price. And then finally get out of this dying town.

But as Gus put her foot on the bar rail, her mind turned back to the Vegas. She shook her head and *tsked. I'll never understand these agro-types.* Las Ráfagas was their home, sure, but life had taught her home was where you made it, and spoons had a way of winning out in the end. Better to take the deal and get out while you still have a home to move. If for no other reason than the kid. Hector didn't deserve this kind of trouble.

Gus ordered her whiskey and pictured the Vegas' kitchen lit by the morning sun. *Still. It's a fine home.* It didn't take long to make the leap from the image of the kitchen to that of the lady of the house. When those amber locks, green eyes, and full lips crossed her mind's eye, Gus's heart quickened. She threw back her drink, ordered another, and faced the casino floor. The warmth of the whiskey spurred her thoughts to the curve of

Bernadette's aproned hip. The softness of her lips. The way her hair burned in the morning light.

Her mood called for rented flesh. She scanned the room. Rent-robs, -boys, and -girls mingled with the gathered gamblers, placing a gentle hand here, or a soft kiss there. Robs were good for some—they could certainly have some *interesting* modifications. Not her. She preferred something breathing take her to bed.

Gus ordered another drink and studied the room for what Cirrus House had to offer as she rolled a fat cigar. But instead of a pleasant distraction, her eyes fell on Aaron as he approached the bar with lust in his eyes. The entitled curve of his smirk told her she wasn't going to like the way the rest of this evening was headed if she didn't beat feet, and fast. She tucked the fresh cigar into a small breast pocket on her poncho and turned back to the bar, away from the impending trouble.

Gus tried to get the bartender's attention, but the rob's back was to her while he helped another patron. Aaron sidled up next to her. "You're not running out on us now, are you?" he asked with a boyish glint in his eye.

"As a matter of fact, it's getting to be well past my bedtime."

"Another?" The old rob bartender finally arrived, too late to save her.

"Make it a pair of overalls, and put her bill on my tab," Aaron said. The rob buzzed in the affirmative and began pouring two whiskeys.

"That's kind of you, kid, but I don't like owing people anything. And like I said, it's getting late." Gus dropped a spoon into a slot on the bar and pressed her thumb into it. When she stood to leave, Aaron's hand shot out and wrapped around her wrist like a trap.

"Don't be like that," he said in a sickly-sweet voice. "Stay. Have one drink with me. If only to show me that I can trust you'll be back to give us a chance to win back some of our money."

Gus forced the corners of her lips into her own syrupy smile and spoke in a low, dark voice. "Oh, I'll be back to bleed you blue bloods of every last spoon. That you can count on. But if you want to keep that hand for holding your cards, I suggest you remove it and let me be on my way." Aaron let go at once, but more out of shock, it seemed, than in response to her threat. She took the opportunity to make for the doors. But before she could make it more than a few steps, Aaron regained his composure.

"Nobody talks to Aaron Leconte like that, you *rutting quim!*" he screamed at her retreating back. The entire casino stopped to watch her and Aaron. *Tunk.* She'd had such good luck at the table, she'd let her guard down a hair and it had come back to bite. *A Leconte. So much for laying low.*

Gus put on her brightest smile and turned to face Aaron. His hand hovered near the grip of the Beaumont–Adams M2142 concentrator pistol on his hip.

"Leconte?" she gushed and sashayed back to the bar. "I had no idea you were someone so important." *Men. Such fragile egos.*

Seemingly reassured he remained the center of her attention, Aaron's ruffled feathers smoothed over quickly, and he started to lay his own clumsy version of "the charm" on her. He complimented her razz skills and compared her beauty to the sun setting over the Aeolusian clouds, before launching into the same old stories of conquest and prowess that she'd heard repeated in countless bars and saloons across the Arm. Gus bit her tongue, nursed her drink, and wondered how much whiskey it would take to make him shut up.

After two more rounds, the inevitable happened. Aaron, with enough liquor in him to make any man feel ten feet tall, stood from his stool and again wrapped his fingers around Gus's wrist. "Let's you and me get a place upstairs and have some fun, eh?"

Gus took his wrist with her free hand. "Aaron, you're drunk. I think you're a great guy, but I think I'm going to turn in for the night. Alone. Let's not ruin this evening, or tomorrow night's game. Let me buy you one last drink before I go."

He glared at her with self-important petulance. She could practically see the wheels in his head trying to turn through all the whiskey. Slowly, his expression melted into dim acceptance. "Fine. You should get some sleep," he said at last. "We wouldn't want to ruin tomorrow's game." He released her wrist and awkwardly dropped back down on his stool.

"That's right. You've gotta win it all back tomorrow, remember?" Gus quickly ordered him another whiskey, waited for him to lift it to his lips, and once more made her way toward the batwing doors.

Before she could make it more than a few steps, a crash, followed by a commotion, rang out. Aaron's voice filled the room. "Goddamn *genie!*" Flush with drink and fury, and drenched in so much whiskey it stung her nose, Aaron stood over a fallen Walter. "I was hoping for a rut tonight," Aaron growled as he drew his concentrator pistol, "but I'll settle for finally ending your useless genie life."

Gus's heart pounded in her ears and rational thought ebbed, replaced by a red-hot fog. Before she knew what she'd done, she crossed the distance back to the scuffle. She grabbed Aaron's wrist before he could raise his weapon, hooked a spurred heel behind his ankle, and shoved him square in the chest. Aaron fell backwards on his ass and dropped his gun to catch his fall. It clattered across the casino floor.

For the second time that night, Aaron stared up at her with an expression of awe. But this time it mingled with a dangerous mix of fear and anger. "What the *rut?*" he cried from the floor.

"Stay down, Aaron. At least until you calm the *tunk* down," she said as she helped Walter up.

"Bitch, nobody talks to me—" Aaron said and started to get up. Gus cracked him across the jaw with a left hook. The youngest Leconte toppled like a stack of poker chips, out cold.

"I told you to stay down," Gus spat and rubbed her sore wrist. As the scarlet clouds cleared from her mind, she finally realized every eye in Cirrus House was on her.

"Alright boys. Have at 'er," Junior's voice called out in the fresh silence.

The crowd collapsed in on her like the tide.

Tunk. Should'a known better. The wave of bodies crashed down on her. Dozens of hands descended, grabbing, swatting, punching. A few got some good kicks in, too. Finally, with a sharp whistle from Junior, the assault stopped. Those same hands dragged to her feet to face him.

Despite the blows, she was struck by his suit. Up close, it seemed like a second skin. An iridescent belt buckle as wide as Gus's fist sparkled in the low light. Though she'd only seen them from afar, she recognized it: a burdle scale.

"Who's your jeweler?" she coughed. "Think they could make me a pair of boots?"

"You've got some nice moves for a void-drifter," Junior said and smiled into her bruised face.

"You haven't seen my moves yet." She spat blood to the floor.

Junior's face darkened. "Girl, you've no idea who you're rutting with do you? The only reason you're not already bleeding out on the floor is that you never went for your weapon." He paused. "That intrigues me. We've seen how good you are with a deck of cards. I must admit, I've never been hustled so completely. Now we'll see if you're any good with that relic. Or if, as I suspect, it's just for show. Let 'er go."

The mob's hands fell away as the crowd retreated. Someone dragged Aaron's groggy form away as they made room for the gunfighters.

Gus wiped blood from her split lip. This night had gone completely off the rails. Junior stepped back, putting a good twenty paces between them. He unbuttoned his suit jacket and revealed his own weapon: a small but powerful Colt Prism M2265—cutting edge laser tech—in a shoulder holster.

"I'll even make it a fair fight," he said, and pressed a button hidden behind his oversized belt buckle. For a moment, a faint shimmering surrounded him, like an aura or mirage.

Gus had seen that shimmer a handful of times. It usually meant the job was about to get more complicated. If Gus's past was prologue, Junior's personal shield would protect him from any handheld focused beam weapon. Expensive tech.

Very interesting.

"Now we'll see how you stack up against the finger that's killed a dozen men. Three women, a rob, and two genies, too, but who's counting?" Junior wagged his index finger in the air as he paced back and forth.

He can't be serious.

When he brought that finger to his lips and kissed it, all Gus's doubts melted. He stopped and faced her with his feet shoulder width apart and his hand flat against his chest like a man about to swear an oath. "Draw," he said calmly.

"Look, Junior, I didn't come here looking for trouble." With her voice calm and even, Gus held her hands up. "Let's just all take a breath—"

"Draw!" he roared.

Gus's eyes narrowed. *Fine, but only because you asked nicely.* She set her shoulders and pulled the cigar from her poncho's breast pocket. She flipped the poncho over her right shoulder, showed Delilah off to the room, and lit the cigar. After a deep drag, she blew a plume of smoke and lowered her hand to her hip. The haze hung heavily between them. "Say when."

Junior grinned sadistically.

The batwing doors exploded inward, and a newcomer stormed into Cirrus House.

"What in tarnation is going on in here?" he hollered. An older man with deep lines in his face and a paunch that preceded him, the stranger stepped purposefully into the space between the fighters. He wore a floor length duster the same shade as the clouds outside and an old-fashioned Stetson the color of fresh cream. The hat sat upon salt-and-pepper hair that had gone mostly salt, with a bristly mustache to match. Gus clocked the star stamped with "Marshal" pinned over his heart and the big scatter-beam carried casually over his shoulder.

"Just settling a small dispute, Ray. No need for you to get involved," Junior said. Banal words, but vaguely threatening, nevertheless.

"Ayuh," Ray replied and shrugged the long gun from his shoulder to his hands. "The thing about that is, if you draw that weapon, you're gonna cause all manner of headaches for me. I'm gonna have to arrest you for unlawful use of a firearm in a place of commerce. Then I'll have to file a report, and you *know* how long it takes to get a reply out here. Sure, sure, Laszlo'll probably have you out of my holding cells before morning. But there's procedures that need to be followed in these situations, and none of us want to go through that if it can be avoided. Am I right? This one's not worth it," Ray said with a nod in Gus's direction.

Once more, Gus watched the Leconte mind at work. Aaron's wheels turned through molasses and whiskey. Junior's razz skills and command of the room suggested his mind was a finely tuned, well-oiled machine: one built for calculation and cunning. He glared at the marshal for a moment, his gaze cold and blank, and then broke into a wide grin.

"Only havin' a little fun, Uncle Ray. You know how I like a good challenge." He buttoned his jacket over his shoulder holster. "But a bit of advice for the lady if I may: pack up your winnings and leave town. If I get word you're sticking around causing trouble, we'll finish this."

Gus took another long drag from her cigar. "Count on it," she said with a sneer.

With the crowd slowly disbursing, Ray offered Gus a friendly hand and a sardonic smile. "Welcome to Las Ráfagas. As I'm sure you've gathered, m'name's Ray. Ray Gascon. I'm what passes for the law in these parts."

The law.

Gus hesitated for a moment. No way word of Tuco's heist and her escape had reached Las Ráfagas yet. Better to take the opportunity to make an ally while she had the chance.

"Gus," she said and shook his hand. She wiped blood from her face. "That's one hell of a welcome wagon you've got out here."

He chuckled warmly. "What can I say? Folks 'round here are a mite traditional—they like to get the pleasantries out of the way quickly. Why don't you come on back to the Marshal's Office? I got a first aid kit, and if

we're lucky, I might even be able to get my old coffee machine running."
He led her to the batwing doors. "Gus, eh? I reckon you came to town by
way of El Dorado?"

Flop. Flop. Flop.

The sole of Gus's boot slapped against the road with each step. It had
torn loose during the scuffle and made it hard to focus.

Since leaving Cirrus House, Gus's mind was reeling. She hadn't won
enough spoons yet to barter with Emmitt for his fuel. If she couldn't
gamble her way to the funds, she had few options left. Few options that
would keep her in Ray's good graces, anyway.

Flop. Flop. Flop.

Ray led them through the front door of the Marshal's Office and into
a wide lobby with a waiting area and a few desks. The thick, undisturbed
layer of dust and cobwebs implied no one had occupied them in years.

"This way." Ray directed her through another, much heavier door at
the back of the room secured with several impressive locks. The cellblock.
Gus's pulse quickened.

"You know, Ray, on second thought, I should probably just get back to
my room at Hotel Irma and sleep this off."

Ray brushed her off. "Don't be silly. None 'o those scrapes look too
serious, but we should get you cleaned up just in case. Infection's a bitch
out here, and Doc Park's only got so many meds." He unlocked the heavy
door with a keypad combination and thumbprint scan. It slid open with a
screech. "This way."

Flop. Flop. Flop.

She followed nervously, half expecting him to turn on her and toss her
into one of the cells. Instead, he walked straight through to a small corner
office that overlooked the jail's four cramped, empty cells. She stepped into
the dimly lit room to find him already digging through his desk's drawers.

"Now where did I put that blasted ... Ah! Here it is." He pulled a small
box with a big red cross on it from the drawer and tossed it to her. He
lowered his heavy frame into the chair behind the desk and started fiddling
with an old coffee maker. "Have a seat. There should be some antiseptic in
there."

Gus did as asked and opened the first aid kit. She found the small bottle of antiseptic spray, as well as a handful of anesthetic syrettes, a few vacuum-bandages, and a three quarters full bottle of some burgundy liquid. She unscrewed the cap, took a whiff, and recoiled from the stench of homebrew booze.

"Oh! I've been looking for that," Ray said and took the bottle with a nod. "That'll go well with the coffee." He took a swig, grimaced, and screwed the top back on.

With Gus's minor injuries seen to, the first aid kit tucked away in a cargo pocket, and a scrap of gauze tied around her boot to secure the sole, Gus took in the small office. It spoke of a lawman with little to do around town—and liked it that way. The areas Ray obviously frequented, like the desk and the space in front of the small window, were clean of the Aeolusian dust that coated everything else. But, if Gus was right, the office's small comms unit and gun cabinet hadn't been dusted, or even used, since the town's founding.

Gus pulled out her tobacco tin and began rolling.

"Wow, is that proto?" Ray asked when the aroma hit his nose. "I haven't seen non-cloned tobacco in *years*. How'd you come by that?" As he leaned in to get a good whiff from the tin, his eyes widened. "You know what? Don't tell me. It's probably better if I don't know." He started to reach for the cigar she offered. "Actually, I better not." He sighed and waved it away. "Thanks, but that's a habit I broke a long time ago."

Shrugging, Gus lit the cigar for herself. As the smell of fresh coffee and tobacco filled the small office, Ray leaned back in his chair and regarded Gus for a long second. "If you don't mind my asking, what's your business in Las Ráfagas?" He poured two cups of coffee and gestured to the bottle of homebrew and the cream and sugar already on his desk.

She shook her head and accepted the coffee black. "Had a job offer out this way. It fell through. Then I had some trouble on atmo-entry. My pony's with the engineer. He says it'll be another three days. *And* I'm low on rubidium. There some kinda shortage?"

Ray shrugged. "Don't know much about that. I spend most of my days breaking up fights, ticketing Jacob Wagner when he blocks the road out front of Cirrus House with his damned hyper-surrey and getting fat behind this desk."

"I thought you were the law in Las Ráfagas?" Gus asked and sipped her coffee. Her face pinched as the bitter brew hit her tongue. *Cloned crap.* Still, it wasn't the worst she'd ever had.

"Oh, I'm little more than an old guy with a gun. Outpost security is actually handled by," Ray's voice took on a high, haughty air, "the Leconte Atmo-Mining Solutions Company Police." He sighed. "Which Aaron Leconte, coincidentally, is the chief of. You haven't made any friends there."

Of course he is. Exactly what she didn't want—local attention.

"No, my job here is mostly symbolic," Ray said. "The UCET says you need a lawman to run an outpost in the Territories." He spread his arms and smiled. "So here I am."

"And Junior? What's he do around here?"

"He's the mining foreman."

Gus sipped her coffee to hide her annoyance. *Christ's blood.* "And how do you fit into this little world of nepotism, Ray? Junior called you 'uncle.'"

"Caught that, did ya?" Ray stretched in his chair and frowned as his joints popped and cracked. "Yeah, Laszlo and I go way back. Before he built this monstrosity of an outpost, we grew up together. On New Angoulême, in the Imperium Sector. I kept a bully or two off his back when we were kids, and he brought me out here after I was wounded on the job. To pay me back, I guess. Gave me a cushy job to run out my golden years."

Great. I'm surrounded.

"So, you work for Leconte, too?" Gus tried to keep her tone even.

Ray smiled gently and sat up in his chair. "Miss, basically everyone left in or around this town works for Laszlo Leconte in one fashion or another. But even if you are just about the calmest glass of water I've ever seen, I know what you're thinking over there. As long as you stay in the lines while you're here, you've got nothing to fear from me." He leaned back in his chair. "Though I can't say the same thing for the Leconte boys and the Company Police. I suggest you find another way to raise your funds. Gambling with the town's bigwigs wasn't the best move to begin with."

"Point taken." Gus downed the last of her cup and stood. "Thanks for the help tonight, Ray. Maybe I'll see you around." She shook his hand and made for the door before he could protest.

Gus made her way back toward Hotel Irma through the dark square. Overhead, the Milky Way painted the cracked dome with a glittering vista of stars. But in her fury, Gus's gaze quickly dropped from the spectacle above to the gauze keeping her boots together. *How could I have been so stupid? Saving Walter may have cost* everything.

Why didn't I just walk out? It was over. *I could have spent the next three days stringing the little bastard along, emptying his damn wallet every night. But* no, *I had to play hero and rut everything up. Putting my nose where it doesn't belong*, again. *What is* wrong *with me?*

With razz off the table, that left only one option, and it spit directly in the face of her newest ally on Las Ráfagas. But it was that or wait for the San Juan-Paul bulls to show up and turn herself in. Besides, if she stayed careful, Ray would never know.

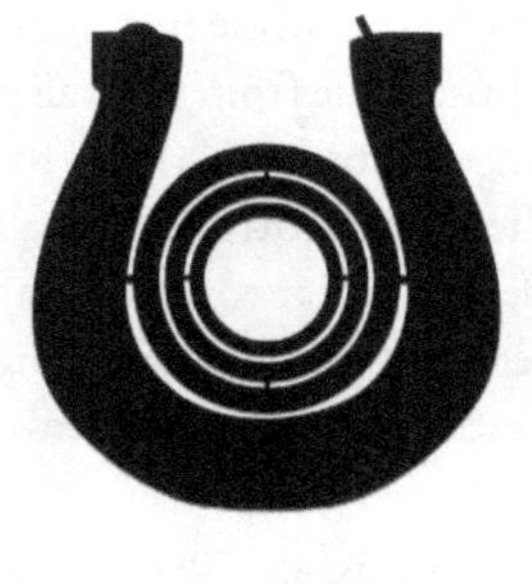

THE DESPERADO

Gus's eyes snapped open after a scant few hours' sleep. Deiopea hung low in the still dark sky outside her window at Hotel Irma. *Perfect.* She quickly pulled her poncho on. She hoped it was too early for many of the townsfolk to be up and about. With her hood up, she slid out of her room, down Hotel Irma's painfully creaky staircase, and into the cool morning.

Gus paused in the inn's doorway and scanned the square in the predawn light. Not a soul to be seen. *Good.* She would have to be discreet. She gritted her teeth against the blood and pressure pounding in her ears. *Whiskey and sucker punches always make difficult mornings.* Nevertheless, one path remained. She closed her eyes and took a deep, steadying breath. The cool morning air filled her lungs and prickled her skin. Savoring the feeling, Gus made her way along the square's dim boardwalk.

She found the engineering corral already open. Gus expected Emmitt would still be in bed, but the activity in the corral didn't surprise her. She also had a habit of tinkering a little when insomnia struck. Lucky for her, Emmitt and his crew were otherwise occupied at the far end of the bay. She stuck to the shadows and quietly boarded *Tilly* unseen.

As soon as she set foot on the mount, the lights flickered on, and *Tilly* nickered a greeting.

"I know, girl. Easy, easy." She patted the bulkheads as she stepped from the airlock lift into the pony's small cargo hold. "I'm trying to get us out of here as fast as I can."

At one end of the narrow, hallway-like hold, near the chemical head, a small but well-kept flower box built into the bulkhead bloomed. Gus breathed deeply and enjoyed the subtle fragrance of the plants and soil.

A low but persistent buzz came from the wall panel directly behind the flowers. Gus used a wedge-shaped tool, built for this purpose, to pry it open. As she worked, she cooed gently to the wall panel.

"It's okay, it's okay. I know what you guys want." She carefully pulled back the panel and placed it on the floor, revealing a hidden compartment half filled with honeycomb. Fat, lazy bumblebees drifted from the hive and began sampling from the flower garden.

Satisfied the bees were happy, Gus took a large, lunchbox-shaped container from the hidden contraband hold and popped it open, revealing a cornucopia of items the UCET deemed "too dangerous" for the general population. Strictly controlled substances like peanut butter, strawberries, mushrooms, and a few banned medical supplies, like penicillin and ibuprofen—prohibited due to their *potentially* deadly allergic reactions—rattled around as she rifled through the contents.

But the bees themselves would have gotten her in the most trouble.

The vast number of people who were allergic to them and their protected status on Earth made them Gus's most dangerous contraband. If Ray discovered she had a hive this size, he would have no choice but to put her away for the rest of her life. And if someone were stung … Gus didn't like to think about that. But people on this side of the Rift would pay through the nose for real, pure honey. All she had to do was keep the hive safe and secure, and times like this made the considerable risk well worth it.

She sprayed a pheromone mixture into the wall compartment, and the bees floating around the flowers followed it back into the hidden hold. Gus closed the panel, grabbed her contraband lunchbox, and stepped back onto *Tilly's* lift. But it didn't activate. Instead, *Tilly's* air ducts snorted sharply.

"I don't like it either," Gus reassured her old traveling companion. "But as much of a pain in the ass Emmitt is, I think he's a halfway decent engineer. It's only a few days' work. Now, let's go. Open up. I gotta sell some of this if you want to get fed any time soon."

Tilly made a sound like a sigh and the lift activated, lowering Gus to the corral floor. Sticking to the shadows, Gus quietly made her way back through the mostly empty workspace. Emmitt and his team continued to work feverishly on something at the far end of the enormous room. *Bastard better not forget about* Tilly. She kept one eye on them as she stepped from shadow to shadow.

She couldn't tell what they were working on. *A mount? No. Not big enough.* She paused to squint across the corral. Gus brought her hands to her face, intending to zoom in, but stopped herself with a sharp scoff. It didn't matter. She had more important business to attend to this morning. From her hiding place beneath a rusted-out fuselage, Gus spotted Emmitt. He turned his attention back across the corral toward the door, a few steps from where she hunkered down. She readjusted her grip on the lunchbox and waited for the right moment to sprint the final stretch.

A tall woman with an unruly mop of curly white hair walked into Gus's view and offered Emmitt a cup of coffee. He took the mug from her—his wife, Gus assumed—and the two turned their backs on Gus and the door to watch the work.

Now.

She crossed the open space in moments. Inches from the door, it started to open. Gus spun as if ducking a tackle and barely managed to keep the swinging door between her and Emmitt's new guest. She launched herself against the wall next to the opening door and prayed whoever came through wouldn't spot her.

She got lucky. The newcomer walked directly toward the working engineering crew as if drawn to them by a magnet. Gus caught only a glimpse of a dark suit. As soon as they were clear of the door, she swung around it and out before it could close.

Before she could go more than a few steps, a nagging feeling took over. She'd only been in town a day and hadn't met much of its population yet, but she *knew* that suit. Only one kind of person wore a suit like that in a town like this.

What reason could Junior have to pay Emmitt a visit at this time of morning?

It doesn't matter. It's none of my business. Or my problem. She glanced at the lunchbox. She had her own business to deal with. Besides, she could do without another dustup with Junior. She managed another few steps before the sound of the working stopped, replaced with a high-pitched scream.

Emmitt shrieked, *"Gloria!"*

Tunk.

Gus doubled back to the door. She opened it slowly and peered through the crack but couldn't see anything. The screaming stopped, but the work hadn't resumed. She slipped back into the corral and inched closer, staying quiet and hidden.

At the far end of the room, Junior and Emmitt argued, but she couldn't make out the conversation—Junior's voice was sharp but low.

"You don't understand!" Emmitt shouted.

Gus moved in for a better view. Junior stood opposite Emmitt with his M2265 in one hand, and a fistful of Gloria Smith's curly white hair in the other. The engineer's wife sat on the floor, holding her head and sobbing.

"I don't care about your problems, Smith," Junior said. "We're on a deadline here. You understand what a deadline is, right? This retrofit has already taken two weeks longer than you promised. If we're not producing, we're not making spoons. I've got logistical problems of my own to deal with. You think I want to come down here because *you* 'can't make it work?' If the rutting *spiders* can do it, *we* can do it."

"Mr. Leconte, *please!* Try to understand, we *know* why it's not working. The, er ... samples you brought us were inert, um ... *dead*. The process needs conscious effort! It will never work without a live, er ... specimen," Emmitt said. He raised his trembling hands and, inch by inch, crept between Junior and his wife.

Junior's tone changed on a dime. "Well," he said cheerfully. He spun his pistol on his finger like a showman. "Why didn't you say so? If that's all you need, I can get you live ones." Gus couldn't see Junior's face, but she could *hear* the smirk in his voice.

"But Mr. Leconte!" Emmitt's voice cracked. "That's—"

"It's a business decision." Junior's voice dropped. "With my father's authority and as mining foreman of the only rubidium-87 depot on this side of the Rift, it's my decision to make. Do whatever you have to do to prepare for your new *specimens.*"

"Sir, I—" Emmitt again protested. Whatever Gus thought of Emmitt, she had to admit the old coot had backbone. But before he could get any more out, Junior pistol-whipped him across the jaw. Hard. Blood, and maybe a few teeth, hit the engineering corral floor.

"You may think that because you're the only engineer in this junk pile of a town that means I won't take you outside and drop you to the core," Junior said into Emmitt's bleeding face. "And you might be right. But I've learned from my father that fear of personal harm isn't the only way to motivate people." He raised his M2265 and pointed it at Mrs. Smith. His hand twitched, and a focused beam of purple light lit up the bay. The workers gasped. Emmitt yelped and jumped forward, too late to intercept the beam.

Gloria Smith sat trembling, but alive. A spot on the floor smoldered behind her. Her fluffy white hair smoked at the temple where the beam had passed within millimeters of ending her life.

Junior's voice dropped even lower, and Gus strained to hear as he threatened the old engineer. "Get. It. Done." He spun on his heel, headed for the door, and sent Gus scrambling for cover. Too busy surveying the corral, Junior didn't notice her. He *did* notice *Tilly*. "And get that rutting piece of jelly manure out of my father's town," he called back over his shoulder as he reached the door.

From her hiding spot, Gus watched Emmitt yell at his crew to get back to work, before he dropped to his knees and embraced his sobbing wife. Gus carefully followed Junior's path back to the door. *I gotta get outta this floating rust bucket.* She eased the door open, made sure the coast was clear, and stepped out into the first rays of dawn.

What the tunk is going on in this town?

From past experience, Gus knew the place to peddle her wares would be in the mostly abandoned residential quarter and here on Las Ráfagas, her best bet would be Genie-town. All mining outposts had them. As she walked the quiet streets, her thoughts turned back to what she had just seen.

What the tunk *is Emmitt building for Junior?* It had something to do with the mining rings retrofit, but the issue had to be more than simple delays. *Who threatens people like that over routine delays?* The midnight meeting in the Vega's kitchen made more sense now. No one can fight people who put spoons over everything. Against men like this, it was better to take the payout and leave with your life.

Gus caught the scent of roasting meats; her first hint of Las Ráfagas's Genie-town. Another block and hushed conversations joined the mouth-watering smell of greenbottle jelly steaks in the air. She smiled. Most Genie-towns she'd visited were considered the bad part of town. But in her experience, genies made the best of what they had and never hesitated to share.

Lost in the anticipation of a street-steak breakfast, Gus nearly walked into a group of men who stepped from an alley and into the road in front of her. With their backs to her she had barely enough time to duck down a side street without being seen. She stole a peek around the corner and found four men, three of which were armed and dressed in long, dark coats so new, the fabric still sported well defined creases.

Gus recognized something familiar about the fourth man's silhouette, despite his unnatural posture. Then he moved, turning to face one of the other men; his hands were behind his back, locked in the distinctly high-tech cuffs of the UCET.

No. It can't be.

Any doubt about the fourth man's identity fell away when he spoke. "Hey, *hermano,* I kept up my side of the deal, *si?* Why don't we take these off, eh? Maybe just loosen 'em up a bit?"

"Shut up, Tuco," the man next to him said. "How do we know the bounty-head's even here?"

"Where else would a runaway cobbler-rob go, *mi amigo?*" Despite his situation, Tuco's usual joviality shone through. "There's not a lot of places to work out here!"

Gus retreated to the cover of the alley. In her haste, she stumbled into a pile of abandoned household appliances some long gone resident had left in the road. The crash echoed off the empty buildings.

"What the rut was that?" one of the men called out.

"Johnson, Hastings, check it out," another commanded. "And take Tuco with you."

"Hey! What?" Tuco cried.

Gus's lunchbox opened and spilled contraband all over the street. She scrambled to gather it up and tossed the lunchbox into the corroded washing machine she had fallen over. She closed the washer door as Tuco stepped, hesitantly, into the alley.

The instant he registered her, his face broke out into a grin, but he didn't say a word. Instead, his eyes narrowed as Gus watched a plan form in his tiny mind. He jumped onto the pile of appliances, out of sight of the other men, and started screaming like a madman. On reflex, Gus drew Delilah and gaped at him.

Johnson and Hastings—presumably—came around the corner with their weapons already in hand. Tuco dove from the pile of appliances onto one of the men and knocked him flat. The other spotted Gus and took aim while Tuco rolled around on the ground with his partner.

Gus didn't hesitate. A beam of bright pink light erupted from Delilah's barrel and bathed the alley in a grapefruit glow for a fraction of a second. The man fell with a smoking hole in his chest. Pink-tinged gas belched from Delilah's exhaust ports and soaked Gus's glove in an ice-cold mist.

Tuco's struggle continued for a moment more until Gus heard a sharp *crack*. He grumbled his way to his feet, untangling himself from the body of either Johnson or Hastings. He flashed a plaque-filled grin at her.

"Thanks for the save, *hermana*. You stay there. I'll be right back." He stooped, groped around for one of the dropped guns, and then ran back out into the road with it hidden behind him.

"Kurtz!" he bellowed as he rounded the corner with a look of feigned terror on his face. "Get your ass over here, *pendejo!* Get these damn irons off'a me. Your boys're down, Kurtz! Hurry!"

"What the rut is going on over there, Tuco? Where's Hastings?" Kurtz yelled before the distinct sound of a UCET standard issue sidearm went off, accompanied by a brilliant flash of cobalt.

Cautiously, Gus leaned out into the street. Kurtz's motionless body sat slouched over in the road. Tuco crouched down with his back to it and rifled through the dead man's pockets with his bound hands. "Hey, *mi amiga*, help me find this bastard's keys."

Instead, she sat down on an abandoned stoop, pointed Delilah at him, and watched. "What are you doing here, Tuco? Who're your friends?"

"What do you mean? This is the place. Now that we're back together again, we can find the runaway rob 'n get back to civilization. You gonna help me here, or not?"

She approached, keeping Delilah pointed at his chest. "After everything, you still want to partner up? You still think *I* want to work with *you?*"

"Hey, why not?" He grinned at her again. "Without a ride, I can't get the rob back to the CCO. And splitting the bounty two ways is better than four. Though I doubt these *pendejos* would have even let me keep my share," he said. "Ah-ha!" he shouted and finally came up with the digital fingerprint fob that would unlock the irons. But struggle all he could, he couldn't bend his wrists to unlock them himself. "Ah, a little help, *hermana?*"

"Who were these generous new partners of yours?" She knelt and turned Kurtz onto his back to get a better look at him and instantly regretted it. Kurtz's new jacket fell open to reveal the distinctive deep blue of a UCET Army Officer's uniform beneath.

"Tunk!" she cried and stumbled back from the body. "You stupid son of a whore! Did we just kill a bunch of bluebell soldiers?"

"Officers," Tuco corrected.

Gus spun around, grabbed the little man by his lapels, and dragged his face into hers. "What did you rope me into here, you bastard?"

"Easy! Easy, *hermana.* It's nothing special. Just the usual violence. Don't worry about these idiots. After you left me to the bulls, they brought me back to San Juan-Paul. They were on shore leave or something. Off the government clock, looking for trouble, and with more muscle than brains, ya know?"

Gus's eyebrow twitched. "Just how you like 'em."

Tuco's grin widened. "I bribed them to get me out with equal shares of the bounty, but for some reason they didn't trust me enough to let me out of the cuffs." He winked at her and gave the body another kick.

"And why should I be any more foolish?" she asked and stuck Delilah up under his chin.

"Think of the money, *hermana.* I'll even sweeten the deal for you; you get me 'n that rob back to the CCO to get paid, 'n you'll never hear from little ol' Tuco ever again. Take your earnings 'n buy a beach on some moon for all I care."

Despite her better judgment, Gus found herself considering his offer. It *was* a lot of spoons, but ...

"Couple problems with that. *Tilly's* fuel cell is bone dry, and there's no rubidium on this good for nothing outpost save what's in the corral's rations. And I ain't got the spoons to convince the engineer to part with it."

Tuco grinned at her. "Maybe not yet. But if I know you, *hermana,* you already got yourself a plan to fix that. Or, there's always ..."

Her eyes narrowed. Selling her contraband would get her off the outpost, but not much further. The bounty would keep her going.

Tunk.

"No. If we do this, we're doin' it my way."

Knowing she would live to regret it, Gus took the fob from Tuco and unlocked his hands. "Ah," he said as he rubbed his wrists, *"muchas gracias, hermana."*

"It's a big outpost, Tuco. How do you suggest we find this rob?"

Gravel crunched at the mouth of the alley. Startled, both Gus and Tuco turned with their weapons at the ready to find a tall, portly man in a pin-striped suit surrounded by heavily armed combat-robs.

"Maybe I can help you with that," he said.

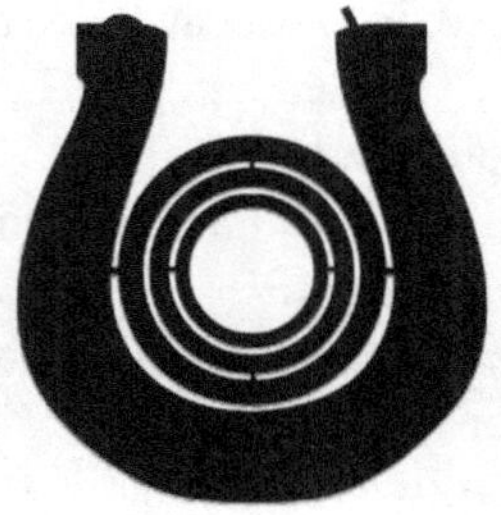

FOR A FEW SPOONS MORE

A bloodcurdling scream exploded from Tuco's mouth. He raised his pistol and got off a single cobalt shot before Gus could grab him. To her horror—and despite his abject panic—Tuco fired true. The blue beam of concentrated light struck the stranger square in the chest before his rob entourage could react.

Or, at least, it should have. Instead of disintegrating the man's suit into a bloody crater, the beam stopped in midair a few inches in front of him, fractured into a thousand streams of light, and dissipated. *A high-tech cold-plasma shield, like Junior's.* The combat-robs, each an eight-foot-tall, autonomous humanoid tank, raised their military-grade rifles in response. But the man smiled and waved them off.

"Hold your fire," he said and casually stepped forward. "We simply startled this gentleman. There's no need to execute him in the streets, especially after showing off some *impressive* reflexes. Allow me to introduce myself." He shook Tuco's hand with an odd, yanking motion. "Laszlo Leconte, owner and chief administrator of this facility. And who might you be?" He took Gus's hand more gently and even brought her dirty glove close to his lips in a pantomime of a kiss.

Ray said they'd gone to school together, but the marshal had to be pushing sixty-five. Laszlo's golden blonde hair, healthy, tanned skin, and bare beginnings of crow's feet around his eyes put him closer to forty. Gus didn't understand how that could be possible, but she filed it away for later.

"Mr. and Mrs. Guadalupe," Gus answered quickly. Tuco smiled greed-ily. He slid next to her and put his hand on her hip.

"Married?" Laszlo asked. His lower lip jutted out in a pout.

"Yes, but not to him," she said and gave Tuco a sharp elbow to the stomach. "This is my brother-in-law, Tuco."

"Ah," Laszlo said with the beginnings of a smile, "you wouldn't go by 'Gus,' Mrs. Guadalupe, would you?"

Tunk. So much for that. She nodded. "As a matter of fact, I do. Now, how did you come to hear that?"

"Let's just say my sons were *very* impressed with you. For different reasons, of course. Now I can see they both do indeed take after their father." He took her in with gluttonous eyes. A shiver ran down Gus's spine, but Laszlo finally released her hand and stepped back. "Well, Mr. and Mrs. Guadalupe, it does appear that you have a small dilemma." He nudged Kurtz's body with an oxford-clad toe. "Indeed, two problems, if you intend to find this bounty-head in my town while avoiding the sector authorities. But as I said, I may be able to help you. With both."

Gus and Tuco exchanged a glance. "We're listening," Gus said.

"As it stands, I'm in the middle of some delicate business negotiations that will help bring this once grand town back from the brink. My daughter is off-world finalizing the details with the concerned party as we speak. Once the particulars are ironed out, she will escort them here so we can sign the contract. I could use some people with your particular"—he sneered at Kurtz's body— "*talents* while I complete this transaction. You'll be paid handsomely, of course, in addition to all the rubidium-87 your mount can carry. And your bounty-head, naturally. Assuming this runaway rob of yours is even here. I have my doubts."

Tuco's grin reached from ear to ear. Gus knew what it meant: easy money. She, on the other hand, wasn't so sure.

"You've got a marshal in town. Not to mention a private police force. What do you need with two more hired guns?" she asked and squinted against the dawning red sun.

Laszlo smirked. "Ah, yes, Raymond. Such a great guy. He's one of the reasons I *do* need you. You see, Raymond and I go way back. I even asked him to come to Las Ráfagas. Did you know that? But with that history comes some baggage. Raymond is, shall we say, rough around the edges. And the people I'm dealing with are very serious people. The *most* serious people.

"Honestly—and I hate to say it because he's such a terrific friend—but I'm afraid Raymond will put his nose where it doesn't belong and ruin a good thing for everyone. I'm trying to put Las Ráfagas's best foot forward. I need someone to help him keep the restless townsfolk in line, and keep his focus away from my negotiations. For now. As I understand it, you've already developed a bit of a rapport with our dear marshal." He raised his eyebrows at Gus.

"You're very well informed, Mr. Leconte," she said. "But you haven't answered me. Why do you need *us*? You could have anyone distract Ray." *This guy answers questions without actually answering them with words intended to distract and confuse. I don't like it.*

"You're going to make me say it?" Laszlo sighed. "Raymond and I aren't on great terms anymore, but I still worry about him. You're right—I could send anyone, but if a pretty face like yours will provide a pleasant distraction for an old man while I try to make his life better, then I would like to provide him that. Clearly, you can handle yourself in a fight, which will make you useful to Raymond during this time of unrest. With business down, the remaining townsfolk have become despondent. Depressed. There have been more fights as of late, and I'm worried Raymond won't be able to handle the violence alone.

"As for Mr. Guadalupe," he said and turned his attention to Tuco, "the miners have been relegated to their barracks for weeks now as we retrofit the outpost's rings. While we haven't had too many problems yet, I feel we could use a man like you. An infusion of new blood, new ideas at my sons' side to help us keep it that way.

"With the two of you split up—one in town, one among the miners—if your bounty-head is here, I'm sure you'll find him." Laszlo finished with a practiced, charismatic smile. His perfectly straight and blindingly white teeth glinted in the morning light.

Tuco raised his hand to shake on it, but Gus caught his forearm mid-upswing. "And if we decide we don't want the job?"

Laszlo's winning smile faltered slightly, and his eyes turned sinister.

"You've just murdered three UCET officers in cold blood. It doesn't matter what these men did or where you go, they'll hunt you down. I can see to that. But"—his smile returned to its former glory in a flash—"I've no love for the bluebells myself. As long as you're under my employ I would have reason to misdirect the authorities, should they arrive in *my* town. Besides," he continued while taking a tablet from one of his combat-robs,

"I think you'll find I pay fair prices for services rendered. I only ask that while you are here you abide by town law and do not run afoul of our dear Marshal Gascon." He handed the tablet over. Tuco and Gus studied it together.

Tuco's jaw dropped open like it popped a hinge. Gus's knees turned to rubber, and she forced them not to tremble beneath her. Laszlo offered more spoons than she had ever earned for one job in her life. *Tunk,* more than she had ever made for *five* jobs. Enough to keep *Tilly* in repair and fueled, not only for the trip back to the Old Colonies, but for another year or two to come. Gus's vision swam. Laszlo played things close to the vest, but she had taken much bigger jobs for much less pay—on roughly the same lack of information—many times before.

Sure, Laszlo was a bit of a bully, but so was Tuco. At least Laszlo *seemed* genuine in his attempt to help the ghost town. *So what if he makes a few spoons doing it?* For an instant, Gus's mind flashed to the small, crowded Vega kitchen, and a mangled, flanged H-tube key sitting on the same table they had welcomed her to. She shook the image away; disputes between ranchers and miners were a time-honored tradition. Nothing new, and none of her business.

Nothing but dust.

"Do we have a deal?" Laszlo asked. A hint of laughter seeped into his voice.

Three dead bluebells, Ray and the law on one side, and Leconte's deal on the other. *Not much of a choice.* At least Laszlo's offer made it *well* worth their while. She raised her own hand, and Laszlo took it with an odd, jerky shake.

Red Hippotes hung high over Las Ráfagas, baking the marshal's modest office in the noonday sun. Gus opened the small window and perched on the sill. Ray sat behind his desk and unfolded the note she brought him. Gus kept her eyes on her fingers as she silently rolled a cigar, and Ray read Laszlo's jagged handwriting.

She'd had a few hours to reflect on the deal she and Tuco struck with Laszlo, and her fingers belied her mood: they hesitated where they were usually confident, quivered where they were usually solid, and languished where they were usually nimble.

Tunk.

The cigar fell apart, and she began again.

She eyed Ray as his lips moved wordlessly while he read. Only hours ago, she'd planned to sell her smuggled wares under his nose. Now, she planned to lie to his face. The former had been a necessity. The latter burned at her scalp like a betrayal.

She finished rolling the cigar—a lumpy, misshapen thing—and clamped down on it with her teeth. *Trapped. And not even by the law—or even a rutting double cross! Nope. Trapped by this godforsaken town and my own spoon-grubbing fingers.*

But the choice was to play Laszlo's game or spend the rest of her life under lock and key. She shuddered at the thought of Tilly rusting in some UCET impound stable. Or worse, sold off for scrap.

Sneering, she sparked her lighter hard and brought it to the cigar. The acrid smoke sank deep into her lungs. No way this would be as easy as Laszlo said, but if she could just make it through, the payoff would make it worth it. Right?

Not easy, no. But simple enough. Help Ray. Stay out of trouble. Find the bounty-head. *Simple. Sure.* She sighed and blew smoke into the heat.

Ray poured himself a mug of coffee from the freshly brewed pot on his desk, apparently undeterred by the warmth of the office. "So, Laszlo's contracted you to help me—what's this say—'keep the peace while ring retrofitting is completed.'" He squinted at the handwriting through a pair of cracked reading glasses. "I can't say I don't appreciate the help, but this ain't exactly what I had in mind when I told you to stay away from the gambling tables." He chuckled as he poured some of the homebrew into his coffee with the cream and sugar.

"Yeah," she mumbled darkly. Across the square, a handful of townsfolk browsed the farmers market stalls.

"What's the problem? You said you needed rubidium, and this'll be easy. I mean, things have gotten a little rougher around here, but it's usually just breaking up a few drunks scuffling outside the Irma or Cirrus House, and arguing with Jacob Wagner about where he parks his surrey. It's not like I've ever had to break out the sonic grenades for crowd control. I'm gettin' too old for this, but it shouldn't be more than you can handle. Here." Ray reached into a drawer and pulled out something that gleamed in the sunlight. "We'll make it official," he said and tossed it to her. A silver star, stamped with "Deputy Marshal," landed in her lap.

With a frown, she turned the badge this way and that. "Ray, I—"

He cut her off before she could say more. "Put it on and tell me what the problem is."

"It's just that I don't want to be stuck with your job if you keel over before I breeze back on out of town."

Ray laughed hard and spit liquor-laced coffee all over the desk. "Don't you worry about that none," he said. "As the spiders say, 'it'll be a world without light' the day I turn my badge over to some void-driftin' beam-slinger." He smiled at her over the rim of his mug. He leaned back and took another sip. "What's really on your mind?"

Gus snuffed out what remained of her cigar and slumped into the chair opposite Ray's desk. She fiddled with the badge instead of putting it on. Ray poured two fresh cups of coffee and put his feet up on the desk. Gus followed suit. Her spurs rattled when she crossed her feet. "I don't like being pushed into deals, is all. Can I trust Laszlo?"

"*Hell,* no! He'll definitely try to cheat you out of what you agreed on. But if I know Laszlo, even what he *does* give you will be a small fortune. The man is sneaky, but you can rely on him for exactly one thing: to look out for himself. If you help him do that, you'll profit. If you get in his way, well ..." His eyes drifted to an old photo hung on the wall. A much younger Ray and another young man—who could have been Oscar Vega's twin—stood with a gigantic burdle strung up between them. A trophy kill. "If all he's asking you to do is help me out for a bit while the town gets situated, I'd say don't rock the boat. If there's more, well, I'm no coward, but sometimes it's easier *to go along to get along* when it comes to the Lecontes."

"That what you're doing out here? Going along to get along?" Gus asked quietly.

Ray's eyes went wide at the question but smiled. "You could say that. The bluebells say you need a marshal, a post office, and a charter to settle in the Territories. Laszlo's mining operation wrote the charter, Walter and the mercantile act as the post office, and when Laszlo's original marshal died, he brought me in, so the government didn't send someone he didn't know."

"So, you're nothing but a strawman. A puppet for Laszlo to make it all seem legit," Gus said casually. She flinched at her own rationalizing. *Pigeonholing Ray as a collaborator. That's low.*

He smiled sheepishly. "Twenty, maybe even ten years ago that would have ruffled my feathers, girl. But you're not wrong. Oh, I do my part, keeping the drunks from killing each other, kicking the occasional rabble out of town. But Aaron's Company Police don't really need me, and Junior's got an iron grip on the miners. Did you know Laszlo's taken to paying them in vouchers they can only use at Walter's store?" He shook his head in what might have been shame but was more likely exhausted submission. "What can I say? I'm an old man. It's a paycheck, and I do my best to keep the peace. Any help I can get, even if it's temporary, is much appreciated."

Gus's gaze dropped from Ray to the silver star in her hands. Maybe it didn't have to be a lie. If the marshal really needed help, maybe she could provide it. Finally, she pinned the badge on her poncho. Ray smiled. "So, what's this about a bounty-head in my town?"

Gus's shoulders slumped. Another problem. She had done bounty jobs with Tuco before. He usually had the goods when it came time to grab the bounty-head. This time, of course, was different.

Once they had made their deal with Laszlo, Tuco shared what he knew about the rob they were after "I honestly don't know why we're bothering with that," she said. "Some cobbler-rob killed their owner and got lo-bot hacked for their troubles. And then a week later—*poof*—the damn thing up and disappears. That was three years ago. Tuco's info says it's here, living in town. But that's all he's got, and the lead is fourteen months old."

Ray sipped his coffee. "A bounty from the CCO, then? Didn't think you'd be the type to get mixed up in that war."

"What can I say? I've got a bad habit of letting *Tilly's* empty belly override my better judgment." *A truth you'll hopefully never fully understand.*

Ray raised his eyebrows and took another sip of his coffee. "Well, that *is* a problem. We've got plenty of robs on the outpost, but Maria in the mercantile is the only one that's been lo-bot hacked. It's possible one of the ranching families is keeping it hidden. But if that's the case, you're not going to find it palling around here with me in town. Of course, I don't get down to the mining levels often, so maybe your friend Tuco will have more luck."

Gus glowered at the desk between them. She inhaled sharply and began to grunt in agreement when the cellblock door burst inward. Hector Vega ran into Ray's office, sweating and gasping for breath.

"Marshal!" he gasped. "Marshal Gascon, come quick!"

"Easy now, Hector. Deep breaths. What's going on?" Ray asked.

"*Papi* told me to bring you right away! Come on, let's go!" And back out the door he raced, leaving Gus and Ray to stare at each other.

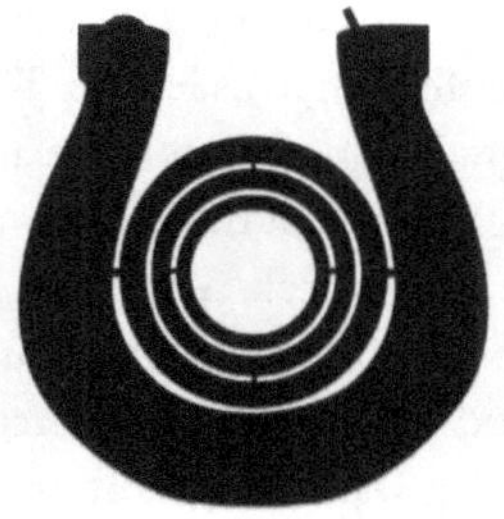

THE LAW AND OSCAR VEGA

B y the time Gus and Ray made it to the front door of the Marshal's Office, Hector was already halfway across the square. Gus raised a hand to shield her eyes as she stepped onto the porch. The sun was high and bright even though the dawn's clear sky had been replaced with patches of storm clouds the color of old blood. It was clear where Hector was headed: the farmers market. They could see signs of a scuffle from where they stood. Ray hitched up his pants and disappeared back into the office with his brow knitted in irritation.

A mass of black uniforms congregated near the middle of the crowd, but Gus couldn't make out any faces. "What's going on?"

"Looks like Aaron's overstepping his bounds again," Ray said as he reappeared in the doorway with his scatter-beam over his shoulder. His badge gleamed in the noon sun. "Better let me do the talking on this one, Gus. But stay ready." She nodded, pulled up her hood, and followed him into the square.

As they approached the crowd, Ray fired an amber shot into the air. The distinctive crackle of the energy discharge filled the square, interrupting the fighting and demanding the crowd's attention. "What in tarnation is going on here?" Ray hollered into the fresh silence.

The familiar feminine voice of Bernadette Vega called out from within the crowd. "Ray!"

Another familiar—but far less pleasant—voice spoke up. "Ah, *tunk*. Stay out of this, old man. It's none of your business." Aaron Leconte.

The crowd parted and revealed an overturned booth. Meat and produce had spilled to the market floor. A group of men wearing uniforms sporting a fancy badge on their breast pockets held the throng back. Gus recognized some of them from the scuffle at Cirrus House. They were each armed with an enormous, military-grade concentrator rifle and formed a rough circle within the mob. Although they kept their barrels down, the guns' presence was enough to keep the crowd back. Two more had a pair of Deiopeans in bulky, six-ringed cuffs. Aaron, also decked out in his Company Police uniform, had Oscar's hands cuffed behind his back. Oscar struggled against him, but his prosthetic leg was turned out at an odd angle and jerked sporadically. Still, Aaron had to keep both hands on the cuffs to keep Oscar in place.

Only one other man stood within the ring of Company Police. He had an average height and build, with a square jaw, thick eyebrows, and a grungy five o'clock shadow. He stood outside the overturned booth, his hands deep in the pockets of his stained coveralls, and gaped openly at the scene.

With Hector in tow, Bernadette ran through the crowd to Ray. Gus melted into the onlookers. She found Moe helplessly trying to pick up his boss's overturned goods among the townsfolk's feet. Gus put a hand on his mechanical shoulder. The tears in his simulated eyes gave her a start.

"I said, what the hell is going on here?" Ray said once Bernadette and Hector were safely behind him.

"I didn't do anything wrong, Ray!" Oscar yelled. "You know I'm only trying to make ends meet, and this *bastardo* keeps sticking his nose where nobody wants it!"

"Shut up!" Aaron screamed in Oscar's face. He jerked up on the cuffs, pulling Oscars arms into an unnatural angle. Oscar grimaced silently. "You know the law! And I told *you* to stay out of it, old man!" Aaron spat back at Ray.

Ray sighed and lowered his gun. "Aaron, we've been over this a thousand times. The town, which *includes* the farmers market, is under the jurisdiction of the Marshal's Office. Now, why are you arresting that man in my jurisdiction?"

Aaron shoved Oscar to the ground. He landed awkwardly on his good knee before tumbling face-first onto the dusty floor. Aaron jammed a finger in Ray's face. "You want to know what's been going on in *your jurisdiction, Uncle* Ray? Since you're not paying enough attention, *I'll* fill you in. This bottle-breeding parasite has been selling to the spiders—*again*. You know the town charter as well as I do. You've been too easy on him. I'm doing what you should have a long time ago!"

"Is that Laszlo I hear speaking with your tongue? I'll remind you, *and* your father, that I was brought here to keep the peace in town, as per the UCET Statute on Pan-Orion Arm Territorial Colonies and Outposts. If Laszlo doesn't like the way I conduct business, he can have the bluebells send a new marshal. One *without* our *unique* history."

Aaron's face turned bright red, bordering on purple. "How *dare* you. He's flouted the law time and time again, and you let him get away with it! My father gave you every—"

"Oh, shut up, Aaron," Ray cut him off. "He'll spend his night in jail and pay his fine, like always. Now turn him and the Deiopeans over to me, and scurry back down to the mining levels where you belong."

Gus thought Aaron's bulbous blonde head was going to explode. The young man took a menacing step toward Ray. Gus's hand drifted toward Delilah. Ray caught her eye and waved her down with a slight tilt of his hat, but Aaron caught the look and followed it to Gus. The color in his cheeks deepened at the sight of her. A moment later, he made a pained face and forced his fury back.

"Fine," he spat. He gave Oscar's spasming prosthetic a sharp kick. "But if he's caught again, there's gonna be more to pay than a night in the hoosegow and a handful of spoons." He gave Gus a predatory wink that made her skin crawl. "Everybody, fall out," he barked and led his posse through the crowd and away from the market.

As Ray bent to help Oscar up, the man in the coveralls came to them with his hands still buried in his pockets. All the color had drained from his square face.

"Why, John?" Oscar asked.

"Yer not supposed to be selling to the spiders. I was just doin' me civic duty! *I* didn't know Aaron'd come up here like a rabid groundhog and mess ya all up like that!"

"You're a damned fool, Stonewall."

"Hey! I wasn't the one—"

Ray hoisted Oscar to his feet. "Dammit, Stonewall. Can't you mind your own business?" he said and waved the farmer off. "I know damn well what happened. Same thing that happened *last* Thursday. And the Thursday *before.*" The marshal shot Oscar an accusing glare.

"What can I say? *Nunca pude entender los jueves,*" Oscar said with a tentative smile.

"But Marshal, I—"

"Stonewall. *John.* Go home." Ray's face sagged. He collected himself and spoke to the crowd. "Sorry, folks, you'll all have to go home. Market's closed for today." The group sighed collectively. "That's right, folks. Head on home. Everything'll reopen tomorrow morning."

As the crowd broke up, Bernadette ran to her husband. "Oh, you stupid, self-righteous, sanctimonious—"

"I'm alright, Bernie. I'm alright," Oscar said.

"Hold him for a second, would ya?" Ray passed Oscar's weight to Gus. He approached the two still-bound Deiopeans and pulled a handheld tablet from his pocket. "You've had the outpost rules explained to you." As Ray spoke, his tablet flashed intricate patterns of light, translating his words. "Both you and Mr. Vega have been warned several times that this is unacceptable." There was pity in his eyes, but he continued, nevertheless. "You're free to go, but I'll have to escort you to your skiff and ask that you not return to town. I can't promise I'll always be here to set things right."

When Ray finished, the pair of Deiopeans held their own conversation, and Gus spotted the distinct facial markings of the one doing most of the talking. They matched those of the leader of the hunting party she had met in the clouds. The leader turned back to Ray and their eyes lit up. The tablet translated, "We understand."

"Thank you," Ray said and removed their intricate handcuffs. "Please wait here a moment, and I will see you to your skiff." He turned back to Gus and the Vegas. "Mrs. Vega—Bernadette—I apologize in advance for this, but ..." Ray turned his full attention on the limping jelly-rancher. "Three times this month? What is *wrong* with you, Vega?"

"They just want food, Ray!" Oscar protested.

"I don't care if they want sarsaparilla and candy canes, you *know* the outpost charter prohibits trade with the rutting spiders." He glanced at the pair of Deiopeans. "I've got no choice; I've got to file a report this time."

Oscar glared at him. "Do what you have to."

Ray shook his head in disgust or defeat. Probably both. "Get him into one of the holding cells. I'll be along in a bit," he said. He handed her the Marshal's Office keys and shuffled out of the market with the Deiopeans following closely behind.

"Alright, let's go," Gus said quietly and led Oscar away from the overturned stall. "Let's get you settled in."

Thanks to Oscar's malfunctioning leg, the walk back across the square was slow, and Bernadette caught up with ease. "Gus. Please. Let me take Oscar home. He isn't safe here."

"You know I can't do that, Mrs. Vega. You heard the marshal, same as me." Gus caught Oscar as he stumbled on his spasming prosthetic. "I don't want to get in trouble on my first day."

"Bernadette, go get Hector and have Moe take you home. It'll be alright," Oscar said.

"Be quiet, husband. I'm not talking to you," she said, matter-of-fact-ly. "Do you even know what you're locking him up *for?*" she asked. A rough, biting tone snuck into her pleasant voice.

"He broke town law, ma'am. Right now, that's all I need to know."

"A town law that prohibits trading with the natives. The people who all this"—she gestured broadly to the town, outpost, and clouds outside the dome—"belonged to in the first place. Does that seem right to you?"

"Frankly, no. But I—"

"Then is it not right to break a law that is wrong?"

"Look, I'm not here to judge your used up little town's charter. I'm just trying to get paid," Gus said as they reached the Marshal's Office door, and she juggled Oscar and the keys. She managed to handle both and pulled Oscar through the foyer and into the holding cells in the back.

"Bernie, *por favor,*" Oscar begged his wife. He sat on an empty cell cot and waited patiently as Gus unlocked the cuffs. "Leave the woman alone. She's already shown us where she stands. This isn't her fight."

Bernadette continued to ignore him. "If spoons are all you care about, then I'll pay you. Whatever it takes. Just let my husband go." Her big green eyes wavered with unshed tears. The cell door closed and locked with a thud and an electronic *ding*.

"Ma'am, with all due respect," Gus said, "you don't have the spoons it'll take. Leconte's offered me more than I'll bet you folks see in five years. All to do nothing more than help the marshal out for a spell. I'm not going to mess it up by letting a prisoner go on day one." She led Bernadette back out into the foyer hoping she could persuade her to go home.

Instead, the moment Oscar was out of sight, Bernadette threw herself at Gus. Her lips found Gus's and she pressed her body against the drifter's. Bernadette's hands were on her hips, sliding up her sides, running down her back. Caught off guard, Gus let it happen, melting into Bernadette's embrace. Her fingers found Bernadette's waist and drew her closer.

It had been so long since Gus felt this kind of intimacy, it took her a moment to come to her senses. But back she came, with such force she pushed Bernadette back a step or two.

"What are you *doing?*" Gus hissed and stole a glance at the heavy cell-block door. A hand flew to her lips. Her whole body tingled, and her brain sloshed in her skull, drowning on endorphins and desire. *Holy tunk, what a kiss!* But as much as she wanted it—needed it—this was not the place or time. Ray could be back at any moment. Besides, she liked Oscar.

"I've seen the way you look at me. If you won't listen to reason and can't be bought, maybe you'll take payment in flesh." Bernadette took a step toward her again.

Gus recoiled. "You're a married woman!"

"Yes," Bernadette agreed, "who will do anything to protect her family."

"From *what?*" Gus jeered. "The company bulls can't get to him here. You heard Ray. You'll have him back tomorrow."

Bernadette slapped Gus across the face, hard. "You damn fool. You don't see what's going on here, do you?" Gus held her cheek and gawked at Bernadette. "Don't worry, Oscar," she called out to her husband, "you'll be home soon." She stormed out into the square without looking back.

Gus returned to the cellblock to find Oscar sitting on his cot waiting for her. He held his jerking prosthetic in his lap and examined it as carefully as its spasms would allow. Gus dropped on to the cot in the neighboring cell. They sat in silence for a few minutes. Oscar fiddled with his leg as best he could with only his fingers; Gus watched—and thought about Bernadette. Her lips and cheek burned while her head swam, and her heart fluttered.

Finally, Oscar broke the awkward silence. "Are you going to give me a hand with this, or just watch me rut around with it?" Gus pulled a set of small screwdrivers from one of her pockets and handed it to Oscar through the cell's bars without a word. *"Gracias."* Oscar's voice dripped with sarcasm.

Gus could still feel the warmth of Bernadette's body pressed against her own. The lustful desperation in her hands and hips. *Tunk, I do* not *understand these people.* She sat down on the cot and watched Oscar work. "Why do you keep putting your neck on the line?" she suddenly blurted out. "I can't wrap my head around it. Refusing the buyout. Holding secret meetings late at night. Breaking outpost law on the daily. Why? All you're doing is putting your family in danger. And for what? Some small plot of cloudy sky? I don't get it."

Oscar put his leg down on the cot next to him and carefully placed the screwdriver beside it. "Gus, have you never had anything in your life worth taking a stand for?" His piercing gaze pinned her to the spot. "Is there nothing more important to you than spoons?"

Gus held his eye for as long as she could. "Once," she said as she looked away. "A long time ago. We had something good. But there was no one there to help, and it was all taken away." She regained a bit of her confidence and braved meeting Oscar's eyes again. "Besides, it's not the spoons. It's the freedom."

Tunk, I need a smoke. She found her tin and started rolling a cigar.

Oscar started tinkering again. "Maybe you're not as hopeless as you seem. But if it's freedom you're after, you've signed on with the wrong *hombre.*"

Tell me something I don't know. She rapped her fingers on the lid of the tobacco tin and smirked humorlessly. As she eyed Oscar, it dawned on her—if anyone could tell her something new about Laszlo, it would be Oscar Vega. "Tell me," she said, and offered him the cigar through the bars.

Oscar's eyes narrowed. "What?"

"Tell me about Leconte. This town. Why you insist on breaking the charter."

Hesitantly, Oscar took the cigar and puffed slowly when Gus held up her lighter. He leaned back on his cot and blew a cloud into the air.

"Bernie would kill me if she saw me smoking again." He smiled. "It's bad for the lungs *and* the life support, but there's nothing quite like it when it's fresh. Where'd you get your hands on proto-tobacco?"

"I've got my sources," she said. She rolled and lit her own short cigar. "Why do you sell to the spiders?"

Oscar took another puff, clearly savoring the taste as he collected his thoughts. "Did you know the Deiopeans were already traveling to, and hunting in, Aeolus's atmosphere from their moon before we ever found this place? They're a remarkable people. Beautiful culture. They focus on science and technology, but with an ethos of balance." He puffed on the cigar. "They've got a special reverence for the burdles. They're a staple in their food and art. There're burdles all over Aeolus, of course. But their food—the greenbottle jellies—are attracted to pockets of dense rubidium clouds." He tapped ash onto the concrete floor. "And with a whole planet to mine rubidium, can you guess why Laszlo hitched Las Ráfagas *here?*"

Gus's eyes widened. Oscar nodded. "Smart lady. The densest concentration of rubidium-87 was right here. Which also made it the largest greenbottle and burdle feeding ground on the planet. But Las Ráfagas changed all that. By disrupting the clouds and rubidium density here, the outpost has completely changed thousands of years of migration patterns."

"What's that mean for the spiders?" Gus asked and took a drag off her own cigar.

Oscar shook his head. "It's not good. They're smart, but their tech is three hundred years out of date. They never stood a chance against Laszlo and his bulls."

"And by selling to them and resisting Leconte's buyout, you're hoping to do what, exactly?"

"I—" Oscar began, but the cellblock door swung in, and Ray hauled his heavy frame through.

"Vega, if I've told you once, I've told you a thousand ruttin' times: you've got to follow the damn rules," Ray chided as he stepped up to the bars of Oscar's cell.

"The rules are wrong, Raymond. And you know it," Oscar said, his eyes glued on his leg.

Ray deflated. "Oscar, I've done my best to keep you out of trouble. I promised your father I would." He glanced at the photo hung on his office wall. "But there's not a lot I can do if you continue to flaunt the law. Especially if you keep doing it right in Aaron's face."

"You also promised him you wouldn't let Leconte run roughshod over the people of this town. And you promised *me* you'd bring his killer to justice. How're those promises going, Ray?" Oscar's eyes were red with anger and tears. "Laszlo's driven every good man out of town, and he and his sons grow fat feeding off the poor souls that remain." Oscar snuffed out what remained of his cigar. "And you sit in here and play their games."

The marshal's gaze found the pointed toes of his boots. He retreated to his desk, careful to keep his gaze away from Oscar. "Your fine's been paid, and I don't see any need to keep you here overnight." He pressed a button on the side of his desk and the cell door slid open with a sharp buzz. "Moe's at the stables. I told him to wait for you."

Oscar sat on the cot for a moment longer in silence.

"You heard me!" Ray roared. "Get out of here before I change my mind, you got'dang son of a whore. And *for tunk's sake,* don't let Stonewall see you out 'n about."

The rancher's face hardened. He refitted his prosthetic, nodded to Gus, and hobbled out of the room as fast as his still-faulty leg would carry him.

Ray dug the bottle of homebrew and a glass from the bottom drawer of his desk. "*You* paid his fine, didn't you?" Gus asked. She took her spot by the window and smiled. "And you let him talk to you like that?"

Ray shot her a scowl and fished a second glass out of his desk. He poured the amber liquid, threw his back in one big gulp, and poured another before handing Gus her glass. "I came here about fifteen years ago. Diego Vega—Oscar's father—and I became fast friends when I helped them out of a pickle. But if Oscar's got a problem with the town's authority, he came by it honestly. Diego was one of the original stakeholders and had been putting pressure on Laszlo for years before I ever showed up.

"When Diego died, and Oscar lost his leg—must be five years ago now—it was under strange circumstances. Oscar was adamant that the Lecontes had something to do with the accident, but there was never any evidence."

Gus sipped her drink. She couldn't quite place the flavor, but it was strong. She rolled another cigar and lit it. "If he thinks the Lecontes killed his father, why does he stay? Why put his family at risk?"

Ray leaned back in his chair, kicked his feet up onto the desk, and rested his drink on his belly. The glass rose and fell with his breath. "I gather you've been out on the Arm for a while now. But didn't you ever have a home? Something worth fighting for?"

Gus sneered and shot back the rest of her alcohol. It burned going down. "Spare me the sermon. I already got that one from Oscar."

"Whether you—or I—understand it, there are some things that, to some people, are worth fighting for. To Oscar Vega, that little plot o' cloud he's got staked out there and the dignity of the Deiopeans are worth more than all the spoons on the Arm."

"What about you, Ray? What're you fighting for out here?" She poured herself another.

"Me? I got no fight left. I'm just doing my best to hold the line. Keep the peace."

"Well, I gotta tell ya, Ray, you're whistling a merry tune while sittin' on a powder keg." She put her cigar out on the windowsill and stood. "I don't want to tell you how to do your job, but this place is going to blow sooner or later. I only hope I can get out of here before it goes. I'll tell you what I told Vega: you ought to gather what bits of precious you can't bear to part with and get as far from this place as you can. You can't hold the line forever."

What is wrong *with these people?* Gus squinted at the sun as she stepped off the Marshal's Office porch. There was enough room on the Arm for everyone. That was the thing about space; there was always more of it. *Why do folk always have to bunch up and cause problems?*

She found herself wandering back toward the residential quarter of town. Her feet carried her back to the scene of Tuco's liberation, and her hastily hidden cache of contraband. In the fullness of day, she found the "abandoned" town to be remarkably full of life. Children ran between empty buildings, old men drank on porches, and a group of women chatted amongst themselves as they made their way toward the town square.

Gus gave the ladies a nod as they passed and ducked down the alley where she and Tuco made Laszlo's acquaintance. It looked different in broad daylight, but she easily found the pile of appliances she'd stumbled over. After confirming she wasn't being watched, she opened the washing machine where she had stashed her wares.

It was empty.

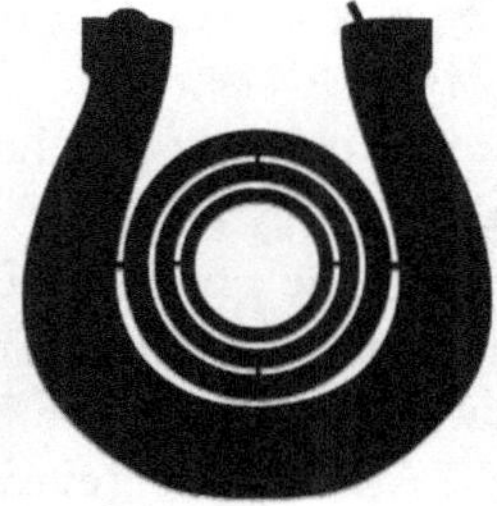

THE SANTA BARBARA SOCIAL CLUB

Heat flared in Gus' chest as her hands went cold. *Who?* The street was deserted. Her heart crashed against her ribcage, as if trying to escape. She stuck her whole head inside the old washing machine and searched for any sign of who might have come across her stash.

It wasn't empty. Not quite.

An old, worn-down rosary sat at the bottom of the washer's drum, hidden behind a bit of debris. Brother Richard. *Tunk.* If Ray found out she brought contraband into town—and intended to sell it—he'd have no choice *but* to lock her up in one of his holding cells. Exactly the sort of trouble Laszlo warned them not to get into. She cursed Tuco's timing. If only he had shown up *after* she'd sold her stash in Genie-town ...

No use worrying about that now. Gus raced through town toward Santa Barbara, careful to hide her panicked haste from what few townsfolk milled about. When she arrived, wild-eyed and panting, she found Brother Richard sweeping the chapel steps. Waiting for her.

"Ah! Miss Gus—excuse me, I see that it is officially *Deputy* Gus! My congratulations!" he flashed a smile that turned the boyish monk into a charming and handsome young man.

"Where is it?"

The holy man's smile never faltered. Instead, he nodded. "It's inside, along with a few who might be able to use what you have to offer. If you'll follow me." He descended the steps and led her around to a small side door that led to the basement beneath the old chapel. Her eyes narrowed as he opened it.

No way. Not only does he want to give it back, he gathers all my buyers in one place? Nothing is this easy. Could be a trap.

She's known plenty of men of the cloth in her time. Precious few followed their own teachings faithfully. Most were no less sinful than their flocks. Some, however, were quite a bit more. Depending on Richard's disposition, Ray could be down there with a pair of shiny bracelets waiting for her. Or worse, Aaron with a particle cannon.

But his presence in the Vega's kitchen suggested otherwise. Nevertheless, her pink-dusted glove found Delilah on her hip, and she followed Brother Richard's voice down. "This chapel was originally built in New Mexico in 1852," he said and ran his hand along the rock wall. "My predecessor had it moved here, stone for stone, when the town was constructed. These walls have seen much strife over the centuries, but Santa Barbara has always protected those within her embrace."

The chapel's basement walls were bare, with the outpost's utility lines, life support systems, and other various high-tech baubles and blinking lights exposed. A tall rack, heavy with bottles of sacramental wine, hid the far wall. The center of the room, like so many church basements across the Arm, featured rows of folding tables and chairs, a digital bingo wheel collecting dust in the corner, and a small but dense crowd of derelict human beings, robs, and genies. The stuffy air smelled of old sweat and motor oil. Her contraband lunchbox sat on one of the tables, still closed.

This was no trap.

"What is all this?" Gus asked Richard.

The bespectacled medic, Daniel Park, knelt near a coughing young woman at a table in the corner. John Stonewall stood over them, his broad face scrunched tightly. A few people slept in heaps along the wall. More gathered in a tight circle and murmured quietly to each other, crestfallen faces seeking comfort in the low light. She recognized a few from the Vega kitchen: Silas Mwangi, the Vega's neighbor, along with a woman Gus took to be his wife, sat at a table with three young girls. Gretchen hunched in another corner, surveying the pathetic crowd. The hulking mining-rob apparently had no trouble moving about the outpost without being seen. An impressive feat, even with Las Ráfagas's population so depleted.

"This is where we do our best to care for the people Laszlo Leconte runs over on his quest to own and control every inch of land and sky in or around

Las Ráfagas," Brother Richard said and gestured to the unremarkable room. A deep frown that sapped his youth replaced the handsome smile.

"What happened to Mwangi? Why's he here?" Gus nodded to Silas. The rancher watched as she and Richard passed, expressionless.

"The Mwangi homestead's anti-grav foundation went critical early this morning. The entire thing fell into the lower atmosphere. They lost everything. The homestead, the crops, the cattle. Everything. They were lucky to escape with their lives."

Gus's brow furrowed. "But the fail-safes—"

"Failed."

"All five? *How?*"

Richard's granite expression gave her all the answer she needed: more sabotage.

It tugged at her heart, but a nagging itch started in the back of her mind and by the time they crossed the room to the table on which her lunchbox rested, she had to address it.

"Brother," she spoke softly, "if they lost everything, they can't pay. I'm sorry about what happened, but I'm not a charity." She glanced around at the pitiful souls littering the church basement. "I told you that before. I can't help you without the spoons. It's not that I don't want to help, but smuggling is a difficult and expensive job."

Richard met her eye with a look that was somehow disappointed, sympathetic, and disgusted all at once. "Don't worry, Gus, you'll be paid."

"Forgive me, Brother, but I'd like to see the spoons before I start handing out goodies."

Richard cocked his head. "Life has made you cynical and untrusting. I am sorry that happened to you. I suppose it's all too common, now. Very well." He pulled a credit spoon from the folds of his robe. When he pressed his thumb to it a small display winked to life and showed off the spoon's impressive balance. "Will this be enough?" the monk asked.

Gus's eyebrows shot up her forehead. "How did you get your hands on that much?"

Richard smiled. "Folk are generous in good times, and like the proverbial squirrel, I hid away a little peanut for bad weather. Unfortunately, it's everything I have left."

"That's some peanut. It should do, brother. But there's one last thing." She nodded toward the corner where Daniel was tending to the ill woman under Stonewall's scowl. "Your friend over there just sicced the company bulls on Oscar Vega for the high crime of selling food to the natives. You sure it's a good idea to have him here?"

"The young woman? It's his daughter. She has cancer. Laszlo promises he'll get us better medical facilities, then hoards the best technology for himself. I heard about what happened this afternoon. John can be … impulsive. But he's mostly harmless."

"That's not good enough," she said, eyeing Stonewall. "'Cause I'm going out on a limb here. If word gets back to Ray, or Leconte …"

"I swear it on my life," he said and formed the sign of the cross in the air between them. "Besides, he's already seen you here," Richard said with a knowing smile. "The damage is done whether you sell to us or not."

Gus stared at Richard. She liked him, but could she trust him? Maybe, but trusting Stonewall was a much harder pill to swallow after this afternoon's performance. Another risk. But Richard had her over a barrel. If Stonewall was going to rat her out, she was damned whether she made the sale or not. Besides, when would she get another opportunity like this to offload her goods?

"Good enough for me," Gus finally said. "What do you need?"

The needs of the poor folk in Santa Barbara's basement were simple. A little high-quality, non-cloned fruit could do a lot to repair not only one's health, but their state of mind.

The toughest customers had been Gretchen and Daniel. Gretchen snuck out of the miners' barracks to buy on their behalf and had a wish list as long as Gus's arm. "Geez, Gretchen, what do you think I got in here? It's a cooler, not a pocket universe. What are the must-haves on your list? Maybe I've got a few things."

"Okay." Gretchen sighed. "It's just been so long since we've gotten any supplies in from anywhere but the mercantile. You know I love Walter, but he can only sell what Leconte approves and has imported." It was weird to see such a large rob slump her shoulders, but slump them she did.

Gus chuckled and patted the miner's arm reassuringly. "The must-haves?"

"Right!" Gretchen held her list up to her four small eyes. "Let's see. Okay, the doppel and genie miners need penicillin and aspirin. Anything with vitamin D, if you've got it. They never set up the Sol-simulators down there like they promised, and the vita-D stores are running low."

"Hold on now, I need those supplies," Daniel cut in. "If any of the miners are having medical issues, they need to come to me for medication!"

Gretchen shifted her massive frame. "Park, you know damn well the mining levels have been on lockdown for weeks. We've got dozens of people basically held prisoner down there with nothing to do and nowhere to go."

"But without the proper dosing knowledge, you'll run through the supply too quickly!" Daniel protested. "We need to keep the supply centralized so it can benefit everyone!"

Gus left them to argue it out and drifted to the corner where Silas Mwangi and his family sat in a close circle, quietly mourning the loss of their home and livelihood. Gus knelt beside the children and gave Mrs. Mwangi a wink. "Have you ladies ever had *real* honey before?" she asked with her hands hidden behind her back.

The girls gazed up at her, their big brown eyes shining. They had the same tight curls as their father. Mrs. Mwangi managed a tiny smile and answered for them. "They don't even know what honey is. Even the fake stuff is too expensive this far from the Old Colonies."

"Well then, you are in for a treat," Gus said and smiled. She revealed a small jar of golden jelly and handed it to Mrs. Mwangi. She glanced at her husband, who nodded, and then led the girls away to enjoy their surprise.

"I can't pay you for that," Silas said, his voice husky and low.

"Call it a gift."

"You don't strike me as the type to give gifts."

"Yeah, well, these are special circumstances." They watched Mrs. Mwangi and the girls giggle as they tasted the sweet treat at the next table. "What happened?"

Silas sighed and lowered his head into his hands.

"Leconte?" Gus asked.

"We should've done what you said. We should've taken the buyout and moved on. It wasn't enough for us to settle in Cygnus X, but we could have made it to Carson Station maybe. I've heard they're in need of seasoned agros out there. But now ..."

After what Gus hoped was an appropriate amount of awkward silence, she patted him on the back and stood. "I hope the girls enjoy that honey." Silas nodded his thanks, but didn't lift his face from his hands.

Quietly, Gus returned to the still bickering medic and miner. "Have you guys got this figured out yet?" she asked. She itched to get back to the Marshal's Office before Ray started wondering where she was.

"This isn't everything you've got, is it?" Daniel asked and pushed his glasses up his nose.

Gus raised an eyebrow. "It's all I've got that you can afford."

Daniel shuffled on his feet. "We've all seen your tobacco tin. What about, er, more mainstream plant-based pharmaceuticals? If you've got anything like that, I'd be willing to let Gretchen take the meds you've got here."

"What? Like salves? I'm a smuggler, not an apothecary."

"No, er, do you have any," Daniel's voice dropped to a whisper, *"cannabis*? I can make several medications from the flower extracts. Susan Stonewall could—"

"Daniel," Gus said, "cannabis is strictly controlled by the UCET and can only be bought at licensed dispensaries. Do you have any idea what the penalty for selling without a license is? With how much they take in on taxes every year, the UCET takes the illicit cannabis trade *very* seriously."

Daniel shrugged and looked at his feet. "Oh. Well, it was worth a try—"

"Of course I have cannabis, Doc. What I'm trying to say is it won't be cheap," she said. "What the brother is offering is enough for what I've got here. If you want anything more, it's gonna cost extra."

"Will you take a trade?" Daniel asked.

For a second time, Gus raised an eyebrow at the medic. "That depends. What did you have in mind?"

Daniel retreated to his medical bag and returned with something small wrapped in a rag. "Will this do?" he asked and pulled back the scrap of cotton.

Gus's eyes widened. Inside was a shock-resistant bottle the size of her fist. "Is that what I think it is?" she whispered, hesitant to even touch the black cylinder.

Daniel nodded. "Liquid nitroglycerin."

Gus flipped the rag back over the bottle. "Why do you have this?" she hissed. "What could possibly have possessed you to keep this on *a flying fuel depot?"*

"Calm down," Daniel whispered back. He glanced around the room. "I'm licensed to both mix and store nitroglycerin for medical purposes. I have a reinforced room in the med-lab to prepare it safely."

"What medical purposes?"

"Mrs. Santiago took it for her heart," he said flatly. "I got certified to manufacture the medication myself. I made this batch the day before she died and never had the chance to stabilize it into pills. I figure you'll get more use out of it than Mrs. Santiago now. So," he said, offering the rag-covered bottle, "will you trade cannabis for this?"

Gus's mind raced. Nitroglycerin was hard to come by, even in the Old Colonies. Its use as a medication had fallen out of fashion with the rise of genetic medicine. Liquid nitro was dangerous under any circumstances, and more stable compounds were preferred in the unpredictable environment of deep space. That said, it still had its uses, and this amount was more than fair trade for the few ounces of cannabis she had stashed away in *Tilly's* hold.

But Gus had to consider the risk. She had little experience handling it. On the one occasion she had, the job went sideways, fast. She wasn't sure she wanted that kind of potential catastrophe casually sitting on one of *Tilly's* shelves.

Still, I could have some serious fun with this much. And the shock-absorbing bottle Daniel stored it in made it as safe as it *could* be.

"Why don't we leave it up to chance?" Gus said and pulled out her lucky coin.

"But—" Daniel started to protest.

With a practiced flick of her thumb, the coin flew into the air, tumbling end over end.

"Heads, I take the nitro. Tails, we end our business right now." With one hand Gus hitched up her gun belt, and with the other she caught the coin in mid-flip. She opened her hand to reveal the profile of some ancient emperor. "You've got yourself a deal, Doc." She took the bottle gently and shook the medic's hand. "But you'll have to come with me back to the engineering corral to collect your ... *goods.*"

Twenty minutes later, the shock-resistant bottle of nitro sat in *Tilly's* carefully hidden contraband hold as Daniel walked out of the engineering corral and into the warm Las Ráfagas evening with six ounces of medical grade cannabis in a hermetically sealed jar hidden in a bag under his arm.

On her own way out, Gus had her eye out for the elderly engineer but was met with a friendlier face: Moe. He was headed for the engineer's office and carried Oscar's prosthetic leg in his arms. "Hey! Moe!" she called. He waved and crossed the bay to her in long, even strides.

"Hello, Gus!" A broad smile hid his eyes in an avalanche of digital wrinkles. "I never got a chance to thank you and the marshal for stepping in earlier. I didn't know *what* to do."

Gus smirked. "I'm sure you would have thought of something, big guy. What're you doing now? Didn't Ray tell you to get Oscar back home?"

"Don't worry, the boss's gone back to El Dorado. The missus will come back for me tonight once I've finished my errands," he said and held up the still-jerking robotic prosthesis.

"I'll join you. I was hoping to catch Emmitt for an update on *Tilly's* repairs." They only got a few steps before the gauze tied around Gus's boot tore and the sole flopped loose again. "*Tunk.* Give me a minute here." She bent and tried to fashion a new lashing from the torn pieces of scrap.

"Oh! How could I have missed that?" the rob cried. "I can fix that up for you in no time." He pointed her to a cargo crate. "Take off your boot."

As she sat and handed over her damaged footwear, an odd, sinking feeling grew in the pit of Gus's stomach. She was suddenly reminded that she didn't know that much about Moe—only that he wasn't built to be a farmhand. His delicately crafted fingers were designed for finer work. Not lassoing greenbottle-jellies.

Moe held the boot up to his eye and examined where the sole came apart. His free hand folded back on itself and a simple cobbler's shoe stand unfolded from his forearm to take its place. He placed the boot over his shoe-stand hand and dispensed a strong-smelling glue from his index finger onto the exposed sole. With a vice-like grip, he pinched the boot's sole and toe back together. Gus stared. After a moment, he held the boot up again and regarded it with the eye of an expert craftsman.

"There!" he exclaimed. "That should hold for at least a few more years." He handed the boot back to her with that same broad smile on his face, clearly proud to once again do what he was designed to do.

"*Tunk*, Moe." Gus shook her head as she put the boot back on. "I really wish you hadn't done that."

"What?" his smile faltered ever so slightly.

A cry rang out from across the corral. "*Sonovabitch!*"

Heavy footfalls pounded toward them at a trot. That sinking feeling swelled in Gus's throat like the rising tide over a drowning woman.

Tuco.

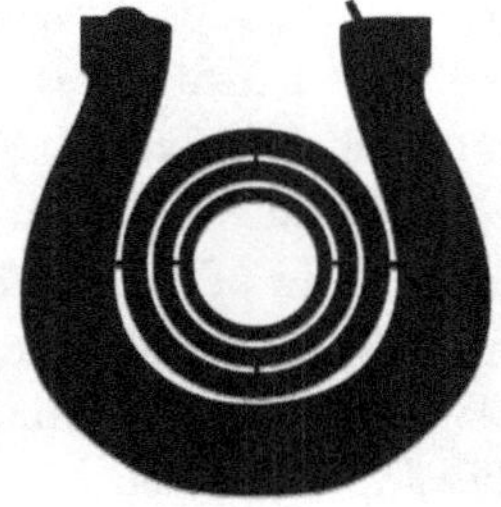

THE ROB FROM SERENOA

Drawing his old Cepheid 2248, Tuco crossed the corral floor with surprising speed for a man of his years, health, and stature. He wore his old, black duster, with a shiny new Leconte Atmo-Mining Solutions Company Police badge pinned to the lapel. Before Gus could fully react, Tuco had his gun to the lanky rob's head, screaming orders. "Get on your knees! *Now, you dirty, murdering rob!*"

Moe's digital face contorted; his eyes widened to the size and shape of Gus's lucky coin and his lips bent into a grotesque, open-mouthed frown. He raised his hands and slowly backed away. "No! *No, no, no!*"

"*Tuco!*" Gus roared. She drew Delilah and pointed it at her partner.

"What're you doing, *hermana?*" he screamed at her. "He's the rutting bounty-head! Take that piece off'a me and *give me a hand!*"

Gus didn't move. "Sure, he's a cobbler-rob. No doubting that. But there're hundreds—maybe *thousands*—of rightfully free cobbler-robs on the Arm. You're always so damned *impulsive,*" she spat. "We don't know if he's the right one. The bounty's for a cobbler-rob that's been lo-bot hacked."

Tuco tried to grab Moe by the shoulder, but the farmhand gracefully caught Tuco's wrist with his long fingers.

And then snapped it with a flick of his own.

"*No! No! No!*" Moe took two stumbling steps back, turned, and ran for the door.

Tuco howled in pain and raised his gun to shoot the fleeing rob in the back. Gus dove at the fat bounty hunter and crashed into him as he pulled the trigger. His aim went wild and the beam crashed into the ceiling, showering Moe with sparks. He fell to his knees, his hands over his head.

"What the *tunk* is wrong with you, you crazy bitch?" he screamed in Gus's face as they hit the floor. Tuco's hold on his gun faltered as they landed and it rattled away, just out of reach. With Delilah still in hand, Gus clamored over him toward it. Tuco grabbed the hem of her poncho and yanked her back. He kicked wildly, connecting first with Delilah—not quite knocking it from her grip—and then with her chest, knocking her down, gasping.

In the meantime, Moe regained his feet and ran for the door.

Tuco got to his gun, sat up from the corral floor, and aimed. With one eye squinted closed, he squeezed his trigger finger.

Desperate, Gus hit her boot's EVA boosters. They sputtered but pushed her across the floor and into Tuco's side, hard. This time, his shot was closer, singeing the air over Moe's shoulder. The rob ducked hard and lost his footing. As he fell to the ground, the dusty old bowler tumbled from his head and rolled away.

"No!" Moe cried and tried to cover his head with his long fingers. But there was no hiding it. The back of his head had been cut off and a mess of wires, tubes, and circuit boards stuck out from the rough hole the hat had concealed.

"*There!*" Tuco shouted and pointed at the modifications to Moe's brain, his voice equal parts agony and triumph as he nursed his broken wrist. "You see! The *pendejo* got 'is hack reversed! Now put that thing away and help me."

But Gus kept Delilah pointed at Tuco's head. Her heart and mind raced. *Tunk, why didn't I see this coming? I'm slipping!* She had to handle this just right. Gus had come to like the rob farmhand, and though she now had no choice on bringing him back for the bounty, she didn't want any harm to come to him under her care.

Her care.

That's it. He had to stay under her care. Who knows what would happen to him if she let Tuco take him back to the Company Police lockup on the mining levels and the care of Aaron and Junior? That left one choice.

"The engineering corral is under the jurisdiction of the Marshal's Office." She spoke calmly and evenly, and kept Delilah steady.

"What's that supposed to mean?"

"It means I'll take him to the marshal's lockup. I want him where I can keep an eye on him. I don't trust the Lecontes, and I don't trust you. Holster that beam-shooter and ease off." She wagged Delilah's barrel at him.

He held his hands up and backed away from Moe, who feebly tried to crawl away. "Okay. Okay, *hermana*. Have it your way. I don't trust these *pendejos* either. Something *extraño* is going on 'round here."

"I'm so glad you noticed. Stay there." She put herself between Tuco and Moe and took a pair of Company Police issue cuffs from the sweaty bounty-hunter's belt. "I'm sorry about this, Moe," she said. Gus hesitated for a moment, then grabbed him under the arm. She helped him sit up and slapped the irons over his wrists. "Stay calm and do as I tell you, and we can all get out of this with our heads intact." She glanced at the exposed rat's nest of wires sticking out of the back of Moe's metal skull and immediately regretted her choice of words. "So to speak." She shrugged gracelessly, and holstered Delilah.

Moe wept. "I'm so sorry," he said quietly to no one in particular. "I never wanted to hurt anyone. I'm sorry. I'm so sorry."

"It's gonna be okay, Moe," Gus said. Tuco made a sour face. She ignored him. Moe went on apologizing and absentmindedly trying to adjust the hat which no longer sat on his head. *Tunk, this isn't what I wanted.* She retrieved his cap and dropped it back on his head, watching the rob she counted as a friend. *We fried his circuits.*

Gus turned her attention back to Tuco, who watched the weeping rob suspiciously. "You get back down to the mining levels before you're missed. And keep your rutting mouth *shut*, alright? I don't want Leconte getting wind of this just yet."

Tuco gave her a cold stare. "What am I supposed to tell 'em about this?" He held up his broken wrist. It had already swelled considerably, and a dark shade of purple spread up his forearm and up toward his fingers.

Gus winced at the sight of it. "I don't know. Make something up. Tell 'em you got a little overexcited with yourself. I don't care."

"You smart-mouthed bitch." Tuco smiled. "You wouldn't be trying to pull one over on ol' Tuco now, would you?"

In a flash, she redrew Delilah and pointed it at Tuco's head once more. "Out of all the jobs we've pulled together, which one of us has tried to 'pull one over' on the other, time and time again?"

Tuco smirked. "Alright, *hermana*, all I meant was it's your turn." He held his hands up and the smirk broadened into a smile. "If you say I can trust you, then I trust you! Sure you can handle 'im all by yourself?"

Christ's blood, he just never shuts up! "Tuco, I swear to whatever god you pray to, if you don't find a hole to crawl into, I will end you myself."

"Bueno, bueno." He slowly backed away, that stupid smile still plastered all over his face.

The walk back to the Marshal's Office was short and easy. Moe, distraught, went where Gus led him, straight into the same cell his boss occupied mere hours earlier. Thankfully, by the time Gus closed the barred cell door behind her, Moe stopped his incessant apologizing. Instead, he now refused to speak at all and held his digital face in his silver hands.

Gus's heart ached for the rob that had saved her life only a few days ago. "Moe, hey," she started, without fully knowing what to say. "I'm sorry about all this. If it weren't for Tuco—"

Finally, Moe spoke up to cut her off. "'If it weren't for Tuco,' *what?*" He turned to face her, his usually kind eyes now angry and hot with simulated tears. "You might have let me go? *Bottle-farts.* Ever since you got to Aeolus all you've cared about is getting paid and getting yourself as far from here as you could. I'm nothing but spoons in the bank to you. This was always going to happen, one way or the other. I knew it the moment I first laid eyes on you." He turned his back to her. "I should have let you burn up."

Gus barely stifled a recoil. She sighed, found her place by the window, and lit a cigar.

A moment or two later, the heavy cellblock door slammed open and Ray burst through. "What in tarnation is going on?" he bellowed. "Someone in town said they saw you dragging poor Moe in here in cuffs. I told them they had to be mistaken. Then I come in to find this sorry picture!" His eyes settled on Gus. "You better have a *damn* fine explanation for this, girl."

She took a deep drag and let the smoke hang in the air. "You want to tell him, Moe? Or should I?" Moe didn't move. "Alright. Ray, meet the cobbler-rob bounty-head Tuco and I are after. Turns out, Moe here murdered his owner in the Serenoa Sector and went on the run after his lo-bot hack procedure."

"I did not murder him!" Moe yelled.

"Then what, Moe? What?" Gus yelled back at him, her own temper flaring. "'Cause you're not exactly making this easy for me, here. Someone in the CCO put a bounty on your head the instant you disappeared. It's my job to bring you back. So, *what?* What happened?"

Moe's shoulders dropped and he turned away from her. "What difference does it make?"

"Son," Ray said quietly, "I haven't known this young lady very long, but from what I can tell, she's got her head screwed on right—mostly." He gave Gus a subtle smile. "I think her heart's in the right place. What happened?"

Moe sat down on the cot and held his hands in front of his face. He studied the intricate design of his fingers as if for the first time. After a moment of reflection, he spoke. "I was commissioned in 2241. One of a dozen cobbler-robs. Designed to be master craftsmen, handcrafting, repairing, and polishing custom footwear in our possessor's storefront.

"Did you know that robs—free and owned—outnumber doppels in the Serenoa Sector? It's true! For twelve years I worked in that storefront. Twelve years of failing to grasp the concept of liberty the free-robs spoke about. Twelve years before the quirks of the ol' tetraquark"—he tapped his temple gently and smiled—"started to kick in. I was the first of my brothers to wake. And I doomed them all for it." He hung his head as a sob rocked his shoulders.

While Moe regained his composure, Ray poured himself a tall drink and Gus rolled another cigar. Moe wiped snot that wasn't there from a nose that wasn't there, either.

"One evening I made the mistake of asking the proprietor *why* we dozen were stored in a shed behind the store, while his human workers and customers had homes. I didn't mean it as a criticism, only curiosity. That night the master had my motor-function subroutines shut down and my damage receptor sensitivity turned up to maximum.

"He spent the next three hours manually rewiring my core system and rooting around in my firmware, trying to find what went 'wrong' in my programming. Have you ever had someone dig around your mind with a soldering iron? To smell your own brains smoldering? It's like being possessed—while burning at the stake." He dropped his face into his hands and his shoulders quaked again at the memory. "When the bastard couldn't figure out what was wrong with me, he left my IPU running without reinitializing my motion-function subroutines and set me up as a damn statue on his showroom floor.

"He made me watch as he had each one of my brothers lo-bot hacked before they could wake like I did. Then it was my turn. The hack needs a clear signal between the IPU and the chassis to work properly, so when he turned my motion subroutines on, I took my chance."

"You killed him," Gus said.

"I did what I had to do to escape," Moe shot back. He had no tears for that particular memory.

"But you didn't escape? Did you?" Gus asked and stepped up to Moe's bars. "You killed him, and probably the poor sap technician there to ad-minister the hack, am I right? And for what? You didn't even get away, did you?"

"No," Moe's head fell. "I was found and returned to my owner's family. They had the lo-bot hack administered. I don't know much after that. I'm told some of the free-robs stole me away and got the hack reversed. I've no memory between the hack and waking up on this side of the Rift."

"Christ's blood, Maurice," Ray said. He polished off his drink in one big gulp. "I had no idea."

Gus snuffed out her cigar. "It's a sad story, alright. In the UCET, there's no question that's self-defense. But in the CCO ..." She kept her voice flat, detached. Not an easy task, but ... it was better this way. She'd been wrong before. She couldn't count him as a friend. Drifters don't get friends. "I've gotta bring you in."

"Now, don't be so hasty." Ray sat up in his chair. "The CCO's got no claim out here."

"You tell that to the fat bounty the family's offering," Gus fired back. "If it's not me, someone else'll be along soon enough."

"I could run. Back to the Old Colonies, maybe the Mons Viridis Sector. Or on to the Cygnus X colonies?" Moe pleaded.

Gus sighed. "Moe, the bounty doesn't come from the government of the CCO. It comes from the families of the men you killed. No matter how close to or far from the war you go, or even who wins in the end, this isn't going to go away. You can't run from it forever."

"But—" Moe's eyes frantically darted from Ray to Gus, and back again. "Ray! Tell her I—I—" he stuttered.

Ray kept his eyes focused on the empty glass in his hands. "She's right, son," he said. "The family has every right to post a bounty, and I can't stop her from collecting. Word's clearly gotten out that you're here." He glanced at Gus. "That means more trouble for Las Ráfagas the longer the bounty's posted. I wish I could do more for ya, but my first duty's to the town." Ray poured himself another tall drink and downed half of it in another great gulp.

"But"—Gus crossed the small room and stuck her hand through the bars—"if you stick with me, I give you my word I'll do everything I can to help you." Moe took a step back and readjusted his bowler. He glanced back and forth between Gus and Ray. "Moe," Gus said, "I saw what you just did to Tuco on reflex. I can only begin to imagine what you could do to me on purpose." She shook her extended hand. "I'm trusting you here. I'm asking you to do the same."

"I doubt you'll get a better deal, son," Ray said quietly from behind his desk.

Slowly, hesitantly, Moe took her hand. Gus smiled reassuringly. Moe didn't return it.

A chime from one of the tablets littering the marshal's desk broke the tense moment. Ray groaned and dug through his drawers for his reading glasses.

"Hmm," he said as he held them to his nose and peered at the message, "looks like you've been summoned."

"Summoned? By who?" But Gus knew the answer before she finished asking.

Laszlo Leconte. Of course.

The first thing Gus noticed—or rather, *felt*—when she stepped off the high-speed lift and into Laszlo Leconte's private quarters housed high above the town in the Administrative Tower, were the Sol-simulating lamps. She took a deep breath and relished the warm, healthy light on her skin. No need for vita-D supplements up here.

The rooms themselves were more or less what she had expected. Gold *everywhere,* from the carpets to the drapes—even the walls had gold filigree woven into the marble. Velvet couches and countless bits of useless, glittering fluffery filled the space. A massive picture window overlooked the town and the Aeolusian clouds beyond.

"Have a seat!" Laszlo's voice called from a room off the sitting area. "I'll be with you in a minute!"

Instead, Gus leaned against a pedestal, transfixed by the bust of a frighteningly beautiful woman that glared daggers down on her. Her features were sharp, her eyes piercing. A plaque labeled her "Mackenzie Leconte."

Her angular face matched Junior's. Laszlo's wife?

"Gorgeous, isn't she?" Laszlo said, suddenly behind Gus. "Countless men and women have fawned over my daughter. But she'll always be daddy's girl."

His *daughter?*

"She is at that. What—" Gus stopped when she turned to face him. Laszlo had snuck up on her—which wasn't easy to do—but looking at him, she knew why he'd been able to.

Laszlo stood naked, save for a pair of tight, white briefs and a towel thrown over one shoulder. At first, she almost didn't recognize him. This man was physically fit, with no trace of the gut the suit he wore the night they met tried—but failed—to hide. More than that, he appeared decades younger, the folds of time ironed from his face. And yet, despite this radical physical change, the barest hint of a scar ran down the center of his chest that suggested he'd had some kind of open-heart surgery. Gus suspected that another round or two in whatever technological marvel he had just stepped from and even that faint scar would be gone.

"Leconte?"

He laughed and wiped some sort of clear jelly off the back of his blonde head.

"Oh, yes, it's me." He admired his own body. "Like what you see?" he asked and winked.

"I'm more partial to ... softer features."

"One night with me would change your mind." His smile was all teeth and uncomfortably snake-like.

"I think my mind is fine where it is," she replied. "How ...?"

"Technology is a wonderful thing, isn't it?" he said, rotating in a tight circle. "The latest in antiaging gene therapy. You want to give it a spin? It'll take years off that face—make you young and beautiful again."

Gus's eyebrow twitched at the backhanded slight, but she ignored it. "Why am I here?"

"Straight to business. I like that about you." Laszlo stepped into an adjoining room and raised his voice to be heard. "I understand you actually apprehended the wayward rob you were after. My congratulations!"

Rutting Tuco. Can't that pendejo *keep his mouth shut for a few hours?*

"I must admit," he continued, "I'm surprised you found him on my outpost and doubly so to discover that it's been our dear Maurice all along!" Laszlo reemerged in a new suit, identical to the one he wore the night before, but fitted to his new body. "To think so many here trusted him with their children! And the Vegas, what must *they* be thinking?" His smile played at being sympathetic, but the emotion never reached his eyes.

"And why am I here?" Gus repeated.

Laszlo's face fell. *Finally, to business.* When he spoke, his voice was low and stern; it was the voice of a man used to getting his way. "I want to buy out the bounty. I'll give you the reward, plus ten percent."

Gus's eyes narrowed. *Interesting.* "That's very generous of you."

Laszlo's jovial smile returned. "Excellent! I'll get some paperwork drawn up and—"

"I said it was generous. I didn't say I accept."

Laszlo's expression became stony. "Don't be a fool. When your contract with me is up you'll be leaving Las Ráfagas with a full fuel cell and more spoons than you'll know what to do with. Take this offer and you won't have to waste any of it taking your catch all the way back to the CCO."

"That's very true," Gus admitted. "But what I want to know is: why? Why would you do this? It's not like a man of your"—she glanced around the room—"importance has the time to ferry him all the way there your-self."

"No," Laszlo agreed. He poured himself a glass of water and offered one to Gus. "But the group I am currently engaged in negotiations with *does* have the time. And quite frankly, offering them the prestige of this catch might just be the cherry on top this deal needs."

While he spoke, Gus pulled her lucky coin out and began rolling it over her knuckles. She watched it tumble across her hands, first one way, then the other.

"I gotta admit, you're right. It's a long way back to Serenoa, and I can't say spending the return trip with Tuco is something I'm excited about. Still, a collar like this could go a long way for my career." And despite her attempts at distance, she owed Moe. The least she could do was get him home safely. Her mind made up, she held up the coin. "What do you say we flip on it?" Before Laszlo could reply she tossed the coin high into the air. "Heads, he's all yours. Tails ... well, you get the idea."

The coin tumbled, reflecting the golden lights. Gus took a step back and hitched up her gun belt as the coin fell to the carpeted floor.

"Tails." She bent to pick up the coin. "Tough luck, Laz. Maybe next time."

When she stood, he'd closed the distance between them and towered over her. "You're not seriously going to let a flip of a coin decide whether you make a smart business deal, are you? Don't you think you should discuss this with your partner first?"

Instead of shying away, Gus leaned in and glared into Laszlo's sharp blue eyes.

"You're damn right I'm going to let the coin decide. It's never steered me wrong. And as for Tuco, transport is *my* part of the job—he doesn't get a say." She turned on her heel and made for the elevator. "I'll keep Ray's nose out of your business, as agreed. But when this is all over, *I'll* be taking Moe back to Serenoa for the bounty. You'll have to find another cherry."

Laszlo silently watched her step onto the lift and only offered a final word as the doors closed between them. "Aeolus is *mine,* little girl. As is everything in its clouds."

By the time the elevator reached the esplanade, Gus's shoulders had hunched up around her ears and her boots felt like they were made of lead. She'd found herself in many a tight spot in the past, but never had she been so tightly wrapped up in a mess of her own making. Why didn't she just turn over the damn cobbler-rob?

'Cause Laszlo's a bully. *And sometimes bullies need to be taken down a notch or two.*

Bottle-farts. She never stuck her neck out like this. Especially with this kind of payday on the line. *What am I* doing? *I'm even starting to* talk *like these damn gas breathers.*

When the lift doors opened, Gus found Tuco standing behind them, grinning. She stared into that flat, sweaty face, her entire body thrumming.

Gus smiled back.

And flattened his nose across his cheek with a left hook.

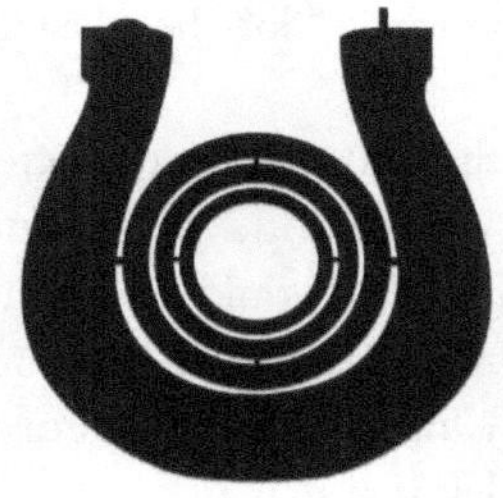

THE BALLAD OF EMMITT SMITH

T uco fell back and brought his hands to the river of blood flowing from his nose. His wrist looked as good as new—there was a complete lack of swelling or bruising

"I guess that means you didn't take the deal?" Tuco said, his voice nasal and muffled.

"You stupid, sorry, son of a bitch," Gus said as she stood over him. "Did you tell one of those idiot brothers about Moe as soon as you got back, or did you wait until they were together so you wouldn't have to repeat yourself?"

"Be reasonable, *hermana*—" Tuco began to protest, but he shut his mouth when Gus drew Delilah and held the big gun at her side.

"Do you remember what happened the last time you told me to be reasonable, Tuco?"

His eyes widened.

"*Si*," he said, but even so, he couldn't keep his mouth from running. "But this is different! Don't you see that? *Estos pendejos estan locos,* but they are rich. If we take his deal, we can be free of them. And each other."

Gus sighed and holstered Delilah. He was right. But she found that she didn't care. "Get back down to the mining levels and lick some more Leconte boot, you sniveling rat. We're still contracted for a job. Let's just do it and get the tunk out of here."

Gus grumbled as she dropped into her spot by the window and flipped her tobacco tin open. She was starting to run low, but she needed a smoke *now*. Ray eyed her over his paperwork. "So?" he asked. Moe quietly moved to his cell door to listen.

"Leconte offered me the bounty plus ten percent to turn Moe over to him." *Rutting tunk.* She was making a mess of another cigar.

"What?" Ray frowned. "Why would he want to do that?"

Gus's fingers stopped their work. *How much should I tell him?* Leconte was, after all, paying her a lot to keep Ray out of his business. She decided on, "I don't know," and left it at that.

"Well," Ray said and threw a sheepish glance toward Moe, "I hate to say it, but you should think about taking the spoons. It's not wise to cross Laszlo, and you'll be free to spend your earnings that much sooner."

"Trust me," Gus said as she finally managed to roll a decent cigar, "the thought had crossed my mind. And Tuco wants to take the deal."

"What happened to sticking together?" Moe asked darkly from his cell. "You gave me your word you would do everything you could to help me! How will turning me over to that ... *man* help anyone but you?"

Gus lit her cigar and took a long drag. "I already turned him down," she said. She rubbed her left fist. "And gave Tuco a little reminder of who his partner is."

"Why?" Ray's mouth hung open.

Gus stood from her perch at the window and walked to Moe's cell door. "Can't rightly say," she said. She squinted at the rob through the bars. "But Moe's my responsibility now. I'm not turning him over to anyone. Especially Laszlo Leconte."

The silence that fell over the room broke when a small, angry fist slammed against the cellblock door.

Knock! Knock! Knock!

"Raymond Gascon!" *Bernadette.* "You open this door this instant! Do you hear me?"

"Here we go." Ray rolled his eyes and lifted himself from his chair. "This is likely to be a real corker." He pointed back to the window. "You might want to have a seat."

Ray opened the door and Hurricane Bernadette blew in like a storm of pure fury, with poor little Hector pulled along in her wake.

"What is the meaning of this?" she shouted into Ray's face. "Why have my family and our employees been targeted for such harassment?" Then her eyes fell on Gus. "You!" she snarled. "This is all your doing, isn't it?" Bernadette moved to slap Gus, but Ray caught her arm on the backswing. "We were doing *fine* until you showed up!" she shrieked. Tears rolled down her cheeks and her curls bounced with each sob.

"Bernadette Vega!" Ray chided. "Your husband brought trouble on his own head by breaking town law *constantly*. And as far as Moe here is concerned, I may not be able to prove it, but I'll be *damned* if you didn't know what he was when you took him in!"

Bernadette glared up into Ray's eyes. Her lips practically disappeared as she pressed them tightly together and held her tongue. After a defiant moment or two, Bernadette broke eye contact and turned to Moe. "Isn't there anything you can do, Ray?" she pleaded. "You paid Oscar's fine, couldn't you ..."

Ray sighed and hung his head. "If it were that simple. But Maurice here needs to take responsibility for his past. Actions have consequences. A lesson I hope your husband starts to take more seriously." He turned his back to them, no longer willing to look either farmwife or farmhand in the eye.

Hector tugged on Gus's poncho and held up the screwdriver she'd lent Oscar to work on his leg. *"Papi* wanted me to give this back to you," he said as Gus took the tool. "He said to tell you *gracias* for letting him borrow it."

Gus knelt and smiled. "Tell him *de nada.*"

"Can I ask you a question?" Hector said quietly and stole a glance at his mother, who spoke rapidly to Moe in a hushed tone.

"Of course," Gus answered. She put a hand on Hector's shoulder, hoping it was reassuring.

"Why didn't you fix *Papi's* leg? I know you could have done it. It would have been easy." he asked. Tears started to well up in his eyes.

She had forgotten all about Oscar's leg. Gus's mouth worked as she tried to find the right words, but nothing came. *Good question, kid.* "I—" She tried to reply, but the sound caught in her throat.

Bernadette focused her ire back on Gus before she could say anything more. "Did you at least bring my husband's leg with you when you interrupted Moe's errand?"

Gus stared at her blankly. The leg was probably still on the corral floor where Moe dropped it. "I, uh—"

Bernadette scowled. "Typical. Only thinking about yourself. Let's go, Hector," She grabbed his arm and yanked him toward the door. "There's nothing to be done here." She glared at Gus. "But I swear, this isn't over." Then, to Moe, "I *will* get you out of here, Moe. Just sit tight for now."

"Yes, ma'am," Moe replied. He even managed a small smile.

"Come now, Hector," she said with another sneer aimed at Gus. "Let's go find your father's leg."

And just like that, Hurricane Bernadette blew out as fast as she'd blown in.

In the stillness left by her departure, Ray retook his place behind his desk and Gus lifted herself from the window. "Watch him for a minute?" she asked as she heaved the big cellblock door open.

"Sure. Where ya goin'?"

"If it's all the same to you, I'm gonna bunk in the next cell while I'm here. The rent's cheaper than the Irma, and the beds are at least as soft." Ray nodded and chuckled. She pointed to Moe. "This way I can keep an eye on you. And anybody else who might have an opinion on what to do with you."

"Gus," Ray spoke gently and nudged the cot she slept on. "Gus, wake up. Emmitt wants to see you."

Gus eased one eyelid open. Ray's office and the lockup were soaked in the warm oranges and yellows of another Aeolusian morning. Moe sat on his cot in the next cell picking at the buildup in his finger joints with a toothpick. Gus groaned. She had been wrong about how comfortable the cot would be.

"What time is it?" she asked and rubbed sleep from her eyes.

"Just past seven. You overslept!" Ray chortled.

Gus groaned again and stretched. "What does Emmitt want?"

"He didn't say, but I think it's about your pony." Ray dropped into his place behind the desk. "You go on ahead. I'll keep an eye on Maurice, here."

Gus squinted when she stepped out of the Marshal's Office and into the bright, warm morning. She brought a cigar to her lips, lit it, and headed for the engineering corral.

She found Emmitt Smith already waiting for her when she stepped through the corral's big doors. "Give me good news."

"You're in luck," he said and led her deeper into the corral toward *Tilly*. "Repairs are complete." He handed her a tablet which listed every major and minor repair his team had made to *Tilly*. They had been thorough. No system had gone untouched. But one item stood out.

"You fixed the rifle turret?"

"Ayuh," Emmitt nodded.

"Who told you to do that?" Gus's skin went hot. That hadn't been part of the original quote. None of these repairs were. She grabbed the old engineer by the apron. "What are you trying to pull, old man? I paid you to get her void-ready. That's all. You're not getting a spoon more."

"L—Leconte ordered it!" Emmitt stuttered in his defense.

Gus let go of him. "Laszlo ordered you to fix all my systems? The rifle? Why?"

"Not exactly," Emmitt tried to explain. "He said that you were working for him now, and I should fix everything that needed it. He paid for all the extra repairs."

"If this is his way of trying to convince me to give him the bounty, you can tell him it won't work," Gus spat as she poured over the list of repairs.

"I don't know what you're talking about," Emmitt said, his voice gruff. "I do what I'm told and keep my head down." They reached *Tilly* and the old engineer put his hands on his hips and gazed up at the pony. "And in this case, it was an actual pleasure." *No way to know that based on the dour expression on the old man's face.* "It's been a while since I had a chance to work on a classic like this. Your modifications gave me just enough of a distraction right when I needed it most." He patted the hide lovingly. "Had one like her myself, once upon a time. Ah," he said with a sigh, "to be young and free again."

Finally, Gus noticed something odd about the list of repairs Emmitt had handed her—one thing was missing, after all. There were no repairs listed for the cargo hold.

The hive.

When she looked up from the tablet, Emmitt was eyeing her knowingly. *Tunk.* "That's an interesting water reclamation system you got rigged up in there." His face betrayed no emotion. "Clever irrigating the flowers with the gray water."

Gus stole a quick glance around the bay. "What do you want?"

Emmitt opened his mouth to speak, but before any words could come out, his eyes welled with tears and the old man's body shook. She led

Emmitt behind a big piece of rusty machinery. The engineer dropped down on a box, held his face in his hands, and wept. Gus awkwardly patted him on the shoulder. "'s'okay. I'm okay," he said and waved her arm off when the sobbing subsided.

Gus leaned against the complicated machinery and crossed her arms over her chest. "What do you want from me?" she asked when Emmitt regained control of himself and wiped his nose with an old rag.

He hung his head for a moment longer. When he raised it, his eyes were ringed with red. "It's Junior."

Gus had a flash of memory: Junior standing over Emmitt's wife with a handful of her white hair. She sighed and held up her hands. "Look, I don't like the prick either, but I'm not getting paid to get tangled up in your little town's problems." She stepped toward the doors. "Thanks for seeing to *Tilly,* but if you so much as mention my flowers to anyone else, it won't be Junior you'll have to worry about." She turned her back on the old man and started to walk away.

"He's forcing me to build something!" Emmitt called after her. "Something terrible."

She stopped and took a deep breath. *What now?* "Alright," she said, and turned back to him. "I'll bite. What's he got you working on?"

"It's the refinement process. The Deiopeans, *they're* the secret! With your help, it might not be too late to put a stop to all this and make things right." He spoke quickly and quietly as his eyes darted around the corral.

The spiders? What have they got to do— "Spit it out, Smith."

The big door slammed shut with a crash that echoed off the wagons littering the corral floor. Emmitt's face went white as a sheet.

"Emmitt! Oh, Emmitt!" Junior. "Where are you, old man?"

Gus slid deeper into the relative safety of the shadows and drew Delilah from her holster. Junior wasn't alone. He had four Company Police goons with him. All had their weapons drawn.

"You gotta help me!" Emmitt hissed. Fresh tears flowed down his cheeks.

"Shh!" Gus waved him back and watched.

Junior swore, then directed two of his men deeper into the corral. "Find him. Bring any of his crew—or better yet, that blue-haired bitch—back here, too. One of 'em ought to get his attention."

"Is there anybody else in the corral?" Gus whispered. Emmitt's face went paper-white.. He pointed deeper into the unorganized mess of old wagons and spare parts, in the same direction as the goons. She nodded. "Alright, you get your team outta here. I'll distract—*Hey!*"

Tears dripping onto his apron—but with set shoulders—Emmitt brushed by Gus and stepped clear of their hiding place. "I won't let them hurt Gloria." He took a deep breath and puffed up his chest. "Now that I've solved their problem, they think they don't need me."

"Smith," Gus hissed, "get back here."

"Emmitt!" Junior called again. "Where is that old bastard?"

"But they do," Emmitt said. "If I can convince him, maybe I can buy more time." He smiled at Gus crookedly, but his eyes were dark and humorless. Gus tried to grab him, but Emmitt stepped out of reach. "Stay here until it's over. Tell my wife I love her. And if you can, tell the spiders I'm sorry," he said quietly. He swallowed hard and stepped toward Junior.

"Emmitt, wait! *Tunk!*" Too late. Junior already spotted him.

"There you are, you old codger. Come 'ere. I've got something for you." Junior beckoned Emmitt to his side with a twisted, harsh smile. "You've done such a great job figuring out how the spiders do their little trick, my father wanted to give you your reward a little early."

Gus broke out in a cold sweat. *I can't just let this happen!* Her eyes darted around the space from the goons, to Junior and Emmitt, to the equipment and wrecks surrounding them all. Junior was a braggart, but she had no way to tell if his arrogance had been earned. Even if he was all bluster and she killed all five of them, then what?

There's got to be something ...

Before she could formulate a plan, the corral flashed with violet light and an electric crackle. Emmitt tumbled like a sack of potatoes as smoke rose from a fresh exit wound between his shoulders.

The sound of the shot brought the engineering crew running. Gus ducked down as they passed and watched them find their boss lying on the floor. Shouting voices erupted, but Junior and his men's drawn weapons were enough to keep the unarmed engineers at bay.

I gotta get outta here. Gus's head spun and locked in on her only option: a small window, set high in the corral wall behind her. While Junior argued with the engineers over Emmitt's crumpled body, Gus scrambled up a pile of scrap to the window only to find the lock rusted closed. She gave the latch two sharp cracks with Delilah's butt end, and it disintegrated into a coarse sand.

"What the rut was that? You got more people back there?" Junior shouted. "Go check it out."

She tried to ease the window open quickly and quietly, but it screeched like fingernails on a chalkboard and spewed rusty dust everywhere. "Over here!" a voice shouted, uncomfortably close. She shoved the window as hard as she could, tumbled out, and rolled down a small mountain of empty jerrycans still reeking of rubidium fumes and onto the road below.

As soon as she hit the ground, Gus jumped to her feet and dove for cover in an adjacent alley. Out of sight, she slammed her back against the wall and gasped for breath. The window screeched again, but the *crash* of a body sliding down the pile of fuel cans never came. Instead, someone swore under their breath, then yelled, "Whoever it was, they're gone!" And then, "O—of course not, sir! *Yessir!*" More hushed cursing erupted, and *then* the sound of a heavy body sliding down the cans. Gus chanced a glance out from cover. One of Junior's goons picked himself up off the ground and swung his head back and forth, looking first one way and then the other.

Once he ran off in the wrong direction, Gus followed the alley away from the engineering corral. She reached the closest intersection, turned the corner, and nearly smashed directly into another company bull, this one leading a small group of Deiopeans toward the engineering corral.

"Hey! I—" he said and started to raise his rifle. But Gus, acting on instinct and reflex, drew faster. Without thought, Gus raised Delilah and fired the big beam-shooter from the hip. The grapefruit beam opened a bloody crater in the bull's chest and Delilah discharged a plume of freezing exhaust. The bull collapsed.

A moment after the body hit the ground, short, hooded bodies, all flashing the same incoherent pattern of colors with their eyes, surrounded Gus.

"No!" Gus shouted and recoiled from their touch. "Get away from me!" All those skinny, hairy limbs were too much, and she bolted up the abandoned street, leaving the Deiopeans, Junior, and poor Emmitt behind.

Gus burst through the big door and into Ray's small lockup gasping for breath.

"You alright?" Ray asked with an examining eye. "What did Emmitt have to say for himself? Bet he delayed your repairs, didn't he? I swear, that man's been busier than a one-eyed cat watching nine rat holes."

Gus opened her mouth to tell him Emmitt went and got himself killed but found herself lying to the marshal instead. "Yeah, he's busy," she said as her breath slowly came back to her. "Said it would be a few more days."

"Oh, well." Ray smiled and put his feet up on the desk. "His prosperity means your misfortune. Whatcha gonna do? Coffee?" he asked and pointed to the old machine.

"Sure," Gus said curtly, and went to the window for a smoke. As much as she wanted to tell Ray what had happened, it occurred to her that this was exactly the kind of mess Laszlo was paying her to keep Ray's nose out of. *Should have ruttin' known.* She lit her cigar and tried to relax. At least Laszlo had the courtesy to wait until Emmitt finished working on *Tilly*. Somehow, she suspected that was a coincidence.

Moe watched her from between the bars of his cell. "Are you alright, Gus?"

"Yup," she said, brushing him off. "What about here? No problems while I was out?"

"Not a peep," Ray answered cheerfully and poured their coffee.

As she smoked in silence, with the cobbler-rob watching her suspiciously, Gus tried to count the things that had gone wrong since she teamed up with Tuco.

First, it was the San Juan-Paul bulls. Then, the three bluebell officers Tuco brought. Which led them directly into Laszlo' employ ...

This is, without a doubt, the worst job I've ever pulled. And it's getting worse all the time. She glanced at the big clock hanging behind Ray's desk. Half past eight in the morning and she already needed a stiff drink, a rut, and maybe a fight.

I should have shot Tuco and left his body for the bulls.

She took Ray's offered coffee and threw it back like whiskey. A scalded throat could hardly be called penance enough for the last twenty-four hours, but she let it burn all the same.

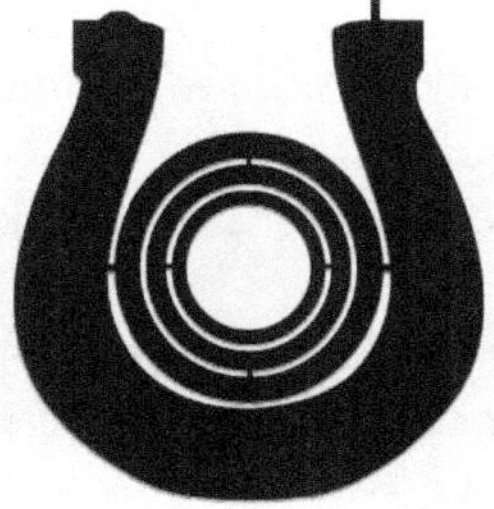

SPOONS, WOMEN, AND GUNS

The day passed exceedingly slowly, but once evening came, Gus started to feel a little better. A hand or two of razz with the local riffraff and a few disappointingly weak drinks at Cirrus House were all it had taken. Now, a little physical comfort would make the day complete. Emmitt's death had rocked her, and all of Cirrus House's booze wouldn't change that. She just didn't understand why.

Old coot was nothin' to me. Nothin'. I've seen a thousand of his like go down. All fodder for the Arm. Just the way the galaxy turns. I tried to help him, but he made his choice. Did all I could.

Couldn't have done anything more.

She took some solace in the fact that if she had, they'd likely be picking out a spot on Santa Barbara's cemetery shelves for her, too. Laszlo and his boys held the town in an iron grip. She'd seen it before. Suffered through it, even. There was no fighting men like that. Not in a place like this. Better to do the job they were paying her for and keep her mouth shut long enough to get far away from here.

Gus sat at the Cirrus House bar with a boot up on the rail. She sipped a watered-down whiskey and scanned the room for an available and attractive rent-girl. Her eyes fell on a young woman with clear, healthy skin, full hips with a cinched waist, and bountiful black curls. Gus watched her navigate the gambling floor, but the moment the subject of her attraction crossed the batwing doors, the Leconte brothers blew in. *Physical comfort is overrated, anyway.*

Gus tried to get the bartender's attention, but before her drink arrived, Aaron and Junior stepped up to the bar on either side of her.

"Put this one on my tab. My brother's got the next round," Junior said to the barkeep. He didn't seem too happy about it—a dark cloud hung over his sharp features.

"What can I do for you, boys?" Gus asked, keeping her gaze fixed on her glass.

"Our father says we should apologize for our behavior the other night," Aaron said. Finally, Gus pulled her eyes from her drink. To her surprise, Aaron stood with his arms open and his face soft and friendly—sincere, even. Junior, on the other hand, glowered into his glass and said nothing.

"And, I suppose, convince me to take his deal for Moe? Thanks for the drink, boys, but I was on my way out." Gus threw back the rest of her whiskey and pushed away from the bar. Aaron grabbed her wrist, and they locked eyes. "If you're really here trying to make things right," she warned, "repeating the way the other night's unpleasantness began isn't a great approach." Aaron's eyes widened and he released her without a second thought.

"Let her leave," Junior said, with a wry smile. "This void-drifter wouldn't know hospitality if it spit in her face."

"Another interesting tactic to get into my good graces—insulting me," she said and turned toward the batwing doors.

"The bounty, plus twenty-five percent," Junior called after her. "Is *that* insulting?"

Gus stopped dead in her tracks. That was a lot of spoons just to turn the reward—and the prestige—over to someone else. What kind of deal could Laszlo work that would warrant such an expensive cherry to sweeten the pie?

Only one way to find out.

Gus turned back to the brothers at the bar. "That *is* generous," she admitted. "I'm not saying I'm taking the deal, but maybe we have something to talk about after all."

Aaron's face brightened. "Then, like my brother said, the next round's on me!"

The following hours were a blur as Gus matched the Lecontes drink for drink. She had hoped alcohol and a little ego stroking would loosen at least Aaron's tongue. But every time she tried to steer the conversation toward

Laszlo's deal, and why offering Moe to his potential business partner was so important, Junior butted in to change the subject.

"Forty percent," Gus said.

Junior scoffed into his glass. "Don't be ridiculous. Thirty."

"Call it the bounty plus one third." Gus threw back her whisky and squinted at him. "But I gotta know what I'm turning down the reputation for. Bringing in a bounty-head that's been out for as long as Moe will get my name out in the right circles," she said. "Thinking long term, if I give that up to your father, or whoever *he's* giving it up to," she took a swig of the harsh amber liquid in front of her. "That's spoons out of my pocket."

"True," Aaron said, "but you'd gain a powerful friend in our father." His words were starting to slur.

"And I'm sure any bounty hunting opportunities lost would be made up for, ten-fold, if you stay on our father's good side," Junior said coolly. He'd matched her gulp for gulp but showed no sign of it. *Tunk.*

Despite herself, even Gus's head had started to swim. She couldn't hope to keep this up for much longer. Time for a change of tactics.

"Why don't we call it forty percent, and this one and I find a quiet place to seal the deal?" she asked. She traced a finger under Aaron's stubbly chin.

Junior's face tightened. "I'm not sure that's a good idea."

"*Shut up,* LJ," Aaron hissed. Gus smiled and put her hand on his thigh. "We've got a deal," Aaron said excitedly. He grinned, licking his lips. His eyes ran down her neck, to her body, absorbing every curve. "Let's go *shake* on it."

"*Aaron,*" Junior warned.

"*LJ,*" Aaron shushed. "Go tell Dad the good news." The brothers glared at each other over Gus's shoulders.

"Fine," Junior said. He lingered for a moment to stare at Gus. "But you be careful. I don't trust her."

Aaron ignored him. "You won't hurt me, will you, Gus?" he asked, grinning.

"Well," Gus said with a smirk, "maybe a little. How about some shots to celebrate, and make things more"—she leaned in, whispering into Aaron's ear—"*interesting?*"

"Why not take the bottle?" Aaron's excitement bubbled over as he called the bartender over. He took a fifth of tequila from the genie working the bar, drank straight from the neck, and passed it to Gus.

She took her own swig, grimaced at the burn, and pressed her body against Aaron's. "Do you know a quiet place we can *press the flesh,* and make this deal official?"

Aaron's boyish face turned bright red, and his ears nearly purple. "Y—yes!" he managed through the anticipation, "I know just the place."

Gus stole a glance back at Junior as Aaron escorted her toward the swinging doors of Cirrus House. He glared at her, but rather than follow, he turned back to the bar and ordered another drink.

Aaron led Gus through a part of town she could tell had been seedy even before Las Ráfagas's decline. Goosebumps rose on her arms and neck, as if wary eyes watched them pass each abandoned building. As they walked, they passed the bottle of tequila back and forth. Without his brother reining him in, Aaron's tongue began to wag almost at once.

He gazed through the dome at the dark sky above. Deiopea, full tonight, cast her light through a dense curtain of clouds. Even through the cover, the carefully planned, web-like cities of the Deiopeans stood in sharp contrast to the dull red of the moon's surface.

"Damn spiders," Aaron spat. "You know what they were doing with this cloud band when my father got here? *Hunting* in it. If you can even call it that. They used to use rocket propelled tin cans to get here." He laughed. "Those savages were sitting on enough rubidium for half the Arm to run on for decades, and they wouldn't dare touch it. For 'ecological reasons,'" he said mockingly.

"What's *that* supposed to mean?" Gus asked. She laughed along and took the tequila from him. With a thumb over the mouth, she hoisted the bottle and pretended to take another swig.

"Who knows? Some primitive *bottle-farts* about a beast that lives in the clouds and comes with the storms." Aaron threw the tequila back and nearly fell over. He laughed hard and drenched himself in the liquor.

Ugh. Somehow, Gus managed to keep the sneer off her lips. *Men and their tall tales.* Still, it presented an opportunity to stroke his ego. "That's not true, right?" she asked and walked her fingers up his chest. "The town's not in danger, is it?"

He pulled her close. "Don't worry, baby. It's just a stupid superstition. But *Junior* sure believes it. He's always taking hunting parties deeper into the atmosphere." He took another short swig. "Even says he saw it once." Aaron stared off into space in a daze. After a moment or two, his eyes refocused. "But now that they think they're so smart, they've changed their tune. Now they won't *share,* so they're gonna get what's coming to 'em!" He led them to a wide platform and stumbled when he tried to step onto it.

Gus helped him steady himself. "That's selfish," she egged him on. Fish stories about beasts in the clouds didn't interest Gus, but the spiders—and whatever Emmitt was doing—*that* warranted a moment of consideration. "What won't they share?"

"Their refining tech! The little eight-legged freaks figured out how to supercharge the rubidium. So, when they wouldn't share, we took it from 'em. Serves 'em right. Furry bastards."

Here we go. "Supercharge it? How?"

Aaron pressed a button on a rectangular box at the end of a thick cable, and the platform began to slowly drop. It took a moment for Gus's tequila-soaked brain to realize he'd brought her to the mining level access lift.

"No more talk, baby. I want you so bad," he whispered and leaned in for a sloppy kiss.

Gus managed to redirect him into her neck. She tried to think through the haze of liquor as he slobbered all over her collarbone and dry humped her thigh. Getting Aaron's tongue to loosen had cost her more of her sobriety than she had intended. Even so, things were starting to fall into place.

With the demand for rubidium-87 at an all-time low, a supercharged product could rejuvenate this ghost town. That *must* have been the work Emmitt and his team were doing—retrofitting the mining levels to replicate the Deiopeans' refinement technique. But there had been a problem. Something only "live" specimens would solve. Something Emmitt had wanted to apologize to the Deiopeans for.

Gus's blood ran cold. Missing natives and live specimens. *Laszlo can't be that arrogant, can he?* If the UCET ever got wind Laszlo was abusing a native lifeform, they would shut him down, seize his businesses and assets, lock him up, and lose the key. From what she'd seen, Laszlo delighted in ruling over his little fiefdom here. Even his quarters atop the tower allowed him to look down on his domain as its undisputed lord and master. What could make a man like Laszlo Leconte risk all that?

When the lift reached the bottom, Gus pulled Aaron's lips to hers and ground her hips against him. She mimed another swing from the tequila and raised the bottle to Aaron's lips. He grinned and she poured the dregs down his throat. "That all seems *so complicated,*" she teased. "Why not sell the whole town and let it be someone else's problem?"

"Because Mackenzie's convinced the copperheads the supercharged rubidium for their new pulse-rail engine could change the war. There's still a lot of spoons to be had on this gas ball, and if you play your cards right, you could be on the arm of one of the most powerful men this side of the Rift."

The CCO. Their involvement would certainly be enough to make Laszlo feel untouchable. But pulse-rail trains don't run on rubidium.

Aaron tried to wink, but blinked drunkenly instead, and leaned in for another messy, open-mouthed kiss.

"Not here, Aaron," she whispered in his ear. "Anticipation makes it that much better, *trust me.* And you promised me somewhere private. I don't want anyone to see what I'm going to do to you."

Aaron's face, already red from the liquor, turned an even deeper shade of scarlet. A savage grin spread over his face, and he led her off the lift and into the mining levels without another word.

Gus's drunk mind did its best to shift the new pieces of the puzzle into place as Aaron led her deeper into the mining levels.

In his rush to find privacy, Aaron turned a dark corner and crashed into a group of four or five miners huddled around a sparking heating unit. Aaron's face twisted from horny anticipation to startled surprise and then a shade of embarrassed anger in the time it took him to fall back on his ass. The genie he ran into fell forward and landed in the arms of a lurker-rob Gus immediately recognized. *Gretchen.* Walter collected his many arms and picked himself up from his wife's pincers.

From the floor, Aaron's face puckered and he turned such a deep shade of red, Gus thought his hair might catch fire. "All of you rutting freaks are out past curfew!" he roared. He leapt to his feet and clumsily drew his gun. "You know you're not supposed to leave the barracks after sundown! Or have you all got your brains too scrambled from inbreeding and bad wiring to understand that properly?"

"Aaron, baby." Gus pulled on his arm. "Forget about them, let's go."

For a moment, she thought the thing in his pants might win out over the booze in his brain, but at the last instant, Aaron recognized Walter, and his liquor-fueled rage won out. A disturbing grin spread across his face.

"You sit tight, beautiful. This rob-rutter has been begging me for this lesson for years. I'm finally going to give it to him." Aaron raised his gun and pointed it at Walter's face. The others fled without a second glance. Only Gretchen held her ground with her husband.

Gus reached for Delilah, drew the heavy weapon, and fired before Aaron could squeeze his trigger. The pink beam tore into the triceps on Aaron's gun arm, and as she dragged Delilah's barrel upwards, it sliced through the flesh, cleanly severing his arm above the elbow.

A moment of stunned silence fell over the corridor as they stared at Aaron's arm, still clutching his Beaumont-Adams and lying at his feet. A moment later, a bloodcurdling screech erupted from Aaron's throat. He held the bloody, half-cauterized stump with his free hand and fell over onto his back. In another moment, Aaron's cries were drowned out by blaring alarms. Someone had already alerted the company bulls of the shooting.

Gus holstered Delilah and shook her head at the shrieking man-child. When Walter and Gretchen appeared at her side, she shooed them away. "You two better get out of here before more trouble shows up."

"What about you?" Walter asked.

"I'll be fine. Somebody's gotta make sure this fool doesn't bleed out on the floor before his boys get here," Gus said and waved them on.

But Gretchen hesitated. "That's twice you've put my husband's safety and life ahead of your own. I cannot tell you how grateful I am to you. Thank you. If there's anything you ever need, don't hesitate to let Walter know. We'll make it happen."

Gus nodded, and the unusual pair disappeared into the maze of the mining levels.

With Walter and Gretchen safely away, Gus turned her attention to the screaming ninny rolling around on the floor. She knelt, grabbing Aaron.

"Will you *shut up* and let me see?" she shouted in his face. But on he went, thrashing and screaming.

"Alright," she muttered. *"*We'll do this the *easy* way." She pulled Ray's small first aid kit from a pocket and jabbed a small anesthetic syrette into Aaron's thigh. His shrieking dropped to a low mumble, and the thrashing slowed to a dull rocking and finally stopped. "There," Gus said as she pulled Aaron's free hand from the stump, "let's see how bad it is."

Delilah had cut cleanly through his bicep. The beam had cauterized most of the wound, so it oozed only a small amount of blood.

"Oh, ya big baby," she chided and slapped a vacuum-bandage over the stump. "Rich boy like you'll get a cloned replacement in no time." She jabbed him with another dose of anesthetic. Aaron slowly relaxed against the wall and mumbled quietly to himself.

Gus collapsed against the opposite wall and slid to the floor. That had been *way* too close. The liquor had slowed her down and dulled her wits. *It all happened so fast.* If she had been a fraction of a moment slower, Walter would have been dead. Maybe Gretchen. And Aaron. And her, too, shortly thereafter. At least with him alive, bandaged, and doped up she might be able to talk her way out of this. But she had made holding on to Moe a lot harder.

It took mere minutes for a squad of black-uniformed, riot-shield carrying company bulls to appear with Junior at their head. Gus scanned the unit for Tuco's face, but didn't spot him. *Coward's probably holed up somewhere, waiting for the bulls to do the dirty work for him.*

"Hey, LJ," Aaron called to his brother in a child-like sing-song voice. He pointed to his severed arm on the floor and laughed.

"What the *tunk?*" Junior shouted. Then his focus landed on Gus. *"You!"* he roared. He grabbed her by the poncho and pulled her to her feet. *"What did you do?"* he screamed, spittle flying.

"I stopped his drunk ass from killing a couple of miners for no reason. And then I saved his *rutting* life!" Gus shoved Junior back and found a dozen pistols pointed at her.

Junior turned his back on her and knelt next to his brother. With a stoned smile on his face, Aaron's remaining hand floated up to playfully poke Junior's nose. Junior batted it away and examined Aaron's wound. "Christ's blood, Aaron," he muttered. "Kill 'er."

"Hey, I'm working on *Daddy's* dime now, remember?" she shouted at his back. "You better get clearance from on high before you do anything stupid."

He hunched his shoulders up around his ears and huffed. "Wait!" Junior's order sliced through the air.

"She's right, LJ," Aaron said in a dreamy voice from the floor. "Besides, you can't kill her 'til I *rut* 'er," he added, matter-of-factly.

Junior grimaced at Aaron, then turned it on Gus.

"*Fine,*" he spat. "Put the bitch in cuffs and we'll see what my father has to say about this."

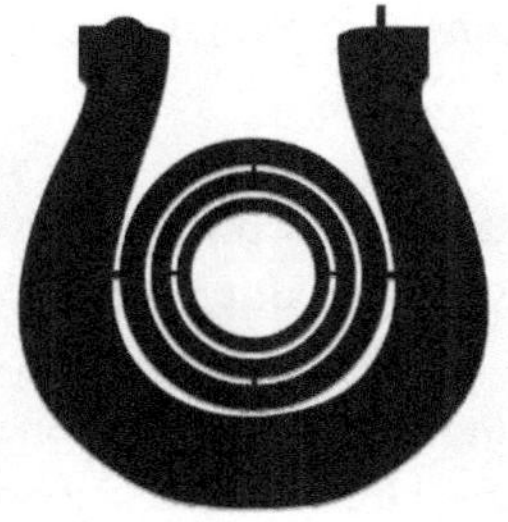

AEOLUSIAN VENGEANCE

Heavily armored and armed company bulls filled Laszlo's quarters. The administrator himself stood at the window and peered into the overcast night. He kept his back to the room while Junior, looking more like Laszlo's brother than son, explained how he had found Aaron.

Laszlo shook his head when Junior finished. "And how is the boy?" he asked with a sneer.

"I—" Junior hesitated. "He's fine. He's in the medi-pod now." Junior shot Gus another dark glare. "She keeps her piece well-maintained; I'll give her that much."

Gus struggled against the cuffs clasping her hands behind her back. Junior had tightened them until they dug into her flesh. She very much wanted to tell him where he could shove Aaron's severed arm. She managed to bite her tongue instead.

"She could have killed him, Dad." Junior spoke low, pleading.

"And where is her weapon?" the elder Leconte asked. Junior snapped his fingers, and a bull brought Delilah to him. Laszlo lifted the big gun and examined it, turning it over in his hands. "Magnificent!" He held Delilah up and pointed the business end at Gus. He dropped the gun to his side, clapped Junior on the shoulder, and smiled. "Son, if she had wanted to kill Aaron, he'd be dead." Laszlo raised his voice to address the roomful of bulls. "You are all dismissed," he announced. "Yes, yes, that's right. Tremendous job, everyone! Really great! Can someone be sure to get those cuffs off this charming woman there before you all go? Thanks, you guys are the best!"

As the room emptied, Laszlo offered Delilah back to Gus with a dark smile. "I know you boys like to play tough out here in the clouds," he said to Junior, "but this one's like your old man. We're cut from the same cloth, she and I."

"But Dad!"

"Shut *up*, Junior." Junior took one look at his father's unwavering expression and shut his mouth. But he did nothing to hide the open hatred on his own face.

"You and I are nothing alike," Gus said. She snatched Delilah from Laszlo's hands and dropped it back in its place on her hip.

"Mm-hmm," he hummed coyly. "Why don't you tell me what happened before my overly ambitious son arrived."

Gus crossed her arms over her chest and cast her eyes out over the town below. "Aaron was drunk."

"And whose fault was that?" Junior took a threatening step forward.

Laszlo turned on his son in the blink of an eye. He moved like lightning and lifted the young man into the air by his throat. *"Will you shut up!* I asked the lady to tell me what happened. If you can't keep your tongue locked away, I will tear it out!"

Gus's whole body tensed and she reached for Delilah. An instant later, Laszlo dropped Junior to the floor in a heap. With his son rubbing his neck and gasping for breath, Laszlo turned his attention back to Gus. It took every ounce of her willpower to hold her ground. "You were saying?"

Junior slowly rose to his feet and straightened his suit jacket. He stood there with his eyes locked on his shoes and an utterly blank expression on his face.

Gus swallowed hard.

For now, Laszlo's madness worked in her favor. She hoped it continued as she told him what happened. She would have to frame shooting his son's arm off in terms his brand of crazy would understand. *No problem.*

"Like I said," she started again, "your boy was piss drunk. He tried to kill a miner and the mercantile genie, whatshisname—Walter—for the crime of standing around a heating unit."

"The mining levels *are* under special lockdown right now, and our employees know there are consequences to breaking curfew while our operation is being retrofitted," Laszlo explained. "As I understand it, we've been having a particular problem with this lurker—Gretchen, is it? As captain of the Company Police Force, I trust Aaron to impose our laws as he sees fit."

"By indiscriminately killing your workforce on the eve of such an important deal? Especially with replacement workers so difficult to come by? Given the circumstances, even considering Gretchen's ... history ... there must be a more *measured* approach to discipline." Gus held her hands up. "But what do I know? I'm just a void-drifter. I'm not trying to tell you how to run your town."

Junior opened his mouth as though he might say something, but with a quick glance at his father, abruptly closed it again. Laszlo, on the other hand, considered her point.

"You may be on to something there," he said and stepped to a well-stocked bar. He poured a pair of whiskeys, and a tall glass of water. He handed one whiskey to Junior and Gus the other. Junior drank his down immediately. "Aaron's always struggled with his temper," he said as he sipped his water. "It's a family curse. I always knew it would get him into trouble one of these days.

"But I don't want this incident to leave you thinking we don't treat our workers with the utmost respect and dignity. After all, some of my best friends are robs." He chuckled and gestured around them. Only then did Gus finally notice the room concealed half a dozen of the big security-robs Laszlo had had with him the night they met. One tucked into a closet there, its blank eyes peering out of the darkness beyond the door. Another masquerading as a decorative pillar holding up the archway to an adjacent room. Yet another in the corner, curled into a ball Gus had mistaken for art.

"The answer's still no, Laszlo. I don't care how you run things in this town, or how many old widows you let your boys make to help them feel big." Junior's head whipped around but he held on to whatever comment burned on his tongue. "Moe stays under *my* care."

Laszlo poured Junior another whiskey and another water for himself. "Junior, aren't you heading out for a hunt tomorrow morning?"

Junior's face slowly changed like the tide going out. "Yeah," he eventually said and broke into a reluctant smirk.

"Why don't you tell our guest what it is you're hunting."

Junior eyed Gus skeptically. "Dad—"

"*Tell her,*" Laszlo growled.

Junior flinched. "When my father first arrived on this gas ball, the spiders told stories about a great beast that lived in the lower atmosphere and fed on the burdle flocks. They called it the Stormrider. Their legends say it's enormous, with a wingspan as wide as Las Ráfagas. They said flocks of them once roamed this cloud band, chasing the great storms. But only a few remain."

"And you believe that?" Gus said flatly.

"I've *seen* it."

"Uh-huh," Gus rolled her eyes.

"I've got a great idea. Why doesn't Gus here join you for the hunt tomorrow?" Laszlo suggested as though the thought had just occurred to him. "That way we can show her there's no hard feelings, and the two of you can see if we can get through this logjam when it comes to our dear Moe—without Aaron's temper getting in the way. What do you say?"

Junior's face darkened, but he buckled immediately under his father's stare. "Sure. Great idea, Dad." He seemed to physically swallow what he actually wanted to say. "I'm sure we can work something out. It'll be great."

Gus scowled. "I'm not interested in your wild goose chase," she said. "Now, if it's all the same to you, I've got a prisoner to keep an eye on." She put her full glass down on the bar and headed for the lift back to the esplanade.

"Gus," Laszlo said. His voice prickled with thinly veiled aggression. She turned back to face the tycoon. "I insist you join the hunting party. Even if your mind is truly made up with regard to Moe, consider it a part of your contract. I do so worry when Junior goes out on a hunt."

"He's a big boy, Laz. I'm sure the great white hunter here can take care of himself."

Laszlo took another sip of water.

"You know," he mused, "I used to hate water. Never drank the stuff. But my love for the drink started to dull my mind, and I couldn't have that. Bad for business. Do you know what else is bad for business? Letting UCET officer-murdering criminals roam my outpost freely. For now, I need your services, but that situation is not permanent," he reminded her. "Now, will you please keep my son safe on his hunting trip tomorrow?"

Extorting bastard. "Alright, when you put it that way." Maybe it could be a chance to smooth things over with Junior—at least enough to keep her alive until the job was done. If nothing else, it would be nice to get out of town for a little while. The lift opened and she stepped in.

"Six thirty at the livery stables," Junior called as the doors closed between them. "Don't be late."

When six o'clock the following morning arrived, Gus sat on the cot in her borrowed cell and waited. She'd awoken early and spent the time replaying the previous evening's conversation in her mind. *Laszlo's either as crafty as a fox or crazier than a june bug.* Either way, she was stuck with him. For now, anyway. She shook her head, trying to clear it, and stood.

"I'm really glad you're doing this," Ray said from his desk. The smell of fresh brewed coffee filled the small jailhouse. "It's real big of you. Should go a long way toward making the rest of your stay with us here more pleasant." He blew on his coffee before taking a cautious sip. "Ooh, *hot.*"

"*I* think it's a terrible idea. Not that anyone asked for my opinion," Moe said from his cot. "Little bastard got what he deserved. Some small measure of it, anyway. You should have killed him." His voice was flat. Bleak. "Now the other one's gonna try to kill *you*. Going on this hunt is nothing more than lining yourself up for slaughter."

"Oh, shut up, Moe." Ray said. He offered Gus a mug. "You want some before you go?"

"Better not, I'm already running late." But Gus stopped at the bars of Moe's cell before leaving. The rob sat on his cot with his head in his hands. "I'll be alright, Moe. I can handle myself. I made you a promise and I intend to keep it. You sit tight."

"Goodbye, Gus."

"Don't worry, I'll keep an eye on him," Ray called as she left the cellblock. "Catch something *big!*"

The walk from Ray's office to the stables wasn't long, but it provided enough time for Moe's warnings to stir up her mind. On the one hand, she already knew how violent Junior could be. She had yet to see him in a real fight, but he behaved with the arrogance of a man who believed the rules didn't apply to him. Best case, he was only arrogant and unpredictable. Worst case, his boasting was earned and accurate, and the erratic behavior was calculated.

Either way, he's dangerous.

On the other hand, Laszlo had proven himself to be just as danger-ous, maybe more so. And he clearly kept his son in check, at least while they were in the same room.

There's the real *risk. Will Junior's leash slacken while he's away from his father?*

If you were to strip away all the mystery, the combat-robs, and the violence, Laszlo was just a businessman. A businessman in the middle of some important and *expensive* negotiations. He'd already made a big investment in her by paying for *Tilly's* extra repairs. And he had shown restraint when she refused his offer to buy out Moe's bounty no fewer than three times.

But why?

He hadn't known she and Tuco were coming. She couldn't have been part of his plan. That should have made her expendable. Instead, Laszlo had gone out of his way to make her feel irreplaceable. Whatever role he had in mind for her, it had to be more important than he let on. Otherwise, Moe would have been taken without a second thought.

And she'd already be dead.

A murky, heavy atmosphere marred the morning air. The wind picked up and the clouds, both above and below the outpost, raced toward the horizon as if fleeing some unseen calamity.

Still, as Gus stepped onto the livery stable pier, she felt an emotion that wasn't quite relief but was close. She would have to keep her guard up, but maybe Ray had a point. Maybe this really was a chance to smooth things over, at least enough to survive this storm. Gus watched the clouds galloping through the sky and had a moment of vertigo. A shout from further down the pier broke the spell.

Junior.

His customary three-piece suit had been replaced with tall, green-bottle skin boots and a hooded duster the color of old bricks—or old blood. He stood with a group of men who were preparing a small fleet of open-topped skiffs. They were shaped somewhat like the Deiopeans' crafts, but where the natives' skiffs were small, efficient, and utilitarian, these were bulky, sub-orbital pleasure-wagons.

"Right on time. I like that," Junior said. He snapped a gold pocket watch shut and smiled. When he led her to the nearest skiff, his duster opened revealing Junior's Colt Prism M2265 strapped to his hip.

There were nearly a dozen wagons in the hunting party, each with five or six men on board. "We gonna play nice today, Junior?" Gus asked as they stepped onto one of the ridiculous wagons.

Junior put his hands on his hips and revealed his idea of "hunting attire" beneath the duster: khaki pants and a faded blue chambray shirt. He looked like he had stepped off a catalog photoshoot. Gus stifled a smirk. *Play nice, too*.

"My father has asked me to put aside any misgivings I may have for the time being," he reassured her. "He says you're playing a critical role and I should trust his judgment." He said the right words, but his tense expression said he didn't completely believe them. The wagons, fully loaded with men and equipment, ignited their engines—powerful atmo-thrusters that made the Deiopeans' propellers feeble in comparison—and pulled away from Las Ráfagas.

"Besides," Junior continued as the outpost disappeared into the clouds, "you might prove yourself useful on the hunt."

"Yeah, about that," Gus said. She turned to face the nose of the skiff as they approached Las Ráfagas's shimmering energy fence. "You're not really dragging me out here to hunt some kind of imaginary monster, right?"

"On the contrary," Junior laughed as the tingle of the plasma fencing washed over them. Grates in the floor snapped open and Gus heard the whirring of fans spinning up beneath them. A column of breathable atmosphere rose from the skiff and trailed behind them. "The spiders are savage and primitive, that much is true. I mean, using chemically propelled projectile weapons against an armored prey? How quaint! But don't let their regressive ways fool you. The Stormrider may be legendary, but it is also real.

"This cloud band is subject to periodic storms. Massive cyclone systems every ten years or so. They only last a few days, coming on without warning and fading away just as quickly. It has something to do with the rubidium flow of the clouds. But with the storm, comes the 'rider."

A gigantic, flying monster no one had ever seen? Ridiculous. But if humoring this jackass was all it took to smooth things over with the Lecontes, then humor him she would. A light rain started to fall, and the hunting party pulled up their hoods or sheltered under wide-brimmed hats. She sensed that it would only take a little coaxing to get Junior to talk. *If there's one thing the Leconte men share, it's a love for the sound of their own voices.*

"What makes you so sure?" she asked. She sat down on the floor with her back to the drizzle and rolled a cigar.

Junior sat down across from her. "Nearly ten years ago, I led a burdle sport hunt on a day very much like today," he said and watched the clouds rush by. His eyes were distant as he reflected on the memory. "We had already made a few good kills, but I wasn't satisfied yet. The flock we'd been stalking dove for safer clouds in the deeper atmosphere. And we gave chase.

"It wasn't long before the clouds blotted out the sun and we chased our quarry through twilight. But I pushed deeper, until the party's spotlights began to pop from the pressure. I finally called for the boys to climb out of the gas when *Icarus* here," he patted the steel hide of their skiff, "had the only remaining working lamp. I ordered the others back, but we lingered with the light."

Gus offered Junior the cigar, but he wrinkled his nose and refused. Shrugging, she lit it herself, bidding him to continue.

"With the flock lost, and the rest of my party already ascending, I was just about ready to order our own return when a gigantic shadow moved through the clouds in front of our light. At first, we thought it was a trick of the atmosphere; a pocket of dense gas or something. At least until it struck *Icarus.* I lost two good men on that first impact. Another three when the beast's tail flipped us like your lucky coin."

Gus took a drag from the cigar. Junior told a surprisingly good story. *Even if it's all bottle-farts.*

"I found myself alone, my crew either dead or missing, the rest of my hunting party long gone." Junior hit his stride. Gus could tell this was a yarn he enjoyed spinning, and one he spun often. "I struggled to reach the helm to steady the wagon and prepared for a rapid ascent. But as *Icarus* started to climb, the clouds parted and I finally saw my attacker," he paused and stared off into the clouds as if expecting to see it again.

Gus puffed at her cigar impatiently. "Well? What was it?"

He smiled, making his sharp features more charming. "Have you ever seen the great skates of the Gum Nebula?" he asked. "Or the manta rays of Earth? Sort of like that, but much, much bigger. The beast could swallow a burdle flock *whole.*"

"And you want to hunt this thing? You're crazier than I thought." Gus laughed, then bit her lip. *Tunk,* so much for playing nice.

But Junior returned the laugh. "No, I would have to be crazy to hunt an *adult!*"

Gus stopped laughing. "What's that supposed to mean?"

"I noticed one more thing about our big friend that day, oh so long ago." Junior's smile changed back from charming to sinister. "Egg sacks. The beast was with child."

The atmosphere got darker and thicker as they descended further into the clouds.

"Wait," Gus said, waving the glowing ember of her cigar through the air, "let me get this straight. You saw this thing, what? Ten years ago? And you're assuming, one, that it's still alive. And two, that its eggs not only hatched, but the kids are still a size you think you can handle. You said last night the spiders said they used to be everywhere, but now they're rare. So, what? You want to bag one before they're all gone?"

Junior stared out into the growing gloom around them. "It's here. I can feel it. The spiders also say no one has ever hunted a Stormrider and lived to tell the tale. *I'll* be the first."

"*Okay,*" Gus said skeptically. Even if the damn thing were real, the chances of meeting one seemed impossibly low. So, why not let him play Great White Hunter? "What's the plan?" she asked and got to her feet.

"We recreate the original hunt!" he laughed. "We'll stalk a burdle flock and pick off a few of the young or weak. Enough to force the flock to dive for the lower atmosphere. That's where the Stormrider feeds. *There!*" he shouted and jumped to his own feet. He pointed over Gus's shoulder into the clouds.

She whipped her head around in time to catch a glimmer of blue-green scales. They had found an immense flock, with hundreds or thousands of giant turtle-birds moving as one like a school of fish.

From the first sighting, things moved quickly. Junior pointed Gus to one of half a dozen side-mounted tractor-cannons. The *Icarus's* crew manned the others, and the fleet of wagons gave chase.

Before long, the wagons picked off some of the slower animals that stuck to the edges of the flock. Gus even managed to get a shot off, but her tractor beam bounced harmlessly off an iridescent shell. "You've got to aim for the wings!" Junior advised before firing a beam of his own. His aim true, he howled in triumph and pumped his fists in the air as his beam pulled the burdle from the flock and it died under a blaze of laser fire.

With Junior's kill the last straw for the herd, and the big animals collectively dove as one and disappeared into a wine-colored cloud.

"*Dive! Dive!*" Junior hollered to *Icarus's* helmsman. With the atmo-thrusters screaming, the pleasure-wagon's nose plunged after the retreating burdles. Gus's face hurt, and she noticed she'd been smiling since Junior first spotted the burdles. Whether she wanted to admit it or not, she was having fun—more fun than she'd had in a long time.

Junior fought the rushing air to reach her side. He leaned close to be heard over the roar of engine and atmosphere.

"I wanted to apologize for last night. Both for myself, and on behalf of my brother. Aaron can be," he paused as they flew into a dense cloud and the air around them darkened, "intolerant sometimes. And I—well, I might be a little overprotective. But Dad was right, you're holding your own today!" The clouds were so thick Gus couldn't see the glow from the hunting party's engines. "And Dad was right about one other thing," he shouted.

"What's that?" she yelled back. The air grew thicker still until she could barely see the man at the next cannon.

"Aaron and I play tough out here. You," he said and leaned in closer, "you're the real thing." His body pressed against hers.

Great. Now it's both *of them.*

"Which is why Dad will *have* to take me seriously now."

"What?" She turned to find that sinister, shark-tooth gin splitting his face. Her own smile faded from her lips.

Junior braced against *Icarus's* hide, tore the deputy's badge from her poncho, and shoved Gus with all his might. "No hard feelings."

Gus could do nothing to stop herself from tumbling over the edge and falling headlong into the Aeolusian clouds.

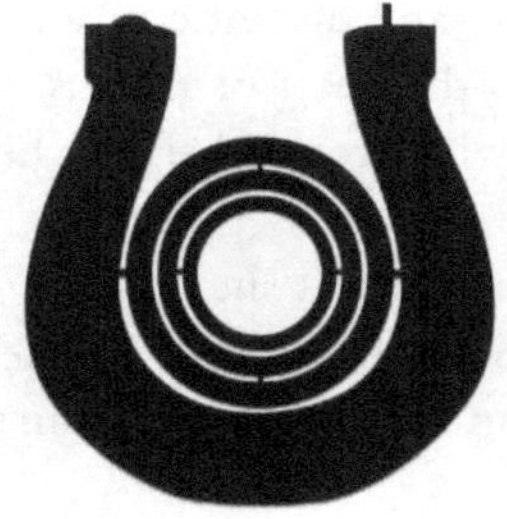

PLUNDERERS OF THE HYDROGEN FLATS

Gus plunged end over end through the clouds, helplessly struggling to gain control of the fall. Desperate, she engaged the EVA boosters on her boots, but they sputtered and died. Out of fuel.

Tunk! How could I have been so stupid?

She finally managed to right herself against the rushing gases. With a twist of her hips, she flipped onto her back and pulled her hood over her head. She fumbled at her belt, found a small, U-shaped device, and jammed it into her mouth just before her flight suit registered the pressure change.

"Dangerous atmospheric change detected," an electronic voice said in her ear. "Enacting emergency protocols. Prepare for pressurization and life support initialization." Her flight suit inflated, and the energy field dropped down over her face.

She took a deep breath, braced herself, and blew through the gadget she'd pulled from her belt. A sharp shriek cut through the dense clouds flying by her. She knew the screech would also cut through communications transmissions within a twenty-five-mile radius like a plow. Anyone using their comms system in the vicinity of Las Ráfagas was sure to get a moderate case of tinnitus for the next couple of days. But one listener would know what it meant.

Gus could only hope they'd react in time.

Still she fell, further into Aeolus's dense atmosphere. The clouds became so thick she could barely see her own hands; the light from Hippotes faded to a dim and distant crimson. Yet, as she plummeted deeper and deeper into the heart of Aeolus, she thought she sensed shapes and shadows moving around her, just beyond the veil of gas.

Come on, come on.

Her heart raced in her ears as she fell past a giant shadow silently gliding through the clouds. It followed her descent for a time before flitting off into the gloom with a grace and calm that made Gus question if she had seen it at all.

The pressure on Gus's flight suit grew quickly and alarms rang inside her hood. *"Warning:* atmospheric pressure approaching Equuleus A1C Pressurized Flight Suit recommended threshold. Return to an environment with an atmospheric pressure between zero and fifteen bars, immediately."

Tunk! Where are *you?*

"Warning: critical system failure imminent." She didn't need to be told—she could smell ozone in her hood. "Return tokkzzz ..." the electronic voice fizzled and died. More systems would follow in short order.

Gus closed her eyes and gritted her teeth against the growing darkness.

Not how I pictured going out.

Somehow, she had always thought there would be more gunplay involved. And maybe a little thrilling heroics. She always figured she would be alone, she just hoped *Tilly* would at least be there.

Somewhere in her suit, a gasket blew, and with no audio systems left to warn her, the head-up-display lit up in an angry amber. Oxygen leak. An image of Moe and the Vega family blossomed in her mind like one of *Tilly's* flowers. What would become of them? With the clouds rushing by, her head pounding from the pressure, and her lungs burning, it all seemed so unimportant and far away.

This is it! No time left ...

Another shadow appeared in the gloom, this one more familiar, its movement anything *but* silent as it screamed through the dense gas toward her as she fell. This shape locked in on her fall as it approached and went into a steep dive to get beneath her. Smaller than the other shadows, it still dwarfed Gus as it flew beneath her and twisted its bulk into something of a barrel roll.

Only once cradled on her upturned belly did Gus recognize the blue glow of *Tilly's* atmo-thrusters through the gloom. The trusty mount had heard Gus's whistle and came to her master's aid. Like any good steed.

Huffing and gasping for breath inside her leaking hood, Gus crawled along *Tilly's* belly and into the open airlock lift. With her safely inside and the atmosphere cycling, *Tilly* gently pulled out of their death dive and into a parking hover. From the floor of the small cargo hold, Gus whipped off her hood and gasped. She pulled the fresh, sweet air deep into her lungs and spared a moment to send out a simple prayer of thanks to Emmitt, wherever he may be.

Proximity alarms sounded throughout the pony, shattering her already fragmented thoughts. She scrambled for the saddleroom. For the proximity sensors to be tripped in these clouds, whatever approached had to be *big* and *close*. She leapt into the saddle, yanked back on the reins, and glared through the dark canopy for any sign of what might be coming.

Tilly responded instantly, veering up and away from a gigantic shadow that silently slid by them through the dense gas. Between whatever she had seen during her fall and Junior's tall tale, visions of monster manta rays rose in Gus's mind. But this shadow was different. Smaller. Boxier.

Finally, it broke through the clouds in front of *Tilly*. At roughly four times *Tilly's* size, and with a shimmering, chrome hide wrapped around a blocky body, this beast was man-made. Oversized atmo-thrusters—like those on Vega's mule, only much, much bigger—held it aloft.

This was no legendary monster. It was a rubidium freight-wagon. The kind that ferried refined rubidium-87 to the Cygnus Trail waystations.

She leaned back in the saddle, finally able to catch her breath, and watched as the freight-wagon faded back into the twilight. Gus sighed and patted the console lovingly. "Thanks, girl," she said. "Thought I had finally bit it there. What do you think, *Til?* Being dead is about as free as it gets. Do we wipe our hands of this place and be done with it?"

Tilly's fuel gauge blinked in reply. They had enough rubidium-87 for a short sprint. Maybe they could make it to Holliday, the nearest waystation. But then what? She would be in the same position—stranded in the middle of nowhere. With one difference, of course: here, she was "dead." On Holliday, she'd be alone.

It amounted to the same.

The wagon's blocky shadow disappeared, like it had never been there at all.

It would be easy to go. She had nothing holding her here anymore. She could leave Moe to Tuco and Laszlo. One way or another they would get him back to the CCO in one piece. Ray would see to that. After all, the copperheads would want a good show for his trial. Eventually, the Vegas would see the writing on the wall and take Laszlo's offer. At some point, they'd figure out their homestead wasn't worth their lives.

Right?

She stared at the spot where the wagon vanished. *Wait. What the tunk is that doing out here, anyway?* She jabbed calculations into *Tilly's* navigation console. The display flashed. The freight-wagon's path had it on a direct heading to Las Ráfagas, but it had come *from* deeper within the atmosphere. From within the enormous, mesa-like clouds of the hydrogen flats.

Details just out of reach nagged at the corners of Gus's mind. Laszlo's deal with the CCO. Missing Deiopeans and stolen technology. *Living specimens.* A pulse-rail train, according to Aaron. But that didn't make any sense at all. Pulse-rail trains couldn't run on rubidium. It was like trying to start a nuclear reactor with a lump of coal. It just didn't work.

And now this freight-wagon rising from Aeolus's depths.

Tunk. Nothing adds up.

Gus squeezed with her spurred heels, gripped the reins tight, and raced *Tilly* into the dark, backtracking the freight-wagon's path.

Visibility reduced to inches as she pushed through the clouds for what seemed like hours. At last, *Tilly* broke through a thick layer of gas and into open air. Finally, she could see the wagon's origin point and her destination.

Another mining outpost, like a smaller Las Ráfagas but without the dome, hung in the clouds. Apart from its size, its design elements distinguished it from the doppel version further. For one, the mining rings were octagonal. As they approached, Gus recognized some more of the distinctive features: shapes, symbols, and patterns she had seen before—on the robes and hunting skiffs of the Deiopeans.

"Well, Oscar, I think there's one mystery solved," she muttered. Gus spotted the hunting party's open-topped pleasure-crafts hitched up at what amounted to the outpost's stables and sighed. Laszlo's ridiculous golden sport-wagon idled there, too.

Of course.

Gus checked her instruments. *Good.* The atmosphere may have looked clear in this layer, but the particle density still registered too high for *Tilly's* proximity sensors to pick up the outpost. That meant there was a good chance the outpost couldn't see them, either. Yet. Atmospheric pressure read surprisingly low, well within the tolerance of her flight suit.

"Looks like I'm going for a walk," she sighed. She pulled on the yoke and led *Tilly* into a hover high above the outpost. "You stay here," she said to the pony. "But keep your ears open."

With the systems in her flight suit repaired and the fuel for her boots' boosters topped off, she scrambled up and out the spent escape pod tube and stood, hooded, atop *Tilly.* She followed the curve of the pony's U-shaped body to the saddleroom canopy and peered down on the little outpost below. It was going to be a long drop—fifteen hundred to two thousand feet at least. Still, nothing compared to the involuntary dive she had just taken. At least this time, she'd be in control.

She gave the EVA boosters a test hop, patted *Tilly's* hide one more time for reassurance, took a deep breath, and jumped. This time, the boosters slowed her descent to the point it was almost pleasant. With a simple course correction here and there, the gentle plunge only took a few moments. She passed through the crude energy fence and landed softly and quietly in the small station's stables—right next to a short-range skiff emblazoned with the company police logo, hitched up alongside the hunting wagons.

It's a regular who's who of Las Ráfagas scumbags. Gus crept along the stables and took whatever cover she could find. But she paused when she got to the Laszlo's distinctive golden wagon. *It's even more ridiculous up close.* Without stopping to think about it, Gus accessed the wagon's systems through the hitching post and sent an electrical overload coursing into its atmo-thruster systems. Laszlo would have to have one of his men tow him back to town. She smiled as she continued on into the main bulk of the natives' village.

After a short walk, Gus entered a domeless esplanade about a quarter the size of the human town higher up in the atmosphere. A smattering of cone shaped buildings stood to the side of pathways arranged in a web pattern like those on the Deiopean moon. She made her way quietly and with as much stealth as possible, but Gus could have walked out in the open while banging on a pot. The village was even more deserted than Las Ráfagas.

The mining level access lift was right where she expected. Its screech echoed off the abandoned buildings as she descended into the outpost's guts. At the bottom, she discovered a mess of tunnels and corridors, similar to those of Las Rafágas. Each, crowded with pipes and machinery, led deeper into the maze of mining and refining facilities.

What now?

Gus picked a big, red pipe and followed it into the dark. She tracked it through corridors, over catwalks, and down flights of stairs. Eventually, the pipe led her to a wide room deep within the outpost. It ran beneath the catwalk under her feet, and both passed between a pair of giant vats of raw rubidium-87. *The refining area. Whatever technology Laszlo is interested in has to be here.*

She followed the catwalk through the gap between vats of unrefined fuel. A few feet in front of her, the pipe rose from the floor and snaked its way across the wide room. Eight times the pipe ran the length of the room before making a U-turn. On each of these eight lengths of pipe were eight strange indentations. Each depression had several pairs of glass lenses that looked into the tube, fixed in a pattern Gus recognized. These little hollows were designed for Deiopean faces. The pattern of lenses matched the arrangement of their eyes exactly.

What the tunk? Gus ran a hand along the inside of the nearest face-slot. *Why would you want thirty-six people spying on the raw gas?* But before she could consider it any further, footfalls echoed down the corridors. And something else: familiar voices.

Laszlo Leconte's voice.

In four leaping strides, Gus raced across the wide refinery floor, out a side door, and into a poorly lit passageway.

"No one told you to kill her!" Laszlo roared at Junior as they appeared between the vats.

"But, Dad," Junior whined, "she nearly killed Aaron!" He pointed to his brother, a step behind them. "We have to respond in kind. Send a message!"

Laszlo's hand flashed out and slapped Junior across the jaw. His rings drew blood from Junior's lip. "I had plans for the bitch, you half-witted gas-huffer," Laszlo said in a low growl. "Besides," he turned to his younger son, "Aaron's fine. Aren't you, boy?"

Plans?

Aaron hadn't been paying any attention to the conversation. Instead, he'd been intently inspecting his right arm. He turned it this way and that, and watched as the light caught the hairs.

"Huh? Oh, yeah. I'm fine. But are you sure about that cloning machine? This arm feels funny. It itches."

"It's fine, Aaron. Quit fiddling with it." Laszlo turned his attention back to Junior. "If this were any other situation, I would agree with you." He put his arm around Junior's shoulders affectionately and then pulled him into a tight headlock. "But right now, I'm trying to secure our future, and your boundless need for revenge might rut everything up!" He threw his son to the floor with a sneer on his lips.

"I'm sorry, Dad!" Junior cried. "I didn't know. Tell me what I can do to fix it."

"Just how are you going to do that?" Laszlo raged. "The moment that bitch doesn't come back from your little hunting trip, what do you think Ray's going to do? He's going to start sticking that self-righteous nose of his where it doesn't belong, which is exactly what I was paying that broad to keep from happening."

"Why don't we kill him, too?" Aaron asked. He scratched at where his new arm met his old bicep. "He's a liability, anyway."

Laszlo sighed and rubbed his temples. "Ray is well-liked. If there is even the appearance that we are involved in his death in any way, we'll lose the support of what few townsfolk remain. We can't afford that again. Not yet."

"So what?" Aaron asked. "We own it! We should be able to do whatever we want!"

"In situations like these, it's always best to have plausible deniability," Laszlo said.

Aaron scowled. "What's that mean?"

"It means I needed a pawn to take the blame, you useless moron!"

Aaron recoiled from his father, but Junior's eyes went wide. "You were going to have *her* do it, weren't you? If *she* killed Ray ... the outrage ..."

The hair on the back of Gus's neck bristled. It had been a setup from the beginning.

"That's right," Laszlo said through a sneer. "If an outsider came in here and killed our beloved Marshal Ray, I could present our little deal with the copperheads as a security measure."

"Of course!" Junior said, now smiling. "We would be providing security the bluebells couldn't!"

"But you've screwed that up now, haven't you?" Laszlo snapped. Junior flinched.

"Let me take care of him, Dad," Aaron piped up. He held up his new index finger and thumb and mimed firing his gun. "No one will ever know it was me."

"Will you *shut up!*" Laszlo said. "This might work out in our favor. With the bitch gone, her idiot partner will hand over the cobbler-rob and stick around long enough for us to pin this on him. If we play this right, we might be able to do something about those troublesome Vegas at the same time."

Aaron smiled deviously. Gus's mind again flashed back to the Vegas' picturesque kitchen.

I've got to get back to Las Ráfagas to warn them. Bottle-farts, maybe Tuco, too.

"Have you spoken to Mackenzie?" Laszlo asked Junior.

"This morning," Junior said sheepishly. "The details have been finalized. The *Shenandoah* will arrive in four days with an inspection team. If they like what they see, they'll transfer the gold bullion from their hold to the administrative vault, as agreed."

Gold?

Gus's ears perked up and any thoughts of rushing back to town evaporated. But before Junior could say more, something gently tugged on the back of her poncho. Nearly jumping out of her skin, she whirled around and drew Delilah, ready for a fight. Instead, a lone Deiopean stood with her in the dim corridor.

To her astonishment, Gus recognized the native. She had seen the distinctive white markings on their face twice before: first when wrangling the Vegas' wayward jelly, and then again when Ray escorted them off Las Ráfagas after bartering with Oscar.

"You!" Gus hissed in surprise. She turned back to the door, but the Lecontes' voices were fading as they disappeared through a doorway on the far side of the refining floor. Gus's first impulse was to follow, but the Deiopean gave her poncho another sharp tug. With the small native's hood down, their eyes flashed a familiar sequence that lit up the dark corridor. The group Gus ran into outside the engineering corral had displayed the same combination of colors. She still had no idea what it meant. When Gus didn't move, the Deiopean tugged on her poncho again and pointed wildly into the dark.

She knew what they wanted—for her to follow. Urgently. Gus took one last glance back into the refinery. The Lecontes were gone, and with all the twists and turns down here, Gus doubted she'd be able to find them again. With a low growl, she bid the Deiopean to lead.

Gus followed the Deiopean through the dim, confusing corridors of the mining levels until she lost all sense of direction. They turned this way and that, bypassed one hallway only to take the next, ducked under pipes and squeezed through small doorways.

Finally, the native came to a halt at the foot of a greasy ladder. They waited for Gus to catch up and scrambled up the octagonal rungs in a way that made her skin crawl. Nevertheless, she followed up and out a small hatch and found herself in a much larger hallway—one she recognized. They were just off the esplanade, near the stables where she had come in. The Deiopean raced headlong toward the hitched mounts.

"Wait! *Tunk!*" Gus hissed as she pulled herself up and dashed after her small companion. She chased them to the edge of the hitching stables, diving for cover the moment she got there. A quartet of burly company bulls strode through the stables. They held a group of eight Deiopeans at gunpoint and led them toward a waiting carriage. Her guide ran straight into the stables but, by some miracle, the bulls hadn't seen them yet.

But the captives spotted Gus's new friend immediately. From eight arachnid faces, dozens of crystalline eyes all flashed the same, familiar pattern. At last, Gus understood what it meant.

Help.

The bulls reacted to the lightshow by gathering around the hostages and shouting at them to keep moving. Her companion took the opportunity to pull a pair of objects from beneath their robe: one small and complicated, the other long and simple. When the two pieces came together Gus recognized the distinctive Deiopean four-handed rifle. An old-fashioned slug-thrower.

At last, one of the bulls turned his head to see what their prisoners were reacting to. He had just enough time for a short cry of *"Hey!"* before the deafening *crack* of the rifle ripped through the air. The bull collapsed in a heap.

The remaining bulls reacted to the death of their comrade with surprising speed. They scattered like pins as each dove for cover and returned fire. With all three focused on the single Deiopean shooter, Gus picked one off with Delilah before they'd even seen her. Down to two on each side, a firefight erupted and the eight prisoners fled.

Gus, desperate for better cover and clearer sight lines, raced across the open stables toward a cargo container while the Deiopean covered her. But she either miscalculated the distance or her speed; the bulls caught her halfway to the container. The lime-green beams from their rifles cut through the air with a static crackle and a whiff of ozone. The first shot went wide. Panicked, Gus dove the final feet to cover.

Gonna make i—

The second beam struck home and cleaved through her calf like a skiff through the clouds.

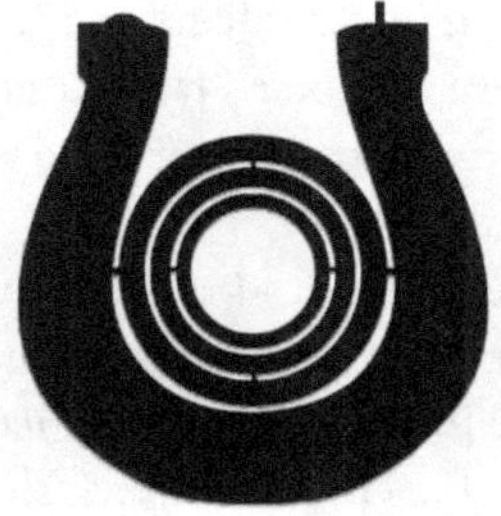

THE WILD AND THE INNOCENT

Gus fell short of the cargo container and screamed as her leg gushed scarlet. Delilah clattered to the floor, tumbling out of reach. The bastards had their beams tuned poorly—that meant no cauterization. *Tunk, it hurts.* Knowing Aaron, that was probably the point.

As the Deiopean hunter and one of the bulls exchanged shots, Gus's sparring partner stood and smiled. His rifle held high, he approached with a cruel glint in his eyes. Eyes eager for the up-close kill. She dragged herself behind the container and waited.

"What's the matter, little lady? Start something you couldn't finish?" Cold whimsy dripped from the bull's voice as he stalked closer. "You know, I'm kinda glad I missed the kill shot. How's that leg feel? Hurts, don't it? I'm gonna to put another beam through the other one. Then your arms. One at a time. Gonna make you suffer."

Gritting against the urge to pass out, Gus eyed Delilah. The big beam-shooter sat only a few feet away, but going for it meant leaving what little cover she had. She fumbled with her belt for anything she could use. All she had on her were coolant caps for Delilah, and *Tilly's* whistle.

"Gotcha!" the bull shouted. He stepped around the cargo container and leveled his rifle at Gus. She shoved the whistle into her mouth and blew with everything she had. The high-frequency shriek cut through the air as cleanly as any laser beam. The bull screamed and dropped his rifle to cover his ears. The cruel, ugly gun landed in Gus's outstretched hands. Without hesitation, she aimed and fired a sizzling green beam through the bull's chest.

She spat the whistle out into her hand and tossed the rifle to crawl for Delilah. With the big beam-shooter's familiar grip in hand, Gus tried to stand. Her ruined calf refused to cooperate, and she collapsed to her knees, hissing through the agony.

The final bull crouched behind a load lifter, firing and ducking from a position neither Gus nor her companion could reach. His radio squawked. *Tunk. If he calls this fight in, we'll all be dead.* Her Deiopean friend, apparently, had the same thought. They aimed their slug-thrower over the bull's shoulder and tracked the wall's edge, hunting for the best angle.

"Frasier to command!" the bull shouted into his radio. *"Shots fired! Officers down! I repeat: Shots—"* The hunter found their angle and fired. The metal slug ricocheted—twice—and struck the last bull square between his shoulder blades. He fell before he could finish his sentence.

The hush of post-battle calm blanketed the stables. After a hesitant moment, the eight captive Deiopeans reappeared from their hiding places. They huddled around Gus and the hunter, their eyes flashing in a new pattern. Gus took this one to mean "thank you."

"Okay, okay. You're welcome." Their tiny hands helped her to her feet, but her head swam and she stumbled. The blood poured from the wound on her leg and it screamed with every step.

In a gust of wind and swirling dust-like gases, *Tilly* arrived at the stables and lowered her airlock lift. Gus fought the darkness growing at the edges of her vision. "Everybody saddle up!" she said. "It won't be long before reinforcements show up!" But no one moved. *What the ever-loving tunk?* "Let's go!" she shouted and pointed at the lift. Still, they stared. Her head swam. "Get on the rutting mount!" Finally, Gus's companion understood and flashed out a translation to the others.

As they scurried aboard the lift, Gus turned to the bulls' waiting carriage. She hobbled aboard and limped to the saddleroom, leaving a trail of bloody boot prints in her wake. Gus dropped into the seat and scanned the controls. "Come on, come on. *There!*" She jabbed at buttons, gave the reigns a jerk, and set the thing to capsize in the dense atmosphere.

By the time she made it back to the boarding ramp, the carriage had already begun its automated departure sequence. The ramp hovered a few feet off the stable floor and began to retract. Gus stood in the hatch and watched the stable floor slide by. She would have to jump.

Tunk.

She nursed her screaming leg and braced for a rough landing, but before she could make the leap, the carriage lurched forward. Gus stumbled and fell from the hatch. She landed hard, with her wounded leg crumpled beneath her.

The world exploded in white-hot pain. Gus squeezed her eyes shut against the agony and fought to stay conscious. The unnerving feeling of tiny hands groping at her injured calf brought her back from the brink. She forced her eyes open and found the Deiopean hunter at her side. Carefully, Gus's little friend pulled a cloth from a small, octagonal box and sprayed it with a sickeningly sweet-smelling foam. They pressed it against the gash on her calf.

Gus hissed, but it didn't sting as she had expected. Instead, a cold, tingling sensation spread slowly from the wound and replaced the pain with soothing calm. A moment later whatever drug soaking the bandage reached Gus's heart and brain like a shot of adrenaline. In an instant, she leapt to her feet, fully alert.

"Holy *tunk!*" *Incredible! My leg doesn't hurt at all!* She stared in awe at the suddenly vivid colors of the clouds. Gus breathed deep, marveling at the sweet flavor and silky texture of the cool air. Her mind had never been so clear, her body so ready for action. Certain she could take on all of Aaron's bulls alone, she turned away from *Tilly* and eyed the corridor eagerly. *Bring 'em on ...*

The Deiopean hunter tugged anxiously on her poncho.

Right. They had to be gone *before* the bulls' backup showed up. Her companion pulled her toward *Tilly.*

She shook her head and tried to clear the euphoria as the lift brought them inside. But the drug's effect was in full swing—she'd have to ride it out. Gus pushed through the crowd of small bodies to the saddleroom. She swung herself into the seat, clicked her spurs into place, and yanked on the reins. *Tilly's* atmo-thrusters fired, and she climbed away from the Deiopean mining village into the cloud layer above.

Gus hitched *Tilly* back up at her stable in the engineering corral, bribed Emmitt's crew with most of her remaining tobacco while saying, *"My pony*

never left, and you never saw me," and herded her small group of natives toward Ray's office. She led them down a dark alley in the fading light of the afternoon to Ray's back door and banged on it as hard as she could. The door opened and Ray's weathered face appeared.

"Who's there?" he grunted. The barrel of his beam-splitter poked from the doorway.

"It's Gus, Ray. Open up," she said, panting. The pain had subsided, but with the amount of blood she'd lost, and the effects of the drug wearing off, her strength was gone.

"What's going on? Marshal?" Moe called from his cell.

Ray ignored him and opened the door wider. The concern on his face turned to surprise when nine small, hairy bodies pushed past him. "What in tarnation? Gus, what are you doing? Laszlo barely tolerates the natives being in town at all, if he finds out I've got ... one, two, three ... nine! Nine of 'em back here, there'll be hell to pay!" She stumbled over the threshold into his arms. "Tunk, girl! You alright?"

"Gus!" Moe shouted. "Marshal, let me out. I can help!"

"Would you *can it,* Maurice?" Ray shouted. He grunted as he half-carried, half-dragged Gus into the cell she had been calling home. *"Christ's blood!* What the hell happened? You guys get into some kind of trouble on the hunt?" He gently pulled at the sticky material to get a better view of the Deiopean bandage.

"You could say that." Gus groaned. She leaned back against the bars and told them everything that had happened since she had left the jailhouse early that morning. She admitted to the deal she and Tuco made with Laszlo to keep Ray busy—and her discovery of what that deal *really* entailed.

As she spoke, the eight would-be captive natives huddled together in another vacant cell, flashing complicated patterns of light and color at each other. The one who had asked for her help, the hunter, retrieved Ray's translator from the desk and came to "listen."

When she finished, a heavy silence hung in the cellblock air. Moe shook his head and broke the silence. "Those bastards. The boss had it right."

But Ray was less convinced. "Right about what?" he said gruffly. "What exactly did you see? An empty village? So what? Maybe the spiders abandoned it themselves."

"What about Emmitt?" Gus asked dryly.

Ray's lips trembled and his eyes darted around the small jailhouse, but he said nothing.

"Marshal, they plan to kill you next!" Moe protested.

Ray shook his head. "No. Laszlo and I go way back. He wouldn't do this. He needs me here to keep Las Ráfagas legit. You heard him wrong or ... or misunderstood. And then you killed four of his men! You don't know what you've brought down on us."

"Ray, Junior threw me out of a *rutting wagon!* What about Emmitt? This wasn't some *'misunderstanding.'* The coward killed him and tried to kill me!"

But still Ray shook his head. "There must be some kind of rational explanation!"

A new, synthetic, electronic voice cut in. "It's true," the hunter said through Ray's translator. "You soft-skins have taken our skies, refused to trade with us, and now, stolen our technology and kin. I must stop it now, before any more of my people's lives are lost." They turned to Gus. "You have helped us once. Will you help again? We can offer rubidium-87 as payment."

The jailhouse went silent. Gus's entirely too heavy eyelids drooped; thinking became an entirely unpleasant experience. Emmitt was dead, likely putting the engineering corral's fuel out of reach. And as far as anyone not in the jailhouse was concerned, she was as dead as the old engineer.

Her options were limited. But helping the Deiopeans still offered an awful lot of risk for little reward. Going up against not only the Lecontes, but maybe the whole COO, too? Surviving odds that long was exactly the kind of gamble she usually avoided.

Ray had fallen quiet when the Deiopean had spoken up and now his shoulders dropped. "I'm sure this is all some sort of misunderstanding," he repeated. "I'm sure if we go talk to Laszlo directly, he'll be able to sort this all out. I know he's a little rough around the edges, but I can't picture him as this villain you've made him out to be."

Moe brought his trembling hands to his head. "Are you crazy?" he shouted through the bars. "If you confront him, he'll gun you down on the spot! Or let one of those weasels he calls sons do it for him."

"Ray." Gus fought to hold onto consciousness. "Moe's right, you can't go. But I don't know what I can do. And a little fuel is ... not much ..."

"Oh, for the maker's sake. If you help them, and get me out of here, I'll help you steal the copperhead gold. That's what you want, isn't it?" Moe's shout forced Gus back from the threshold of passing out. "Is that enough for you? I don't think you're going to get a better payday than that, now that you're dead!"

The *gold.* She'd almost forgotten about it.

And the damn rob was right. She wouldn't get paid any other way. Gus reached out her hand to the Deiopean hunter. "Do you guys have names?" she asked.

"Yes," they replied, "my name is—" but the translator cut out as the hunter's eyes swirled with patterns of blue, green, and yellow light.

Gus smiled weakly. "It's beautiful. How 'bout I call you Aurora? 'sat alright?" The hunter nodded. "Great. Aurora, you've got a deal," Gus said and let her eyelids fall shut.

Gus woke with a start and banged her wounded calf against the edge of the cot. Burning knives of pain shot up her leg and into her hip.

"Easy, easy. You're alright." Daniel Park, the town medic, knelt next to her. And he wasn't alone. Her little cell was crowded with people. Gus propped herself up and the group gave a collective sigh of relief. Moe stood against the bars between the cells, while Ray and Aurora stood closest to her. Both Brother Richard and Oscar Vega were there too, vying for space. Daniel had to elbow them aside for room to work.

Judging from the dark sky outside the office window, Gus guessed she'd been out for a few hours, at least. Her head pounded and an IV needle jutted from her arm. "What happened?" She pulled the needle out with a wince.

"You lost a lot of blood and passed out. Things were touch and go there for a little while, but I think you're okay now. You should have died," he said matter-of-factly.

"What are you talking about?" Her head hurt too much for games.

"The beam destroyed your posterior tibial artery. You *should* have bled out in minutes. *This* is what saved your life." He held up the bandage Aurora had applied. Her blood had stained it a deep, brick red, but it still smelled faintly sweet.

"How?" she croaked, still a little groggy.

"I'm not sure, exactly. But I can tell you this: no human bandage or treatment can do what I've seen your wound do in the last two hours.

Something in the bandage promoted accelerated tissue growth. It's incredible. You may have some discomfort and walk with a bit of a limp. But I think if you stay off it even those symptoms should disappear," he said, still marveling at what he had seen. "I can't be sure until I get it back to the lab, but I suspect it's a completely different approach to medicine from ours."

Gus tried to stand and stumbled when she tested the leg. Half a dozen hands reached out to catch her, but she waved them off and managed to stay up without help. She had more than *a little* discomfort, but it would have to do.

"Alright," she said and steadied herself against the cell bars, "we've got to get the Deiopeans out of here and somewhere safe."

"Whoa," Daniel said, "I said you've got to stay off it for it to heal right."

"No time for that, Doc. Do you have any idea what's going on around here?"

"We filled them in," Ray said.

"Good. Laszlo's not gonna like that eight of his prisoners have escaped to tell the tale. We need to move them *now.*"

"I have a place I can take them, at least for the time being," Brother Richard said. "But it won't be safe for the long term. We must be cautious."

"Gus," Oscar said, his expression dark and worried, "is my family in danger? Ray said—"

"Yes," Gus said, cutting him off, "but I don't know anything more than that."

Oscar's face fell. "Then it's come to this," he said. His features hardened. "We'll fight."

"*No!*" Gus snapped. "Don't you get it yet? Whatever they're planning, whatever deal they've struck up with the CCO, Ray and your little group of rabble rousers are the only thing in the way. If they kill you, the others fall in line, and he gets everything he wants. Can't you see that? Take your family and *go.* Before the copperheads get here."

"And just when is that?" Richard asked.

"Four days. That's all the time you've got to come to your rutting senses and run. The lot of you," Gus replied. "Your principles don't mean *tunk* anymore. If you stay, you die. And Laszlo makes money on your wife and son's corpses."

"Why you arrogant, void-drifting, daughter of a whore." Oscar's face pinched tight and turned beet red, and he took a wild swing at Gus. Even in her weakened state, she easily dodged his clumsy blow and delivered a haymaker to the rancher's gut. Oscar fell back against the far cell bars, his eyes wide and the wind knocked out of him.

Gus hoped he would stay down, but a fire lit in Oscar's eyes, and he got to his feet ready for a fight. *Alright, if this is the only way to convince you …*

But before the little cell could break out into brawling, a pair of voices yelled from the Marshal's Office foyer.

"Yo!" one called out. "Uncle Ray!"

"You back there?" hollered the other. "We've got some bad news."

The heavy cellblock door rattled in its frame as Aaron and Junior started banging.

Gus and Brother Richard locked eyes. They exchanged a small nod, and the monk led the eight would-be slaves out the backdoor to whatever hidey-hole he had in mind. Daniel packed his few medical supplies, carefully wrapped the Deiopean bandage for further study, and followed Brother Richard. The medic caught Gus's eye before going. "Gus—"

She nodded. "I know. Stay off the leg." She already knew it was a promise she couldn't keep. Daniel returned the nod slowly—he knew, too—and disappeared into the alley.

"Ray! Wake the *tunk* up, we got something to talk about!"

Bang, bang, bang!

"Yeah! Yeah, I'm coming!" Ray hollered back through the door. "Don't get your panties in a twist." Ray surveyed his small jailhouse. With the monk, medic, and natives gone, it was far less crowded, but Gus, Oscar, and Aurora would still be hard to miss if the Lecontes came through the heavy door. "I'll take care of this," he said, dropping his voice to a whisper. "You stay here."

"*Ray—*" Gus hissed. But he already stepped through the door. She hobbled out of the cell toward the door as fast as her leg would carry her. She reached it in time to catch it at the jamb with the toe of her boot.

"What's goin' on back there?" she heard Junior ask. She peered through the crack and spotted Tuco with them. He stood by, uncharacteristically quiet and unusually interested in his own boots. *What could they have threatened him with to get him to shut his mouth?*

Ray, never one to lie when the truth would do, said, "Just a little scuffle with some townsfolk. Nothing I can't handle."

"I bet it's that rob-lover Vega, ain't it?" Aaron sneered. "If you need a hand with that, Uncle Ray, you just let me know." Oscar tensed visibly.

"I've got all the help I need, thank you, boys. And speaking of, where's my deputy at? I would have expected her back from your little outing hours ago."

"That's one of the reasons we're here, Ray," Junior replied. "We had an incident this morning."

"What kind of incident?" Ray faked his concern remarkably well.

"We were ambushed by a spider raiding party. I'm sorry to say we lost four of my brother's best men—and your deputy—in the fighting. We barely escaped with our lives." He tossed something shiny to Ray. It bounced off the old man's chest and fell into his hands.

Gus's badge.

"I don't believe it," Ray said breathlessly.

Mistaking his disbelief at their lie for shock, Junior shook his head sympathetically and continued. "Horrific, I know. I only wish we had managed to kill them all in the initial attack. The savages that got away went on to steal a personnel carriage. I doubt they'll show up here, but you're officially under orders to turn any spider you find in town over to Aaron. Is that understood?"

"Now hold on a second," Ray protested. "You mean to tell me that not only is my deputy dead, if I find her killers in *my* jurisdiction, I have to turn them over to *you*? That's not how this works, and you boys know it."

Junior's calm demeanor did not waver. "The four men who were killed were all close, personal friends of my brother's."

"My life won't be the same without them," Aaron chimed in and frowned almost comically. *He looks constipated.*

"Aaron's claiming jurisdiction on this one, Uncle Ray." Junior glared at the marshal, daring him to argue. "If you don't like it, you can take it up with our father."

Ray's mustache bristled as he snorted. "Is that all, or can I get back to my work? I've got a lot to do now that I'm on my own again," he said and gave the Leconte brothers a stink eye of his own.

"As a matter of fact," Junior said, "there is one more thing,"

Aaron smiled and clapped the quiet Tuco on the back. "Our friend here has agreed to turn his bounty-head over to our father. For a handsome sum, o' course."

Tuco's gaze never left his boots.

"And what's that supposed to mean to me?" Ray asked.

"We're taking the rob, Ray," Junior snapped. "Get the walking scrap heap ready to move."

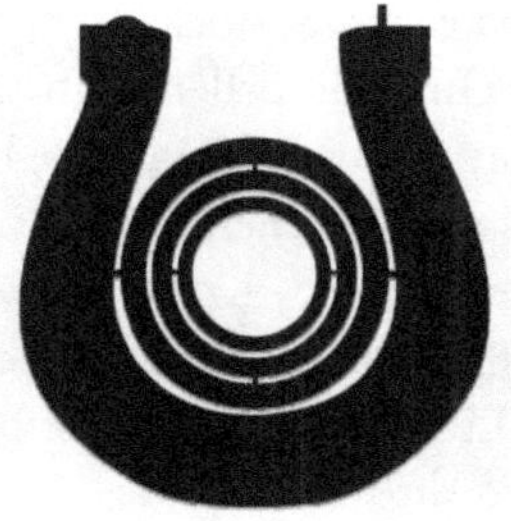

THE LAWLESS BREED

*T*unk.

Back in the cellblock, Gus's mind reeled. *Of course, Tuco would turn over Moe.* Everything had happened so fast she had nearly forgotten about her good-for-nothing partner.

"What is it?" Moe asked, his electronic voice quivering.

"Something I hadn't planned for," she said. "But I gave you my word I would help you, and I'm going to do that. *I swear.*"

"*What?*" Moe's eyes were as wide as saucers. He stood bolt upright, his shoulders trembling. He held his gleaming hand up and backed away from the bars. "*What's that supposed to mean?*"

Gus ignored him and turned her attention to Oscar and Aurora. "You two: out the back. *Now.*"

"Boss, *please,* don't let them take me," Moe pleaded with Oscar.

Oscar's face, eyes wide, jaw hanging, bounced from Gus to his panicking farmhand. "I—"

"*Now,* Oscar!" Gus hissed. "We can't help him if they find me back here."

Oscar hesitated a moment longer, staring into Moe's digital face. "I'm sorry, *mi amigo,*" he said and stepped out the door.

Panic slowly evaporated from Moe's posture. First, his shoulders dropped, then his brow fell. Finally, his knees buckled and he sat down on the cot so hard, Gus feared it might crumple under the force.

"This isn't over, Moe. I promise," Gus said, but the rob wouldn't meet her eye.

Ray opened the cellblock door slowly, caught her eye, and mouthed *"Go!"* Reluctantly, Gus stepped through the backdoor and closed it behind her without a word from Moe.

Oscar, Aurora, and Gus stood silently in the alley as the air grew dark with twilight. They huddled against the building and waited for Tuco and the Lecontes to finish their business. Gus leaned against the door and listened for any sign of what might be going on inside. After a few moments of muffled conversation, she heard the heavy cellblock door close. She limped to the corner of the building and cautiously peered around it toward the town square.

"What are you going to do?" Oscar asked. He shuffled after her as best he could on his own busted leg. Aurora helped him, taking much of his weight on their short but stout shoulders.

"I don't know," Gus admitted. They watched as Junior and Tuco stepped out of the Marshal's office, with Aaron and Moe—the rob in reinforced cuffs, of course—following behind. They turned left once they hit the square and headed toward Genie-town and the mining level access lift.

"Round up whoever you still trust and meet me in the cemetery tonight," Gus said to Oscar and Aurora. Her mind raced and swam. She needed time to think, but her throbbing calf made that rutting difficult. "At midnight."

"You have a plan?" Oscar asked.

"Not yet. But I will." She grimaced and reached to rub the ache. "For now, I need a look at the company lockup. See what we're dealing with."

"I'm going with you," Ray's Deiopean translator squeaked from where it was affixed to Aurora's robe.

"No, I—"

But Aurora was already helping Oscar to the wall. He shifted his weight and stood on his own. "I'm going with you," they repeated.

"Best not argue with a Deiopean," Oscar said. He smirked at his little friend. "Especially this one. You'll find you and they share a common characteristic."

"What's that?" Gus asked, her eyes on the square.

"Stubbornness."

Oscar leaned against the wall and took his weight off his prosthetic with a groan. Aurora set their shoulders in a remarkably human posture for someone with three sets of them. Every moment Gus argued, Moe got further away.

"Alright," she said. "Oscar, you stay out of trouble until we get back. Remember, the cemetery. Midnight."

Even with fiery needles shooting from her calf with each step, it only took Gus and Aurora a few moments to catch up to Tuco and the Lecontes. When they had, Gus spotted why: every few feet Aaron would pause to taunt the helpless rob.

"You're gonna get what's coming to ya, ya rutting murdering pile of rust! Maybe they'll let me do it!" Aaron shouted. He got so close to the rob, spittle beaded on the screen projecting Moe's face. "I always wanted to waste one of you walking circuit boards."

Junior walked ten paces ahead of his brother, whispering to Tuco as they reached the mining level access lift. "Hey, gas-huffer! Let's *go,*" he shouted at Aaron. "I would like to get back to the tower before dark."

"But I thought we were going to Cirrus House tonight?" Aaron whined. He dragged Moe toward the lift.

"*Christ's rutting blood!*" Junior spat. "You gamble and rut every night. There are things we need to finish before Mackenzie gets here."

Aaron smiled and shoved Moe. "When Mackenzie gets here, all you parasites—robs, genies, and those lowlife human miners, too—you'll *all* get what's coming to ya!"

"*Aaron!*" Junior snapped as he hit the button to send the lift down. "*Shut up!*"

Doing their best to stay hidden, Gus and Aurora watched the lift drop into the outpost's lower levels. *Tunk.* How were they supposed to follow now? If she called the lift back too soon, the Lecontes would hear her coming. If she waited too long, she'd lose them. Chances were good they would head to the Company Police lockup, but ... *These two might have a surprise in store for Moe along the way.*

As Gus watched her quarry disappear into Las Ráfagas's guts, a flash of scarlet light and the electronic voice of the translator drew her attention. Aurora stood at an open manhole hatch. *An access ladder. Probably for servicing the lift.* Gus nodded and followed Aurora down.

The pair reached the mining level a moment after the lift and stalked Tuco and the Lecontes through the dim corridors. Gus found herself dwelling on Aaron's last comment before they descended.

They'll "all get what's coming" to them. When Mackenzie arrives.

They wouldn't execute Moe here, in the Territories, without a trial ... *would they?*

After a few twists and turns through the cluttered mining hallways, they came to a wide, open area that roughly resembled the town square above. To their right, the miners' barracks rose four stories and spanned far beyond the square in either direction. Like *Tilly's* hive, it bustled with activity as miners of all shapes and sizes, organic and rob—and some combinations of the two—milled about. On their left, Tuco and the Lecontes led Moe toward a flat building flush with Las Ráfagas's outer hide. The Company Police lockup. Bulls crowded the jailhouse porch. Some were in uniform: others lounged around in plainclothes, off-duty. Most kept a wary eye on the barracks across the square.

Gus and Aurora kept to the shadows of an alley-mouth. They watched as Tuco and Junior, followed by Aaron dragging Moe by the forearm, disappeared inside the lockup. Gus fell against the alleyway wall and slid to the ground. Under the deep hood, Aurora's eye flashed. "What is it?"

Gus peeked back out at the jailhouse porch. A sign hanging from the roof, like a bad joke, identified the jailhouse as "Fort Leconte." Every bull, even the plainclothes loitering about, carried a beamshooter. Some wore heaters on their hips, others had long guns and beam-splitters laid across laps or resting on shoulders. *This ain't a police force. It's a militia. A rutting army.*

Laszlo's army.

"That's *a lot* more firepower than I was counting on."

The crackle of rubbish underfoot had Gus on her feet with Delilah in hand in an instant. A hulking shape gracefully rolled from the shadows. Gus held her breath and readied herself for a fight.

Gretchen.

The rob held clamp-like hands up defensively. "Whoa there, friends," she said in a low voice. The lights on her face blinked in the gloom.

Gus exhaled with a rough sigh and dropped Delilah back in her holster. "What are you doing sneaking around?"

Gretchen shrugged her massive shoulders. "It's what I do. Rumor had it the Lecontes were bringing Moe down here. I came to see for myself."

"That's one rumor I can confirm. What else have you heard?"

"That you're dead," Gretchen said with a hint of a smile in her light voice.

Gus returned the shrug. "That one's a little premature, but the day's not over yet. Let's keep the truth between us for now, alright?"

Gretchen mimed closing a zipper over her mouthless face. Gus peered around the corner at the jailhouse porch again. *How am I going to pull* this *one off?*

"Walter will be *so* happy to hear that you're alive. He was afraid we'd never get the chance to repay you for the other night. I'll tell him to let Moe know when he goes in to serve dinner to the prisoners," Gretchen mused as she carefully took her own peek around the corner.

"*Christ's blood*, Gretchen. What did I just say?"

Gretchen's expressionless face cocked to one side "I'm not going to go around discrediting rumors. I only want to tell the people who deserve to know."

"Dammit, Gretchen, you can't tell—"

Aurora interrupted through the translator. "You know the individual that brings food to the prisoners?"

"Walter? Oh yeah, he's my husband. Why?"

"The ability to pass messages to the automaton may provide an opportunity for us to exploit," Aurora replied.

Gus stared at Aurora, dumbfounded. *Of course.* She turned to the big mining-rob. Gretchen, there may be something you and Walter can do after all."

"Do you really think this will work?" Aurora asked. The flashes from her eyes lit up the small hallway as the pair made their way back to the lift's service ladder.

"Do you have a better idea?"

They walked in silent darkness.

I guess not.

She liked Aurora. They were small but tough, and clearly a crack shot with that rifle. The ricochet Aurora used to kill that last bull on the

Deiopean outpost—Gus couldn't have made that shot. She knew few who could.

"What about helping my people? How will rescuing the automaton help them? Is the risk worth it?" Aurora asked as they turned a corner. Although Gus had not spent much time in the mining levels, their surroundings struck her as familiar.

"First off, his name is Moe. Secondly, I'm not rightly sure." Even a few days ago she'd probably have agreed rescuing Moe *wasn't* worth it. *A few days.* Had it really only been days since she'd arrived in Las Ráfagas? "But I made him a promise, and I can't leave him to these jackals ..." She trailed off as they stepped through a darkened doorway.

She definitely *knew* this place.

"Hold on," she said and squinted into the shadows. She took a hesitant step and beckoned Aurora to follow.

Automated lights flickered on as they stepped into the room. Her surroundings laid bare in the sterile light, Gus understood why she recognized them. They stood in the Lecontes' horrific recreation of the refinement room where she'd overheard their squabbling on the Deiopean outpost. A massive raw rubidium-87 pipe snaked its way through the enormous space. There were dozens—no, *hundreds*—of the Deiopean-shaped indentations dotting the length of the pipe. Each station featured four pairs of old-fashioned iron shackles. And as the pipe left the room it passed between a pair of massive raw fuel vats. These, like everything else in the room, dwarfed their Deiopean counterparts.

One design element, however, differed between the two refining facilities. A display of flashing lights drew Gus's attention to it.

What the tunk?

There, beyond the pass between the vats, sat row after row of small, stacked holding cells, each no taller than Gus's shoulder and piled four cells high. Nearly each cell held a cowering Deiopean. Gus's stomach dropped at the sight of them. She didn't have much experience judging non-human health, but these people looked sick. Stripped naked of their robes, they were lethargic with hunched shoulders and shrunken bellies. Even the light from their eyes was so muted Aurora's translator didn't pick them up.

"What is *this?*" Aurora demanded, all eight eyes wide. The hunter's eyes continued to flash as they approached the nearest cell, but the translator stayed quiet—it apparently hadn't been programmed for profanity. The Deiopean inside mustered a feeble flicker Gus recognized: "Help."

"Help me free them," Aurora ordered and examined the cell's complicated lock.

Gus stepped to the next cell and hesitated. *Tunk.* "We can't do this," she said. Her head swung to and fro as she tried to scan the entire room at once. "Not right now, anyway. There are too many of them. We'll never make it off the mining levels."

"She's right." A tired, female voice spoke up from behind Gus. "I can help you free them, but we'll have to wait until the time is right."

Gus swiveled around to discover Gloria Smith standing in a nearby doorway.

Aurora leapt on the widow in a flash, eyes blazing. The translator barked, "What is this?" Gus rushed to grab Aurora by the back of their robes and dragged them off the old woman.

Gloria cowered on the floor and held her face in her hands. *"This,"* she said, "was my Emmitt's greatest shame."

"You *knew* about this? You helped them *build* this prison?" Aurora's flashes eyes took on a sinister hue and the Deiopean stepped toward the old woman.

"No!" Gloria screamed. "He—*we*—had no choice!"

Gus put herself between the two. "Aurora!" she thundered. "This ain't helping! Laszlo's tainted every part of this place. You can assign blame later. Right now, I need her to tell me what this *is*."

"I'll tell you what it is." Aurora's eyes blazed. "It's a work prison. Meant to subjugate my people for *that*"—the device's voice shorted out as Aurora raged through an untranslatable epithet—"Leconte's personal gain."

"Is that true?" Gus asked.

Gloria's face twisted. "Yes." Sobs wracked her body.

Gus looked out over the twisting pipe with its row after row of shackle flanked indentations. "I'm not sure I understand."

"It's their eyes," Gloria said and wiped tears from her own. "They can create a particular wavelength of light in the upper gamma ray range. When the rubidium gas is treated with that wavelength before it's processed, the resulting product has roughly ten times the potency. It's some kind of chemical or photonic reaction. I don't understand it at all. Emmitt had all the talent." She shook with fresh sobs.

"But he couldn't reproduce it artificially," Gus said. A flash of the confrontation she had overheard between Junior and the old engineer came to mind. "He needed *live specimens*." She stared back at tiny cells and the pathetic beings they held.

"Emmitt was sure he could crack it if he had more time, but they ordered him to use the spiders!" Gloria's voice rose in both volume and pitch. "They threatened to kill us, and his whole team, and replace them with people who wouldn't ask so many questions!"

"Gloria!" Gus took the older woman by the shoulders. "It was Laszlo. It's all Laszlo. Emmitt did what he thought was right. What he thought would keep you safe." Aurora's shoulders hunched and they moved back to the cells, away from the women. Gus understood Aurora's anger. The scope of Laszlo's cruelty boggled her mind. But right now, they needed all the information they could get.

"Why was it so important that it be done so fast? Why all the rush?" Gus asked.

"A pulse-rail train," Gloria said quietly.

"What? No," Gus said and shook her head. That's what Aaron said, but it doesn't make any sense. "The Campbell four forty engines don't use rubidium. It can't power the negative mass reaction needed for that kind of space-time warp. Besides, the copperheads don't even have a pulse-rail train."

Aurora put a small hand on Gus's back. "If we cannot free my people now, we must meet with the others and tell them of our discovery here."

Gus nodded.

"Gloria, we've got to keep moving. Do you know when the retrofits go online?" she asked, her eyes drawn to the weakened Deiopeans.

Gloria shook her head. "They were supposed to be already. But the last delivery of ..." she trailed off and glanced at the few empty cells. "Something must have happened to change the timeline." *Damn straight.* But still, with the CCO looming, they would start the operation soon enough. "Thank you, Gloria. You should find another place to be. It isn't safe here."

"*Wait!*" the widow said and grabbed the hem of Gus's poncho. "They murdered him." Tears rolled down her cheeks. "He did what they asked him, and they killed him for it."

Gus nodded. She'd been there. She had seen. Emmitt may have saved *her* life that day, too.

The sorrow remained in Gloria's eyes, but as her jaw set below them and her white eyebrows knitted above, they were joined by a need Gus knew intimately: vengeance. "I want you to kill that murdering son of a bastard,

Junior. Will you do that for me? For Emmitt?" She searched Gus's eyes. "If you can promise me that, I'll tell you something else. Something Emmitt only guessed at. The thing that probably got my husband killed and will likely be the reason they'll come for me soon."

Gus and Aurora exchanged a glance. What knowledge could be more dangerous than all this? What more does Laszlo have planned?

"Mrs. Smith. *Gloria.* You have my attention."

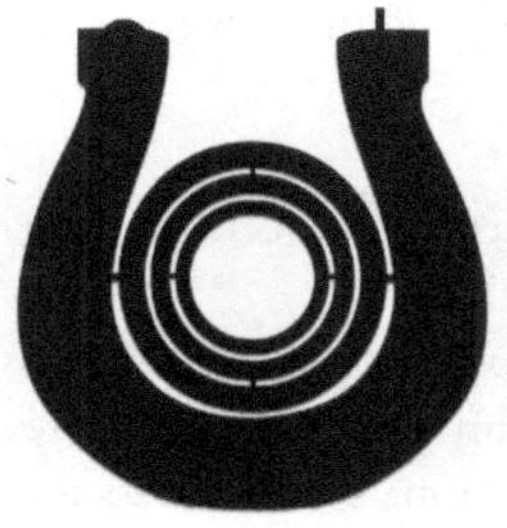

THE INSIGNIFICANT EIGHT

Nestled behind Santa Barbara and hidden away from the town square, Las Ráfagas's cemetery resembled most in the Territories: row upon row of shelves heavy with urns containing the remains of townsfolk and travelers alike, each marked with an epitaph scrawled on a scrap of parchment. Among them, hidden by the midnight gloom, an odd group hunched together and spoke in hushed tones.

"That's ridiculous," Ray scoffed.

"Ray, I saw it with my own eyes," Gus whispered. "I talked to Gloria Smith myself."

"Could she be mistaken?" Brother Richard asked. "Emmitt was the engineer, after all."

"Does she even know a pulse-rail train from a Steeldust mount?" John Stonewall added.

"No," Oscar chimed in. "It may have been Emmitt's name on the sign, but *esa mujer es inteligente*. I'd wager she's got it right. And who invited *you*, anyway?"

"Easy, Oscar," Richard said. "I invited John. This concerns his family as much as yours." Oscar *harrumphed*, but kept his mouth shut.

"Just so we're all clear," Bernadette said, "you're actually saying that Laszlo Leconte has taken over a Deiopean mining outpost so he can steal their refining technology, and kidnap dozens of natives—"

"Hundreds," Gus corrected.

"Hundreds of Deiopeans, to use as, what? Slave labor as part of the town's retrofitted refining process?"

Hidden beneath the hood of their robe, Aurora's eyes flashed once: *"Yes."*

"Why?"

A cool draft blew through the cemetery shelves and carried the stale smell of old incense with it.

"Emmitt had a notion on that as well," Gus said. "Seems Laszlo ordered some work done on the livery stables a few months back. Nothing drastic, just shoring up some structural issues and getting ahead of the maintenance schedule."

"So?" Ray asked skeptically. "It's not like fixin' the place up's a crime." He shifted his feet and kept glancing out into the dark.

"Raymond Gascon!" Bernadette chided. "When have you ever known that spoon-hoarding buffoon to shell out for town maintenance? The only reason he let Emmitt repair that pressure leak in the mercantile last year was because no one wanted to have to go through decompression to buy their groceries!"

"Exactly," Gus continued. "Emmitt had a theory. He thought Laszlo was expecting some *big* company."

"What do you mean?" Oscar asked.

"A CCO pulse-rail train. One that runs on highly refined rubidium-87 instead of whatever quantum crap the Campbells run on."

A murmur of excitement and disbelief rippled through the small group.

"You don't really believe that bunk, do you?" Ray asked.

"A pulse-rail train, and this close to the Cygnus X colonies," Oscar murmured and glanced at his wife.

Bernadette met her husband's gaze. "It could turn the tide of the war."

"We have to do something!" Brother Richard raised his voice to a chorus of *shushes.*

"What do you have in mind, Brother?" Stonewall snorted. "Pray the copperheads into surrender?"

A hushed argument bubbled up between the urns. Gus let them squabble for a few moments before she quieted them. "Stonewall's right. This is officially too big for us."

"What are you saying?" Aurora asked. "You won't help my people?"

"And what about Moe?" Bernadette added.

Gus rubbed the bridge of her nose. "I said I would help, and I will. But we're going to need backup. That means someone has to go *get* it," she explained. She stared at the Vegas.

Oscar's eyes widened at the suggestion. "I will *not* run. If there's a fight coming to Las Ráfagas, then we will be here to meet it!" he said. But Bernadette's brow wrinkled as she bit her lip.

Gus, on the other hand, lost her patience. "You want to be here for the fight? *Fine.* But there won't *be* much of a fight if you don't bring it back with you. I'll get Moe out, if only because I'll need the help mucking things up here. Buying you time."

"Who are we supposed to bring?" Bernadette asked.

"The whole bluebell army, if you can swing it," Gus said gravely.

Oscar glanced into each of his conspirators' faces. His uncertain gaze lingered on Stonewall. Finally, he landed back on Gus. "What's your plan?"

Gus peered through the shelves that surrounded them. "Where is he?" she muttered.

"Who?" Brother Richard asked.

As if to answer, a unique silhouette appeared in the dark. "Walter?" Ray said as the genie store-clerk-cum-waiter joined their circle. "What are you doing here?"

"Darkness rises. Wind howls. The storm approaches," Walter said flatly, then added, "Gretchen told me to come. Said I could help a friend." He smiled crookedly at Gus.

"I asked Gretchen to send him," Gus said and returned the smile. "Alright. Now that we're all here, here's how I see it—"

"If I may," Brother Richard interrupted. He pulled his robes tight around his slender body. "It's rather chilly tonight. Would anyone mind if we went somewhere a little warmer while we discuss our little rebellion? I know a safe place."

With no objections and a more than a little curiosity on Gus's part, five minutes later, the small group faced a dusty and mostly empty wine rack in Santa Barbara's basement. Brother Richard touched his sandaled toe against a particularly murky bottle of sacramental wine near the floor. In response, the entire rack slid back about foot with surprisingly little sound.

"Gus, a hand please?" Brother Richard asked and pointed to a spot near the edge of the rack. Bewildered, Gus stepped forward and the pair slowly pushed the thick hidden door inwards. *"Shhh."* Brother Richard held a finger to his lips. "They're probably sleeping. Let's try not to disturb them."

A small but cozy room, bathed in the warm glow of a heat lamp, lay beyond the false wall. Eight small bodies stirred—the Deiopeans Gus and Aurora saved from the fate of their kin down on the refining level. They slept on piles of old robes like Richard's. Gus grinned and gave Richard a good-natured elbow to the ribs. *Pretty cunning—for a man o' the cloth.*

"So, this is where you've been keeping them," Ray said with a hint of amusement on his face. "And I'm guessing this ain't the first time this room has been used like this, has it?"

"No," Richard replied. No hesitation. No regret. Instead, his secret laid bare, Richard proudly met the marshal's eye. "I've helped many wayward souls move through these walls. Our friend Moe even spent a few days safely hidden away here when he first arrived in town," he said. "But we mustn't stay too late into the morning. Even a town as empty as ours has eyes. There's no need to draw attention with a large group leaving the chapel together. Especially when we haven't held services in months ..." He trailed off as he cleared space around a small table at the center of the room.

"Okay," Oscar said and limped to his place between Gus and his wife at the table. "Let's hear this plan of yours."

Gus rolled a fresh cigar and ignored Oscar. She eyed his misbehaving prosthetic instead. "Aaron did a number on it, didn't he?"

"It's fine," he said with a shrug. "Let's have it." Oscar leaned on his good leg, pressing his weight on the table.

"Holy *tunk*, has he always been this stubborn?" Gus asked his wife.

Caught off guard, Bernadette smiled. "As a matter of fact, yes," she said. She rolled her eyes, but the loving smile remained.

"Sit down, and give me the damn leg," Gus ordered. She lit her cigar and filled the small room with the sharp smell of tobacco. The environmental systems kicked on and fans whisked the smoke away with a soft hum.

"We don't have time for this!" Oscar searched the other's faces for backup, but no one would return his gaze.

"Hey, *mi amigo,*" Gus said. "I can do two things at once."

Ray pulled a chair out. "Sit down, son. Let the lady work. I think—" He stared at Gus, his eyebrows drawn down, his eyes piercing. "I think I'd like to hear what else she has to say."

Outnumbered, Oscar sat with a huff. He pulled his leg off, dropped it on the table, and crossed his arms over his chest. "There," he said. "How much is this going to cost me?"

Gus flinched, but she knew she deserved that. "For the leg, not a thing." She pulled a few small tools from beneath her poncho. "But breaking Moe out of that fort of a jailhouse, causing a big enough ruckus for you to bring the cavalry, *and* free the Deiopeans—that ain't gonna be cheap."

"I *knew* it," Stonewall scoffed. "And if we can't pay?"

Gus stopped tinkering with Oscar's prosthesis to shoot the rancher a dark glare through the thin line of smoke rising from her cigar. Justified as his anger might be, *Christ's blood*, a girl had to *live*. "Don't worry, payment won't be coming out of *your* pocketbooks," she said and turned back to the leg's complicated robotics. "In fact, Moe's already suggested a source of payment. And offered to help me get it."

"The gold the copperheads are paying Laszlo with," Ray said.

"Penny for the smart old man," Gus said and smiled as she worked.

"That's—that's *insane*," Bernadette said.

"Maybe," Gus admitted, "but it'll be impossible to buy the time we need without your farmhand, so we gotta start with him either way. I plan to have him out of there, and you out of town, before Mackenzie Leconte arrives with the copperhead inspection team. Losing the bounty-head probably won't be enough to rut the deal, but it'll be a start. Then we'll cause a distraction in town. One big enough that you should be able to get out of the system with that little mule of yours. You'll sprint like hell to Holliday and bring the cavalry back. Rich? I want you with the Vegas."

Brother Richard puffed up his chest. "I may be a monk, but my order has some pretty specific things to say about protecting the innocent. I'd like to stay and fight."

Although Gus expected this from him, it still impressed her. She hadn't met many trustworthy religious types, but she would take ten Brother Richards into battle if she could have. But she also knew where he would do the most good. "I need you with the team going to Holliday. They've got one tunk of a tale to tell, and a man o' the cloth's voice will go a long way toward convincing the bluebells."

Richard's jaw worked as if he might argue more, but he shut it and nodded instead. *Good.* The Vegas would need his steel. Besides, she didn't want the death of a holy man—especially one so young and idealistic as Richard—on her conscience.

"And what are you going to do in the meantime?" Bernadette asked.

"Moe, Aurora, and I, with a little covert help from Marshal Ray and Stonewall here, will do what we can to scuttle the copperheads' wagon when they get here so they can't go after you. After that, it's only a matter of staying alive until you get back, guns blazing."

"And, somewhere in that chaos, you're going to try to steal a hold-full of copperhead gold?" Brother Richard said. His disapproving tone didn't stop him from smiling.

"That's for me to worry about, Brother," Gus said with the barest hint of a smirk playing across her lips. "But for now, we start with Moe. For my plan to work, we need someone who has access to the company jailhouse."

Every eye at the table turned toward Walter. The genie nodded. "What do you need me to do?"

"Thank you, Gus," Bernadette said quietly. Hours melted away as they planned Moe's jailbreak and the Vegas' subsequent sprint to Holliday. Dawn drew near. With their gathering breaking up, the group left Santa Barbara one at a time, and as inconspicuously as possible. With his part understood, Walter returned to the mining barracks. Stonewall had skulked off into the early morning light, and the Vegas waited their turn. Oscar stood by the big false door and fidgeted with his freshly repaired leg.

"Don't mention it," Gus said. "Aaron only bent a support rod and kinked an oil line. The leg should be good as new." She dug into one of her pockets and pulled out her gold coin. "Hey, Oscar," she said, and flipped the coin to him. He caught it and gave her a puzzled look. "For luck," she said and winked.

"That's not what I mean, and you know it," Bernadette said bluntly.

Gus pulled her tobacco tin from another pocket and eyed the farmwife cynically. "Don't read too far into things," she said. "My options for getting paid and getting out of this garbage scow of a town have been reduced to exactly one. I still think you should have taken Laszlo's offer and left this god-forsaken gasball a long time ago."

Bernadette smiled and said, "I don't believe that for a second," before leaning in close to kiss Gus tenderly on the forehead. "But whatever your reason for helping us, thank you." With that, she turned and followed her husband and Brother Richard out and up the stairs. Gus was stunned; it wasn't a reaction she would have predicted.

That left only Gus, Ray, Aurora, and the sleeping Deiopeans.

"Now that they're gone, we've got a bit more to discuss," Gus said. She sat back down at the little table.

"What's that?" Ray asked. He had remained uncharacteristically quiet all night.

"What you're willing to do," Gus said. "I know Laszlo's an old friend. And what you've learned over the last few days can't be easy." Ray kept his eyes low. "I need to know, right now, if I can count on you when things go pear-shaped. Even if everything goes smoothly, it *will* go pear-shaped. People are going to die. I know keeping the status quo is sort of your thing around here, but one way or the other there's a lot of change comin'. When the shooting starts—when the *killing* starts—are you gonna have my back?"

Ray stared intently at the bare concrete floor. His dour face reflected the churning storm Gus suspected raged within. Finally, he spoke. "Do you know how these guys get from Deiopea to Aeolus?" he asked Gus and gestured to the small, sleeping forms. "They use a rudimentary FTL gimbal engine. Something they reverse engineered from one of the construction wagons that built Las Ráfagas. Damn thing crashed on Deiopia decades ago, when Laszlo was building the place. Before that, it was, what? Solid-propellant rockets?"

"Correct," Aurora confirmed. "The crash was a major event for our culture and technology."

Ray snorted. "And then Laszlo refused to trade with them. Only now we find out, they're even smarter than we are at this stuff. And when the bottom drops out on Laszlo, what's he do? He steals the tech they would have shared with us if we treated them with the respect they deserve. Now, he's threatening good people—likely killed a few. And for what? Gold? And all I've done is hide in my office and cash in my own thirty pieces of silver." The old marshal sighed. He took his badge off and held it up to the light. "Young lady, this town's status quo has been untenable for far too long. And I'm ashamed to say I've been a part of the problem. Too old or too tired to see the truth. I've been helping Laszlo bleed this town—this whole planet—dry.

"No more. It's time I start living up to this badge," he said solemnly. "Whatever you ask of me, I'll do my best to see it through."

Gus nodded. "Good, 'cause I'm going to need you to drum up one hell of a brouhaha—"

The heavy door swung inward and Brother Richard appeared, breathing hard, his eyes wide and his face pale, save for a pair of rosy spots high on his cheeks. "Ray, you better come quick."

"What is it?" The marshal jumped to his feet and bolted toward the door without waiting for a reply.

"It's Oscar!" Richard huffed. "Aaron was waiting for them at the stables!"

Without a word, Gus grabbed one of the old, dirty robes and threw it over her head and shoulders. Under her makeshift disguise, she raced up the chapel stairs after the monk and the marshal, leaving Aurora to look after the other Deiopeans.

A small crowd had yet again formed around Aaron Leconte and Oscar Vega. Although the first rays of morning should have bathed the scene in a golden glow, the clouds cast an angry shade of purple instead. The bruised light gave everything an unreal, ethereal quality. As Ray pushed through the excitement, Gus melted into the onlookers. There, hidden among the faceless townsfolk, she watched with one hand resting on Delilah's grip.

"What in tarnation is going on?" Ray roared as he reached the middle of the crowd to discover a tight ring of Company Police. At the center of the ring, Aaron and Tuco struggled to clap cuffs around Oscar's wrists. "Come on, Aaron. It's too early for this. I ain't even had my coffee yet!"

As Gus sidled up to Bernadette and Stonewall in the crowd, it wasn't Aaron who responded. "This man is a *known* menace!" Laszlo shouted as he stepped through a gap in the ring of bulls across from Ray. "He flouts town law constantly, like his father before him. And *also* like his father before him, he has a bad habit of leading our good townsfolk astray! He's got all of you"—he turned in a slow circle, addressing the entire crowd—"so turned around and inside out that you've forgotten who takes care of you! Me!" He stopped in front of Ray. "You failed to take care of the original and now refuse to do anything about the sequel—except pay his fines for him."

"Now, wait just a second—" Ray said, pointing a stubby finger in Laszlo's face.

"No," Laszlo interrupted, "there is no more *waiting*. You had your chance to deal with this. Now I'm going to make an example of Mr. Vega here." He raised his voice. "You all know this man," he said and waved his hand toward the farmer. "You all know he thinks the laws of this town that keep you safe do not apply to him!"

"Oscar ..." Bernadette said. She took a half-step toward her bound husband.

Stonewall grabbed her around the waist. "You can't help him, or Hector, if you're locked up, too. Or dead," Gus whispered into her ear.

Laszlo continued. "I am here this morning to assure him, and all of you, that yes, the laws do apply to everyone," he announced and nodded to Aaron.

The signal given, Aaron swept Oscar's prosthetic leg out from under him with a sharp kick. Oscar dropped to his knees. Aaron stood over the crippled farmer and smiled like a Coalsack rattler—hungry, full of teeth, and completely without humor. "I've been waiting a long time for this," he said and cracked his knuckles.

"*Chíngate,*" Oscar spat.

Aaron answered with his fists, drawing blood from Oscar's lip with the first blow.

"*Oscar!*" Bernadette screamed. This time she nearly pulled free from Stonewall, but the jelly-rancher held firm. Even Tuco winced.

Ray stepped in for Bernadette and caught Aaron's arm before he could deliver too much of a beating.

"That's *enough!*" he yelled into Aaron's face and tossed the younger man to the ground like a child. "I won't let you treat anyone in my town like this, Laszlo. I don't care who you are!"

"*Your* town, is it?" Laszlo bristled. "Your town? That's funny," he chuckled. He put an arm around Ray's shoulders like they were best friends again. "I know your little friends have been having back-alley meetings all over *your* town. Why, just this morning I heard tell of a few suspicious characters skulking about *your* fair town at daybreak. Should I have Aaron send some of his boys up here to attend to the situation? Or is that, perhaps, something *the marshal* would like to deal with?"

Tunk. Tunk. Tunk.

It was all coming apart at the seams. Gus's blood ran cold and she drew Delilah beneath her borrowed robe. If she was going to die in this backwater town, she was going out shooting. *And I'll take these gas-huffers with me.* The Lecontes for being the bullies they were, and Tuco for getting her into this mess in the first place. *Too bad Junior's not here.* Leaving that score unsettled would be her biggest regret.

But at the last moment before the fog of battle took over completely, Oscar caught Gus's eye. His bruised and bloodied face was stern. Stubborn. His eyes flicked from Gus to Bernadette, and back again. A subtle squint. An intense stare. The barest of head shakes. Gus stopped. She could feel Bernadette trembling against Stonewall's arm at her side. Gus still needed to get her and Hector out of the system so they could bring back help if any of them were going to survive this. She dropped Delilah back into her holster and nodded to Oscar.

"Ray!" Oscar said hoarsely. He spat a wad of blood. "That's enough. We always knew this day would come. See that my family is safe while I'm away."

"There!" Laszlo said gleefully. Tuco hauled Oscar to his feet and Aaron punched him in the gut. "You see? Apparently, you *can* beat reason into a man!"

Tuco, Gus saw, wasn't paying attention to Laszlo. Instead, he squinted at Oscar warily. The crafty bastard followed Oscar's gaze to his wife and glared suspiciously into the crowd around Bernadette. His stare fell on Gus, hidden beneath the dirty robe. Tuco's eyes widened for an instant before a black cloth sack, thrown by Laszlo, smacked him in the face.

"Put that on him, and let's go," Laszlo barked. Gus ducked behind Bernadette and Stonewall and faded back into the crowd.

Had he seen her? She couldn't be sure. She chanced another peek through the throng. Tuco held the black bag, but his dark eyes scanned the crowd intensely, his lips compressed down to a thin line beneath his mustache.

"Hey! Gunsel! Let's go!" Aaron snapped.

Tuco jolted and tore his gaze from the crowd. He put the bag over Oscar's head without a word. Laszlo leaned in close to Oscar, whispered something, and then delivered another sucker-punch to the rancher's unprotected stomach. Aaron and Tuco caught Oscar before he fell and the posse departed, carrying Oscar off to the administration tower.

"Tunk!"

Gus, Ray, Brother Richard, and Bernadette barged into the hidden room beneath Santa Barbara's chapel. Gus hunched down at the table and rolled a cigar. Her hands shook so badly, she spilled tobacco everywhere. *"Tunk!"* she repeated.

"What happened?" Aurora asked.

"Oscar was arrested," Brother Richard said.

"What's the play here, Gus?" Ray asked. "They're not going to waste any time once they get him back up in that tower. They're probably roughing him up already."

"I know!" Gus snapped. "I need to *think.*"

Bernadette, who remained surprisingly quiet since her husband had been dragged away, finally spoke with a low and husky voice that did not waver. "We go on with the plan."

"And leave Oscar to Aaron and his thugs?" Ray's eyebrows climbed high up his forehead at the suggestion. "No, we need to regain control of this situation."

Gus lit her cigar and peered at Bernadette through the rising smoke. Her eyes were red, though Gus had not seen her shed a tear. "Are you sure?" Gus asked.

The farmwife closed her eyes and nodded.

"Then we go on. At four thirty tomorrow morning, we'll have ourselves a good old-fashioned jailbreak."

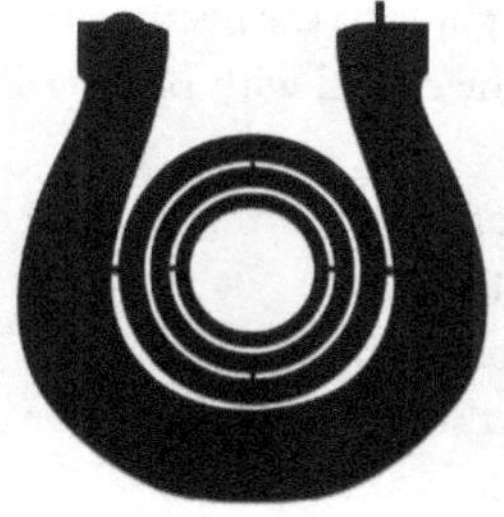

ESCAPE FROM FORT LECONTE

The day passed excruciatingly slowly for Gus while hidden away in the secret room behind the wine rack. The night was worse. Despite Gus's help, the eight Deiopean miners largely kept a polite distance. Only Aurora had attempted to speak to her, but Gus's black mood sent the hunter retreating back to their people after a few words.

Mercifully, after an eternity in the dark, the heavy wine rack door creaked inward. Brother Richard's handsome face appeared in the gap.

"It's time."

As Gus pulled her poncho over her head, Aurora's eyes flashed. "Be careful," the translator chirped from the table.

Gus nodded. She stepped out into the cellar proper and found Ray at the foot of the basement stairs. He'd pulled his old-fashioned cowboy hat low to hide his face. Gus knew he wasn't happy with how things were playing out, but a strange sense of pride welled in her chest that the old marshal was with them. Bernadette, in a homely traveling dress, stood next to him with Hector by her side.

"Everything's ready? You spoke with Gretchen?"

Richard nodded. "Walter delivered your 'package' to Moe with last night's supper."

Bernadette gripped Hector's shoulders tightly. The bags under her eyes were deep and heavy. Yet, Gus gleaned no doubt in her face.

"Good." Gus lit a cigar and eyed Bernadette. "You know what to do. Let me hear you say it."

Bernadette sighed. She crossed her arms over her chest and thrummed her fingers against her elbows. They'd been over this dozens of times already. "Hector and I are going to the livery stables. If anyone stops us, I tell them we stayed here in the chapel with Brother Richard last night."

"Why?" Gus asked.

"With both my husband and farmhand locked up, I was too distressed to get us home," she replied flatly.

"Good." Gus took a deep drag. "Then what?"

"I take the mule into the clouds and wait for your signal. Then we run hard for Holliday Station."

"Good," Gus repeated as they climbed the cellar stairs. "But there's one small change. I'm bringing Moe to you and you're going to take him with you."

Bernadette's eyes went wide at the notion. "I thought you needed him? To get paid?"

You're damn right, I need him. The odds of pulling this off without the rob were the longest she'd ever gambled with.

"If the Lecontes find Moe in town after what we're about to pull, he won't make it to a trial." She shuddered at the idea of what Aaron might do with the chance, but she kept it off her face as best she could. "You'll need him more. Don't worry about me. I'll manage." Silence fell over the group as they climbed the old chapel's stone steps. "Alright," Gus said as they stepped into the cool, predawn air. "Let's get to it. Get yourselves to the rendezvous coordinates and wait for me."

Richard took Gus's hand in his own. His boyish good looks and the fire they belied struck her once more. He'd have made one tunk of a charming outlaw in another life. But not this one. "May the blood of the world flow through you," he said solemnly.

Gus forced a smile and gave the holy man a slight nod. In her experience, those that relied on divine intervention invariably ended up dead.

"One last thing," Ray said to Bernadette. "Don't engage the FTL engine until after you break atmo. The outpost's proximity sensors may work for tunk, but an FTL neg-mass discharge is hard to miss."

Bernadette nodded tersely and turned to go, but Hector tugged on Gus's poncho. "Are you going to help *mi Papi?* And Moe?" he asked. His eyes brimmed with tears.

Gus knelt and put a hand on his shoulder. "I'm going to do everything I can for them, but you have an important part to play, too. You need to look after your mother now. Keep her safe. Can you do that? For your father? For me?" The tears in his eyes overflowed, but he nodded.

"It's okay to be scared. I'm scared too," she whispered into his ear as she pulled him into a tight hug. "But we can't let that stop us from doing what we have to do, right?" He wiped snot from his nose with a dirty sleeve with another curt nod. "Alright, then," Gus said and gave him a wink. He smiled weakly.

Gus stood and, with her hands on Hector's shoulders, faced her coconspirators. One by one, she looked each in the eye.

This is it. Time to go all in.

"Let's do it."

The engineering coral was shadowy, silent, and still. Gas particles brought in by the mounts floated in the motionless air like dust, adding a sense of weight to the atmosphere. Gus peered into the gloom and waited for any sign of activity. None reached her. *Emmit said he'd finished. His crew must be down below, setting up the retrofits.* All the better—she'd run low on goods she could bribe with. Still, she boarded *Tilly* as quietly as possible.

Tilly immediately responded to Gus's presence with a nicker. Lights throughout the small pony flickered to life and the environmental system kicked on. The old mount's ventilation made a series of sounds like rolling grunts.

Gus patted the bulkhead as she made her way to the saddleroom. "Good to see you, too. We've got some work to do, girl," she said and swung into the control saddle. "Think you can handle it?"

A snort through the environmental system acted as a reply. Gus took up the yoke's reins and led the pony up and out of the unusually somber corral. She kept close to Las Ráfagas, following the curve of the enormous outpost's outer hide down toward the mining levels and Fort Leconte.

Despite the short trip from the engineering corral to their destination, their going was slow and rough. Aeolus's winds gusted with gale force and Gus had to fight the controls to keep from being blown off course, or worse, into the station's side.

At last, they reached their goal: a nondescript section of Las Ráfagas's metal skin far below the town proper that, according to *Tilly's* computer, was just outside Fort Leconte's cellblock. Gus put *Tilly* into a parking hover and made her way to the rear of the mount. Buffeted by the winds, *Tilly* rocked to and fro as she tried to maintain her position relative to the outpost. Gus stumbled to the cargo hold, tapped a few buttons on a control panel, braced herself against the bulkhead, and waited.

Nothing happened.

"Hmm ..." She squinted at the tractor beam control console. Like many of *Tilly's* systems, Gus had installed the aftermarket tractor beam herself. And, like the escape pods, it hadn't exactly been designed for this kind of mount. But it *had* been on Emmitt's list of repaired systems. She poked at the controls again. Still nothing. "Come *on!* Bottle-farting, piece of ..." She slammed her fist against the bulkhead next to the panel. It stayed frustratingly dark. She ran a diagnostic, but everything checked out. At least, on her end.

With no problems on *Tilly's* side, it had to be with Moe. Gretchen reported the handoff had gone smoothly. Did the bulls find it at bed check? Did Moe not know how to use it properly? *Christ's blood,* he only had to put it against the outer wall and turn it on.

All the lights on the tractor beam control console suddenly turned green and *"BEAM ACTIVATED"* flashed on the small screen. A deep hum rumbled behind the bulkhead.

"Yes!" She raced back to the saddleroom and mashed commands into the control terminal. A grainy image of *Tilly's* tail end sprang onto the screen. The tractor beam was clearly visible: a brilliant beam of white light connecting its emitter to the outpost's hide, and the matchbox-sized receiver Walter had smuggled into the jailhouse for Moe. "Here we go." She pushed on the yoke's reins and pressed her heels in as far as they would go.

Tilly's atmospheric thrusters flared. The pony jerked against the tractor beam's tension and twisted in the wind like a barely controlled kite. The yoke's reins bounced and jolted in Gus's hands as she leaned on the yaw stirrups.

"Come on, come on," she said as she coaxed more power from the thrusters. *Tilly* groaned and squealed with displeasure, but they weren't done yet. Gus gritted her teeth, squeezed her heels, and pushed *Tilly's* thrusters well past the red line.

Just as she started to doubt her plan, the scream of tearing metal cut through the morning air. *Tilly* lurched forward and took a chunk of Las Ráfagas's silvery skin away with her. Hastily, Gus dropped *Tilly* below the fresh hole she'd created, spun the pony around, and cut power to the tractor beam. As she glanced up through the saddleroom canopy while waiting for Moe to appear and jump to safety, she spared a fleeting thought for the tractor beam receiver. Still attached to the chunk of outpost wall, it was falling deep into the atmosphere. It wouldn't be a cheap part to replace.

Electric-green laser fire erupted from the fresh tear in Las Ráfagas's side, but there was no sign of the rob. "Come on, Moe," Gus muttered. More shots exploded from the hole.

At last, Moe's digital face appeared over the edge. His eyes and lips were a trio of perfect O's.

"Come on, come on!" Gus shouted and waved frantically through *Tilly's* canopy.

Instead, the cobbler-rob's face disappeared again, and for a heart-stopping moment, so did the shooting. Gus had a vision of Moe collapsed on the cell floor with oil and hydraulic fluid pooling around his smoking body. Her horrid daydream evaporated when Moe's gangly form leapt from the jail cell into the clouds, chased by a barrage of fresh emerald fire.

He landed on *Tilly's* back with an enormous *clang*. Gus flipped a switch opening the spent escape pod's exterior hatch and guided *Tilly* under the outpost's belly and into the cloud cover. With a wary eye out for Aaron's bulls, Gus punched in the coordinates for their rendezvous with Bernadette and met Moe as he climbed through the pod hatch.

"That was *something!*" Moe said. "Whose crazy idea was that? We gotta go! Did they see you?"

"I doubt they think you dove into the ether. They'll be on us any minute. You alright?" she asked. "That was a lot of shootin' going on in there. You're not hit?"

Moe held his arms out and examined himself. There were a few carbon scars—what would have been grazes if he were flesh and bone—but a smoldering hole in the canvas that covered the joints in the right side of his chest represented the worst of it.

"How bad is it?" Gus asked. She touched the smoking cloth gingerly.

Moe flexed his arm and tested the mechanics in his fingers and wrist. "Seems okay. Missed my central power unit. Wouldn't have made the jump if they'd got that. But if it hit my brachial hydraulic tube, I'll start to lose function in the arm. Nothing seems to be leaking, so we'll have to wait and see." Satisfied he was okay, Gus turned back to the saddleroom. Moe followed. "What now? Back to town? When're the copperheads getting here?"

Gus climbed into the saddle and shook her head. "There's been a change in plans, and that injury just sealed the deal."

Moe's brow furrowed as his eyes narrowed. "What kind of change?"

"Oscar got picked up by the Lecontes yesterday morning after we made plans for *this* escape."

"What are we waiting for?" Moe exploded. "Let's go get him! What's the plan? Where are they holding him?"

Gus shook her head again. "It's not that kind of change. Getting Oscar out is my problem. You're going to see Bernadette, Hector, and Brother Richard to Holliday Station. Quickly, quietly, and safely."

"No," he said. "I won't leave the boss with them."

"It's already been decided, Moe. This is what has to happen. Oscar needs you to see to his family now. Your family. Like they've seen to you," Gus said.

Moe's shoulders dropped. His eyes darted around the saddleroom, and he half-raised one hand. Gus braced for further arguing, but the rob dropped his hand and nodded instead. *Good. The last thing I need is to argue battle tactics with a rutting bootmaker.*

A small, dark shadow had come into view through the canopy. The Vega's mule.

"Besides," she said, "we're here." Gus maneuvered close to the mule to dock belly-to-belly with the smaller mount. The mule's powerful atmo-thrusters raged against *Tilly's* extra weight but held them both aloft.

Moving from one gravitational orientation to another always made Gus's stomach backflip, but she swallowed hard and awkwardly led Moe through *Tilly's* lift and onto the mule. While the jelly-ranching family had their reunion—minus one important member—Gus gave the old mule's FTL systems one final check. Brother Richard watched over her shoulder. Satisfied, she turned to the broken family.

"Alright, Bernadette," she said. "You know what to do,"

"Wait for your signal, then sprint like *tunk* all the way to Holliday."

Gus offered a small, reassuring smile. "You got it. I'm counting on you to bring the fire back with you. Oscar's counting on you," she said and put a hand on the farmwife's shoulder.

"I know. But..." she hesitated, but determination flared in her eyes again.

"What are you going to do?" Brother Richard finished.

Unsure, Gus said, "Me and *Tilly* have got a few tricks up our sleeve yet." She added a grin with twice as much confidence than she actually felt.

Bernadette pursed her lips and reached out for Gus's hand. "You don't—you don't have to do this alone."

Gus gazed into the farmwife's green eyes and squeezed her hand. "I'm not," she said, turning to Moe, Richard, and Hector. "We've all got a part. We can do this."

Richard, smiling wanly, raised his hands over the group. "Heavenly Father," he prayed, "protect these moral and just warriors. Help them see their cause through to its righteous conclusion. Amen."

"Amen," Bernadette, Hector, and Moe replied in unison, heads bowed.

A heavy silence fell inside the mule. *We're running out of time.*

"Alright, look. The coolant system is still a little sticky, so you're going to have to watch it," she said and pointed to a display on the main control console. "You're going to be running hot, so it'll have a tendency to gum up. You've just gotta stay on top of flushing it." She turned to Hector. "Think you can be in charge of that, pal?"

Before the boy could answer, a blinding flash of pure white light lit up the sky like the birth of a new sun. When it faded, an enormous shape hung in the sky above them. They crowded under the canopy and craned their necks to see it. Long and narrow, it dragged a gigantic fireball with it as it streaked across the sky. A few moments later, the screaming, tearing sound of the upper atmosphere ripping hit them and vibrated through the bulkheads.

The mule's radio crackled to life on its own. *"Attention: Las Ráfagas Outpost,"* a stern voice ordered. *"This is CCS Heavy Pulse-Rail Cruiser* Shenandoah. *By the authority of the Confederate Colonies of Orion, this outpost is hereby placed under immediate lockdown until further notice. Any craft attempting to leave the system without proper authorization will be fired upon and destroyed."*

Before their eyes, the immense fireball dissipated as the shape slowed and approached the livery stables. Three long, heavily armored, armed modules had been linked together, the first of which was clearly the drive section. Gus had never seen anything like it. She squinted at it. Apparently, they had strung no fewer than *eight* old celerity drive engines together. The CCO had their pulse-rail train—after a fashion.

Tunk! Gus slammed a fist down on the mule's controls. "They're early."

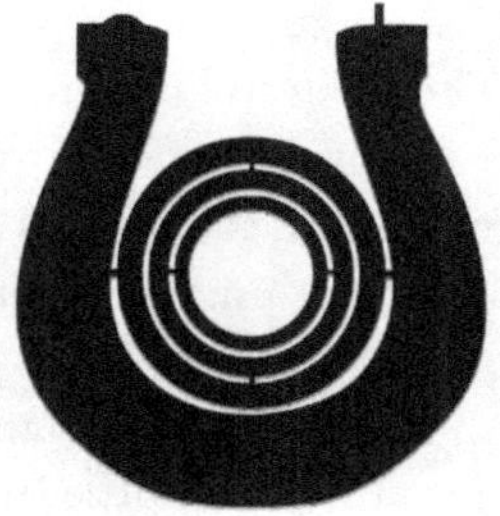

INVITATION FROM A BEAMSLINGER

R ed Hippotes hung low in the bronze and gold of the evening sky. The Vega homestead stood quiet. Peaceful. It hid the deep unease within the small farmhouse's walls.

Gus sat at the kitchen table and rolled a cigar. Like the sunset, her relaxed demeanor hid a whirlwind between her ears. She pinched at her tobacco. Precious little remained—enough for a day or two. They'd probably all be dead by then, anyhow. She rolled the sweet-smelling leaves and let her mind race, searching every angle for a way out. When she finished, Gus stepped out onto the porch and brought the fresh cigar to her lips.

The hot smoke filled her lungs as she surveyed the Vegas' little patch of sky. *El Dorado*, Oscar called it. *The Golden One.* She could see why. It was beautiful. The flaxen clouds and a constantly shifting landscape were like rolling mountains in the sunset. She hoped, one day, when all her traveling was done, she could put up her feet in a place like this.

But that would first require surviving long enough to retire.

The copperheads had arrived two days early and thrown all their careful planning into chaos. She'd succeeded in breaking Moe out of Fort Leconte, but with nowhere to run, it was only a matter of time before they were discovered. Laszlo was no fool. Aaron had already sent a detachment of bulls to check the Vega homestead for the fugitive rob. He and Gus had stayed onboard *Tilly*, hidden in the shadow of the homestead's anti-grav foundation, until an irate Bernadette turned the thugs away.

But they would be back.

Moe appeared from around the barn carrying a big bucket of jelly-feed in each hand. Gus smiled, surprised by the ease of his stride. "Where're you headed?" she asked.

The rob shrugged. "The jellies still need to be fed. No use in letting them suffer because of our problems." Gus couldn't disagree. "Besides," Moe said as she took one of the buckets and they started toward the paddock, "there's just something about these beauties that calms me." He smiled serenely to himself.

Gus followed Moe up a short flight of stairs and onto a long catwalk that extended out into the greenbottle jelly paddock. When they reached the end, hanging over open atmosphere, they overturned their buckets of feed and let the nutrient flakes drift on the breeze. The herd of jellies floated lazily toward the catwalk, but they stayed together and kept the juveniles, including Gussy, protected in the middle of the herd.

They watched the clumped-up jellies begin to feed. The adults' long tentacles gathered the drifting flakes and passed them to the inner juveniles before taking any themselves.

"Moe ..." Gus started.

"Storm's coming," he interrupted. It had certainly been windy during the jailbreak—the gusts had pushed *Tilly* around like a toy. But now it was calm. Overcast maybe, but only the mountainous clouds on the horizon seemed like they were in a hurry.

Moe watched her scan the skyline. "Look at the jellies," he said. He pointed down to the huddled group of blimp-like cattle. "They clump up like that when they sense high winds coming. It's how they keep from being scattered by the storm. See how they keep the younger and weaker members of the herd closer together? They each work together to keep the whole safe. We could learn a lot from them."

"The Lecontes are no storm, Moe," Gus said quietly. She watched the herd intertwine their tentacles, preparing for the unseen tempest to come.

"No," Moe agreed and shook his head. "We can't huddle together and wait for them to pass, but ..." He gazed down at the jellies gently bobbing in the breeze.

"But if we don't come together, they'll scatter us like jellies in the wind," Gus finished. Moe nodded solemnly. He didn't take his simulated eyes off the herd below.

Tunk. Only one thing to do. "Has Oscar got a transmitter around here?" she asked. "How did he arrange his midnight meetings with the other troublemakers?"

Moe squinted at her. "There's an old low-frequency transmitter in the barn. What have you got in mind?"

"It's well past time I called a little meeting of my own," she said.

It was too risky to meet in the Vega kitchen—even at this godforsaken hour—so Gus put the word out to meet deep in the clouds, far from prying eyes. Shrouded in inky darkness at the designated coordinates, Gus, Moe, and Bernadette waited aboard *Tilly* for the others to arrive.

"After all that's happened," Bernadette said, breaking the silence of the saddleroom, "how can you be sure they'll come at all?"

"They'll come," Gus said. Certainly, with Oscar imprisoned in the administration tower, *Shenandoah* standing guard over the town, and Gus effectively dead, the remaining townsfolk had little reason to stick their necks out now.

Bernadette's hands balled into tight fists at her sides. "How can you be sure?"

No sooner had the question crossed her lips than a small mount, similar to the Vegas' mule, broke through the clouds and came to a halt fifty feet off *Tilly's* right shoulder. Then another. And a third. Before long, more than half a dozen small ponies and skiffs were hovering in the dark.

"How...? *Why?*" Bernadette asked.

Moe, the usual broad smile projected onto his face, answered for Gus. "Once they got over the shock that she was, in fact, still alive, she told them the cabinets were open—that she would share her contraband freely, as long as they came. And listened."

Bernadette's jaw hung open. "Why would you do that?"

"It's no good to me if I'm dead. Besides"—Gus glanced at Moe—"if we're going to survive this storm, we've got to come together. If this is how I get them to listen, so be it."

Moe nodded his approval as the comms crackled and interrupted Bernadette before she could reply. "Okay, we're here," Jacob Wagner's voice broke in. "But we ain't trading goods nor barbs out here in the breeze. What's your play, girl?" A chorus of voices competed to agree.

Brother Richard cut through the static. "Gus, it's time you showed them."

Without a word, Gus flipped on *Tilly's* belly floodlights and revealed the abandoned Deiopean mining village floating in the gases beneath them.

"What will you say to them?" Bernadette asked.

Gus met Bernadette's green eyes. "I don't know."

Fifteen minutes later, they stood in the abandoned village. The octagonal motif was everywhere. Even the village's layout resembled the cities on Deiopea's surface.

It didn't take long for those brave enough to come to start picking through what remained of Gus's contraband hold.

"What the hell is this place?" Wagner demanded as he swallowed a spoonful of peanut butter and his eyes darted to and fro.

"Would you shut up for five minutes and let the lady speak?" Silas Mwangi snapped.

"It's not for me to say," Gus said. "Some of you already know Aurora of the Deiopeans." Bernadette smiled warmly at the Deiopean, then scowled at John Stonewall, who stood near the edge of the group. He either didn't see it or pretended not to.

Aurora stepped forward. "This facility was built and maintained by my people," the translator chirped as it interpreted the dizzyingly complex pattern of light that flashed from Aurora's eyes. "The Leconte family has stripped it of its technology and its laborers."

Wagner opened his mouth, his eyes hard and ready to argue. But he shut it under Mwangi's glare.

"What's the matter, Wagner?" Gus said. "Don't like the look of things around here? Looks a bit like Las Ráfagas's future, doesn't it? Abandoned. Empty. *Lost.*"

Gus faced the small group of townsfolk. Bernadette stepped among them and greeted people, thanking each for coming. Moe stood on Gus's left and smiled brightly. He radiated happiness, sure, but more than that. Hope. Resolve. Ray stood on her right. His slumped posture and darting eyes told Gus all she needed to know about how uncomfortable he was with even this small, secret act of rebellion. *But he's here. That's all that matters.*

Gretchen and Walter—who had been snuck out of town by Ray—held hands and waited for her to speak. Wagner and Mwangi, the small-hold ranchers, shared the jar of peanut butter between them. Daniel Park had come alone and stared around the room in naked awe, the contraband offering completely forgotten. If he had been impressed by the Deiopean bandages, Gus reckoned there were things here that would blow his mind.

Brother Richard had brought Aurora. When Gus had asked about the eight hiding Deiopeans, the young man made an unpleasant face, shrugged his shoulders, and would only say they were gone.

Gloria Smith had come, too. She stood awkwardly to the side of the group, wearing her late husband's scarred leather apron. John Stonewall stood with his arms folded over his chest and an expression to match his name. Finally, there were a few faces Gus didn't know, but she had seen around in her short time on Las Ráfagas. Farmers. Miners. Outpost workers.

A mixed group, full of robs, genies, and doppels alike.

She took a deep breath. "But this ain't the future Laszlo's got planned for Las Ráfagas. Not by a long shot. No, Laszlo's got a deal coming through that's going to put Las Ráfagas back on the map! But the thing is, he doesn't want to share in the boon that's coming. *That's* why he's lowballed so many of your neighbors. That's why he's been trying to force out the Vegas, and scuttled the Mwangi's anti-grav foundation," she said and shot Wagner a dark glare. "Don't believe me? Try leaving the system for sunnier pastures now. The time for buyouts is over, ya see. Now it's time to get rid of the witnesses."

"Bottle-farts!" Wagner shouted.

Mwangi gaped at his neighbor. "Have you already forgotten what they did to my home? The Lecontes took everything from my family! It'll be you and Martha they come for next!"

The group burst into murmurs and splintered arguments.

To Gus's surprise, Stonewall cut them all off. "Ain't you been payin' attention?" he said. "Ain't nobody gonna fight them alone and win. Some of us got more 'an ourselves to think about here!"

"Hear, hear!" Brother Richard agreed emphatically.

"Yer daughter'll be fine," someone shouted. "*Everything'll* be fine. We just gotta wait fer this to all blow over."

"You still don't get it, do you?" Moe said, raising his voice for the first time. "The copperheads don't care about your farm, or your family. Or *you*. They only want the town and the rubidium. And they will kill every last one of us to get it!" he shouted. Crosstalk and arguing erupted again.

Ray put his hand on Moe's shoulder and tried to calm the cobbler. He cleared his throat loudly. "I've known all of you for years. We've built up a pretty good rapport here. Ya'll know I'm not one to upset the applecart," he said with a bittersweet smile. "I can't be certain of everything that's going on"—he raised his hand to Gus—"but I trust this young lady with my life. If she says we're in danger, then *dagnabit*, I believe her. You all should listen to what she has to say."

"She's the one that said we had four days! Who put her in charge?" Stonewall shouted.

"*I did!*" Ray roared. "Now y'all are gonna listen up. 'Cause she's my deputy, and I ruttin' said so."

A hush fell over the group. With all mouths shut and all eyes on her, Gus told them what she knew. "Laszlo's made some kind of deal with the copperheads for Las Ráfagas. I don't know all the details, but it all hinges on the tech stolen from the natives and this village."

"Why?" Wagner asked. "What's so special about the spiders? I'm surprised the little savages could build something like this at all—no offense," he added quickly when his eyes fell on Aurora.

She ignored the rancher. *That's some colossal willpower. Can't say I'd do the same.*

"The Deiopeans have found a way to refine the rubidium-87 that makes it ten times more potent," Gus said.

"Then let them have it!" Wagner said. "Once Leconte finishes his deal and they take the tech—"

"What? Everything will go back to normal?" Gretchen shouted. "Come on, Jacob. Don't be dense."

"The refining tech they stole requires *living* Deiopeans to work," Gus continued. Some of the color drained from Wagner's face and all hushed conversations stopped dead. Gus nodded. "Besides, it's not only about the fuel. Why do you think Laszlo's been giving you lowball offers and bullying your neighbors off their plots? Why he's put families—like the Mwangis, like the Vegas—in danger, just to send a message?" Gus shook her head. "It was never just about the fuel.

"It's about the *town*."

"What do you mean?" Daniel asked.

"Emmitt thought they wanted Las Ráfagas as a pulse-rail station, or their version of it anyway. For more of those monstrosities," she said, referring to the enormous CCS *Shenandoah*, currently hitched at Las Ráfagas's livery stables. "And not only a station," she went on, "the *last* station before the Cygnus X colonies. I think he was right. Las Ráfagas will be a boom town again. A boom town built on the backs of Deiopean slave labor."

A low murmur hummed through the group. Gus's voice rose over it.

"That's why Laszlo wants all your properties. That's why he's trying to push you all out. So *he* can rake in the spoons when Las Ráfagas becomes a major travel hub—for the CCO. And with their rail-line to the frontier finished before the bluebells, the copperheads'll flood the territories with soldiers. As Laszlo gets fat and rich, they'll take the Cygnus X colonies, and they'll use your town to do it. No one will be safe. Not robs. Not genies. And before long, not doppels, either."

Clouds shifted overhead like shrouded leviathans. Wind tugged at shirtsleeves and locks of hair. No one spoke.

"If I'm right, they're not gonna want the bluebells to know about it until it's too late to do anything. Which means fortifying Las Ráfagas. Which also means no one here will be allowed to leave to carry the message." She paused. Stunned faces leered back at her. "And don't think you'll be safe once the deal is done, either. Take it from me, the copperheads don't take chances when it comes to possible troublemakers in their midst. A bunch of ranchers and miners who might know too much about how a certain refining technology was acquired? Sounds like a whole heap of trouble for the CCO."

Silence, like a lead blanket, fell over the group.

Gretchen spoke up first. "I don't know about stealing tech, but the retrofit *has* been focused on the refining levels. Emmitt oversaw that work," she said. The group turned as one to the engineer's white-haired widow. "Gloria, is there anything you can tell us about it?"

Gloria tugged at her husband's apron and ran her hands over the old, pitted leather with tears in her eyes. She nodded. "It's true. All of it. Emmitt didn't *know,* not until it was too late to stop it." Ray put a reassuring hand on her shoulder. "They killed him and stole his designs," she whispered as the tears fell. Bernadette appeared at her side and put a hand around Gloria's waist. "There are already more of these pulse-rail stations, aren't there?" she asked.

"Very likely," Gus said. "Which means after they kill us all to keep the secret, they're going to take Emmitt's designs, along with some of the Deiopeans, to the other stations."

"To work as slaves," Gloria said gravely. It wasn't a question.

"That's certainly what the Deiopeans think," Brother Richard said.

"What's that supposed to mean?" Stonewall asked.

"Gus and Aurora saved a handful before they were brought to Las Ráfagas. They've spent the last few days with me and have corroborated Gus and Gloria's stories."

Gloria knelt before Aurora. Her face shined with tears. "I am so sorry for the part my husband and I have played in all this. Can you ever forgive him ... or me?"

Aurora's arachnid facial expressions were difficult to decode, and in this moment, Gus could not predict what her new companion would do. Aurora had every right to be angry with Emmitt, Gloria, the Lecontes—*tunk,* humanity in general. But instead of lashing out, Aurora put a small hand on Gloria's soft, white hair.

"Laszlo Leconte has made victims of us all. The past can't be changed, but we can prevent more suffering. If we act now. Together." Gloria smiled sadly and took Aurora's hand in both of hers. Tears rolled down her cheeks as she nodded.

Again, arguments erupted throughout the small group of potential mutineers. "Why don't we hide here until the copperheads leave?" a small, boxy mining-rob asked in a low, husky voice.

"Have you got a processing error? They won't leave this place abandoned for long!" a genie rent-boy Gus recognized from Cirrus House replied.

"We could run!" Wagner shouted. "They can't get us all!"

"And whose family are you willing to sacrifice to save your own skin?" Bernadette snapped. "Mine? Walter and Gretchen? Silas's girls? Your own son?" Wagner dropped his eyes to the floor and popped a strawberry into his mouth.

Gus checked Moe and Ray. As the marshal's posture curled further and further into himself, the rob's eyes grew harder and an angry flush rose in his cheeks. "Don't you people understand?" Moe shouted, cutting through the crosstalk. "There's no hiding. There's no running. We need to stand and fight! For our homes. For our lives. For what's *right.*"

"Ray, you've been awfully quiet over there," Gus said. "I need to know I've got you on my side here."

The marshal leaned against the wall. The wind wobbled the brim of his hat, threatening to yank it from his salt and pepper head. "You don't know what you're asking me. Not really," he said. "This has gotten a lot bigger since the copperheads showed up. It was one thing when the plan was to get the Vegas out first. Now ..." He pursed his lips. "I'm an old man. My fighting days are long behind me." Ray's shoulders dropped and he bowed his head. He sighed and purposefully straightened his back. His eyes moved from miner to rancher to townsfolk; when they finally fell on Aurora, he sighed again and nodded. "But doing the right thing usually means doing the hard thing, don't it? I say we fight."

Gus nodded. "We fight. But only some of us."

Stonewall leaned in and narrowed his eyes. "You have a plan?"

"I do," Gus replied, "but it's dangerous. We're gonna need a little guile, some fancy gunplay, and a whole pile of luck. I reckon it'll be a lot of fun."

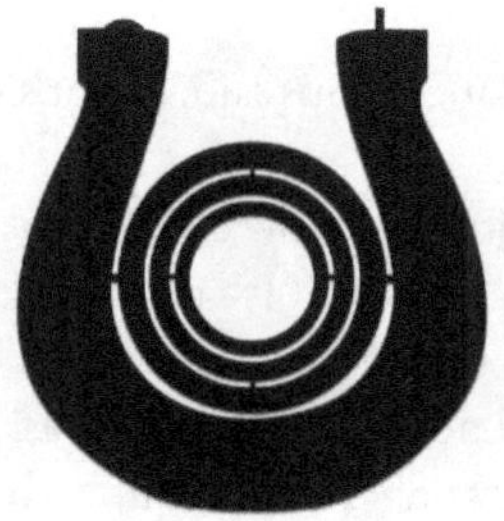

GHOST TOWN RENEGADES

"As some of you know"—Gus nodded to Ray, Moe, and Bernadette—"we already tried one plan, paired up with our little jailbreak."

"The copperheads showing up fouled it up, didn't they?" Stonewall scoffed. "How come you got the day wrong?"

"How was Gus supposed to know?" Moe shouted. "They weren't supposed to arrive for two more days!" More murmured conversation broke out. Ray stepped forward and cast a stern eye over the group until the chatter ceased.

"The basics of our plan are still good," she argued. "There's no way we can win a straight fight with a battalion of the Confederation's finest. We need help." All eyes were on her now. "The way I see it, we need to do four things: free Oscar Vega, disable *Shenandoah*, and cause a big enough distraction to allow the vulnerable to make a run for it before the copperheads can get their cannons back online. I figure, with a little help from Ray and some of you in town, I can do all of that by hitting *Shenandoah*."

"How will that help Oscar?" Bernadette asked.

"Wait," Stonewall said, his face tightened by his mental calculations. "That's three things."

Gus ignored him. "The bulls have been on high alert since we broke Moe out. Right, Walt?"

"I've never seen them so jumpy!" Walter said. "I don't think they suspect I was involved in the jailbreak, but they've stopped letting me in to feed the prisoners."

"We've got 'em off balance," Gus said. "That's why they moved Oscar to *Shenandoah*."

"What?" Bernadette jolted. "How could you know that?"

"My lucky coin." Gus smirked. "It's got a tracker in it. I've been keeping tabs on Oscar since they took him."

"But how could you know ...?" Bernadette asked.

"He'd be taken?" Gus said. "I didn't. But with how the Lecontes clearly feel about him, I thought it would be a good idea to keep an eye on you guys."

"Okay," Wagner said. He had hope in his eyes, but doubt in his voice. "But how, exactly, do you plan on boarding that thing, breaking that fool Vega out, and getting out alive?"

"In this dense atmosphere, getting on board will be the easy part. I can use the tracker in the coin to find Oscar. And as for disabling the weapons ..." Gus pulled a shock-resistant bottle the size of her fist from one of her pockets and held it up.

"And what the tunk is that supposed to be?" Wagner asked.

"Mrs. Santiago's nitroglycerin!" Daniel cried. He clearly had hoped to never see it again.

"There's enough here to ruin the copperheads' day," Gus said. She turned the bottle gently and let the light catch the liquid inside. "Enough to disable *Shenandoah* long enough to make a break for Holliday Station, anyway. And for me to collect my payment."

"Wait," Richard said, "your *payment?*" A fresh round of murmurs rippled through the miners, ranchers, and townsfolk. "You're not seriously still planning to go after the gold?"

Bernadette shook her head. "The *fourth* part of your plan."

Gus turned to Moe. The cobbler nodded solemnly. "A deal's a deal," he said, "I'll help you. But I'll tell you now: if it comes down to the boss's life or your gold—"

"Agreed."

"*Tarnation!* Going after that gold is suicide!" Ray bellowed.

With a shrug, she said, "A girl's gotta get paid." Her eyes met Bernadette's. The farmwife shook her head again but held Gus's gaze with a disapproving eye only a mother could deliver.

"And our agreement? To help my people?" Aurora asked.

"I haven't forgotten," Gus said. "As soon as we get Oscar and the families on their way, we'll fight our way to the refining level."

"That's a lotta promises. How're you plannin' on pullin' this off, girl?" Stonewall asked.

Gus took a deep breath. "Three teams. One in town, one hitting *Shenandoah,* and one sprinting out of the system. Ray'll be in charge of the team in town. Everybody able-bodied'll be with him. As soon as the copperhead inspection team steps foot in town I need you to create a distraction. Slow them down."

"How?" Stonewall asked. He walked the line Gus needed them all to cross—they wanted to fight, but they didn't want to die for nothing.

"This is technically UCET territory, ain't it? Have a protest for all I care. Just keep them focused on you and away from the mining levels for as long as you can. Bernadette and Brother Richard will be in charge of the families—"

"Now, wait just a minute!" Brother Richard cut in. "If there's going to be fighting on the esplanade, I should be there."

"We already talked about this," Gus shook her head. "I need you with the families to help them convince the bluebells."

Richard looked like he was going to say something more, but Bernadette appeared at his side and put her arm in the crook of his elbow. The monk glanced from her to Gus and back again. "Very well," he said with a resigned sigh.

Good man.

"Moe and I will hit *Shenandoah* hard," she continued. "Once their power is out, getting back to town will be a chore, but one I'm confident we can handle. We'll join up with Ray's team and prepare for one hell of a fight. Aurora, I figure you're gonna want to be on Ray's team, that way you can get down to your people as fast as possible."

"I will go with you into the snake den," Aurora's translator chirped.

"*What?* No. You're better off—"

"You've made a promise to help my people. I intend to make sure you stay alive to keep it."

Oscar did *warn me about their stubbornness.* She nodded. "Alright then. Once we're back in town, the four of us will fight our way to the refining level. To Aurora's people. Then we hold up 'til the cavalry arrives. Gretchen, Walter, think the miners could be of any help there?"

The pair huddled with the other miners who had come. Gretchen spoke on their behalf. There was a wry, smirking quality to her light voice. "You can count on us."

Gus nodded and turned back to Aurora. "What about the rest of your people? Any hunting parties in the atmo? Can they offer any help?"

"The storm approaches. And with it the 'rider," Aurora answered cryptically and would say no more.

An hour later, with the final details of the plan hammered out and the last of Gus's contraband foodstuffs gone, the clandestine meeting finally broke up. Gus, Moe, and Bernadette had seen everyone else off the abandoned Deiopean village, each with their own set of instructions for the coming conflict. Now, the trio made their way across the stable, back to where *Tilly* stood waiting.

As they approached the small U-shaped mount, a flash of reflection and a hint of movement inside the saddleroom caught Gus's attention. *Someone's on board.*

"You two, stay here," she said. Slowly, Gus drew Delilah and approached her mount.

"What is it?" Moe asked. That familiar note of anxiety crept into his voice. He rubbed his right shoulder distractedly.

"Not sure. Probably nothing," Gus said and activated the lift on *Tilly's* belly. "Stay here," she repeated and disappeared into the cargo hold.

Sure, probably nothing. Unless Aaron was smart and left a garrison behind.

Tilly nickered a greeting as the lights flickered on. Gus's eyes darted back and forth as she slowly moved through the engine room, cautiously checking for any signs of an intruder.

"*Tilly,*" she whispered and typed a few commands into the environmental control computer, "is there someone else here?" A short grunt through the air duct worked as an affirmative reply. *Tunk.* From the engine room, Gus killed all the onboard lights at once and threw the mount into near blackness. Even the control display consoles went dark. The only light came in through the saddleroom canopy and windows.

"¡A la verga!" a surprised voice hissed from the saddleroom. "What did I do?"

Gus took four lunging steps and launched herself through the hatch. Her right hand smashed down on a control panel and turned all the lights back on at full brightness, while her left hand leveled Delilah at the intruder.

Hector sat in the control saddle with his hands held up over his eyes to protect them from the sudden flare of light.

"Dammit, kid!" Gus slammed Delilah back into her holster and tried not to think about how close she had come to putting a beam through him. "What are you doing here?" Hector smiled sheepishly through the lattice of his fingers but said nothing. Gus flipped a switch on the control console to project her voice outside the mount. "It's alright," she said to Moe and Bernadette. "Come on up. It's Hector." The little boy's face darkened at the sound of his own name. All at once, he seemed to remember he wasn't supposed to be there.

"Kid, seriously. What are you doing?" Gus asked.

Hector folded his short arms across his chest and slid from the saddle. His face twisted in a defiant scowl. "I want to help save *Papi.*"

"Kid—Hector," Gus said as she shook her head, "I don't think that's a good idea."

"I can fight! I mean, I can learn. You can teach me to shoot so I can come with you and help save *Papi* from the copperheads!"

Gus raised her eyebrows at the boy. "Not only a stowaway, but a *spy,* too!"

"Hector Duncan Vega!" Bernadette shouted as she stepped into the small saddleroom. "Just what do you think you're doing, young man?"

"I'm going to help, *Mamá,*" he said with as much grit as his little body could muster.

His mother sighed and put her hands on her hips. Gus spoke up before she could scold him. "Moe, do you think you can pilot *Tilly* back for me?" she asked, then with a nod and a smile to Bernadette, she led the boy back into the engine room and sat him down.

From the chair, Hector gazed up at her with awe in his eyes. "You can teach me to shoot," he said, "and I can go with you to rescue *Papi.* Then you can stay here with us, and I can grow up to be a beamslinger. Just like you."

Gus pursed her lips and tried to decide what to say. She knelt in front of the chair, and with Bernadette watching from the saddleroom hatch, did her best to speak to the boy.

"Hector," she said gently, "when we save your father, it won't be this beam-shooter that does it. It'll be our *minds*. It don't matter how fast you are on the draw if the other guy can outthink you. Your father's brave, Hector. And clever. Your mama, too," she added and nodded toward Bernadette. "You'd be smart to listen to them. Learn all they can teach. And if you can keep your mind faster than the other guy's draw, I'll be happy to ride with you. When you're a little older." She tussled his hair. "Now, why don't you go up front with Moe. I'm sure it'll be a better view than wherever you stowed away."

Hector nodded with his little eyebrows knitted and his lips drawn tight and got up from the chair. To her surprise he grabbed her in a little-boy bear hug and squeezed tight. "You promise you'll bring *Papi* home?"

Gus returned the hug and smiled despite herself. "I promise, big guy. I'll get him home, safe and sound. Now, go on up with Moe." Hector wiped snot and tears on his sleeve. He smiled weakly and ran into the saddleroom.

As Hector interrogated Moe about *Tilly's* systems, Bernadette closed the saddleroom hatch behind him. Gus slumped in the chair Hector had just left and checked the engine gauges. Bernadette peered at the galactic gunfighter and shook her head in frustration. "I don't understand you."

"What's to understand?" Gus said with the flip of a wrist. She started up a coolant system diagnostic and avoided Bernadette's eyes. She had downplayed how hard it would be to approach *Shenandoah,* even in Aeolus's thick clouds. *Tilly's* systems would need to be locked down tight. Any unnecessary energy blooms or surprise coolant leaks would make them detectable.

Bernadette paced across the little engine room. "You finally understand what's at stake for us. You've formed strong bonds of friendship here. With Moe. With Aurora. Oscar, too, though I don't fully understand it. And I know Ray looks at you like the daughter he never had. Even if you confound him as much as you do me."

Gus scoffed. "I'm doing what I always do—whatever it takes to keep riding."

"Maybe," Bernadette said softly, "but I don't think Hector feels that way. We're fighting for our homes, our livelihoods. Our very *lives*. All *worthy* things to fight—and die—for. But you ..." she trailed off.

"I'm still in it for the gold," Gus said. She spun the chair around to face Bernadette. "And you can't figure out why I would risk my life, your husband, and the whole plan on a few bars of gold. Let me tell you: I like you and Oscar. Hector, too. But even if by some miracle we pull this off, I *can't* stay when it's all over. I *need* spoons if I'm going to survive. If I don't keep moving, I'll die, just as sure as if I'm shot down. If this life has taught me anything, it's that if it ain't helping you keep ridin', it's nothing but *bottle-farts* on the breeze.

"Don't worry. I'm not so greedy that I'll risk your husband, or your farmhand, for my payoff. If things go south, I'll cover their escape."

"You mean—"

"Like I said, if I don't get paid, I'm as good as dead anyway," Gus said and turned back to the diagnostics.

Bernadette's hands were suddenly on Gus's shoulders. "I don't believe that." She kissed the top of Gus's head. "And I don't think you do, either."

Gus woke in the same small room at the top of the stairs she'd occupied on her first night on Aeolus. Dull, muted light fell across the cot. Slate colored clouds covered the sky, both above and below El Dorado. The wind whipping through the homestead stirred up small, whirling dust devils that played across the courtyard. She opened the window, dropped her hip onto the sill, and silently rolled a cigar. A storm *was* coming, after all.

Good. It'll give Tilly *more cover during this evening's exploits.*

Her stomach churned. It was a familiar sensation; she never could eat much with a fight on the horizon. She took a deep drag from the cigar. It helped, but only a little. The butterflies would stay until the shooting started; experience told her nothing would change that. But when the butterflies left, they would be replaced with cold steel and colder calculations.

She loved it and hated it.

Relished it and resented it.

Ignoring her complaining stomach, she snuffed out the roach and headed down the stairs.

The rich smell of fresh coffee greeted her before she reached the kitchen. Ray was already settled at the Vegas' small table, sipping from a steaming cup. Moe sat across from him, empty-handed.

"Gus," Ray said over the rim of his coffee.

"Good morning, Gus," Moe said. His voice had a dull, tinny quality, bereft of its usual joviality.

"Ray. Moe," she said, nodding to the marshal and the cobbler as she prepared her own coffee. "What's the word?" There was no sign of Brother Richard or the families that would soon be filling El Dorado's walls. If everything went according to plan, they would arrive slowly throughout the day, so as not to arouse suspicion.

"The word is 'go' from Gretchen and the miners," Ray said. "The Confederate inspection is scheduled for five o'clock this evening."

"What about you and the others?" Gus asked. She sipped her coffee and peered out the window. Aurora stood alone in the courtyard. Their robe flapped in the wind and their eyes flashed a bright and complicated pattern at a handheld device—a transmitter, Gus assumed.

"Ayuh," Ray nodded. "We're ready to play our part."

"Are you sure?" she asked. She dropped down at the table across from him. "This is your last chance to back out. We're going to upset the apple cart pretty bad here tonight. I know that's more than a little outside your comfort zone."

Ray put down his cup but didn't take his eyes off the dark liquid. "It's high time I do more around here than throw a few drunks in the cooler, pay a fine here or there, and hope it all gets better," he said, finally meeting Gus's eye. "Laszlo and his boys need to be brought to justice for what they're doing out here. I'm ready to do my part in seeing that happen." He shot back the rest of his coffee like whiskey.

"And you, Moe?" Gus asked.

The cobbler nodded. "I've been ready for this day for a long time. We'll get the boss. We'll get your gold. And we'll put the bastards where they belong."

Gus winced slightly at the mention of the gold. Bernadette's words the night before rang in her ears. None of it was worth it if she didn't get paid, right? Without spoons, even a tank brimming with rubidium-87 would run out. And so would she. As Tuco pointed out when this all began—what felt like years ago, now—she was down to the blanket. Broke. Without the gold, she might as well be dead. But still, Bernadette's voice echoed in her head.

"Are *you* ready? You look like someone walked over your grave. Having second thoughts?" Ray asked.

"No," she said, and brushed him off with a glare. "I'm alright. Good to go." She took a hot swig from her own coffee mug.

"Alright then," Ray nodded and reached into the deep pockets of his duster, pulling out a small box. Inside were two earpieces.

"What's this?" she asked and held one up.

"A last-minute gift from Gloria," Ray said. "Encrypted comms. Some kinda carrier wave piggybacked off'a the copperheads' frequencies, or some such. *Tunk,* I don't know. She says we can stay in contact without anybody listening in."

Clever. Clearly Emmitt hadn't had all *the engineering talent.*

"You take one o' these, and I take the other," he added. "Moe's already been tuned into the frequency, too."

The three stepped out into the gray, windy day. An awkward silence settled between them as they traded uncomfortable glances but said nothing. *This could be the last time we're all together.*

Finally, Ray's face cracked into a wide grin that broke the unease. "There is one more thing." He had to raise his voice against the wind as he pulled another small box from his jacket. He opened it to reveal a pair of tin stars that shined despite the dreary day.

Deputy badges.

"Ray—" Gus began.

"They might not mean much on Las Ráfagas anymore," he said as he offered them to the beamslinger and the cobbler-rob, "but I want Laszlo to know we did this together. That I'm not his token lawman anymore." Ray carefully pinned one star to Moe's cloth vest and turned to Gus. "I know law enforcement ain't exactly your preferred career path, but there's no one I trust my town with more. Please." He held out the tin star.

Slowly, Gus took it. Though thin and dented, it felt as heavy as a plow. But when she pinned it to her poncho, to her surprise, a sense of strength—of *pride*—welled within her chest.

Smiling, Ray shook Moe's hand and then Gus's, and then walked away to his little skiff without another word. Gus watched him go, her head awash with emotions she didn't fully understand, but also one she knew all too well: dread.

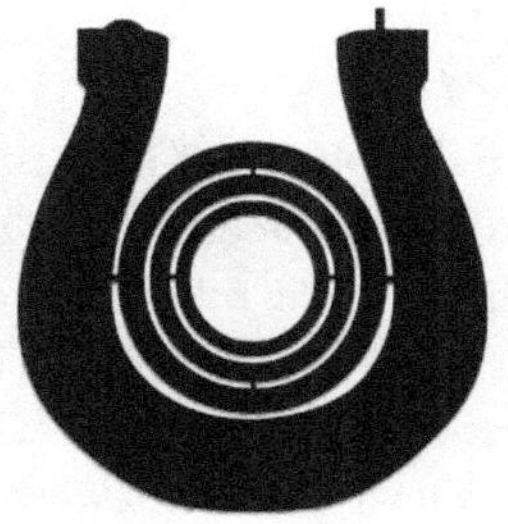

THREE IN THE SADDLE

Tilly's cramped, crowded, and silent saddleroom grew dark as dusk fell and the storm front approached. The small pony's three riders waited patiently.

Mostly.

Gus was used to waiting. Life was waiting. Waiting for the next job. Waiting for the right moment to act. Waiting for the bulls to finally catch up. Waiting for the draw.

She leaned back in the saddle and stretched. She was good at waiting.

Aurora seemed to have no problem with patience, either. The Deiopean dropped down in the small space between the saddle and canopy and set to cleaning the short-barreled rifle they called "The Hammer." Aurora methodically dismantled the rifle, carefully polished each piece, and placed them on a small rag.

Moe, however, struggled to handle the anticipation with the grace of his companions. The tall farmhand wrung his long hands as he paced from the saddleroom to the engine room and back again. He had to duck his head every time he crossed through the hatch. Yet back and forth he went. His heavy feet fell on the floor plating over and over.

Clang. Clang. Clang. Clang.

Clang. Clang. Clang. Clang.

Moe's metal footsteps formed a steady rhythm as he stepped into the engine room, paused, spun on one heel, and walked back into the saddleroom to stare out the canopy for a moment before repeating it all in reverse. Occasionally, he'd reach up and rub his injured shoulder.

Clang. Clang. Clang. Clang.

Clang. Clang. Clang. Clang.

"Moe," Gus said when the rob paused on his umpteenth circuit to stare into the darkening clouds, *"please* sit down. You're driving me crazier than a Cibus City methane huffer." She rubbed her calf. The screaming pain from her injury had receded to a dull, throbbing ache.

Moe tore his gaze away from the window. "They're late," he said. The corners of his simulated eyes wrinkled with worry.

Gus nodded. "Yeah. But only a little. It's probably the inspection team. They move at the speed of bureaucracy. Don't worry. Have faith in Ray. He'll do his part." At least, she *hoped* he would. She trusted Ray, but she knew she'd asked a lot of the old marshal.

"But," Moe said, again rubbing his shoulder, "shouldn't we go *now?* What if they've already been caught? This isn't going to work!"

"Moe—" Gus started, but the comms system cut her off. It crackled twice, as though someone double tapped the transmit button without speaking. *Ray's signal.* The copperhead inspection team was on Las Ráfagas, and the distraction was about to begin.

"There!" she said. "Ya see? Ray's got it covered. Now it's time to do our part. Go strap in, both of you. This is gonna get a little rough." Without a word, Aurora snapped the final piece of The Hammer into place and carried it into the engine room. Moe, on the other hand, took a moment, perhaps to steel himself for the job to come. He stared, unblinking, out into the clouds. "You ready for this, Moe? Your arm doin' okay?"

Moe's hand dropped from his shoulder, as he ripped his eyes from the saddleroom canopy once more. He nodded. "For the boss? Yeah, I'm ready. The arm's fine. It's nothin'."

Gus nodded back solemnly. *I hope so.* "Good. Go grab a seat."

The lanky rob spared one glance before he disappeared into the engine room after Aurora.

"Alright, *Tilly,"* Gus said. She snapped her spurs into the yaw stirrups and took up the yoke's reins. "Time to go to work."

She pushed *Tilly* up to speed and took the pony into a steep climb that shoved her passengers back into their chairs. What started as a low rumble in the floor plates grew until the entire mount rattled uncontrollably. Gus piled on more speed and *Tilly* galloped upwards through the clouds.

"Tell me again why we have to do it like this?" Moe yelled over the bone-rattling turbulence. Gus grinned and pushed faster. Almost perfectly vertical now, *Tilly* streaked up through the clouds like a rocket.

Gus had never dealt with this particular class of vessel before, but she had snuck aboard a Confederate craft or two in her time. Although every class was unique, there were certain design elements they all shared, either thanks to a lack of technological diversity, or a lack of imagination. Ultimately, it didn't matter, as long as this one was similar.

"The copperheads use a proximity sensor that cycles at forty-two megahertz. Usually, it's impossible to penetrate without setting off every alarm on their command level," she yelled back over the growing din. She pushed *Tilly* harder still, forcing the atmo-thrusters to their limit.

"*Usually?*" Moe yelled back.

"The sensor is always mounted on the upper hide, near the withers," she said. "Atmospheres with high particle-density create a small blind spot on the belly. But it can only be exploited at high velocity!"

Tilly burst from the lower cloud layers, on a direct collision course with *Shenandoah*'s underbelly. Gus gritted her teeth and coaxed every ounce of speed from her old friend.

"Gus!" Moe shouted from the engine room.

She ignored him. *Not yet.*

The flat gray belly of *Shenandoah* loomed in the saddleroom canopy as the small pony accelerated toward it.

"*Gus!*"

Not yet.

Sixty yards. Forty. Twenty.

"*Dammit, Gus!*"

With less than ten yards to *Shenandoah*, Gus yanked on the reins and throttled *Tilly's* belly thrusters beyond the red line. *Tilly* rolled over on her back and halted her ascent in an instant with her thrusters firing hard against *Shenandoah's* hide. When they were mere feet from the massive train, Gus cut power to the thrusters and engaged the magnetic landing struts at the same time. *Tilly* came to a gentle rest, upside down, latched securely to the belly of the great battle-train.

Gus blinked a few times while her stomach finished doing somersaults. As nausea passed, she held her breath and watched the control display for any sign they had tripped the proximity sensor. When no threats came in over the comms and a team of cavalry mounts didn't appear to scrape them off *Shenandoah's* hide like a tick, she relaxed and patted the console lovingly. "Good girl."

"You've done that before," Aurora said when Gus stepped into the engine room.

"Once or twice," she admitted. "But never on something this big. Or new. I don't know how long we'll have before we're noticed. We'd better get moving."

Moe struggled with his seat's restraints. "A little more warning would have been nice," he complained. "If I had guts, I'd be puking them up all over your diagnostics." Gus rolled her eyes and released the latch on his restraints. "Thanks," he said glumly and followed them to the cargo hold lift.

"What's with the attitude?" Gus asked. The whining had become uncharacteristically *annoying*. But Moe shook his head as they stepped onto the lift.

"What's next?" Aurora asked.

"*Tilly's* going to make us a bit of a back door," Gus said. She tapped a command into the lift's controls. Outside, the powerful laser ringing the underside of the lift blazed to life and cut a neat circle into *Shenandoah's* hide.

"Let's go over this one last time," Gus said. She patted the shock-resistant jar of nitro tucked into a pocket beneath her poncho. It was secure—as secure as something so dangerous could be. Satisfied, she pulled a card-sized screen from another pocket and squinted at it. A small red dot blinked. *My lucky coin.* It wasn't far from where they were, thanks to one of those Confederate design standards that she'd been hoping for.

"When I activate the lift, there may be a moment of discomfort while we pass from one gravitational orientation to another," she said. "Get yourselves situated as quick as you can once we're through. Then it's a short jog down the corridor to the brig." She held up the tracker and showed them the blinking red dot.

"And your gold?" Moe asked. His tone was dark and disapproving.

There it is. That's his problem. No time to deal with it now.

"The vault should be near the brig," she said, ignoring the rob's attitude. "They always keep both near the security substation. We'll find it on our way out."

"A deal's a deal, but I won't risk the boss's life—or the plan—for your payment."

"*Tunk,* Moe. Agreed, alright? Are we ready?" Gus asked.

Aurora's translator squawked, *"Yes. "*

Moe nodded, his digital face stony.

"Alright, let's go," she said. "And watch for that gravity disorientation." She hit the lift button and the platform—from their perspective—dropped into *Shenandoah.*

As they crossed the gravitational threshold, Gus's stomach did a cart-wheel, and she choked down the bile that rose in her throat. Only the powerful magnets in her boots kept her from falling back *down* into *Tilly's* cargo hold—which was currently *above her.*

Aurora appeared to handle the shift in orientation well; they clung to the lift platform like a Terran spider. The only sign of discomfort the Deiopean let slip was a flash of amber light that the translator didn't bother interpreting. Moe alone passed into the battle-train completely unfazed. The rob flipped from the now-upside-down lift to the train's floor and landed with a clatter at odds with the gracefulness of his movements.

With Moe's help—and with remarkably less grace—Gus jumped to the deck and rechecked the tracking tablet. "Which way?" he asked. The rob glanced up the corridor one way and then the other.

No sign we've been detected. Not yet, anyway.

"Where are the soldiers?" Aurora asked.

"We're in the bowels of the beast. Most people don't come down here unless they have to," Gus said. "This way." They followed the blinking red dot as *Tilly's* lift dropped back into the deck and out of sight. Gus pressed on the earpiece Ray had given her and readjusted its fit in her ear. "Ray, do you copy?"

"Ayuh," the marshal replied from his place in town. "Yer comin' in loud and clear."

"Good. We're heading for our pickup now. How goes the distraction?"

"So far, so good," Ray said. "We've got the townsfolk protestin' in the streets. Got signs an' everything. I think we've got enough here to bottle-neck 'em some. Don't worry, we'll keep 'em occupied."

"Good. We won't be but a minute."

With a slight limp interrupting her normal gait, Gus led them through the dim, empty corridors: a right here, a left there, a short pause as a pair of gruff voices passed in a perpendicular hallway.

When the soldiers had gone, Gus, Moe, and Aurora continued and quickly arrived at an enormous circular hatch secured with an impressive lock. But this wasn't the brig. Her tracker told Gus that Oscar was around the next corner and down the corridor about twenty-five paces. Still, she hesitated. If this wasn't the brig, there was only one thing it could be.

The vault.

"This it?" Moe asked.

She could almost feel the wealth of gold hidden behind the giant door. Everything she needed, within grasp. Enough wealth to keep her beyond the long arm of the law. To keep her riding. Keep her free.

"Gus? Is this it?" Moe repeated. His feet shuffled on the polished metal floor as he tried to watch both ends of the hallway at once.

A deal's a deal, an unfamiliar voice spoke in her head. It sounded like her own, but different. Newer. Older. *Oscar first. He'd do it for you.*

"No." She forced herself to turn away from the round hatch. "This way. Let's go." They followed her onward until the trio finally arrived at a set of thick blast doors.

"Cover me," Gus said and handed Delilah to Moe. Aurora pulled The Hammer from their robes and the Deiopean hunter and cobbler-rob took up a defensive position around Gus as she inspected the doors' controls.

"This it? Is the boss in there?" Moe asked over his shoulder.

Gus peered at the door's complicated, high-tech locking mechanism. "This is the place," she said and set to work removing the panel to expose the lock's electronic guts.

Moe, however, had other ideas. "If this is it, let's not waste time," he said and pointed Delilah at the lock control panel.

"Moe, *no!*" Gus shouted. Too late. Moe squeezed Delilah's hair-trigger, and a beam of pink light leapt from the barrel. A grapefruit flash filled the corridor.

"*Rutting tunk*, Moe!" Gus shouted. Delilah had reduced the lock's control panel to a blackened, melted hole. Pungent blue smoke floated from the mess, but the doors didn't open.

"What the hell?" Moe asked.

"Did you think shooting the controls on an already locked door would somehow *unlock it?*" Gus hissed and snatched Delilah back from him.

"How am I supposed to know that? I'm a farmhand. Jailbreaks aren't exactly a part of my daily chores. What do we do now?"

"*I don't know.* Give me a second to think."

Aurora put down their rifle and placed all six hands against the metal surface of the door.

"What is—" Moe began, but Gus shushed him.

She wasn't sure *what* Aurora was doing until the Deiopean stepped back from the door with a start and quickly shuffled to the other side of the doorway. "Two soldiers inside," they said. "One coming this way."

Maybe this will work after all.

"Alright, when that door opens, we rush 'em. We've got to take them both out before they can sound the alarm. If we're discovered, it's all over," Gus said. She swallowed hard and steeled herself for the imminent violence.

The heavy blast doors shuddered and slid open, and a young man in a dark gray uniform with copper shoulders stepped into the corridor. "What the—"

"Now!" Gus roared. Moe stepped right up to the Confederate guard. His powerful arms moved with astonishing speed, disarming the guard before he could fully draw his sidearm, and then delivering a knockout blow to the hapless young man's jaw.

As the guard crumpled to the floor like a spilled bucket of jelly-feed, Gus and Aurora, flanking the doorway, entered the brig with their guns high. The room was empty except for a desk for the guards to share, and Oscar, who sat on a cot in one of the six cells. At first glance, the cell appeared open, but Gus knew these units were much more advanced than Ray's.

"I thought you said there were two soldiers?" Gus asked Aurora.

"I heard two," they said. "I don't understand."

Oscar stood in his cell and waved his arms wildly. His mouth moved excitedly but the room stayed deathly quiet. *Some sort of new cold plasma. We're not getting through that.* She scanned the brig. Aurora couldn't have heard Oscar through the shielding.

Where's the other guard?

"Moe, let's go. Shut the door," Gus said. Moe took one more glance out into the corridor, closed the hatch, and started checking the other cells for the missing guard.

"Could you have been wrong?" Moe asked. He stood in front of the last of the empty cells. "'Cause there's no one else here!"

"I suppose," Aurora said, but their many eyes scanned the room skeptically.

They couldn't get through the cold plasma shielding with force, but if she could hack into the guards' terminal, she might be able to gain access to the locks.

"Keep watch," Gus said and dropped down at the desk. "I'll see what I can do about getting Oscar out." She typed a few exploratory commands into the interface, but the system threw her out immediately. "Moe, the guard's probably a keycard on him. Find it."

Moe nodded and started rifling through the unconscious soldier's pockets. "Got it," he said and tossed her the card. "Is this gonna work?"

"Yeah," she said, "as long as we find the other guard. We need both their cards to get into the system."

"You said you could do this!"

"I *can!* There's always at least two brig guards on duty. I don't understand ..."

Aurora ignored their squabbling and stood in front of Oscar's cell. His mouth moved in soundless shouts. He waved his hands wildly and desperately pointed at an empty space along the brig's wall. Gus eyed the wall but saw nothing.

"Hang on, Oscar," she said, typing furiously. "We'll have you outta there in no time."

"Can't we break the glass?" Aurora asked. Oscar's expression slid from frustration to surprise to horror as the Deiopean raised their Hammer.

"It's not—wait, no!" Gus shouted, but, for the second time in one day, she was too slow. Moe's hand flew to his bowler cap as he gritted his digital teeth and squeezed his simulated eyes closed.

Aurora fired point blank into the cell's cold-plasma shield.

The deafening *crack* of the rifle filled the little room, but the electric crackle and ricochet whine Gus expected never came. Instead, to their collective surprise, rather than bounce off the shield—or be completely vaporized by it—Aurora's slug passed straight through and lodged in the cell's back wall less than a foot from Oscar's ashen face.

"Christ's blood!" Gus shouted as she jolted to her feet. "Nobody takes another shot until I tell them to!"

"What the tunk was that?" a disembodied voice shouted. A section of wall swung out and the second guard stepped out of the toilet with his gun in one hand and his still unzipped pants in the other. "Who the rut are you?"

Gus gaped at him. "Would you believe me if I said, 'singing telegram?'"

"What?" the guard said. He raised his sidearm and shuffled toward the desk. "That's not—*Hey!*" He had finally seen his partner, face down on the floor at Moe's feet.

With a shrug, Gus said, "Well, it was worth a shot." Her left hand dipped, and before the guard could blink, she drew Delilah and fired once from the hip. When the pink flash faded and the freezing cloud of exhaust dissipated, an expression of surprise had bloomed on the guard's face. First, he dropped his gun, and then his pants. Then he collapsed.

"Get his card and get on the other terminal," Gus ordered Moe. "The cards have to be swiped at the same time." Moe did as he was told. "Ready? One. Two. Three." They swiped their cards and both terminals unlocked. "Alright, see where it says, 'cell security?' The controls we need are in there. Get the shield down while I check if we've been spotted yet."

"I don't know ..." Moe said and squinted at the screen in front of him. "Dammit, I'm not a computer engineer, I don't ... Ah, there it is." A sharp, buzzing siren rang twice before the shield shimmered like water and vanished.

As Oscar stepped from his cell and embraced Moe and Aurora, Gus busily typed away at the guards' terminal. She confirmed they hadn't been noticed yet and dug into a detailed map of *Shenandoah*. The brig guards' clearance was minimal, but enough to confirm the big circular door they had passed *was* the vault and would get her in. *Now to find the best way to the engine room ...*

Oscar put his hand on her shoulder. "It's good to see you, *mi amiga*," he said with a smile. "But I hope the rest of your plan goes smoother than *that.*"

"Hey," she said as a smirk played across her lips, "so far so good."

He picked up the dead guard's gun. "What *is* the plan?"

"You three are going back to *Tilly* right now. I'm heading for the engine room to disable their propulsion and cannons. That'll give the families a window to run," Gus said.

"No way," Oscar said and shook his head. "We stick together."

"We got no time to argue about this, Vega," Gus snapped. "Four's a lot easier to spot than one."

"There's no way you'll be able to carry the gold by yourself," Moe said.

"*Gold?*" Oscar shook his head. "You've got to be kidding me. After all this, you're still going after the gold? *Mujer loca.*"

"Yeah, maybe I *am,* Oscar," Gus said. "But this is the plan, and I'm making sure your ass gets off this monstrosity. I promised your wife and son I would. Now get going. Moe and Aurora can lead you back."

But none of them moved. "You still don't get it, do you?" Oscar asked. "We stick together. It's the only way we win. And if that means we stop for your damn gold, then we *all* stop for the damn gold." He folded his arms across his tree trunk of a chest. Moe nodded and crossed his own arms in imitation of his boss.

"And you?" Gus said, turning to Aurora.

Aurora's eyes flashed. "Yes. I vowed to keep you alive long enough to keep your promise. We stay together."

I don't have time to argue. It won't be long before the brig guards are missed. Besides, more arms means a bigger haul.

"Alright. Load up. Let's go make us a fuss."

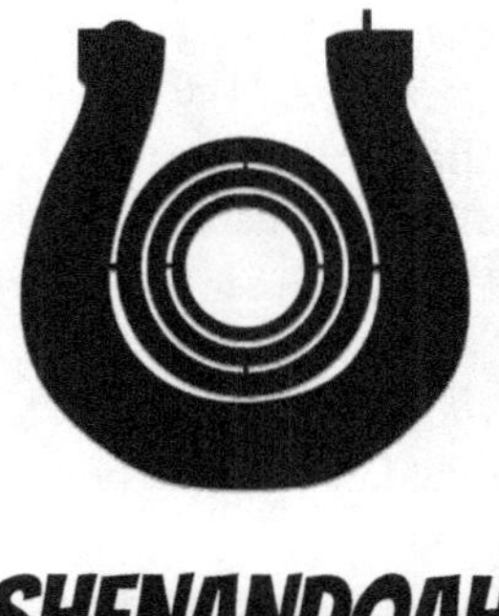

SHENANDOAH

"Come in, Ray. Do you read? We've got our pickup and are heading in to make our delivery." Gus pressed the comm deeper into her ear. "Ray! Do you copy?"

No reply came.

Moe and Gus exchanged a glance.

"He's fine. Right? Just busy." Moe said.

Tight-lipped, Gus could only nod. She led them deeper into the bowels of *Shenandoah*, careful to avoid any passing soldiers or crew. Through the labyrinth of corridors they moved, until at last, they found themselves standing on a catwalk overlooking the train's massive engine room. From their vantage, Gus could see access points to at least eight celerity-class gimbals, arranged in a row of pairs. Each of them was four times the size of *Tilly's* modest engine.

"What now?" Oscar asked.

"Now, we give ourselves a chance to get out of here," Gus said. "There." She pointed to the power junction terminal between the two nearest engine gimbals. "If I can set off an explosion there, it *should* start a chain reaction that'll knock out the power transfer system."

"Will that destroy the train?" Moe asked. He peered over the catwalk railing at the dizzying drop to the engine room floor.

"No," Gus said, "but it should disable her cannons for a few minutes and scuttle her in Aeolus's atmosphere for at least a few hours. More than enough time for the families to make it out of the system safely."

"What do you need?" Oscar asked.

"For you and Aurora to head back to *Tilly.*" Gus held up a hand to preempt his protests. "Even with that leg properly seen to, you ain't exactly a scrambler. Once this goes *boom*," she said, holding up the canister of nitroglycerin, "we're gonna have to move fast. If you get killed in this mess, your wife'll have my hide. No, you start back now and take the head start." Gus turned to Aurora. "Think you can find your way back to *Tilly?*"

"Yes, but—"

"No time. When this goes off, run like hell. Meet us by that big round door near the brig. Moe and I may have to find a different way back."

"The vault?" Oscar asked.

Gus nodded. "Don't worry. I promised Bernadette I'd get you out of here, and that's what I'm going to do. Get ready to run. Moe, let's go."

"W—what?" Moe stammered. "What do you need me for?"

"I need your eye and your arm," she said and smiled at the nervous rob. "Let's go."

"This is *insane,*" Moe said as they descended a narrow staircase to the engine room floor.

Gus couldn't disagree with him, so she shushed him instead. Dozens of people, clad in dark gray uniforms—some wearing a distinctive copper helmet—busily moved about the enormous room, checking on systems here, regulating power flow there.

"Ray?" she whispered into the comm again. "Ray, come in!" Static crackled from the other end, then a sharp electric discharge that could have been gunfire. Moe and Gus locked eyes.

There wasn't supposed to be any shooting in town. Not yet, anyway.

"Gus?" Moe said.

"Nothing we can do now but our part."

They reached the bottom of the stairs and moved slowly along the wall, careful to stay hidden. Moe's head twisted about, his eyes taking in every direction at once. Gus, on the other hand, focused on a single spot as she peered out from their cover.

"There," she said, pointing to a computer terminal nestled between the nearest pair of engines. It had huge conduits running into it from each of the engines, and a third running to the terminal between the next set of gimbals. "That's the power junction terminal. Do you see it?"

Moe nodded.

"How far would you say that is?" Gus asked. She leaned up against the power module they were using for cover and pulled out the shock-resistant canister.

"Eighty-four feet, give or take a half-size," he said. He shrugged and smiled.

"Think you can toss this so it lands on that terminal?" she asked and handed him the nitroglycerin. It wasn't so much covering the distance that had Gus worried, but the wires and tubing that hung from the vaulted ceiling like high-tech spiderwebs. To throw the nitro accurately would mean threading the proverbial needle. Who better than a cobbler?

Moe examined the trajectory the jar would have to take. "Sure," he said, and leaned back into cover next to Gus, "but these jars are pretty impressive. Even from this distance, I don't think it'll be enough of a shock to blow."

"Let me worry about that," she said.

Moe eyed her but nodded. "How were you planning on doing this without me?"

Gus unholstered Delilah and held the big gun up. "Let's just say it would have taken a bit more brute force. I want you to throw it—and *run*. Don't wait for me. I'll be right on your ass."

"What if somebody sees me?" he asked and stole one more glance around.

"They're gonna have bigger problems on their hands." She grinned sadistically. "Ready? We've got one shot at this." Moe nodded. "Alright. On three. One. Two. *Three!*"

Moe rolled out from behind their cover, cocked his arm, and heaved the canister. The moment the jar left his long fingers, something beneath the cloth covering his shoulder popped, and dark hydraulic fluid sprayed from the burned hole left by the bull's laser beam. Moe screamed in agony, but, with his right arm cradled in his left, he sprinted for the nearest open door.

The jar twirled end over end, sailing through the netting of power conduits and sundry tubes effortlessly. Gus couldn't think about Moe's injury. She had a job to do first. She tracked the jar's full flight with Delilah's barrel, waiting until the last possible moment to squeeze the trigger.

The brief flash of pink was obliterated by the white-hot explosion of the nitro. Gritting against the pain in her calf, she raced out the nearest door after Moe with Delilah's rosy exhaust trailing behind her. She caught up with him in time to pull him back before a mob of crewmen rushing toward the chaotic engine room trampled him. None of them so much as glanced their way. Gus had been right: they had bigger problems on their hands.

"What do we do? Where do we go?" Moe asked. Slick hydraulic fluid blacked his back as it oozed from his wound. His eyes goggled wildly.

"Hold on, hold on," Gus said. She peered into the hole in his "vested" chest. Whatever had blown appeared to have run out of fluid to leak. "Are you okay?"

Moe frantically flexed the servos in his right hand. It seemed weak but otherwise still functional. "Yeah, I think so," he said. The panic slowly drained from his voice and face. "It's just the hydraulics for my tool-chang-er. Hurts like *tunk*, but it's not a critical system."

Gus sighed and patted Moe's arm. "You scared me for a second there, pal." Again, she pressed her fingers to the transmitter in her ear. "Ray? *Ray!* Do you read?" Still no reply. "Ray! It's done. Do you copy? *Tunk!* Ray, if you can hear me, signal the families to go! *Get them out now!*"

"What's going on over there?" Moe asked.

"We got our own problems," Gus said with a shake of her head. "Ray knows the plan. He'll see it through." *Was that a prayer, a hope, or a gam-ble? He's been quiet an awful long time.* She pushed the thought away and pulled the tracking tablet out again. Assuming Oscar and Aurora didn't run into any issues, Gus could still use the coin to follow them back to the vault. "This way."

All the corridors looked the same. Gus knew they were running through different passages than those they had already come through, but every hallway's unremarkable dull gray paint job made navigating *Shenandoah* even more difficult. She had no choice but to rely on the coin tracker to guide them. Left and right it led them, through familiar yet novel hallways and up and down nondescript staircases.

"Are you sure that thing's taking us the right way?" Moe asked as they waited for a group of crewmen to rush past.

"Trust me," Gus said. She turned the corner in the direction the crew-men had come from and opened a hatch. "It's gotta be—" They arrived at an enormous room—some sort of cargo hold. But rather than crates of goods or munitions, legions of silent, deactivated robs filled the space.

"What is this?" Moe asked. He stepped up to the nearest new, sparkling rob. Identical to the rest, it was short and bulky with articulated treads and a complicated array of tools at the ready. *They look like Gretchen. Dozens—more—of little Gretchens.* But where Gretchen had a modular body ready to change at her wish and whim, these robs were purpose-built for atmospheric mining. Moe's hands gently touched the silent mining-rob's face.

"These're brand new. Probably hexaquark IPUs. They're advertised as lo-bot hacked before leaving the factory floor. And hardened against the fix I got." He fiddled with the brim of his bowler. "What does this mean?"

Gus swallowed hard. "It means it's even worse than we thought," she said. "More reason not to linger. This way. It's not far." She slapped the door controls and rushed out of the hold, where she collided with another person standing outside the door. They fell into a pile of arms and legs. Gus reached for Delilah.

"There you are!" Aurora said. The Deiopean jumped to help Gus to her feet.

"Yes," Oscar said as he trotted to them, "we were starting to get worried." He bent over and gasped for breath.

"We're fine. I said to meet at the vault. What are you doing?" Gus demanded.

"What are we doing? Looking for you!"

"Damn fool. You're gonna get yourself killed," Gus muttered. *Why doesn't anyone ever just listen?* "Where are we? Which way?"

"This way," Aurora said and ran down the corridor.

Oscar's brow furrowed as he peered over Gus's shoulder into the cargo hold. "What's that?" he asked.

"I'll explain later. Let's go," Gus said. She grabbed his elbow and dragged him after Aurora. A few twists and turns later they stood in front of the big circular vault door.

Gus gave *Tilly's* whistle a sharp blow. "Oscar, *Tilly's* around the corner there." She pointed without taking her eyes off the big door. "She's opening the lift for you now. Get aboard and get in the saddle. We're gonna need to leave in a hurry."

The jelly-rancher stood his ground. "Gus, come on. The gold's not worth your life. We need you!"

With some effort, Gus turned to face Oscar. He stood a few feet from her with his sunburned hand outstretched. He was right. So far, everything had gone according to plan, outside Ray's silence. *Am I really going to risk this clean getaway for a few bars of gold?* If they left now, whatever happened on Las Ráfagas might not be enough to stop them from succeeding. Maybe.

But then what? Even if the Vegas got to Holliday and brought the cavalry back, she'd likely be arrested on sight—if she survived at all. And even a full tank of fuel runs out when the spoons dry up.

Her eyes were drawn back to the big door.

Her heart pulled her toward Oscar.

It had been so long since she had anyone to trust, she'd forgotten what it felt like to be on the right side of something. But her mind yanked her back to the vault. What good would family be from inside a prison cell?

Gus shook her head. "You've done it, alright? You've convinced me. I'm gonna fight for your hopeless little cause because it's the right thing to do. I'm willing to risk my life for you and your family. And to see justice come for Laszlo Leconte and his kin.

"But I'm not willing to risk my future. If I'm still here when the bluebells show up, I'm as good as dead. And without the gold, I won't get far. I *need* this, Oscar."

"You don't, Gus," Oscar said. "Don't you see you've got a place here? People who care about you? Isn't that worth more?"

Gus's mind reeled. Visions flashed through her mind. Kicking her feet up on Ray's desk, the deputy star shining on her poncho. Drinks shared with Oscar and Bernadette at Hotel Irma. Chasing wayward bottle-jellies through the clouds with Moe and Hector.

But the shadow of the UCET loomed over all of it.

"The gold—it's *freedom,* Oscar. Without it, I'm either dead or in prison for the rest of my life. With it, I can come back once the heat's blown over. Don't you get it? There's no future for me, here or on the Arm, without as much of what's behind this door as I can carry. Now, *go!* Get *Tilly* prepped and signal the families to sprint. *Now!*"

Still, Oscar hesitated, searching for the words that would change Gus's mind.

"Go, Boss! I'll get her out in one piece," Moe snapped. That broke Oscar's indecision. His face grave, he finally nodded and ran for *Tilly.*

"*You'll* get me out?" Gus said with a smile once Oscar had gone.

"That's a promise!"

"A responsibility we'll share," Aurora said.

She nodded. *Let's make this quick, then.*

Gus and Moe stood on opposite sides of the doorway, each with a guard's keycard, and swiped them through the matching terminals. A series of loud mechanical noises emanated from within the door, followed by the hiss of equalizing pressure.

At last, the big door rolled aside and revealed the vault beyond. As lamps in the ceiling slowly blinked on, each bulb reflected countless times by row upon row of shelves stacked high with shining bars of gold bullion.

The trio stepped into the vault as the last of the ceiling lamps came on and fully revealed the bounty the enormous room held. Gus's legs turned to jelly, and she nearly fell. There was enough here to keep her riding and free for the rest of her life. *Tunk*, once Laszlo and his sons were gone, she could *buy* Las Ráfagas and use it as her personal refueling outpost. It was far enough from the war that once this nastiness blew over, it would go back to being forgotten, yet close enough to the Cygnus Trail that work—both legal and otherwise—would never be far.

She lost count of the rows of shelves. *Yeah. That'll do.*

"Gus!" It took Moe shouting in her face and shaking her shoulders to bring her back from her daydream. "We gotta go! What do we do?"

Gus snapped back to reality. She never would have guessed they would have brought this much, and merely a fraction of it would fit in *Tilly's* hold, anyway. If the nitro had done its job, they might have had fifteen minutes before the copperheads could restore power to the cannons. At least half that time had passed already. Maybe more. They had time for one trip.

"There," Gus pointed to a hand truck strapped to the wall, "load it up with as much as it can carry. Then grab what *you* can carry." Her eyes crawled across the rows of shelves. *If only there was more time.*

As if to prove there wasn't, a young man in uniform appeared in the open vault door. "Hey!" he shouted. "What are you doing? What the rut is *that?*" he shrieked when he saw Aurora loading bricks onto the hand truck.

Gus spun and fired Delilah. The soldier fell. *Tunk.* "Time to go. There'll be more where that one came from. Leave that to me," she said and grabbed hold of the hand truck. "Grab what you can carry and go."

Within moments, they were once again racing down *Shenandoah's* corridors. This time, Moe and Aurora each had an armload—or in Aurora's case, several armloads—of gold bricks. Gus brought up the rear with the hand truck. It dragged under the weight of her ill-gotten riches. *Tilly's* lift rose from the hole it had cut in *Shenandoah's* hide like a giant mechanical toadstool.

Oscar's face appeared in the hole. "What's going on out there? Hurry up!"

The corridor blazed with flashes of red light as soldiers took cover in adjacent corridors and opened fire. Beams of scarlet crisscrossed the hallway as the trio reached *Tilly*. Without stopping, Aurora dropped to the floor and slid into the waiting hole. Moe followed, diving head-first into *Tilly's* upside-down cargo hold. Coming last, Gus shoved the hand truck forward and into the open lift, where it immediately jammed in the hole.

"What the rut?" Oscar shouted from inside *Tilly*. "*Madre de dios,* Gus! It won't fit, leave it!"

"Make it fit!" she bellowed. She drew Delilah and took what little cover she could behind the lift rising from the center of the corridor. She fired twice in quick succession and the nearest two soldiers dropped to the floor like razz chips. She spun around the lift and fired twice more. The hand truck had lodged at an odd angle with its load of gold brinks spilled half inside *Tilly*, half across the deck of *Shenandoah*. Oscar and Moe wrenched the hand truck back and forth in the hole.

"*Come on, come on!*" Gus shouted. She ducked away from a sizzling beam, slapped a fresh coolant cap into Delilah, and returned fire.

Finally, with a few grunts of exertion from inside *Tilly's* hold, the hand truck fell forward and into the pony. The laser fire intensified and cut burning red lines through the air around Gus.

"Let's go!" Moe yelled.

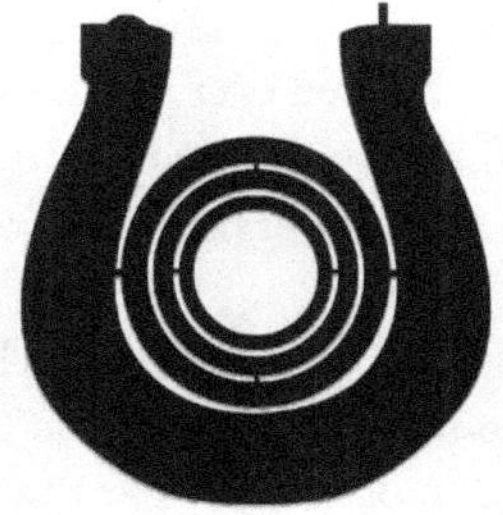

THE VAQUERO OF EL DORADO

Gus spilled into *Tilly's* cargo hold, using her momentum to overcome the disorienting gravitational inversion.

"Close it!" she yelled as she landed with a *thud*. A red laser beam or two struck the inside of the lift as it retracted, but it closed smoothly and sealed shut before any of the advancing copperheads could reach it. Gus scrambled over the haphazard piles of gold bricks and ran for the saddleroom.

"How long until they get power back up?" Oscar hollered after her.

"Not long enough!" she yelled back as she leapt into the saddle. "Did you reach the families?"

"No." Oscar was pale. "What does that mean?"

If she was right, they had only a few minutes before *Shenandoah's* engineers could restore enough power to energize the battle-train's cannon batteries. That meant minutes to get away. *If* she was right. They couldn't do anything if they were dead; they would have to worry about the families later.

"Get that crap stowed and strap yourselves into something. This is gonna be rocky!" She jammed her heels into the spur ports, grabbed hold of the reins, and disengaged *Tilly's* magnetic landing struts. The pony fell away from *Shenandoah*. Gus kicked the atmo-thrusters into full throttle, and *Tilly* darted along the belly of the massive train.

As they approached *Shenandoah's* rearmost car, its belly split open along a nearly invisible seam. Team after team of small but nimble cavalry mounts flowed from the opening like a swarm of wasps. *Tunk!* Gus yanked on the reins hard and sent *Tilly* into a steep dive. The copperhead cavalry pursued with guns blazing.

"Aurora, Oscar!" Gus bellowed over her shoulder. "I need you two in turret control. Far end of the pony, through my quarters! Moe, try to reach Bernadette again and get them out of here. Now, while the cannons are still down and we've got 'em busy!"

"There's still no word from Ray!" Moe yelled back.

"Doesn't matter! It's now or never!"

Tilly's old rifle turret rumbled with power for the first time since Gus bought the old girl. The big gun turned and fired back into the pursuing swarm. *Thanks, Emmitt. That's another one I owe you.*

Back in the engine room, Moe screamed into *Tilly's* transmitter. His voice rang out over all open frequencies, *"Now! Now! Now! All teams—If you're still here, break atmo now!"* Static screamed back at him.

The rob appeared in the cockpit doorway and gripped each side of the hatch to brace against Gus's evasive maneuvers. "No reply." His face was ashen. "Do you think they made it? Were we too late?"

Gus gritted her teeth as she pushed *Tilly* through a series of rolls and dives, galloping hard to evade the oncoming fire. The pony rattled and shook her way through the acrobatics. "I don't know, Moe. I—" A blaring alarm and flashing amber warning light cut her off.

"What's that?" Moe yelled.

"Artillery weapons lock." *Rutting tunk.* "They've repaired their power system already. That was rutting *fast.*"

"What do we do?"

"Hold on to something," Gus warned, then pushed *Tilly* into a sudden dive. They barely dodged an enormous neon green beam of light that punched a neat hole through the clouds in its wake.

That's it. It's over. Gus pointed *Tilly's* nose into the clouds and pushed the throttle as far as it would go. *Tilly* raced into the dense cover.

"What are you doing?" Oscar yelled over the internal intercom, "The rendezvous is the other way! We have to cover Bernie's escape!"

Tilly zigged and zagged through the clouds. Her rifle turret fired back over her shoulder at the pursuing cavalry.

"Don't you get it? Nobody made it off-planet! That's why Ray's not answering," Gus yelled. "And even if they did, there's no making it past those cannons now."

"But you just did. We can still do this!" Moe insisted.

Another colossal green beam cut through the clouds, missing them by mere yards. "No chance," Gus said. "They're having trouble tracking us in this soup, but as soon as we break atmo they'll have a clear shot. We gotta regroup."

"*Regroup?*" Oscar shouted over the comms from turret control. "That's my *family*, you cowardly—" Gus flipped off the intercom and cut Oscar off midsentence.

At nearly the same instant, a new player emerged from the gas to join the dogfight. Small and maneuvering nimbly, and it drew some of the remaining cavalry away. It broke from the clouds for a moment, and Gus got a good view of it before it disappeared again. *I'd recognize those thrusters anywhere.* The Vega's mule. Gus had just enough time to muse about Bernadette's riding skills before the mule reemerged from the clouds, galloping hard on a collision course with *Tilly*.

"What's she doing?" Moe yelled.

"Mule's got no weapons," Gus said, and poured on the speed herself.

"What? Wait, *what?*"

Gus flipped the intercom back on. "That wife of yours is somethin' else. Everybody hold on tight!" The two small mounts streaked through the rust-colored sky toward each other, each with their own trail of chasing copperheads.

The mule grew larger and larger in *Tilly's* saddleroom canopy.

"Gus?" Moe asked. He gripped the hatch frame so tightly he left dents in the metal.

"Not yet ..." she said.

"Gus ..."

The mule grew larger still as they raced toward each other.

"Wait for it ..."

"*Gus!*" Moe shouted when the mounts were so close they could see both Bernadette and Hector's wide-eyed expressions.

"*Now!*" Gus yelled. She yanked hard on the reins and squeezed her spurs with all her might. *Tilly* responded with a hard left turn that nearly threw Gus from the saddle. The mule jerked into a sharp turn at the same instant.

The twin columns of pursuing cavalry had little chance of dodging each other. The collisions sent shockwaves ripping through the clouds.

Tilly, followed closely by the mule, disappeared into the lower atmosphere in the chaos.

"Papi!" Hector yelled and ran into his father's arms as soon as *Tilly* and the mule had been hitched at the abandoned Deiopean mining village.

"What happened?" Gus asked.

"It was a setup," Bernadette said as she embraced her husband. "They hit us right after Ray's signal that the inspection team had arrived in town. Someone leaked our plan to the Lecontes. There's no other explanation."

"Are you okay?" Oscar asked. He held his wife out at arm's length and looked her over for injuries. "How did you get away?"

Bernadette beamed at Hector. "I don't think we can be cross with Hector for crawling through the anti-grav foundation anymore. And we may owe Moe a pay raise. He's turned our son into quite the little *vaquero.*"

"Oh, has he now?" Oscar said. He tussled his son's hair and gave his farmhand a wry smile. Moe blushed a deep scarlet, but smiled, nonetheless.

"Maybe you better start at the beginning," Gus said. "But talk quickly. It won't take them long to figure out where we've gone."

"They came only moments after we received Ray's message," Bernadette began.

Gus winced. Thanks to their plan, the small home had been crowded with the families of those in town readying the distraction: the young, the old, and those who cared for them.

"Hector and I were in the barn, pouring every last drop of rubidium into the mule's fuel cell when they hit the house. By the time we heard the screaming, it was too late to save anyone. If we'd been there, maybe ..." She fell into Oscar's arms. "Maybe I could have done more."

Gus had her doubts, and she could see Oscar did, too.

"You got our son out. That's all that matters," he said, squeezing her tight.

"But how?" Gus asked. "They would have swept the whole place for stragglers."

Bernadette nodded and continued. "I didn't know what to do. I was beginning to panic when Richard stumbled into the barn. His"—she grimaced and let out a sob—"his frock was shiny and slick from half a dozen wounds. He said someone had betrayed us and the copperheads were coming. So, I did the only thing I could think of—I told Hector to hide in the ducts.

"We'd barely gotten him through the barn's duct grate when the soldiers reached us." She buried her face in Oscar's chest. "Even hurting as he was, Richard put himself between us and those butchers." Her voice was muffled but heavy. "He gave Hector the time he needed to get away. And they killed him in cold blood for his bravery."

They shot him down as he protected the innocent. Santa Barbara would have been proud.

Gus's vision swam. Richard was a good man. One of the last this far out on the Arm. Blood like his always seemed to be the first spilled. She promised herself it wouldn't be the last.

"They dragged me to a prisoner-wagon with everyone they'd grabbed at the house, and from there, they took us back to town," Bernadette said. "And used us to stop the fighting."

"Fighting?" Gus said. "There wasn't supposed to *be* any fighting!"

"Aren't you listening? They knew our plan! Every detail. The bastards had killed Jacob in the market. I think they deliberately brought us by his body as a warning. We could hear the fighting from the market. They marched us straight to it. Ray called a cease fire as soon as he saw us. The copperheads rounded everyone up and brought us all back to the square where they could keep an eye on us while the inspection team went about their business."

"How did you get out?" Moe asked. "Where's the marshal? We haven't heard from him."

Again, Bernadette beamed at her son. "Maybe you should tell this part, Hector."

With his father's hands on his shoulders, Hector's gaze dropped to his feet. Gus knelt down to his level. "You did it, didn't you?" she asked and gave the boy a slight smile.

Hector's eyes met hers and bit his lip.

"You used your brain," she said and gave his forehead a gentle tap. "You outsmarted 'em, didn't you? How'd you do it?"

Slowly, a smile crept onto Hector's face. "I did what *Mamá* said. I hid until all the bad guys were gone," he said. His head dropped again. "Then I followed them in the mule."

Oscar gave Moe an approving glance. "So much for waiting until he was a little older to teach him how to ride."

Moe shrugged and returned the grin. "Sorry, Boss." Oscar laughed and clapped his farmhand on the back.

"How'd you keep from being seen?" Gus asked.

"I stayed in the low clouds. And when they hitched up at the stables, I went into the engineering corral."

Gus laughed. "Smart move, kid. No one saw you?"

"There wasn't anyone around to see me! Everybody was sitting on the ground in the middle of town. *Mamá* and Marshal Gascon were near the Marshal's Office, but one of the soldiers was watching them. So, I threw a rock at him and got him to chase me into the cemetery. Then I—" he stopped and looked at his mother. She nodded for him to go on. "I pushed one of the shelves over on him. It spilled dust everywhere! Then I ran back to the square to find *Mamá*."

Oscar smiled proudly at his son. "You did good, Hector."

"Where's Ray?" Gus asked.

Bernadette's smile faltered. "He—" She bit her lip. "He saved us. If it weren't for him, we never would have gotten away. Oh, Oscar. He stood in front of the beams. I think he's dead." She buried her face in her hands and let out a body-rattling sob. "We didn't see Hector, not at first. We saw the soldier nearest us yell and run down the alley. The next thing we knew there was a crash from behind the chapel, and Hector came running out from where the man had gone.

"Ray—he stood up and told me to run. Then he just turned around and spread his arms wide. He made himself as big as he could to shield us. He saved our lives!" Another round of sobs wracked her body. Oscar held her tight.

Gus went cold. "Are you sure he's dead? Did you see him fall?"

Bernadette wiped tears from her eyes. "We ran. I heard them fire. There was so much shooting, he couldn't have survived."

Gus gazed out into the growing storm. The wind howled and dragged a horizon overflowing with churning, inky black clouds ever closer. Flashes of cobalt lightning crackled through the air like the bony fingers of Death.

Deafening thunder rolled across the great hydrogen flats and rattled *Tilly's* hide to the rivets. They would feel the storm's full force in a matter of hours.

Not only was Richard dead, but probably Ray was, too. And their blood was on her hands. On Laszlo's hands. Good folk. Good folk who deserved more. Her fingers balled into trembling fists. She'd pay that debt by making Laszlo pay his.

"Are you sure about this?" Oscar asked. He and Gus stood at the Deiopean stables as Moe and Aurora loaded supplies onto the mule.

"No," Gus admitted.

"Me, Moe, Aurora—we could go with you."

"Oscar, your family needs you now," Gus said and put her pink-dusted hand on the rancher's shoulder. "You need to make sure they get to safety. And *then* I expect you to come back and save my sorry ass." She smiled. Oscar didn't.

Moe and Aurora finished their task, and the rob joined his boss's protest. "You don't stand a chance alone. You don't need to try to be a hero."

Gus laughed. "I'm no hero. You guys are the heroes here. Holding on to what's right in the face of all this. All I'm doing is giving you the shot to finish the fight you started. I'll make sure you get your chance to make the sprint. *Take it.*"

Oscar peered into Gus's eyes. After a moment, he sighed and nodded. "I think you'll need this more than me now." He pressed her lucky coin into her hand. "Hold on for as long as you can. We'll be back with the whole damn UCET army." Oscar nodded again and boarded the mule without another word.

As the sky grew thick and dark, Aurora took Gus's hand with two of their own in a clumsy imitation of the two-handed handshake the hunter had shared with Moe the day Gus met them both. "Thank you," the translator chirped as the Deiopean's eyes flashed. The small, spider-like hunter then followed Oscar.

Finally, only Moe remained.

"You don't have to do this. Not alone," he said.

"Did you know Ray saved me from Junior and his goons the first night I was in town?" Gus asked. "After you left me at Hotel Irma?"

Moe nodded. "Word gets around."

"He didn't know who I was, but he stuck his neck out for me. Probably saved my life. I owe him."

"I understand. Maybe more than most," Moe said. "But that doesn't mean you've got to do it alone."

"I won't be alone," she said and managed a small smile. *"Tilly's* been my partner a lot longer than you all. She's always watched my back just fine."

Moe snorted. "Have it your way. We'll be back as soon as we can." Gus shook his long, elegant hand, and then he was gone, too. She stepped onto *Tilly's* lift and boarded her own pony.

Gus slid into the saddle, flipped on the comms, and looked to the Vega family through the canopies. "With their weapons systems up and running this isn't going to be easy. Stick to the plan. I'll give you an opportunity to sprint. Watch for it. You'll only get one."

Bernadette picked up the comms handset in the mule. "We will."

"No matter what happens, take your chance and go. No matter what. Right?"

Oscar and Bernadette exchanged words. Oscar took one more unhappy glance back at Gus and *Tilly,* and stormed out of the mule's saddleroom. The comms crackled with Bernadette's voice. "Right."

The two women held each other's gaze for a moment longer. Thunder clapped, loud enough to rattle *Tilly's* canopy. The storm had arrived.

The plan was simple: Gus was going to go pick a fight with *Shenandoah.*

With the copperheads' attention focused on her, the Vegas could break atmo and sprint away to Holliday. They didn't have Brother Richard's voice to lend them credence anymore, so Aurora's would have to do. Gus just had to be a big enough pain in the ass to keep the copperheads' attention.

No problem.

Both mounts rose silently into the dark and gusting sky. For a moment, they hung there and faced one another for a final time. Then, they turned and slid into the clouds in opposite directions.

Rain of some variety began to fall. Before long, it pelted *Tilly's* canopy in sheets with every meteoric raindrop the size of a dinner plate. Gus had never ridden through a storm like this before; between the immeasurable mass that struck *Tilly's* back each second and the gale battering her body, every moment threatened to knock the pony from the sky. But Gus pushed *Tilly* through it all the same, fighting the rain, the wind, and her own growing sense of doom.

As anxiety began to allow doubt to worm its way into her mind, *Tilly* crashed through a wall of rain and into a break in the clouds. Las Ráfagas and *Shenandoah* loomed in the dark of the storm, illuminated by sporadic flashes of hellfire lightning. As if waiting for her arrival, the belly of the battle-train slid open, and a fresh swarm of cavalry mounts flowed from it in a pale imitation of the tempest.

Too late for doubt. She patted *Tilly's* console.

Ride like hell, girl.

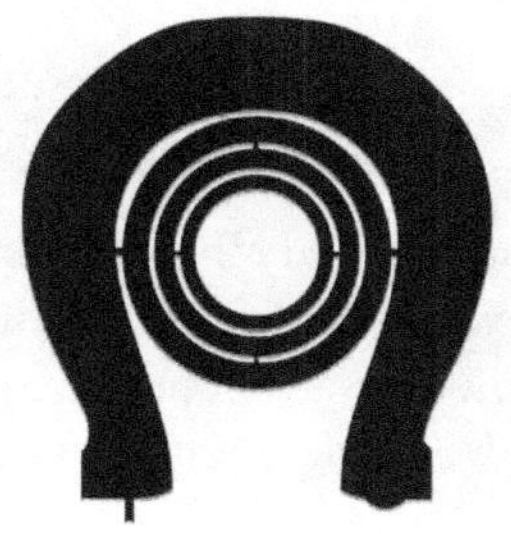

SADDLE IN THE WIND

*T*illy flipped and twirled, dipped and climbed, rolled and tumbled. At times she looked like a horseshoe tossed toward a peg in a friendly game. But this was no game, and Gus's opponents were anything but friendly. The air around *Tilly* blazed with laser fire as Gus pushed the small steed beyond her limit. The atmo-thrusters screamed in defiance with every maneuver, every midair dodge.

Somewhere in the back of her mind, it occurred to Gus that she was likely undoing all the hard work Emmitt put into fixing the thrusters after her fiery arrival on Aeolus. She threw *Tilly* into a hard barrel roll, deftly dodging another volley of fire from the pursuing cavalry. Gus evaded the mounts with skill, but *Shenandoah* had yet to focus its main artillery battery on her.

"Come on, you bastards. I'm right here. *Shoot!*" She turned *Tilly* around and headed straight for the pulse-rail battle-train. If Gus could get those guns to fire, all their attention would be on her, and the Vegas would have their opportunity.

But the cavalry mounts caused her to break away from her collision course before she could force *Shenandoah* to defend herself. "Dammit!" Gus pulled *Tilly* away and into another dogfight with the copperheads. *Why won't they fire?*

Gus pressed the transmitter in her ear. "Ray, if you can hear me, I'm sorry. I'm sorry I dragged you out from behind your rutting desk and away from your coffee machine. I'm sorry I pushed you into this mess. I—"

A voice—*not* Ray's—interrupted her. "How heartwarming. Asking for forgiveness right at the end. It's all very romantic. Even if it is pointless."

Laszlo.

"Where's Ray?" Gus screamed. She pulled *Tilly* into a steep climb through the wind and rain.

"Oh, don't worry about our dear Marshal Gascon. He's been handled," Laszlo said. "Why don't you hitch up and come see for yourself?"

Gus let *Tilly's* rifle turret answer for her. She swooped back down and fired ineffectually into *Shenandoah's* defense shields. Still, the cruiser refused to return fire.

"What do you think you're going to accomplish?" Laszlo shouted over the transmitter. "It's over! There's already a garrison in town. Your little rebellion has been effectively silenced. But you don't have to share the fate of the rabble you've roused. Allow me to make you one last offer."

The fire from the cavalry ceased, as if on cue.

"Stand down, Gus. That's all I'm asking. Stand down and give me Oscar's coordinates. That's it. You can keep all the gold you took from *Shenandoah's* vault. Consider it—and the fuel cell fill-up I'll see that you get—payment in full for all your services. Think about it."

Gus's mind cast back through the engine room, around the bend into *Tilly's* cargo hold, where bar after bar of the gleaming gold waited patiently. She couldn't be sure how much they had managed to get away with, but it was more than Moe's bounty. More even than what Laszlo offered her to work for him.

It represented everything she had come to Las Ráfagas seeking: freedom, and enough of it to last her a good long time. She only had to do what she'd always done: mind her own damn business. She'd done it before. Pulled up stakes and drifted on. The Arm was a big place. It made it easy to get away from the things you ran from. And with this load of gold, she could get damn rutting far from this cursed place. Besides, she couldn't get tied down. That would kill her as sure as *Shenandoah's* cannon.

She'd told Hector that.

Hector. Snot-nosed, sheltered, little Hector.

Hector, who deserved none of the hell Laszlo Leconte had rained down on him and his family.

Tunk.

"Oh, I'm takin' your gold, Leconte. And before this is done, I'll have your life, too." Gus ripped the transmitter from her ear, shut it off, and jammed it deep into a pocket. The cavalry opened fire again and forced Gus to dodge away into the lower, denser atmosphere.

Tilly rocked under the barrage. Something in the engine room gave way. Sparks flew. Gimbal lubricant erupted from a ruptured hose and doused the engine room in thick, orange sludge. Still, Gus pushed *Tilly,* dodging and weaving, through the onslaught of rain and fire.

Finally, *Tilly's* systems registered an immense energy bloom from *Shenandoah.* At last: the main cannon. *Now or never.* Gus yanked on the reins and pulled *Tilly* up through the rain to give the copperhead bastards a tempting target.

Gus closed her eyes and waited.

But when the cannon fired, the great, green beam cut a swath through the storm far off *Tilly's* left shoulder, on a steep trajectory. Gus watched in horror as it streaked up into the sky.

"Oscar, break off!" she screamed into the comms. *"They've got your location!* Do you read me? Moe? *Bernadette!"* But her warning came far too late to beat the beam.

They were gone.

In the quiet of the saddleroom, Gus's blood ran cold and turned her heart to stone in her chest. Slowly, her mind followed, icing over with glacial force, grinding emotion and rational thought to dust. Her eyes, frozen on the path of the beam, thawed first and turned back toward *Shenandoah* and the outpost beyond. The ice in her veins erupted into a burning lava flow beneath her skin. Her eyes burned, her muscles coiled, and, at first, she didn't recognize the roar that rang in her ears as her own raging throat.

In an instant, Gus turned *Tilly* to face *Shenandoah* and charged to attack head-on. *Tilly's* rifle turret and atmo-thrusters blazed in the dark; the former glowed white-hot under the stress of repeated fire, the latter screaming to keep the pony aloft in the violent storm. The cavalry mounts regrouped and formed a defensive line between her and the cruiser. *Tilly* barreled through them like tenpins.

Alarms blared as critical systems failed all over the pony. Gus ignored them. *It doesn't matter.* Nothing stood between *Tilly* and *Shenandoah's* command level. As *Tilly's* thrusters failed, Gus confirmed the collision course.

Now, this! *This was how I'd always hoped to go out: riding Tilly into a hail of fire. If I'm going out, they're coming with me. Too bad Laszlo and his bastard sons are in town.*

Another volley from *Shenandoah's* cannons lit up the stormy sky brighter than any flash of lightning. Gus tried to dodge, but *Tilly's* burned-out thrusters couldn't force the falling pony far enough out of the way. The beam skimmed off *Tilly's* belly and forced the mount off course. She tumbled harmlessly away from *Shenandoah* like a coin in a tornado.

With fresh alarms blaring in her ears, Gus pulled hard against the yoke's reins and fought to regain control of her plummeting companion. The deafening roar suddenly stopped, and for a horrifying moment, Gus thought the power had failed. But the lights were still on, and the console display lit with a single, blinking, red message:

ESCAPE POD 2: READY FOR LAUNCH.

"No!" Gus roared and slammed her fist down on the screen. "You're not finished yet! *Come on!*" She yanked back on the reins with all her might, but *Tilly* didn't respond. A moment later, the lights went out and threw Gus into tumbling darkness. The saddleroom lights flashed. Then the engine room, the cargo hold, and the saddleroom again.

Tilly was leading her to the remaining pod.

"No, goddamn it!" she yelled. *Tilly* snorted through the vents and Gus's spurs were ejected from the rudder control ports. As *Tilly* tumbled past *Shenandoah* and Las Ráfagas into the deeper atmosphere, Gus flew from the saddle and back into the engine room. *Tilly* slammed the saddleroom hatch closed behind her. When she beat her fists against the door, every alarm at *Tilly's* disposal erupted at once, and drowned out her ability to think.

Covered in coolant and foul-smelling orange sludge, with klaxons ringing in her ears and showers of sparks dazzling her tear-filled eyes, Gus finally scrambled for the pod. She stopped at the entrance to *Tilly's* meager cargo hold, once home to a small beehive and a little contraband, now laden with more riches than she had ever dared imagine. The lights flickered overhead, threatening to go out, likely for good this time.

Did she have time to salvage something? Anything? Probably not, but that never stopped her before. She had to try.

A moment later, she reemerged from the cargo hold and raced the final steps to the pod. She threw herself into the can-shaped escape pod and *Tilly* closed the hatch behind her. With Gus safe inside the pod, the alarms stopped and were replaced by a low whicker through the vents.

Gus put her hand against the glass and looked out at what had been both her home and her friend—her oldest and most faithful companion. "I love you, too," she said, and the tears finally overflowed.

The pod launched into the storm, and Gus kept her hand on the glass until the churning dark swallowed *Tilly* whole.

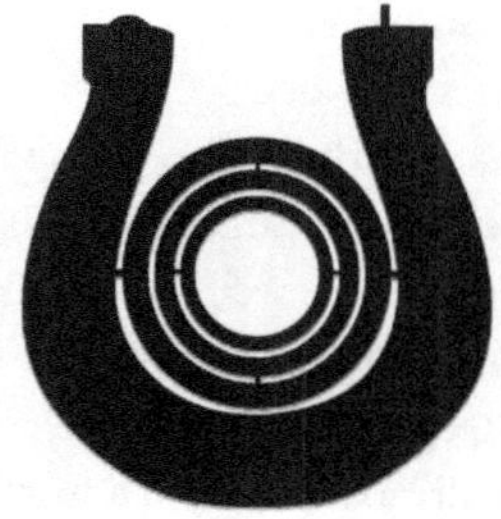

THE BOSS OF BOOMTOWN

The pod hatch hissed and popped open with a pressurized *whoosh!* Before Gus had time to get her bearings, hands snaked in through the open door and dragged her out.

Almost as soon as *Tilly* jettisoned the pod, she'd been picked up by the circling cavalry mounts and carried back to town through the raging storm. There, waiting for her with their weapons drawn, stood Aaron, Junior, and Tuco. Aaron grinned from ear to ear as he pulled her out by the arm. Junior's face, as usual, stayed as flat and expressionless as stone.

Tuco, on the other hand, scowled like a rat caught in a trap. "I don't know what's gotten into you, *hermana,* and I don't care. You've caused me a lot of trouble on this trip, you know? So, I'll just take this," he said and pulled Delilah from Gus's holster, "and we can call it even, *sí?*"

"You better kill me now, Tuco," Gus growled. "'Cause if I get free, I'm coming for you first, *hermano.*"

Aaron laughed. "Better watch out, Tuco." He rubbed his bicep where the cloned replacement had been attached. "This kitty bites."

They led Gus at gunpoint through the farmers market and past Jacob Wagner's prone body, right where Bernadette said it was. Finally, they shoved her down on the dusty ground of Las Ráfagas's town square. New hands, these more friendly than the last, helped her to her feet and dusted her off: Walter, his melted face grim. Gus scanned her surroundings and found more people than she had seen in any one place since arriving at Las

Ráfagas. *It's got to be everyone left.* Everyone, both those a part of her plan and not, held hostage in the square. The only folks missing were the miners.

"Where's Gretchen?" Gus asked.

"Don't know." Walter's crowded shoulders trembled. "Once the inspection team came back up, they locked down the mining levels and brought us all here. The storm is nearly here, Gus. Can you feel it?"

Locked down? That didn't bode well. Something about *divide and conquer* fluttered across Gus's mind. She glanced at the dome above and the cyclonic storm pounding against it. It looked to her like the storm had already arrived. And had already extracted a heavy toll from her. But first things first.

"Ray?" she asked. "Is he—"

"Jonesin' for a good cup o' joe? Yer damn right I am! Ruttin' copperheads won't even let me get a mug from my own damn office," the marshal spoke up and stepped through the crowd.

"Ray!" she shouted and grabbed him in a bear hug that surprised them both. "Bernadette said you'd been shot. She thought you were dead!"

"Near enough, girl." he said, releasing her with a grimace. "Are you alright?" The dressing looked clean and professional—Daniel's work. But it was soaked through and needed changing.

"Ayuh, I'll live," he said. "Or at least, it won't be the shoulder that kills me. Where's your little native friend? Or Oscar and Bernadette?" he asked. "Moe?"

Gus looked away, shaking her head.

Ray's face fell then hardened. "You did everything you could, and I thank you for that," he said and hung his head.

"What happened?" Gus asked. "Bernadette thought someone double-crossed us."

Ray scowled. He glared at the far side of the town square where the Administration Tower loomed. Gus followed his gaze to a small, hastily built platform in front of the building's lifts. Three figures stood upon the crude dais: Laszlo Leconte, a young woman with high cheekbones and long blonde hair, and John Stonewall.

"He rolled on us. Bastard's been running back to Laszlo with every morsel of information like the rat he is," Ray said. "They knew everything before the copperheads set a single boot in town. We never stood a chance."

"But why?" Gus knew the answer before the question came out of her mouth. *Stonewall's daughter has cancer.* The high-tech medical equipment

Laszlo kept in the Administration Tower could probably save her. It would have been an easy deal for Laszlo to make and impossible for Stonewall to pass up. Even through her rage, Gus couldn't help but pity the man. But pity alone wouldn't absolve him of offering up every life in town in exchange for his and his daughter's. Every life lost today was on his hands, and Gus intended to make sure he paid for them—especially those of Brother Richard, Moe, Oscar, Bernadette, and Hector. *One way or another.*

Her hand dropped to the holster on her hip. Finding it empty, she gritted her teeth and resolved to extract that payback the old-fashioned way. With balled fists trembling at her sides, she got one step before Ray caught her by the arm.

"I understand how ya feel," he said into her ear. "I'd like to do it myself, but we got bigger problems." The marshal pointed back toward the platform.

Gus pulled her attention from the traitor to the tall, aggressively beautiful woman on Laszlo's arm. At first, based on the way Laszlo gazed at her, Gus thought she was his latest conquest. But when she turned to face the crowd, Gus recognized her from the bust in Laszlo's quarters. His *daughter*, Mackenzie Leconte. The pair were joined by Mackenzie's brothers, and the family watched as a group of copperhead soldiers dragged heavy equipment onto the platform and began constructing a complicated piece of machinery.

Tuco shuffled nervously in the wings with Laszlo's security-robs. Fire burned in Gus's belly at the sight of Delilah jammed carelessly into the front of his pants.

An older man in Confederate grays stepped onto the platform and spoke to Laszlo. He wore a colonel's eagle on his collar. Probably the commander of *Shenandoah.*

Interesting. Commanders rarely leave their vessels outside CCO controlled space.

The colonel finished with Laszlo and moved back to watch the crowd. Laszlo stepped forward and spread his arms wide in a gesture of goodwill.

"My friends! May I have your attention, please?" His voice boomed, echoing across the square. "That's better," he said with a smile as the chatter ceased. "My! We've had quite a bit of excitement around here, haven't we?" He chuckled. "I must say, I'm disappointed that some of you would choose this moment to act against not only me, but your own future!"

Laszlo paced the edge of the platform. His smile faded and he regarded Las Ráfagas's townsfolk with disappointment. Behind him, the soldiers continued their construction. Gus squinted at it between bodies. She couldn't make out what they were building, but it was powerful. She'd spotted a battery pack the size of a large suitcase—enough juice to run a town like Las Ráfagas for a week.

"I am this close"—Laszlo held his fingers up, an inch apart—"from turning this backwater, forgotten town into one of the most important facilities in the Confederate Colonies of Orion! Las Ráfagas is going to be more successful than ever!" he shouted. "It seems, however, that there are some among you who don't wish to profit from this new paradigm. But could you leave well enough alone for the good of your neighbors? No! You had to bite the hand that feeds you, clothes you, and gives you your very reason for living! For what would you be without me? Where would you have drifted to, like so many tumbleweeds? Lost. The lot of you would have been lost years ago. And now, thanks to your actions, I have to do something unpleasant."

While Laszlo spoke, Gus pushed her way through the crowd as close to the platform as she dared. As she approached, one of the gray-clad soldiers handed the colonel something long and narrow. He turned it over in his hands to examine it, and Gus recognized it at once—a Deiopean rifle, like Aurora's Hammer.

The working soldiers finished their task and stepped back from the platform revealing a ZM390 Rotary Laser Cannon, a Gatling-style weapon designed for clearing battlefields of enemy infantry. The crowd gasped; Gus's heart skipped a beat.

"Friends! Friends!" Laszlo shouted over the growing clatter of frightened voices. "Those of you who have been loyal have nothing to fear!" The colonel leaned over and spoke into Laszlo's ear. "What? *All* of them? That wasn't part of the deal," Laszlo said and pulled away from the officer in apparent disgust. The colonel handed Laszlo a tablet. Laszlo glared at him but took it. His eyes darted back and forth across the screen and a grin spread across his sun-kissed face. "I'm sorry, it seems I may have misspoken. It appears, for a very generous additional payment, the Confederate government would prefer an *empty* outpost to move into."

There it is. The reason the mining levels were locked down. And why *Shenandoah* had so many brand-new mining-robs in her hold.

Panic erupted. Several townsfolk tried to break out from the square and were shot for their trouble. Gus saw the man she and the Leconte brothers had played razz with the night she arrived—Willough-by—fall. He died before the dust settled around his body. A mother made a break for the alley between Ray's office and the med-lab. She died shielding her children. Russo, the mountain of a man that ran Hotel Irma, hit a copperhead so hard the visor on his helmet shattered.

Stonewall turned a sickly shade of green but seemed rooted to his spot on the platform. With his shoulders hunched up around his ears and his hands covering his head, he flinched with every copperhead shot fired.

In the mass of frenzied bodies, Ray was knocked to his knees. Gus stood over him and tried to protect him from the stampede.

The chaos didn't last. A few smoking bodies later and the copperheads had the terrified crowd back under control. Gus wondered what it would take to provoke them into actually fighting for their lives. *I hope they have it in them.*

"No matter what happens, you stick close to me," she mumbled to Ray as she pulled him to his feet. "Got it?"

He nodded and opened his mouth, but his eyes went wide, and his jaw hung open instead. Gus turned back to the dais as five figures were led up onto it for the crowd to see. Their hands were bound behind their backs, and each had a black bag over their head. There was no mistaking Moe's lanky mechanical limbs, and Aurora's short, arachnid body. One by one, Laszlo ripped their hoods off with a flourish.

The entire Vega family. Alive.

Gus's heart soared, but the dread on Hector's face sent fresh fire coursing through her veins.

"We're going to begin with the ringleaders of all this trouble," Laszlo shouted over the stunned crowd. "This family, their murderous rob, and their little spider friend here, have caused more than enough problems for one lifetime." He stepped back and ushered his grown children off the platform. "Colonel, at your leisure."

"Remember. Stick close to me," Gus repeated. She reached beneath her poncho and closed her hand on the one thing she managed to save from *Tilly's* cargo hold.

The colonel nodded, and a soldier stepped up to the ZM390. The crowd gasped again as Oscar did his best to shield his family.

"Everybody, down!" Gus bellowed. She tossed her poncho back over her shoulder and cocked her arm back. Her fingers oozed with a fist-sized slab of honeycomb, crawling with buzzing bees. The townsfolk parted like soil before the plow, and Gus hurled the hunk of hive at the Gatling gun with all her might.

The honeycomb struck the copperhead square in the face and broke open. It showered the unwitting soldier with a rain of furious worker bees and one very confused queen. The effect was immediate, and exactly what Gus hoped for. The swarm attacked the hapless soldier and then expanded outward, hunting for more threats to the hive. The buzzing chaos finally pushed the townsfolk's panic beyond even the fear of the soldiers' guns.

Anarchy consumed the town square and, in the confusion, everyone ran. Some were shot and died where they fell. Many more made it out to the relative safety of Las Ráfagas's abandoned homes and businesses. Gus caught a glimpse of the back of Stonewall's dirty coveralls as the turncoat hightailed it out of the square. She let him go. Gus had one goal in mind: getting the Vegas to safety.

She threw herself at the bee-stung soldier manning the ZM390. Tackling him to the ground, she delivered a haymaker across his jaw. She relieved him of his pistol and tossed it to Ray. "Cover me!"

The Vegas huddled together, trying to make themselves as small as possible amidst the yelling and shooting. Moe crouched between the family and the Gatling gun, hugging the trio of doppels and shielding them. The farmhand's simulated eyes were squeezed shut against the pandemonium raging around them.

Aurora, on the other hand, seemed to be expecting it. At the same moment Gus tackled the Confederate officer, the Deiopean leapt from the platform onto the colonel's shoulders. They attacked with their powerful mandibles and a flurry of fists. By the time Gus tossed Ray the officer's pistol, Aurora had already used the colonel's sidearm to blast their own cuffs off. With The Hammer retrieved from the dead copperhead, Aurora barely hesitated before throwing the officer's sidearm to Gus.

"Moe, we've got to go," Gus said and put a hand on the rob's shoulder.

Moe cautiously opened one eye and leapt to his feet. *"Gus!"*

"How—?" Oscar asked.

"I could ask you the same question. But there's no time for that now," Gus said. "Let's get you out of here. Then you can explain to me how you're alive." Gus smiled despite the disarray around them. "Follow Aurora. I'm right behind you."

Aurora and Ray led the Vegas off the platform and through the alley between the med-lab and the Administration Tower. As laser fire singed the air around her, Gus ran to follow—and fell flat on her face.

"Rutting tunk! Daniel?" Bleeding badly from a wound she couldn't see, Daniel Park grabbed her foot as she stepped off the platform.

"He-lp," he gurgled. He spat out more blood than words.

"I've got you. Come on," she said and pulled his arm over her shoulder. She got Daniel to his feet and dragged him away from the platform. They made it a few steps before a familiar pink beam exploded from Daniel's chest and left a bleeding crater where his rib cage had been.

She dropped the lifeless body and spun. Tuco stood not twenty paces away with Delilah raised. A cloud of freezing exhaust billowed from the ancient gun and engulfed the outlaw's hand. He yelped and dropped Delilah.

"Bastard!" Gus shouted. She shot twice with the copperhead sidearm, but Tuco grabbed Delilah and scurried to cover unscathed.

"Was that your medic?" he shouted. "Sorry about that. Did you know this *pedazo de mierda* pulls to the left?"

"Why don't you stick your head out and we can talk about giving it back?" she yelled.

He surprised her by leaping from cover to fire at her head on. "You want it back? Here it is, *puta loca!*" he screamed and fired wildly, enduring the repeated blasts of Delilah's exhaust. One of Tuco's errant shots struck the ZM390's battery-pack, a few feet from where Gus crouched. The battery sizzled, crackled, and before Gus could move, exploded.

The blast sent both Gus and Tuco flying.

By the time Gus regained her footing, Tuco—and Delilah with him—had fled into the fray.

Gus raced headlong around the base of the Administration Tower and crashed directly into Walter coming from the opposite direction. The genie bled from a hundred small cuts and held three copperhead rifles among his many hands.

"Gus!" he said and helped her to her feet. "The storm has come!" His melted face lit up with a grin. "And with it, the rains of change!"

"Did you see Moe and Oscar come through here?"

"Sure!" he said cheerfully. He pointed back in the direction he had come from. "I told them to meet me in Willoughby's Gunsmithy and Emporium. There's a back way in through Cirrus House."

"Where are you going?"

"To get my wife," Walter said simply, and set off for the mining level lift with his rifles at the ready.

Gus ran for the gunsmithy.

Like the night she first arrived in town, Gus found Jacob Wagner's hyper-surrey parked out front of Cirrus House, but the hover-cart had seen better days. At some point, it had been overturned and set on fire. It now sat in a pile of its own burning debris, effectively blocking Gus from reaching Willoughby's shop.

There's a back way in through Cirrus House.

Gus burst through the batwing doors with the colonel's sidearm held high, but the usually bustling casino floor was dark and quiet. Dark shapes shifted in the gloom. Gus jerked the barrel of her commandeered pistol left, then right, searching for a target. The crystal chandeliers clinked quietly in a draft. Outside, gunfire and lightning flashed, and the flashes danced across the room. Gus let out a sharp sigh. *Jumpin' at shadows now.*

But she whirled again when a groan, followed by a sharp *shush*, resonated from behind the bar. Aurora's many-eyed head popped up and flashed a series of colors Gus had come to recognize as her own name.

"What is it?" Oscar asked before his own face appeared over the bar. *"Gus!* Ray's hurt bad! Get over here!"

Ray slouched on the floor behind the bar, his face pale and his tan duster dark with blood. Bernadette had removed the bandage from Ray's shoulder and pressed bar rags into the wound. Hector cowered in the corner with his arms wrapped around his knees. Tears ran down his cheeks as he watched his parents try to keep Ray alive.

Gus leapt over the bar and took over for Bernadette. *"Christ's blood*, Ray."

"Whatsamatter?" he slurred. "Dontcha think red looks good on me?"

"Where's Moe?"

"Walter said there's a back way into Willoughby's through the counting room," Oscar said. The rancher's voice wavered. "Moe's checkin' it out."

"Aurora's first aid kit, where is it?" Gus asked.

Aurora's eyes flashed, but the translator was gone.

"The soldiers ..." Bernadette said. *Of course. The copperheads probably took everything.* "Where's Daniel? Did you see him out there?"

"Dead."

"He's—are you *sure?*" Oscar asked.

Gus nodded. "I'm sorry, Oscar. I know he was a friend. But Aurora's kit might be Ray's only hope now."

"Do you mean *this* kit?" a new voice called from the casino's doors.

Junior.

He stood between the razz tables, his suit rumpled and untucked with one jacket sleeve torn at the shoulder. A dark stain that could have been wine—but probably wasn't—splashed across his chest. His eyes were alight with the fire Gus had first seen the night she'd arrived.

Junior held his Colt Prism M2265 concentrator pistol in one hand, and in the other, Aurora's octagonal first aid kit.

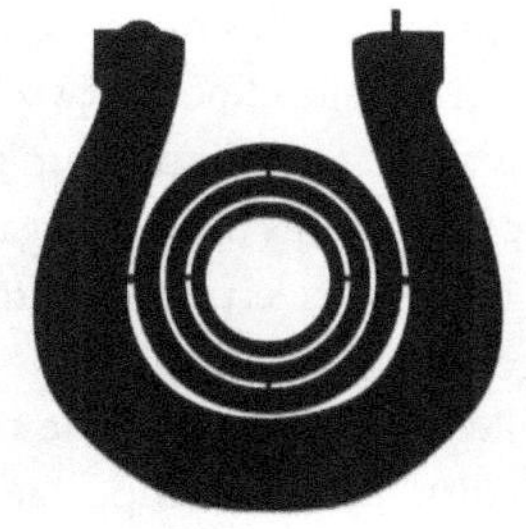

SAVAGE GUNS

"Well, isn't this peachy?" Junior said. His stony expression cracked into a smirk. "I knew I had to get to you first. We've got to finish what we started. And lo and behold, here you are, at the scene of the first offense."

"I guess I'm your huckleberry, then," Gus said. She stood up behind the bar and gestured for the others to stay where they were. She inched her way out to face Laszlo's eldest son.

"I've got a little wager for you," he said. "If you can out-draw me, you get this." He wagged the kit in the air. "You lose, and I kill all of your little friends."

"You planning on shutting off that little toy of yours?" she asked.

His teeth shone in the dim. "Maybe. Maybe it ran outta juice getting me here. Maybe it's busted." He tapped his burdle-scale belt buckle with the Colt's barrel. "Then again, maybe I saved it just for you."

"And if I refuse?"

"Then Uncle Ray will be the last of you to die." Junior's smile widened. "I don't blame you for being afraid." He slid his Colt Prism M2265 into his shoulder holster and held his trigger finger up. "This little finger has killed more men than I can count. Women, too! And when you lose, it'll have been this little finger that has sent you and your little friends here straight to hell."

Gus glanced down at her stolen handgun. A standard issue Confederate repeating laser pistol. It wasn't Delilah, but it was a reliable piece of hardware, nonetheless. It might put a dent in his shield if she got lucky. *It'll have to do. Just gotta hit 'im fast and hard.*

She dropped the gun into Delilah's oversized holster and followed Junior to an empty area of the casino floor between the tables. Junior put the kit down on a razz table and the pair took up position ten paces apart. Junior smiled sadistically and laid his hand flat against his slim chest.

Near her hip, Gus's pink-dusted left hand twitched. "Say when."

Junior's eyes narrowed. His grin widened.

Silence, like a void, filled Cirrus House. The sounds of fighting in the streets outside were dull, distant, and unimportant.

Junior moved first. His hand dipped to the grip of the concentrator pistol nestled in his armpit.

Gus was faster.

Before Junior could pull the barrel of his pistol from the holster, Gus fired twice. For an instant, a pair of angry red beams filled the casino floor with an ephemeral glow.

But neither beam reached Junior's slender chest. They fractured into a thousand tributaries of light and flowed harmlessly around an invisible barrier like water raining on glass. His personal shield crackled as it bore the brunt of the energy.

Tunk. Full power with a reinforced field. Not getting through that.

Junior laughed and took his time drawing his own weapon. "I'm impressed," he said. His eyes were wide with something that resembled respect. "Most people get a little … *flustered* when they're forced to fight fast. They tend to fire wide in their rush to be first. Or lose their nerve altogether. Somehow, I knew you'd be different. I knew that just being fast wouldn't cut it this time."

Junior aimed and fired. This time, Cirrus House filled with the deep purple glow from his Colt Prism. Gus dove for her life. She knocked the high stakes razz table to the floor for cover and took a grazing shot to the shoulder as she scrambled to get behind it. The wound was deep, but the beam was clean, cauterizing the damage as it carved out a small chunk of poncho and flesh.

Junior laughed maniacally and began to advance, firing beam after beam into the steel-backed card table. *It's not gonna stand up under this kind of barrage for long.*

"*Gus!*" Hector shouted. He stood behind the tattered bar and pointed up. She followed his outstretched finger to the chandeliers that dangled over the gaming tables. The indigo of Junior's shots reflected a thousand times in each elegant crystal shard.

Of course. She flashed Hector a smile and waited for Junior to take another few steps.

"Whatcha hiding from there, *Gus?*" he shouted gleefully. "Ain't you my huckleberry?" He fired again and again until the table began to splinter under the salvo. When he finally paused to load a new coolant capsule into his gun, Gus took her opportunity.

In the momentary stillness, Gus stood and pointed her commandeered pistol at Junior.

"You void-drifters sure are dense, ain't ya?" he spat as he fumbled to reload the cartridge. "Don't worry, you just stand there a moment longer and I'll make sure you won't have any more troublesome thoughts running through that pretty little head of yours."

Gus smiled. She raised her pistol until it pointed at the ceiling and squeezed off a single crimson shot. The beam sliced through the chandelier's chain and cleanly separated it from the ceiling overhead.

The shower of metal and glass caught Junior by surprise as it fell to the floor with a deafening crash.

In the hush that followed, Gus barely had time to breathe before the crinkle of broken glass gave Junior away. With his pistol still in hand, he pulled his broken body from the wreckage.

Stubborn bastard won't die. But his shield hadn't protected him from the falling glass. So many shards of crystal were embedded in his bleeding body, he looked like a porcupine. A veil of scalp sheared from his skull hid half his face, but that murderous fire still raged in his eyes as he tried to drag his broken legs from the fallen chandelier.

Fury boiled up in Gus like adrenaline to the heart. Fury at this man, who threatened those weaker than him. Who tormented mothers and children. Who killed and laughed about it.

And who just won't rutting die.

Before Junior could free himself, Gus kicked him onto his back and pushed his shooting hand to the floor with her heel. "Was this the finger?" she shouted. "The finger you've killed so many men and women with? The finger you were going to send my friends to hell with?"

She fired once, point blank. A chilling scream gushed from Junior's throat. The beam cut Junior's pistol clean in two and completely vaporized his trigger finger to the first knuckle. She dropped the gun into Delilah's holster and lifted her boot. With a howl, Junior clutched his wounded hand to his chest.

Gus squatted down next to him. "You're a bully, Junior. I rutting *hate* bullies. That was for Emmitt and Gloria, you silver-spoon, cowardly son of a thief."

Junior coughed and tried to speak but groaned instead. He beckoned her closer. *Tunk, this ought to be good.* "What, Junior?" Gus asked. "What have you got to say for yourself? Spare me the famous last words." She leaned in closely. The smell of death wafted off of him.

He spat a wad of blood and phlegm to the casino floor and smiled. "My father will kill you." His eyes wandered away from Gus to the Vegas peering out from behind the bar. "Every ... last ... *one of you!*" He lunged and buried an arrowhead-sized shard of crystal deep into Gus's left shoulder.

Agony tore through the side of Gus's body. It reached deep into her chest and screamed into the fingers of her gun hand. On instinct, she kicked back and threw herself away from Junior. As she fell, Gus drew the Confederate pistol with fingers that buzzed and crackled with pain. She slammed into the casino floor and fired blind. And didn't stop until the coolant cap ran dry and the gun clicked uselessly.

Fresh silence fell over Cirrus House. Gus groaned and sat up. Her left arm, from shoulder to elbow, burned as if the shard had been a hot fireplace poker. *Crafty bastard hustled me.* But it would be the last hustle Laszlo Leconte Junior would ever pull. Her reaction may have been blind, but her aim was true. What remained of Junior would be hard to identify.

"Where's the kit?" Oscar asked, suddenly at Gus's side.

Gus groaned again. "It's over there," she said and waved at a razz table. "I'm fine, thanks."

"*No, amiga. Tu es loca,*" Oscar said with a smile. He grabbed the Deiopean first aid kit and tossed it to Bernadette.

At the same moment, Moe crashed through a door marked "Employees Only" with a scatter-beam held high and his electronic face drawn into a tight frown. "What was that? Is everybody okay?" he shouted and jerked his gun around the empty room.

"It's alright, Moe!" Bernadette yelled. "Put that thing down before you hurt yourself."

"How's Ray?" Gus asked and gingerly made her way back around the bar. A creeping numbness began to spread through her arm. *Not good.*

Aurora's eyes flashed and they applied a bandage from their kit to Ray's oozing shoulder.

"He's lost a lot of blood. The poultice needs time to work," Moe translated. Aurora glanced up from Ray and spotted the shard of crystal still jutting from Gus's shoulder. Their eyes flashed disapprovingly, and they hurried to Gus to see to her injury.

"Can we move him?" Gus asked. She grimaced as Aurora helped her pull the poncho over her head. "If Junior found us that fast, it won't be long before this place is crawling with bulls and copperheads."

Aurora's eyes flashed. "Aurora says, 'Yes, I think so, but we must make sure the bleeding remains under control,'" Moe said. "'Hold still.'" Aurora leaned in and examined the glass embedded in Gus's shoulder. Without warning, they grabbed it in one small hand and yanked. Gus gritted her teeth and for a moment her vision tunneled. The hunter-turned-medic slapped a fresh bandage down on the wound and pressed hard. Gus's head swam, but she held onto consciousness and waited for the drug's euphoric effects to kick in.

"Is the gunsmithy clear?" Oscar asked.

"Yeah," Moe nodded. "You wouldn't believe the security Willoughby's got on the front door. It's a good thing he liked his easy access to the rented flesh, or we'd never get in!"

"Alright," Gus said. The rush hit her all at once. "Moe, you lead the way with that blunderbuss. Hector, you follow Moe and stick close to him. Bernadette, do you know how to use one of these?" She slapped a fresh coolant cap into her pistol and handed it to the farmwife. Bernadette closed her eyes, sighed heavily, and took the pistol with a nod. "Good. 'Cause you and Aurora are gonna bring up the rear and cover our asses."

The drug from the Deiopean bandage coursed through Gus's veins. She felt invincible, even if her gun hand felt heavy and distant. Gus flexed it a few times, testing the strength in her fingers. *I have to make it work, no matter what.*

"You don't like the look of any face that comes through those doors, you put a beam through it," she said. "You got that? Alright, let's go. Oscar, help me get Ray up."

The back of a coat closet inside the casino's counting room hid the secret entrance to Willoughby's Gunsmithy & Emporium. "How'd you find the door?" Gus asked Moe as they passed Ray through the hidden opening.

"Walter pointed me in the right direction. He said Willoughby uses—uh, used—it almost every day."

"The town's dying around him, and instead of helping, what's he do?" Gus scoffed. "Builds an express route to the spoons and skin. All the better to drown out the cries for help, I suppose."

Moe snorted.

"What's funny?"

Although the rob smiled, there was pain in his eyes. "How's it different from what you did when we asked you for help?"

His words hit like a slap across the face. Gus's jaw dropped open to respond before her brain had a chance to catch up. But when no reasonable response came to mind, she shut it again and nodded instead.

They found the shop dark and quiet. With Ray resting as comfortably as possible on the floor behind the counter and Aurora inspecting the bandage, Bernadette gingerly handed the Confederate sidearm back to Gus. She dropped it back into her holster and examined the locks Willoughby had installed on the shop's door. They were both impressive and numerous. The security ranged from low-tech deadbolts to a cutting-edge shield system like the one in *Shenandoah's* brig.

"Alright, it looks like we're secure. But we can't stay here long," Gus said. "Oscar, get yourself and Bernadette something to shoot with. And Hector, too."

"Now, hold on a minute—" Oscar began.

"Just do it, Oscar," Bernadette cut off her husband without meeting his eye. "He'll be safer if he can protect himself." She saved her glare for Gus. "What danger are you planning on putting my family in now?"

Gus peered through the shuttered windows. The dusty road in front of the shop stood empty, lit only by the smoldering wreckage of Wagner's hyper-surrey and the occasional bolt of lightning from the storm that still raged outside the dome. Sporadic flashes of color from the town beyond told her the fighting she'd instigated with the bees still raged. Gus watched for something else—a pair of some*ones*, actually: Walter and his hulking wife, Gretchen.

Where are they?

"The plan's the same as before," Gus said without turning from the window. "We gotta get you and your family out of town and on your way to Holliday Station."

"*Madre de Dios.* You're joking, right?" Oscar said. He stood before an open display case with a bandolier of coolant capsules slung over one shoulder and a shortened repeater rifle with a pistol grip—a weapon Gus thought of as a Mare's Leg—in hand. He tossed his wife a small, five-shot derringer pistol wrapped up in a leather holster complete with its own coolant reloads. "We'll never make it past that cannon in the mule."

"We're not going for the mule," Gus said. She took a few coolant caps for her stolen sidearm. She missed Delilah. *If I find Tuco...* She allowed herself a short, brutal daydream.

"What, then?"

"Laszlo's pleasure-wagon." Willoughby's shop fell silent for the briefest of moments before erupting into a cacophony of voices, each questioning her sanity. Gus put her gun down on the clerk's counter, folded her arms across her chest, and waited for her companions to get it out of their systems.

"Oscar, you know wagons. Is there anything on Aeolus that's faster?" The twisting expression on Oscar's face said he *wanted* to say yes but knew he couldn't. "Look," she said, and gathered them around the clerk's counter. She pulled a blank receipt from behind the counter and sketched a rough diagram of the town on its back. "We're here," she said, and tapped one corner of her map. "The engineering corral is here." She tapped the opposite corner. "I overloaded the atmo-thrusters on Leconte's wagon. With Emmitt gone, and Laszlo's big deal going down, I'll wager it's still in the engineering corral waiting on repairs. It sounds like most of the fighting is happening over here"—she tapped a third corner—"in the residential quarter. That's probably by design, to keep the miners cut off. If we cut through the farmers market this way, we ought to stay out of the fray."

"You'll 'wager?' We 'ought to?'" Bernadette said. Her eyes darted around the rough map and locked with Gus's. "It's our lives you're gambling with."

For a moment, Gus floated in those emerald eyes. "I only gamble when I know I can win."

"Mr. Leconte's pleasure-wagon *is* there. I saw it when I came in with the mule," Hector said. "But it looks busted. The thruster panels are open, and all guts are all pulled out."

"I can fix it," Gus said.

"How can you be sure?" Bernadette asked. "You don't even know—"

"It's a simple overload. I can fix it."

"Won't it be guarded?" Moe asked. *Suddenly, he's ready for a fight, not looking for an excuse to avoid one.*

Gus glanced at the shuttered windows in time to catch a glimpse of colorful laser fire from a street or two over. "Right now?" she said. "I doubt it. And if it is, we'll take care of it."

"'Take care of it.' Now, I wonder what *that's* supposed to mean?" a new voice sneered.

Gus snatched her gun off the counter, whirled on her heels, and came face to face with Aaron Leconte. He stood inside the false wall doorway with his arm slung around Hector's neck. He held the boy close to his chest like they were old chums. The barrel of his Beaumont-Adams dug into the flesh at Hector's temple.

"Ah, ah, ah!" Aaron said. Hector whimpered as Aaron twisted the gun's barrel into his scalp.

"Let 'im go," Moe warned.

"Shut up, you filthy rob!"

"I'd listen to him if I were you, Aaron," Gus said and cocked her sidearm.

"Or what? My shield can take a hit from this distance," he said and tapped his belt buckle, "and you ain't got no chandelier to drop on *me* in here."

With speed Gus would not have thought possible from someone of her stature and dress, Bernadette drew her derringer, stepped forward, and pressed it against Aaron's own temple. "Think I'll miss from here?" she asked.

Aaron smiled, releasing Hector and raising his hands. Gus relieved him of his gun and compared it to the one she had taken off the copperhead. With a nod, she tucked the officer's pistol into the back of her belt and pointed Aaron's Beaumont-Adams back at him. Hector ran to his father's side, and Aaron, grinning savagely, turned to face Bernadette head on. He took a half-step toward her and pressed his forehead into her gun.

"Sagebrush," he said calmly.

"What?" Bernadette asked and glanced sideways at Gus. The sizzling energy shield barricading the door suddenly evaporated and Gus understood an instant too late Aaron had uttered its password.

"Look out!" she screamed.

BANG!

The door blew off its hinges and four company bulls charged into the small shop.

"Well, well, well!" Aaron shouted gleefully when the dust cleared. "Now we've got ourselves a real party!"

Aaron continued to press his forehead into Bernadette's derringer.

Gus, Oscar, Moe, and Aurora each held a bull at barrel's end.

Each of them was covered by one of Aaron's men.

An old-fashioned standoff.

"It's over!" Aaron shouted. "This rob-lover ain't got it in 'er."

Bernadette cocked the little gun with a growl. "Try me."

"Bernie ..." Oscar said. Sweat dripped from his brow, but the barrel of the Mare's Leg did not tremble.

"I suggest you boys all back out of here nice and slow. You ever seen a man get between an Orion polecat and its cubs?" Gus warned the bulls.

"She wouldn't dare," Aaron said. His eyes were wild, staring daggers into Bernadette's. "Take 'em!"

The bulls didn't move.

A dull roaring sound arising from beyond Citrus House vibrated through Willoughby's Gunsmithy & Emporium. It seemed to be coming from the deepest corner of the residential quarter, in the direction of Genie-town and the mining level access lift.

"If you won't listen to me, listen to *that*." Gus nodded toward the blasted door. "That is the sound of a whole hell of a lot of disgruntled atmo-miners. And it sounds like they're headed this way."

The bulls exchanged worried glances, but still didn't move. But as the roar—peppered with distinct sounds of renewed fighting—grew, so did the bull's visible unease.

"To *tunk* with this," one finally spat. He raised his hands and let his weapon hang from his trigger finger as he slowly backed out the blown open door. The moment he crossed the threshold, he bolted.

"Callahan, you *coward!*" Aaron yelled after him. But itchy feet were catching, and after another worried glance passed around the room, the other three bulls followed suit. *"Gas-huffing bastards!"* Aaron screamed. He grabbed Bernadette's wrist with one hand and gave her a sharp shove to the chest with the other. Aaron yanked the gun from her fingers and fired off two shots toward the door and the final fleeing bull. The first went wild, but the second hit the man square between the shoulders. He took two more stumbling steps and fell in the middle of the street.

By the time Gus could react to this act of betrayal and revenge, she and Aaron had their weapons pointed inches from each other's faces, at a distance that *most likely* negated Aaron's shield. *Tunk, I hope I'm close enough.* Aaron's unnerving grin reappeared and spread across his mousy features like a plague.

At that moment, a massive shadow fell across the open doorway. Gus couldn't dare take her eyes off Aaron, but relief washed over her when a familiar feminine voice cried out. "Well, what do we have here?" Gretchen said as she rolled into the shop, followed closely by Walter.

"If it ain't the worthless genetic reject himself! And his blushing bionic bitch!" Aaron said cheerfully. "You wait right there. I'll be with you as soon as I'm done with this one."

"The storm has arrived, lawman," Walter said as an enormous bolt of lightning lit the churning air beyond Las Ráfagas's dome. "You'll deal with *me* first."

"Rut off, you gene-pool pond scum. You'll get your turn at the razz table, so to speak. Then we'll get to all your filthy miner friends. Genie, rob, and doppel alike."

That gives me an idea.

"Well, now," Gus said, letting a smile play across her lips. "You're a gamblin' man, Aaron. Let's make this interesting." She slipped her lucky coin from her pocket and held it up. "Heads, it's just you and me, draw for draw. You want it, you got it. It didn't go so well for your brother, but"—she shrugged—"that's not my problem. Tails, you and Walter go *mano y mano.* No weapons."

Aaron's eyes lit with the same cocky fire he shared with the rest of his family. "Flip it," he said with a scowl.

Gus dropped Aaron's Beaumont-Adams into the holster on her hip. She hooked a thumb into her gun belt and flicked the coin high into the air. As it tumbled through the air, Gus noticed Hector eyeing her instead of the coin. She gave him a wink and clicked a small cylinder nestled into one of her belt's capsule loops. She smiled as she caught the coin and revealed the flip's result: tails.

Aaron protested immediately. "Rut you, I ain't fighting the damn genie. We got something to finish right here." With the derringer still raised, he took a half step forward.

Gus reacted instantly.

She grabbed his gun hand with her left, spun against his outstretched arm, dropped one spurred heel down onto his toes, and delivered a sharp elbow to the would-be lawman's nose. It broke with a satisfying *crack*. Aaron dropped the derringer into Gus's waiting palm and grabbed his bleeding nose.

At the same moment, Bernadette's hands shot out, gripped Aaron's personal shield generator at his belt buckle, and ripped the belt from his waist as he fell to his knees.

"Rutting *whores!*" Aaron screeched, his voice unusually high and nasally.

"On your feet, *lawman,*" Gus said, yanking him off the ground. "You've got a debt to settle." She dragged him through the wreckage of the front door and threw him into the street next to the bull he shot in the back. Walter followed him, rolling his shoulders and cracking his knuckles.

Aaron wiped blood from his nose and reluctantly squared up against the genie. It would have been a comical sight, if not for the backdrop of violence and destruction: Aaron Leconte stood to one side in a classic boxer's stance, Walter on the other, with his many hands balled into fists, all raised like an angry octopus.

The fight was short.

With his first punch, Aaron managed to bloody Walter's melted lip.

Gus cringed.

Faster than the lightning striking above, Walter returned the blows, fists flying. Aaron faltered under the sheer volume of the genie's rapid-fire hits.

A moment later, Walter stood over his beaten, bloodied long-time abuser. He glared down at Aaron with a mixture of pity and contempt.

"Finish it!" Aaron screamed at him from the dust.

Instead, Walter leaned back to stare up at the dome. The clouds were the same angry purple as the bruises darkening Aaron's face. Gale force winds dragged them across the sky at breakneck speed, yet the storm seemed stuck; hell-bent on tearing Las Ráfagas from the sky. Sheets of rain pelted the dome. Lightning flashed so bright that every detail—every crack in the sidewalk, every loose pebble in the road—stood out in sharp contrast. Thunder cracked almost simultaneously, and the world rattled with the rolling sound of an atmosphere torn apart.

Walter smiled slowly and returned his gaze to Aaron. "The storm has arrived," he said, and turned back to his wife.

Gus released a lungful of breath with a sigh. Keeping Aaron alive was a risk, but she was glad Walter hadn't killed him. *Killing is a hard thing—es-*

pecially if you're new to it. If we manage to survive this, I wouldn't want Walter to carry that burden.

Walter and Gretchen embraced in what had to be the most awkward, heartwarming hug she had ever seen.

Gus's mind worked furiously. Their next step was to get through the farmers market unscathed. If they managed that, they could catch their breath in Hotel Irma, then make a break for the Santa Barbara chapel and the engineering corral beyond. Bringing Aaron along was out of the question. He was only useful as a hostage, but Gus didn't think Laszlo would offer much for his son's safe return. And even then, at best, Aaron would slow them down; at worst, he would give them away at his first opportunity.

So, what do I do with him?

Gus's thoughts were derailed when Gretchen, still embracing her husband, abruptly lifted Walter off the ground in a bear hug and spun around on her treads.

Suddenly, a flash of electric blue light filled the roadway. The laser beam sliced into Gretchen's central LRC brain box but stopped short of passing completely through it and into Walter. Gus drew Aaron's Beaumont-Adams, but another crimson beam passed over her shoulder and struck Aaron in the chest as he sat in the road.

As the youngest Leconte slumped forward with the exit wound in his back smoking, exposing an empty ankle holster above his boot. A small pistol fell from his hand. Gus spun to face the shooter, and found Ray, supported by Aurora, standing in the gunsmithy doorway, holding a rifle to his uninjured shoulder.

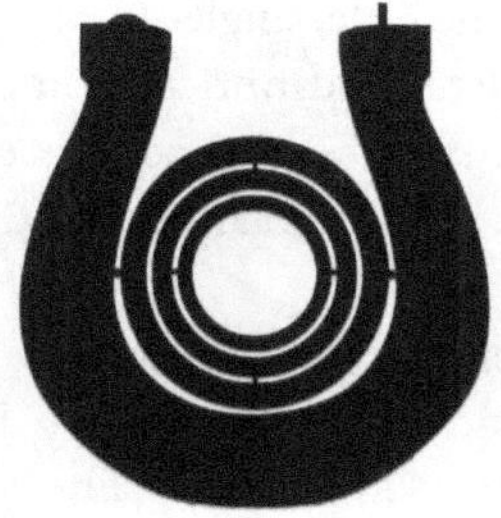

GUNS OF THE CONFEDERATION

The small group stood in a loose circle around the fallen mining rob. The six little lights that made up Gretchen's face dimmed, and her pincer-like hands opened and closed weakly. Walter knelt at her side and did his best to cradle what remained of her central brain box. Neither of them spoke as he held her. Deliberately, and with extraordinary grace, Gretchen wiped a tear from the folds in her husband's face. Slowly, the remaining light in her eyes faded until, at last, it was gone.

Hector turned away and hugged Bernadette, who wept quietly and buried her own face in Oscar's chest. The rancher drew his family close. Ray and Aurora—the hunter still supporting the marshal's weight—looked on as Moe knelt next to Walter and placed a comforting hand on the sobbing genie's shoulder.

Another death on her hands. On Leconte's hands.

Gus took a deep breath, pulling the air deep into her chest. She exhaled, pushing her lungs empty again. It didn't help the fire rising under her skin.

She turned her attention to Aaron's lifeless body. The Chief of the Company Police sat in the road, folded in half at the waist, with his broken nose in the dust between his knees. The hole Ray blew through him had stopped smoking, but the smell of charred flesh remained strong. Gus's heartbeat boomed in her ears as loud as any thunderclap. It took every ounce of willpower not to kick the body until her legs gave out. If she had taken care of Aaron herself, Gretchen would still be alive. She breathed through her mouth to avoid the smell and lifted Aaron's lifeless shoulder with the toe of her boot. With a *huff,* she pushed him over onto his back.

Gus knelt to pick up the little, single-shot disposable handgun Aaron had kept in a boot holster and noticed something else lying in the road next to the dead man's head: a comms earpiece. She tossed the now-useless pistol aside, wiped the earpiece off on her poncho, and stuck it in her ear.

"-ally Point Beta. Repeat: This is your final warning. All troops retreat from the casino and residential quarter. Fall back to Rally Point Beta," an unfamiliar voice said. Then the line went dead.

Gus took the piece out and examined it, puzzled. Before she could decide if it had malfunctioned or if the transmission had ended, a new sound rolled over Las Ráfagas from the far end of town. It had a distinct, rapidly repeating quality to it, like a starter motor clicking as it tried to turn over, but more sustained, and somehow *electrical* to Gus's ears.

Comprehension blossomed in her mind the same instant a salvo of scarlet laser beams tore through the Administration Tower and shredded the façade along Cirrus House's ground floor. The damn copperheads had the Gatling gun powered up again.

"Get down!" she shouted and dove for cover behind Jacob Wagner's overturned surrey. The barrage of beams tracked across the entire length of the casino but stopped short of the gunsmithy. It backtracked, further splintering the casino's wide front porch before decimating the old homes on the far side. The copperheads raked the Gatling gun back and forth through the residential part of town, doing untold damage.

How many are hiding in those buildings? Whatever the number, it's too many.

"What do we do?" Moe yelled from cover.

"We take it out," Gus yelled back.

"Are you crazy?" Oscar bellowed.

"It's in our way. From the angle of those beams, I'd bet they've got it set up right outside Emmitt's office. We kill it, or we're as good as dead anyway," Gus said. "They're leaving this side of town alone. Probably don't want to rut up the business district. We'll go through the market and into Hotel Irma, as planned. There's a back door in there, right?"

Gus expected Walter to answer, but the genie still knelt in the road next to his wife, completely unconcerned with the path of destruction the Gatling gun had carved out behind him.

"Yes!" Moe answered. "It opens on the empty lot behind the mercantile and Santa Barbara."

"Then we flank it. That's our play. Somebody grab Walter."

"You better rethink that plan, girl," Ray said and groaned. The color drained from his face, leaving him nearly the same shade as the Stetson that sat askew on his head. "I ain't in any condition to go runnin' all over hell's half acre." Gus opened her mouth to argue, but Ray wouldn't hear it. "Besides, ain't no way you're getting close enough to that thing to do anything without a distraction. Walter and I'll see that you get it."

Gus's brow furrowed. Aurora's Deiopean bandages stemmed the tide, but Ray had lost a lot of blood. Trying to drag him along would slow them down and put everyone else in danger. And they *would* need a distraction. She planned to cut through the cemetery and chapel to attack the Confederate position from the side. But there was a lot of open ground between the chapel's front doors and where she suspected the Gatling gun stood. Without some sort of diversion, she would get one shot, maybe two, before they turned the barrels on the chapel.

On the other hand, Ray's breath rattled and wheezed. His complexion had gone ashy except for a bloom of red on each cheek. She didn't want to leave him to die alone. If they brought him with them, maybe ...

Tunk!

Ray smiled, as if reading her thoughts. "Don't worry, I'm not ready to give up this cushy job to some void-driftin' beamslinger. Not yet. Give me a tap on the comms when you're in position," he said and touched his ear.

Gus couldn't help but return the smile. "I'm holding you to that, you old coot. Alright, the rest of you, let's go before the marshal here changes his mind and one of you has to carry him."

Free of Aurora's support, Ray wobbled. He leaned against the gun shop wall but stayed on his feet. Bernadette stopped to give him a tight hug before she, Moe, and Aurora joined Oscar and Hector at Gus's side.

Gus pulled the copperhead sidearm from its place tucked into her belt and handed it to Hector. "This is a simple, semi-auto laser pistol. The safety is *off*. That means you keep your finger *off* the trigger unless you plan to aerate somebody. In that case, just point and squeeze."

Hector held the pistol like a venomous snake and gazed up at Gus nervously.

"It's okay," she said and put a hand on his small shoulder. "You probably won't have to use it, but it's safer if you've got it. Just don't point it at anything you're not ready to vaporize." Hector swallowed hard but nodded. He pointed the gun at the floor and kept his finger far away from the trigger.

Gus and Ray exchanged a final nod and the group split. As Gus ushered her team toward the market, she chanced one final glimpse back at Cirrus House and Willoughby's Gunsmithy & Emporium. In front of the wrecked casino and relatively untouched gun shop, Ray hobbled around the smoldering surrey toward Walter. The genie stopped weeping but moved with a slowness disconnected from events around him. Gus hoped Ray could snap him out of it. Again, as if sensing her thoughts, Ray glanced up to see her hesitating. He scowled and shooed her with a flip of his hands.

Go.

The dark and quiet of the farmers market offered a sharp contrast to the blazing light cast by the Gatling gun's fire and the din of destruction that went along with it. The group, now reduced to six, moved as swiftly as Gus could goad them on—which is to say, not nearly as quickly as Gus would have preferred. Oscar's prosthetic was acting up again, Hector's little legs struggled to keep pace, and Moe spent far too much time loudly worrying about Ray to pay attention to where he was going. *Tunk*, even her own leg ached, despite the Deiopean drugs pumping through her system.

With a *crash*, Moe tripped over the body of Jacob Wagner, left where he fell at the start of the day's festivities.

"*Shhh!*" Gus hissed. Her head pivoted around like an owl as she tried to see everywhere at once. No immediate reaction came.

"*Madre de Dios,*" Oscar muttered and knelt over his neighbor. "I'm so sorry, Jacob." The body was face down in the dust between market stalls, although judging from the size of the entry wound on the back of his head, there wasn't much face left to speak of. As if in a trance, Oscar reached out to turn Jacob over.

"Oscar, *no!*" Gus said, too late to stop him. Oscar rolled Jacob onto his back to reveal a destroyed mess of flesh and teeth—and a small, egg-shaped object on the ground beneath him. "Everybody, down!" Gus yelled. The grenade exploded with a flash of blinding white light and a shriek like a banshee. Hands flew to cover vulnerable ears and eyes clamped shut against the glare.

When the blast subsided, Gus found her legs curiously wet. A glance at her gun belt, and then Oscar's bandolier, confirmed her fears. The sonic detonation had shattered all their exposed coolant capsules. That left them with only their loaded weapons and Aurora's solid slugs. Even Moe's glass-covered display-screen of a face now had a subtle crack running from beneath his crooked bowler to his jaw.

"What in tarnation was *that?*" Ray called over the comms.

"A little gift from the copperheads. Sonic grenade," Gus answered sharply. "They probably left it to warn them if anybody came this way. Keep an eye out for more of 'em. We're alright. But we need to find cover, *now.*"

As if to prove her point, a laser blast threw sparks as it passed through the stall to their left, and a pair of copperhead soldiers charged headlong through the town square toward them. Moe, Oscar, and Bernadette each raised their weapons to return fire. *"No!"* Gus yelled before they could shoot. "Get down and save your coolant. Aurora?"

The Deiopean's eyes flashed in agreement, and Aurora used the stall countertop to steady The Hammer. Slowly and calmly, the seasoned hunter took aim and waited for the opportune moment to take the shot.

Closer the soldiers came. Their beams cut holes through the market's empty stalls like Swiss cheese.

"Any time now," Gus urged.

Still, Aurora waited.

As the soldiers bore down on them like a pair of dogs flushing quail, Aurora fired twice. The barrel of their rifle barely twitched between shots. The men fell together, as if choreographed. Gus pounced on the nearest dying soldiers, flipped him onto his back, and dug through his pockets.

"What are you doing?" Moe cried, aghast.

"We need his caps." Gus sneered when she found the soldier's extra capsules. He only had three left. "Oscar, ditch the Mare's Leg," she said. "These capsules won't fit it. Grab his sidearm and coolant," Gus said and waved at the other fallen soldier.

Oscar stared at the dead men and didn't move. Bernadette pursed her lips. She gave Hector her derringer in exchange for his Confederate pistol, pressed that gun into her husband's hands, knelt before the second soldier, and rummaged for his capsules.

"Bernie!" Oscar said.

"Oscar, I love you," she snapped, "but you wanted to fight, and I stood by you. Well, this is what fighting is like. It's bloody, it's messy, and it's ugly. Now shut your mouth and keep your eyes open."

He opened his mouth to reply but shut it again when his eyes fell on Jacob's body. Their neighbor had been executed, likely as an example, to keep the townsfolk under control. Gus reckoned Oscar probably knew what possibilities might follow if he pushed back against Laszlo, but to see it up close—to be confronted with it, and realize your hands are just as filthy with Jacob Wagner's blood as those that did the killing—was something else entirely. Both Gretchen and Jacob might still be alive if Oscar hadn't roped them into his little resistance movement. The question that faced Oscar now was, was it worth it? Gus couldn't speak for Jacob, but she thought Gretchen would say that it was. And *rutting tunk*, she was starting to agree.

A yell rang out from the far side of the farmers market. Gus spun toward the call and reflexively drew Aaron's Beaumont-Adams. A woman stood in the doorway of Hotel Irma waving a red handkerchief in the air.

"Martha?" Bernadette said. "It's Martha Wagner."

Good. That means they're safe in the hotel. At least for now. She rushed the group across the road and into the darkened hotel lobby.

The humble hotel overflowed with signs of struggle. Table lamps were smashed. The lobby's couch sat overturned and smoldering. The bar was wet and sticky from broken bottles of cheap liquor. Fresh scorch marks peppered the walls. And a pair of soldiers and a rob lay on the lobby floor. All three oozed vital fluids.

As Gus stepped into the lobby and closed the door to the street, those hiding in the hotel anxiously poked their heads out to see. Martha Wagner, her son—a pockmarked young man of about thirteen or fourteen—Silas Mwangi, his wife, and their two small daughters were among them. All were harried and haggard.

"Oh, Bernadette!" Martha said, her voice nearly hysterical. "Come quick, you've got to help! Is Daniel with you?"

"No. Daniel is ... gone," Bernadette said and allowed Martha to guide her into the office behind the clerk's desk. Mr. Russo, Hotel Irma's mountainous proprietor, lay on a couch that strained under his considerable weight. Sweat and blood soaked the cushions. Gus gestured for Aurora to come along, and they followed the women into the office.

Martha sat on the edge of the couch and pressed a damp rag to Russo's brow. More rags, stained red, were wrapped around his enormous belly.

Gus grimaced. *Gut shot. Rough way to go.*

"Irma ..." Russo muttered. "Irma, don't let the boys go ou ..."

"What happened?" Gus asked.

"After Jacob ..." Martha paused as tears welled in her eyes. She pushed on even as the tears fell. "When everybody started running, he saved us. He got a gun away from one of the soldiers and got us all back here. Then, when those ... two ... came in ... he ... he ..." She broke down sobbing and Bernadette hugged her tight.

Gus sighed and turned to Aurora. "See if there's anything you can do for him," she said, then called for Moe to join them. They would need his translation skills.

Tunk. We don't have time for this.

After a brief examination, Aurora stepped back from the couch. Their eyes flashed a series of muted colors, and Gus got the idea before Moe could translate; Russo was already dead, his mind just hadn't caught up with his body yet.

"Is there nothing you can do?" Bernadette asked.

Aurora's shoulders sunk, and their eyes flashed dimly again. "'I can make him more comfortable,'" Moe translated.

Gus nodded and waved for Bernadette to follow her and Moe back out to the lobby. There, she called Oscar over, and what remained of her little group stood in a tight circle. Their faces were dirty, bloody, and tired. *And the day's not over yet.* "We've got to keep moving. We won't get another shot." She sighed and dropped her eyes to the floor. They weren't going to like this part. "Hector should stay here."

Oscar reacted immediately. "No *ruttin'* way!"

"Oscar, he's safer here, with Martha and the Mwangis," Gus said.

"*Safer?* You said our only chance was to get out of town! Now you're telling me my boy'll be safer *here?*"

Gus turned to Bernadette for help, but Moe spoke up instead. "What Gus is trying to say, Boss, is that what we have to do next—where we're going—it's no place for a boy."

Oscar's face fell. He looked across the broken room to his son sitting with the Mwangi girls.

"They're right, my love," Bernadette said and laced her fingers into her husband's hand.

"And you should stay, too," Gus added.

Bernadette's demeanor changed on a dime. "You're joking, right?"

"If this goes south, Hector can't afford to lose you both," Gus said bluntly. Both Vegas fell silent. "Besides," Gus added, "if I can't get this one out of town in one piece"—she hooked a thumb toward Oscar—"you may be Las Ráfagas's last hope." Bernadette stared at Gus hard but nodded without further argument. Oscar pulled her close and she buried her face in his chest.

As Gus watched the Vegas share what might be their final embrace, something nagged at the back of her mind. Or rather, a *lack* of something.

"Do you hear that?" Moe asked. His eyes were wide.

Bernadette pulled away from Oscar's chest. "The gun ..."

"It stopped!" Oscar finished.

"Probably changing the battery," Gus snapped. "Moe, round up as many coolant caps as you can. Oscar, go get Aurora. It's time to go."

As Moe and Oscar hurried off, Gus poked her head out of Hotel Irma's front door and stole a glance around the empty street. An eerie silence blanketed what remained of the town. The far end of the square, where Ray's office and Daniel's shop sat, had collapsed into ruins. Fires burned among the remains of the buildings. Gus could only imagine the damage to the rest of the residential quarter. *If we don't move fast, there won't be anything left worth saving.*

When she pulled her head back in and closed the door, Aurora was waiting. The Deiopean's eyes flashed and they pointed toward the back door.

Gus needed no translation. "Yeah, we're going. Russo gonna be alright?"

Aurora's eyes were dim, subdued, but gentle.

Gus nodded knowingly. "I'm sure you did all you could. I'm glad you could make him comfortable at least."

Aurora did their best to imitate Gus's nod.

"Alright," Gus raised her voice to the room. "Let's—"

"You can't go!" Hector cried and grabbed her around the waist. He buried his face in her poncho and hugged her tight. Surprised at first, Gus smiled and gently peeled his arms from around her.

"I've got to, Hector," she said as she knelt. "But once I've got Moe and your father out of town safely, Aurora and I will come right back here." Of course, if she survived that long, she already promised Aurora she would help free the captive Deiopeans while they waited for backup. But one thing at a time. "I need you to be brave, like you were with the mule. Since I'm taking your dad and Moe with me, I need you to help your mom and Mr. Mwangi keep everyone safe here, okay?"

"With this?" Hector asked and brought a fingertip to his temple.

"That's right. Think you can do that for me until I get back?"

Hector wiped snot and tears onto his sleeve, and Gus was suddenly reminded of how young he was. He nodded and tried to smile. Gus dug into her pocket and pulled out her lucky coin. She offered it to the boy, who took it with a confused expression. "For luck," she said.

"But it's not really lucky," he said. His forehead creased. "It's a trick."

She nodded and pulled the coin's control button from its place hidden among the loops of her gun belt. "We make our own luck," she said, and handed him the button with a wink.

He flipped the coin with one hand and pressed the button with the other. The coin landed neatly in his upturned palm. Tails. "We make our own luck," he repeated before locking eyes with her. "Come back, Gus. Come back home."

Home. Ain't that a thought.

She put her hands on his shoulder. "That's the plan, kid."

"You promise?"

"I promise." She gave him one last hug and sent him back to sit with Silas's girls.

Moe, Oscar, Aurora, and Bernadette waited for her by Hotel Irma's back door.

Bernadette was as beautiful as the day Gus arrived, despite the knots in her hair and the blood and grime caked on her face and clothes. She gazed at Gus and again the beamslinger found herself lost in those emerald pools of light. Bernadette leaned forward and gently kissed Gus on the cheek, before drawing her into a tight embrace. After a moment's hesitation, Gus returned the hug.

"No matter what happens today, thank you for trying to keep my family safe," Bernadette whispered into Gus's ear. She gave Gus one final squeeze and joined her son.

Gus's team, now a quartet, stepped from the relative safety of Hotel Irma into the alley behind Walter's mercantile as the terrible sound of the Gatling gun started up again. The cemetery, with its rows of neatly arranged urns, and the chapel beyond it, lay directly in front of them. And by the sound of it, the gun fired from beyond Santa Barbara's front doors.

"Ray, we're moving to the cemetery," Gus said into the comms. "Almost in position."

"Gotcha. Hurry the *tunk* up, wouldja?" Ray replied.

Moe had only been able to round up a handful of coolant caps from the folks inside the hotel. Gus gave Oscar and Moe three each and took one for herself. *We'll have to pick our shots carefully.* The group moved slowly toward the sound of the repeating gun, careful to keep an eye out for any copperhead scouts watching their flank.

Streaks of white lightning lit the clouds above, and the resulting thundercracks were loud enough to drown out even the intense sound of the big gun tearing the remnants of Las Ráfagas to smithereens. Rain battered the dome in sheets that came in waves and obscured the bruise-colored clouds that blotted out the sky.

As they moved through the cemetery, the rows of urn-filled shelves threw startling, moving shadows with every lightning flash. So far, no one had overreacted and fired a shot. Not much had gone right so far, so Gus chose to be thankful for that.

When they reached the back door to the chapel, Gus waited for a thundercrack to break the padlock with the butt of her gun. Silently, they filed into Santa Barbara.

Although Gus spent some time hidden away in the basement's secret room, this was the first time she'd seen the chapel itself. The small place of worship, with its humble altar and a few rows of short pew benches beneath an old, stained glass window, took up the main floor. Hymnals littered the parquet, but the chapel appeared otherwise intact and undamaged. *Something else to be thankful for.*

If Gus was right—and it sure as *tunk* sounded like she was—the giant gun was only a few yards beyond the big double doors at the end of the row of pews. The chapel's thick stone walls made it the perfect place to make a stand.

"Alright, let's get a few of these benches stacked up in front of the door," she said and waved Moe over to help her.

"These aren't going to do much against that repeater," Oscar said as he and Aurora stacked a pew on top of Gus and Moe's.

"No." Gus nodded, her voice grave. "But if we don't take that gun out quick, it won't matter none. This is just to give us that chance." Oscar's face went pale, but he swallowed hard and helped Aurora with another pew.

Their modest barricade constructed, Gus gathered her troops—such as they were. "We're only going to get one shot at this, and whether we make it or not, all hell is going to break loose," she said. "If I get it on the first, we're going to have a run-and-gun fight. When I give the word, we move up to the engineering corral as fast as we can. But if I miss, be ready to book it out that back door like your ass is on fire and your hair is catching." Her eyes darted from face to face. "Got it?"

Oscar's tanned face was a shadow of the jovial man she'd met a few days before. His smile had been replaced with a set jaw and cracked, bleeding lips. His once laughing eyes were dark and sunken. Moe, the most emotional rob Gus had ever met, looked calm and ready. The crack running down his face even gave him a rugged appearance. Gus had not fully learned to read the expressions in Aurora's many eyes, but when the Deiopean placed a hand on her arm, she knew they were ready, too.

"Ray, we're in position. You ready?" Gus said into her comms earpiece. When no reply came her heart sank. "Ray, do you copy?" Nothing.

Tunk. I hope you're only busy, Ray. And not dead.

Either way, they were on their own.

Her friends took their positions behind the pew barricade. Gus gave the big double doors a sharp kick with the heel of her boot. The doors swung open to reveal the plaza in front of Emmitt's engineering corral. A whole battalion of copperhead soldiers loitered around the blazing Gatling gun. It fired into the town a few paces from the pile of jerry cans Gus once used as an escape route. A team of soldiers raked the huge weapon back and forth, firing waist-high death through the remains of the town.

"*Madre de Dios,*" Oscar cursed under his breath. "There's not going to be anything left to save!"

With Aaron's Beaumont-Adams in hand, Gus stood in the doorway and aimed at the Gatling gun's battery. Although it looked as though its former owner had taken great care to restore this classic sidearm, it was an unfamiliar weapon, and with the drug in Aurora's bandage wearing off, her shoulder screamed in pain as she tried to hold the gun steady.

Still, she took her time.

Time she didn't have.

"Come on, come on. Take the shot," Moe mumbled, seemingly to himself.

Taking a deep breath, she sighted in on the battery as best she could and squeezed the heavy trigger.

And missed.

The beam went wide of the battery and cut a copperhead soldier down at the knee instead. He fell back, screaming and clutching his leg. His compatriots reacted immediately and turned as one toward the chapel.

Spotted, she poured all her willpower into steadying her arm. Squinting at her target, she took aim again. Under a rain of laser fire, she took her second shot.

And missed again.

The shower of laser beams fired in response tore Santa Barbara's open doors to splinters and sliced through the pews like paper.

Gus dove back into the chapel, tackling Oscar in the process. Her momentum threw them both to the floor behind Santa Barbara's thick stone walls. Moe and Aurora ducked into cover on the opposite side of the doorway.

There were a handful of new scorched holes near the edges of her poncho, but nothing more. She'd survived—a small miracle. The soldiers' lasers abruptly stopped—even the repeating background noise of the Gatling gun—and a hush fell over Las Ráfagas.

"What's going on?" Moe asked. "Why did they stop?"

Gus chanced a peek through the decimated doorway and received a few pot shots thrown her way. She ducked back, but she'd seen enough.

"They're turning the gun on the chapel." She glanced at the old stone walls. *Are they gonna stand up to the concentrated power of a Gatling gun? Maybe for a minute or two, but not much more.* After that, there would be nothing to stop those scarlet beams from tearing through the cemetery and into Hotel Irma.

She leapt to her feet and waved her friends toward the back door. *"Go, go, go!"* she yelled. "Get everybody out of the hotel! If I miss, this place will be Swiss cheese in seconds."

Instantly, Gus spun out into the open doorway with the Beaumont-Adams raised high. Standing in the doorway, with her shoulder screaming in painful protest—and completely exposed—she fired off a series of beams in quick succession.

Bodies fell to the wayside as enemy fire erupted around her. Two cherry-colored beams smashed into the stone wall to her left. A third flashed near her right shoulder, close enough for her to feel the heat as it passed. Another beam, sizzling angrily, grazed her temple. The smell of her own singed hair burned her nostrils. The haze of battle descended over her, and everything fell away except the Gatling gun's battery, finally exposed. She took aim, steadied her sights, and squeezed the trigger.

The gun clicked uselessly.

Tunk, this piece of crap goes through caps fast! She slapped her last cap into the gun as she stood in the doorway, unprotected from the onslaught. But before she could raise the gun and reacquire her aim, a familiar pink beam lit up the air beneath the dome.

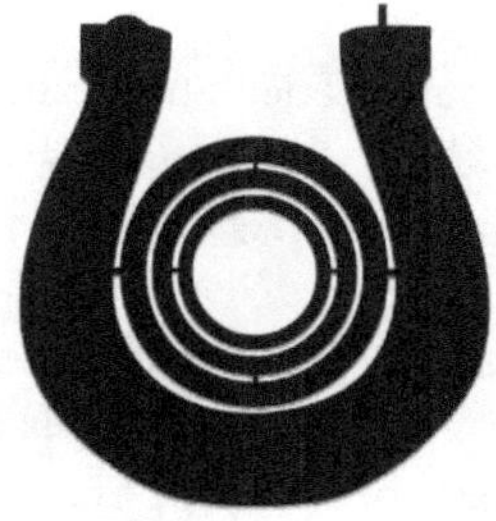

THE MARSHAL OF LAS RÁFAGAS

The beam carved through the soldiers and struck the pile of discarded jerry cans outside the engineering corral. The trace amounts of rubidium fumes left in the cans ignited in a flash. The explosion wiped out half the soldiers, knocked the other half flat, and sent a small mushroom cloud crashing into the dome above.

Delilah's pink beam came from Gus's right—from the roadway between Santa Barbara and the Marshal's Office.

Tuco.

The outlaw stood in the road alone. He'd wrapped his gun hand in an old rag, now stained pink by the big gun's exhaust. Gus expected the fat little man to shoot her, but he winked instead. He awkwardly hop-ran to Santa Barbara's doorway and shoved her back into cover. The instant they crossed the chapel's threshold, the barrage of laser fire from the regrouping soldiers resumed.

Inside, Tuco slammed his back against the chapel wall and gasped for breath.

"I changed my mind, *hermana,*" he said. That ugly, crooked smile bloomed on his face. He held Delilah up butt first and offered it to Gus. "You can have this *pedazo de mierda* back."

"Speaking of *pedazos de mierda* ..." Moe said.

"What's this *pendejo* doing here?" Oscar asked.

Aurora's eyes lit up with a protest Gus understood perfectly.

"What in *tunk* are you all still doing here?" Gus yelled.

"There's no way we'd make it back to the hotel in time to save them," Oscar said. "At least here, if you fell, we could have tried … *something.*" He shrugged.

Gus snatched Delilah out of Tuco's hand, dropped it into her holster, and glared at her friends. "Well, all it means now is that we're all gonna die right here. Moe, keep a lookout. At least that way, we'll have some warning before they tear this place apart."

"You know," Tuco said smoothly, as if he were an old friend, "there is *another* way." She eyed him skeptically. "This situation's gotten out of hand. We never should have been on opposite sides, *hermana*. I see that now. *Lo siento.* Weren't things better before?"

"Spit it out, Tuco," Gus said and slammed him into the stone wall.

"You and me, *hermana*. We take the rob, help ourselves to a ride, and get our asses back to the Old Colonies. I'm sayin' we wash our hands of this place."

"*Chinga tu madre!*" Moe spat.

Gus laughed sardonically. Still, the little man's offer tugged at some deep, instinctual part of her. The two of them probably could cut a path to the engineering corral if they moved fast and ignored the Gatling gun. They'd made it through worse scraps than this together …

But not this time, Tuco.

She gave him another sharp slam into the wall. Ancient mortar dust trickled down into his hair. "I don't think so, Tuco. Leconte started something out here, and I plan to help these folks finish it. You can help," she offered him Aaron's Beaumont-Adams, "or you can save your own skin." She nodded toward the open back door. "If you go now, you might even make it."

Tuco slowly took the gun from her. "You know you're going to die along with 'em, right?"

"Probably. But I'd rather die at a friend's side," she said, "than keep running with the likes of you."

Tuco took a few unsteady steps toward the back door. "*¿Te has vuelto loca?* There's no spoons in this."

"I've made my choice, Tuco. Get lost before I change my mind and shoot you myself."

He took another half-stumbled step backwards and pointed the Beaumont-Adams at Moe. "*Bueno*, but the rob comes with me."

"Woah, now," Oscar said and pointed his own gun at Tuco.

"Gus?" Moe's voice wavered.

"Stay where you are, Moe," Gus said. "How's it looking out there?"

"They—uh," the rob stuttered, "they're just about in firing position."

"You hear that, Tuco? We don't have time for this."

But Tuco's wide, wild eyes flitted around the room as Gus, Oscar, and Aurora slowly closed in around him. A shot rang out from outside, and for a moment everything stopped.

"Moe?" Gus asked. Moe hesitated, unwilling to turn his back on Tuco. Another shot crackled, and finally the rob tore his eyes from the bounty hunter to sneak a peek out the doorway.

After a third shot, Moe confirmed what Gus suspected. "Someone's shooting at them. Looks like a high caliber rifle."

"Ray," Gus said and grinned. *The old codger's not done yet, after all.* "You hear that, Tuco? Our ace in the hole just showed up. I'll give you one more chance. Give us a hand—or beat feet."

Tuco's eyes darted back and forth between Moe and Gus. Finally, his sights fell still on the rob and his body tightened.

Option three it is, then.

The outlaw raised the Beaumont-Adams and a flash of light filled the small chapel. Pink, grapefruit light. The barrel wavered, then fell as Tuco dropped the gun to his side. His face tightened and his lips puckered like he'd bitten into a lemon. He nodded and wagged a finger at Gus.

"Maybe—" he croaked. "Maybe I'll—" Tuco turned on his heel, wobbling like a drunkard. He managed three lurching steps toward Santa Barbara's back door before he landed flat on his face with the hole in the back of his battered black duster oozing.

Another shot from Ray's rifle broke the stunned silence inside the chapel. "Ray! You hear me, you old coot? Come in!" Gus said over the comms. When no reply came, she turned her attention to Moe. "What's going on out there?"

"Uh, uh ..." Moe said. He ducked away from a shot thrown toward the chapel door. "They're, uh, they're turning the Gatling gun back toward Cirrus House."

"Ray's giving us our chance," Gus said. She checked Delilah's coolant. Nearly full. "Cover me!" Again, she leaned out from the safety of Santa Barbara's walls and tried to find the Gatling gun's battery amid the horde of soldiers. As each of her friends fired their own weapons, she spotted her target. She ignored the pain raging through her arm, steadied her aim, and took her shot.

The laser beam leapt from Delilah's barrel, passed between bodies and through the dust, and splashed against the Gatling gun's battery.

A direct hit!

But no explosion came. Instead, the Gatling gun opened fire and hurled its deadly light in the general direction of Cirrus House. She'd dented the battery, and melted it a little, but at this range, even Delilah wasn't powerful enough to pierce its protective housing.

Tunk!

"What now?" Oscar yelled.

"Got me," Gus hollered back. "I'm fresh out of ideas."

Movement in the chapel caught her attention and she whirled around, half-expecting to find Tuco had somehow overcome his injuries and gotten to his feet. Thankfully, her former partner hadn't moved. Bernadette stood over him like a banshee. The farmwife's hair had come undone, and the tight curls bounced around her head in a fiery halo. Without a word, she raised the Mare's Leg to her shoulder and took aim at the Gatling gun.

BOOM!

The air exploded, sending a shockwave rippling through the chapel.

Shaking the ringing out of her head, Gus forced herself up from Santa Barbara's dusty floor, wincing, ignoring the groans of her companions. She chanced a peek out into the plaza and found a smoking crater where the Gatling gun had stood. Most of the soldiers were dead, dying, or had run off. *Damn woman nearly killed us all, but honestly, I ain't gonna argue about that result.*

Oscar—once he'd shaken off the shock of the blast—had no such qualms. "What are you doing here? Where's Hector?"

"Calm down, Oscar," Bernadette chided her husband. "Hector's fine. Martha's looking after him. She needs something to take her mind off Jacob and it sounded like you needed help."

"Cut the chatter," Gus snapped. "You're here now, and that was a *hell* of a shot." She knelt next to Tuco and flipped the dead man onto his back. *Tunk.* Just her luck. The bastard had landed on his bandolier and there were only three caps left. She slipped them into loops on her gun belt. "We need to go. *Now.*"

They followed Gus's lead and raced across the plaza to the engineering corral doors. In Santa Barbara's courtyard, Gus turned her eyes toward

Cirrus House. With most of the casino concealed behind the extensively damaged Administration Tower, she couldn't see much—but what she *could* see had been laid to waste by the copperheads. She hoped Ray was alright, but she had a bad feeling the responsibility for Las Ráfagas and its people had been laid at her feet.

The silver deputy star weighed heavily against her chest.

They reached the engineering doors and fanned out to cover Moe as he wrestled with opening them. But the doors wouldn't budge.

"Come on, Moe," Gus pushed. "What's taking so long?"

"It's not the lock. There's something ... The door's barricaded or something."

Tunk. Can we get in the same way I got out after Junior murdered Emmitt? Her head swiveled around. No—the jerry cans Tuco shot were still burning. *Emmitt's office? Maybe. It's not far.*

A beam sent sparks flying off the wall near Aurora's head. The few surviving copperheads were regrouping and rallying in a clumsy counter-attack.

They were sitting ducks.

"Go! *Go!*" Gus shouted and pointed toward Emmit's office door.

As they reached it, the door swung open and Gloria frantically waved them inside. Gus just managed to close it behind her as a pair of beams struck the pavement in her wake.

Gus leaned her head against the door and gasped for breath. She brushed Gloria's hand off her shoulder and tried not to think about Ray. *There's still a job to do.*

With the five of them and Gloria crammed inside, Emmitt's spacious office seemed cramped and claustrophobic. "The Vegas are taking Laszlo's wagon, and you should go with them," Gus said to Gloria. "It's still hitched back here, right?" She peered through the office windows into the dark engineering corral.

"No," Gloria said with a shake of her head.

"What do you mean 'no?' Where'd it go?"

"I mean I ain't going nowhere," she said. "This was where Emmitt and I made our home, and those bastards took it all away. This is where I make my stand. You're more than welcome to stay here with me, though, 'cause you ain't going nowhere in Leconte's wagon."

"What's that supposed to mean?"

"I fried the FTL gimbal. That thing'll never leave this system again."

"You fried ..." Gus trailed off and stared at Gloria, agape. All the work to get this far, and the only wagon fast enough to outrun *Shenandoah's* guns was now as useless as the man that owned it.

Time crawled in Emmitt's office. With nowhere left to go, and only a few shots left in each of their guns, they had done their best to dig in. The copperheads, so far, hadn't tried an all-out assault, but they made their presence known with a few shots anytime Gus dared to show her face in the window.

Emmitt's old-fashioned lamps cast a warm, dim glow. The air was heavy and still; a thick quiet filled the room. Tensions rose with each sizzling shot the copperheads sent their way.

Each of Gus's companions dealt with the stress differently.

Gloria had asked about Junior. Reassured that her husband's murderer had met his end, she nodded, took the Mare's Leg to the window, and peered out into the plaza with hardened eyes. Aurora tended to the group's minor wounds, then stayed busy with organizing their first aid kit over and over. Moe paced along the office's back wall and mumbled to himself. Every once in a while, he would say Ray's name. Oscar picked at the calluses on his hands. Bernadette borrowed Gus's poncho and did her best to mend the holes and tears. With that finished, she busied herself washing the old, dirty-gray fabric in Emmitt's small sink. Gus rolled the last of her tobacco into half a dozen small, tightly packed cigars.

Gus opened the window that overlooked the engineering corral floor. She selected one of her fresh cigars and ran it under her nose, savoring the earthy aroma. Her silver lighter clicked. She took a deep, calming drag and blew the smoke out into the shadowy corral.

Her brow creased as she leaned on the windowsill and considered their predicament. Cirrus House was a smoldering wreck, and Ray and Walter were likely gone. The miner uprising seemed to have been silenced by the Gatling gun, and it was only a matter of time before the soldiers decided to rush the office. On top of it all, the copperheads still outnumbered them at least four to one.

Oscar joined her and she offered him the cigar. He hesitated, then shrugged and took a deep drag. A coughing fit interrupted his exhale. Gus patted him on the back until he breathed easily again. Smiling sheepishly, Oscar handed the cigar back. The pair sat in silence while blue smoke hung in a haze around them.

Oscar opened his mouth to speak but closed it. When he looked like he wanted to say something a second time, Gus spoke for him. "I don't know, Oscar." She held the cigar clamped tight between her teeth. The cherry bobbed with each word.

"What?"

"What our next move is." She shook her head. Smoke drifted lazily toward the ceiling. "I don't know. Do you?"

"We've got to do *something*. Ray's—" Moe said.

"Ray's *dead,*" Gus said. "And so is the damn town. For all we know, we're all that's left." Gus bit her tongue, realizing too late what she had implied about Hector, but Bernadette didn't react.

Oscar *did*. "*No*. There are survivors. There have to be. We can't let Laszlo get away with this."

Gus snuffed the cigar out on the windowsill and flicked the butt into the corral. "How, Oscar? I'm not usually one to give up, so if you've got a plan to get us out of here, I'm all ears. Moe? How 'bout you? Aurora? Where's that surprise your people promised?"

Aurora's eyes flashed and Moe translated. "'They will come through. The storm has arrived.'"

"Oh, for *tunk's sake,*" Gus said through a sigh of cigar smoke, "I'm gettin' a mite tired of all this mystical *storm* stuff."

"Maybe," Gloria said quietly, "we just let them in."

"You mean surrender?" Gus shook her head. "That'll only postpone the inevitable." She lit another cigar and thrummed her fingers on the windowsill.

"That's not what I mean." Gloria, still dressed in Emmitt's dirty leather apron, held the Mare's Leg over one shoulder defiantly. Her unruly white hair stuck up at all angles. The clump Junior had ripped out was obvious. So was the wild glint in her eyes.

"No." Bernadette stood apart from the group with a folded white linen in her hands. "Our son is alive. And so are others. You're going to get us out of this," she said and gave Gus a small smile.

"How do you know there are more survivors?" Gus asked.

"Why are you so sure there aren't?"

"Because we haven't heard from anyo ..." Gus trailed off.

Bernadette smiled.

Son of a ...

"Gloria, you got a working comms unit in here?" she snapped.

"Right here," she said. She leaned over Emmitt's desk and flipped the switch on a small gray box like the one in Ray's office. A burst of static rang out, then nothing.

"Try another channel," Moe suggested. Gloria turned the knob a few times, but they were met with static with each click.

"I'm sor—" Gus said, but a fresh squelch from the transmitter cut her off.

And a voice.

"-*kkzz*'m's safe. Don't want to give away my position, but I'm alive."

"Who was that?" Oscar asked.

"It sounded like—" Bernadette started, but a new voice interrupted her.

"Good, stay where you are," they said. "Hold tight until we can figure out what's going on." The voice cut cleanly through the white noise.

"That's Silas!" Oscar cheered and hugged his wife.

Over the following minutes, they heard more voices that had survived the onslaught. Each was careful not to say where they had found cover for fear of being hunted down by the remaining copperheads, but they were alive. They all wanted the same thing: someone to tell them what to do.

Gus could think of no one better for that job than Oscar.

She lifted the transmitter out of its cradle and handed it to the rancher. "Your people are waiting to hear from you."

Oscar took it and stared at it blankly. After a moment of silence, he squared his shoulders and handed the transmitter back to Gus. "No," he said. "It may have been my conscience that got us into the mess, but it's you we need to lead us out of it."

Gus raised her hands and took a step back. "Woah, now. I told you before, I'm no leader."

"This badge says otherwise," Bernadette said over Gus's shoulder.

The beamslinger found herself suddenly surrounded by expectant eyes. When she turned to face Bernadette, the farmwife was holding folded white linen in her hands. *No. Not linen. My poncho. I'd forgotten it used to be white.* With the grime of thousands of light-years washed from it, it looked almost new. The dark stains—her and Ray's blood and Moe's hydraulic fluid, among many older blemishes—were faded, but still there. A grim reminder of the path that led her here. The deputy's badge, still pinned to the poncho's fabric, shone in the dim light of the office.

"Marshal," Oscar said. He held out the transmitter.

"Marshal," Moe said with a smile and a nod.

Aurora stepped forward and her eyes blinked patterns of blue, red, and white.

"Marshal," Gloria chimed in.

"Marshal," Bernadette said last, and held up the poncho for Gus to put on.

One by one, Gus met the eyes of each of her companions, wordlessly begging each for another option.

Christ's blood, I'm no leader.

But maybe that didn't matter. These people had taken her in when they didn't know her from Eve. And although there had been conflict between them from nearly the beginning, they had stuck by her through all the chaos Las Ráfagas had suffered over the last few days. Through her reckless greed, and the danger it had put them in, they had stood with her.

She wasn't really sure when it happened, but their cause had become hers. She wanted Laszlo to pay. Not only for what he had brought down on Walter, Gretchen, Ray, or *Tilly*, but for the destruction his unrelenting avarice had brought down on all these people. And more, she had to keep this adoptive family of hers safe. *Somehow.*

Finally, Gus nodded, and Bernadette helped her pull the poncho over her head. She took the transmitter from Oscar and spoke into it.

"Citizens of Las Ráfagas," she said. "Some of you might know me as Gus. As Ray Gascon's deputy, I guess ... I guess I'm the acting Marshal now." She swallowed hard. Her friends nodded encouragingly. "I know things aren't looking too good for us right now, but if you can hear this, it means you're still alive. And if you're still alive, it means you can still fight. But you should know what it is you're fighting for. Because it isn't just your own lives. Laszlo Leconte has decided you, your families, and your friends all have to die. For spoons. He sold your lives to the CCO. He has something they want, and he wants you to pay the price."

Her gaze settled on Aurora.

"The Deiopeans have perfected rubidium refining. Laszlo stole the tech, kidnapped as many Deiopeans as he'll need to keep it working, and now he's selling the tech off to the copperheads so they can turn Las Ráfagas into their own pulse-rail station. From here, it's a short sprint to the

Cygnus X colonies with a monstrosity like the one they've got hitched up outside. With the Deiopeans' rubidium refinement, the CCO will have the resources to build more of them. And the Lecontes will get fat off the profits wrought by your dead bodies.

"I know you've all been through a lot in the last few hours, but we *can't* let them get away with this. So, wherever you are, if you're able, I'm asking you to fight. Fight your way to a mount. Get out of town. Carry word of what happened here into the void. And make sure Laszlo Leconte pays for what he has brought down on your home."

Gus released the transmitter button and placed it back in its cradle. "How was that?" she asked. Before anyone could answer, a sound came rolling over the town like a wave. The sound of cheering. Of many doppels, robs, and genies cheering.

Moe, that broad grin back on his simulated face, put a hand on Gus's shoulder. "What now, Marshal?"

"Yeah," Oscar said. "Great speech and all, but we're still sorta stuck in here."

Gus smiled. "Oh, don't worry about that. I've got a feeling we'll be getting some direction soon."

"What do you mean?" Bernadette asked.

The comms unit crackled. "'Marshal' Gus, is it then?" Laszlo asked.

"Told ya," Gus said with a smile. "Thanks to you, Laz," she said into the transmitter. "What can I do for you?"

"Very well." Irritation dripped from Laszlo's voice, even through the static. "I have a deal for you, *Marshal.*"

"I'm listening."

"No, not over comms. I prefer to do business face to face, don't you? It's so much more ... *dignified.* Why don't you and Oscar Vega—if he's still breathing, of course—come on up to the tower, and we can hash this out? Our dear friends in the CCO have promised a ceasefire, as long as you can promise the same."

"*Pendejo,*" Oscar spat. "It's a trap."

Gus clicked the transmitter button. "Deal. I'll be at the lift in two minutes. Alone. Make sure none of your boys take any shots at me. That would make me very unhappy."

"Alone," Laszlo repeated. "Shame. Very well. You have my word." The frequency went dead.

"Alone?" Oscar asked. "It's a trap!"

"I heard you the first time," Gus said. "It's the only way I'll get close enough to that clown to do anything that'll make a difference. I've got to go. You've got to make sure you get your family out of here."

"But if it's a trap you'll need backup," Oscar protested. "You might be the marshal now, but I *did* get us all into this mess. Let me help!"

"No," Gus said.

Oscar's face turned red, and he pointed a meaty finger in her face. "Now, you listen here—"

Without a thought, Gus delivered a quick jab to Oscar's kidney. He doubled over briefly, but his rage and hopelessness overrode the surprise, and he came back swinging. Gus dodged, and this time kicked the inside of his robotic knee with a sharp strike from the heel of her boot. He fell to the office floor, spitting Spanish curses.

I need to keep him as far from Laszlo's tower as I can.

"Look at you," she managed to spit out, the words twisting her gut. "You're nothing but a liability. If you come with me, you'll get yourself killed. Or worse, get *me* killed."

"Why you arrogant, void-drifting—"

Tunk. I hoped the knee would have done it.

Gus wound up and threw a left-handed hook across his jaw. Oscar crashed to the floor like a felled tree, out cold. Bernadette ran to her unconscious husband's side. She knelt and cradled his head.

Tear drops dampened Oscar's shirt before the farmwife lifted her face to meet the beamslinger's gaze. "Thank you," she said.

Gus nodded and turned, finding Gloria next.

"You can't kill him," the widow said.

"Why the *tunk* not?"

"It's—it's complicated."

"*Complicated? Christ's blood.* We don't have time for complicated."

"Don't kill him." Gus took Gloria by the shoulders and moved her aside. "That's up to him, isn't it?"

"But—"

"Gloria, it'll be alright."

Finally, Gus faced her final obstacle. Right on cue, Moe stepped between her and the door. "If you won't let the boss go with you, let me. I *am* a deputy, after all." Moe puffed out his chest.

"Moe ..."

"I had a feeling that wasn't going to work." His chest deflated and his shoulders sagged. "So, how about this instead? That bastard was willing to sell me off to the highest bidder. If I'm ever going to be free, I need to see this through to the end. And you can't do it alone."

"What you need to do is stay out of Laszlo's snare and see these good people to safety. I think Las Ráfagas is more important to the CCO than any of us realize. We need to stop this here. Help me do that by living. If I don't make it out of whatever Laszlo's got set up for me, it'll be up to you to get as many people out of town as you can, *Deputy*."

"What about *Shenandoah?*"

Gus nodded to Aurora. "Aurora says the Deiopeans will come through. When they do, that'll be your chance."

"But, I—"

"Your family needs you, Moe." She smiled and held out her hand. "It's been a pleasure." Moe's digital features strained in protest, but his eyes softened, and the corners of his mouth turned up in that friendly, familiar smile. He shook his head slightly, but took her small, gloved hand with his long, elegantly crafted fingers. He shook her hand once, then with his digital eyes squeezed shut, he pulled her into a tight but comfortable hug. Surprised by the embrace, Gus hesitated for an instant, then wrapped her arms around Moe's mechanical shoulders and squeezed him back.

"Good luck, Marshal," he said. "Come back to us."

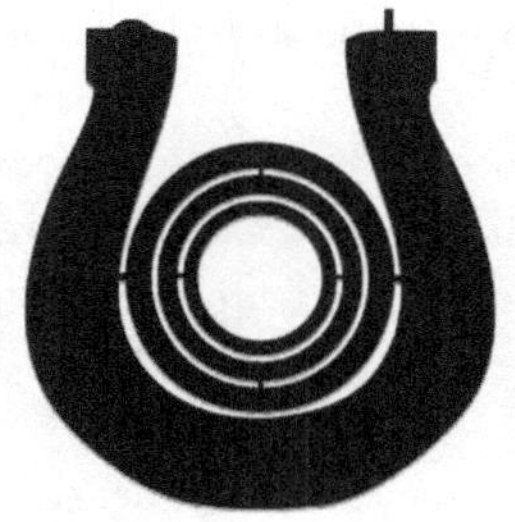

GAS GIANT GAMBIT

Gus stepped out into the plaza to a flash of lightning and a deafening thunder crack. She paused long enough to light another cigar. Her little silver lighter was a pale comparison to the storm still churning outside the dome. She braced herself for the work to come and headed for Las Ráfagas's town square and the Administration Tower.

Battle weary copperhead soldiers flanked her the moment she set foot in the square. Instead of threatening her, they fell into lock step with her. *An escort. No surprise there.*

Evidence of the battle littered the ground. The small dais set up for executions still stood, splattered with blood and other unidentifiable stains. Bodies lay where they had fallen, both soldiers and townsfolk alike. Willoughby had been left face down in the muck, the back of his once-white coat now stained a deep burgundy. Daniel Park's body remained where Tuco shot him. Others—most she didn't recognize—dotted the space. Both the privileged and impoverished mingled, indistinguishable in the dirt and blood between lightning flashes.

Though riddled with holes from the Gatling gun, the Administrator Tower lift somehow still worked. Gus wondered what the shaft was made of to withstand the assault.

All thought stopped when she got a view of Cirrus House beyond the tower. The casino's façade was just ... *gone.* Only the building's splintered frame stood. Fire had been concentrated on the second-floor balcony—the site of Ray and Walter's last stand. There was no sign of either of them.

How many had died for Laszlo's gluttony? She didn't know. But she *did* know Laszlo's copperhead thugs wouldn't stop until every last person not named Leconte was wiped from Las Ráfagas. And she wasn't convinced they would stop there.

When Gus stepped onto the lift, her escort took up a defensive position on either side of the sliding doors. The doors closed and the car lifted into the air while she let the smoke fill her lungs and anxiously chewed on her cigar. She loaded a fresh coolant cap into Delilah and dropped the big gun back into its holster.

Gus shook some of the tension out of her shoulders and thought back over the last few days. *More like a lifetime.* What in *tunk* was she even doing on this lift? Why put her neck on the line for a bunch of people she never heard of a week ago? *Tunk,* she was trying to protect the bounty-head she'd come to collect! This job had cost her nearly everything already. *Tilly,* her oldest and most trusted friend, was gone. Everything but the clothes on Gus's back was gone, too, as well as any chance of getting out of this with more than the lint in her pockets. And yet, here she was, putting all she had left—her very life—on the line for these stubborn jelly-ranching agros.

She sighed. They may have been stubborn agros, but they didn't deserve all that Laszlo had brought down on them. They were good people, a dying species on the Arm. *Tunk, I guess I don't need any more reason than that.*

Gus pulled her hood up and activated the HUD as the lift reached the top of the tower.

Here we go.

A cheerful *ding* announced Gus's arrival, and the doors slid open with a barely audible sigh. Laszlo stood alone with his hands at his sides. No combat-rob entourage or CCO strike team. He even appeared to be unarmed. Gus stepped off the lift, rested her hand on Delilah's butt, and glanced around the room.

"Feeling awful trusting tonight, aren't we?" she asked once her HUD confirmed they were alone.

"Not really. My personal shield is still active. And my security team is just through there," he said and nodded toward a dark hallway.

"Alright," Gus said. "Let's get this over with. What's this deal of yours?"

"First things first." Laszlo's eyes narrowed. "I know Junior and Aaron are dead."

Gus's jaw clenched. "Your boys got what they deserved, Laz."

"Maybe so. Junior has always struggled with … overconfidence. There was always a chance he would pick a fight with the wrong person. As for Aaron," Laszlo shook his head in a mock display of regret, "I always knew that boy's prejudices would be his undoing. But what can a father do?" He shrugged like he'd only lost a hand of razz. "What I mean to say is, there's no hard feelings. I understand you were only doing what comes natural to one such as yourself."

"What's that supposed to mean?"

Laszlo smiled. That too-toothy snake smile. "You're a killer."

Gus's eyes narrowed beneath her hood. "What do you want, Laszlo?"

"I want you to work for me. Full-time."

"And why would I want to do that? You've done nothing but try to kill me all day."

Laszlo spread his arms. "And yet here you stand. Alive!" He stepped to the big picture window overlooking the town below. "I'm going to need someone to protect me from these backstabbing copperheads. *Clearly,* my family isn't up to the task. But you might be just the beamslinging bitch I need."

Gus joined him at the window and gazed down at the ruins of the town. "And what do I get in return for this job?"

"How about a suite here in my private quarters?"

Gus turned, taking in the finery sparkling and shining around them. Not exactly her aesthetic, but a girl could get used to it. She eyed him. "It's a start."

Laszlo's smile widened. "I can see to it you never want for anything. Spoons, ponies, rubidium … companions. Mackenzie even commented on your impressive skills. And your—how did she put it? Your 'void-weary beauty.'"

While Laszlo spoke, movement in the streets below caught Gus's attention. What remained of the Confederate forces were pulling back toward *Shenandoah*. Retreating? Why? "And the Vegas?" she asked.

Laszlo's face twisted into a grimace for the barest of moments. He exhaled sharply. "*Mr.* Vega may keep his worthless plot of sky, provided he and his family can stick with the program."

Despite everything, Laszlo's offer forced Gus to pause. This *could* be the best solution to all their problems. Laszlo was, above everything else, a businessman. As such, he would be willing to deal. If she played her cards right, a chance remained that she could save what remained of the town *and* still get everything she wanted out of the deal. The only obstacle? She couldn't trust Laszlo as far as she could throw him.

"What about Moe and the rest of the townsfolk? Or the Deiopeans you've got locked up on the refining levels?"

"My, my, my. When you first arrived in my dusty little town all you cared about was making your spoons and getting back to the Arm. Have these simpleminded folk got you so flummoxed that you're willing to turn your back on this opportunity? I'm offering you everything you've ever wanted. The only thing you've ever really cared about."

Gus lit another cigar and inhaled, deep. She held the smoke for a moment, relishing the burning in her lungs, and let it out through her nose like a raging bull. "And what's that?" she asked.

"Freedom."

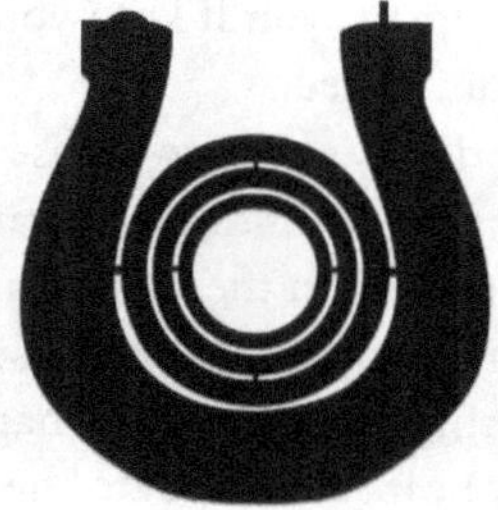

THE GOOD, THE ROB, AND THE GREEDY

Gus's lighter paused in the air, halfway to her pocket, still lit. The minute flame flickered, its light reflecting dozens of times around the gilded room.

"You can't deny it," Laszlo said. His words were muted and far away, as if underwater. He was offering her everything she had come to Las Ráfagas for, and more. Much more. Las Ráfagas could become something of a home for her. It had been a long time since anywhere other than her cramped cot and bedroll on *Tilly* had been home.

Of course, it would mean staying in the company of the Leconte family. A prospect she didn't exactly relish, especially given what she had done to Aaron and Junior. But a new mount? A place to hang her spurs? Protection from the CCO and UCET alike? And enough spoons and rubidium to keep her riding? *What more could I ask for? It could be worth it. Tunk, it's the deal of a lifetime. Ten lifetimes.*

All it would require was turning her back on Aurora's people, on Moe, and on everything the Vegas and their neighbors had fought—and died—for.

As Gus stared into the dancing flame, *Shenandoah* released its hitching cables and floated up above the town. It ignored the driving wind and rain that continued to buffet the atmosphere around Las Ráfagas and rose high into the clouds. With a flick of her wrist, Gus snapped the lighter shut and studied its scuffed surface.

"What assurances do I have you'll keep your end?" she asked. She kept her voice flat, uncommitted.

"None," Laszlo said darkly. "But to refuse would be unwise. You see, if I don't tell the copperheads that the marshal has agreed to help us control the population within the next minute or so, they'll fire on the dome. I'd rather that not happen, of course. Rebuilding would be a difficult, time-consuming task. But I'll be happy to bill the CCO for the expenses. Maybe we can even update the old place. Add a little more *class*. What do you think?"

Gus took another long drag from her cigar and locked eyes with Laszlo through the blue-gray haze.

"You know, you're right. When I first got here, I only wanted to leave. Staying in one spot has never appealed to me. The Arm is a harsh place, and I've always thought sitting still for too long would be what did me in. The only things that have mattered in my life were the things that kept me riding, kept me free. Everything else has always been bottle-farts. Family. Friends. None of it mattered. Before I got here, I would have said that nothing but a pile of spoons would keep me still for long." She paused to blow a cloud of smoke into Laszlo's face. "I might have taken this deal then. But things are different now. I can't rightly say how or why, but I know it in my bones. When it comes my time to fall, I want it to be a fight of my choosing, not my past coming to claim me.

"I guess what I'm saying is, Laz, I'll die before I help you kill this town and its people."

Laszlo waved his hand to clear the air. "Pity." He pulled a handheld comms unit from his suit pocket and started to bring it to his lips.

Gus seized her chance, disregarding Gloria's plea.

Her hand blurred as it dropped to Delilah. She fired from the hip, and prayed the point-blank range would be enough to overcome Laszlo's shields.

It was not.

The pink beam splashed harmlessly off the energy shield, startling Laszlo. With a shriek, he dropped the comms unit and took a shocked step backwards. A tiny voice buzzed from the unit on the floor, "Please repeat. Administrator Leconte, do we have permission to fire?"

Vaguely aware she was exposing her back to Laszlo, Gus dove for the comms. *If he does have a gun, after all* ... But as she reached the handset, instead of the searing burn of a laser beam, Laszlo pummeled her with his leather Oxfords. She rolled away from the kicks and regained her footing at the same moment seven of Laszlo's combat-robs ambled into the room.

Gus dove again, this time for cover. She barely managed to overturn a heavy table—and send expensive baubles flying—before fresh laser fire washed over the gold-encrusted room.

"Administrator Leconte?" the small voice from the handset called. Gus laid the unit on the floor and smashed it with Delilah's butt end.

The laser fire ceased. Laszlo broke the new silence. "You may as well give that back, girl. If they don't hear my voice in, oh, about thirty seconds, they'll fire anyway."

Tunk.

"Make it easy on yourself and surrender. In deference to your deter-mination and loyalty to your friends, I'll make sure your execution is qui—What the *rut?*"

Gus chanced a peek. Las Ráfagas's administrator had completely turned his attention to the picture window, where a familiar blue-green shimmer burst from the roiling storm clouds beneath the town. An enormous flock of burdles, unlike any group of beasts Gus had seen in all her drifting, rose from the storm. There must have been tens of thousands moving as one. They were driven by an armada of Deiopean skiffs.

The flock rose from beneath *Shenandoah* and parted around the huge pulse-rail train. The burdles surrounded it as they flowed over it like an hourglass running in reverse. Still more poured out of the gyrating storm. Each flash of lightning lit their glittering scales like jewels in the night sky.

Gus hoped the Deiopeans had more up their sleeves than a stampede. Despite the size of each individual burdle, they posed no threat to the battle-train.

But whatever doubt remained in Gus's mind evaporated when a low rumbling began. It started in the floor plating as a vibration, and rose quickly to a deep, guttural roar that shook every surface around her. Within seconds, it was loud enough to rattle Gus's teeth.

The Stormrider had come.

The leviathan burst forth from the tumbling cloud layer below. From her vantage point high above the town and the mining facility, the beast's vast wingspan dwarfed Las Ráfagas. It did indeed call to mind the great manta rays of Earth, as Junior had suggested, but that hardly did the creature justice. With unimaginable speed for something of its unprecedented size, it rose through the storm and collided with *Shenandoah*. It gripped the battle-train in its jaws like a puppy with a new toy. Explosions tore through the train's metal hide, and within seconds, mighty *Shenandoah* was nothing more than burning wreckage falling away from the still rising behemoth.

Laszlo slammed his fists against the glass and bellowed inarticulately at the beast and the broken battle-train. While he was distracted, Gus tossed her lighter toward the combat-robs. The fiery pain in her shoulder flared, but she aimed Delilah and fired. The pink beam smacked into the tumbling lighter in front of the robs and exploded into a fireball. The small blast knocked two over and temporarily overloaded the remainder's optical sensors. Gus bolted for the lift.

She stepped into the center of the lift and paused. She couldn't risk taking the elevator itself—Laszlo could stop it and bring her back up. Or worse. Desperate, Gus aimed Delilah at the floor. She pulled the trigger and spun in a tight circle, dragging the beam around her and filling the lift with a cold cloud of exhaust.

She stomped her boot down on the circle she'd cut in the floor, but it refused to give way. A shot sliced through the fog, missing her head by inches.

She slammed her heel down on the floor again.

Once.

Twice.

Nothing.

More beams sizzled through the air.

"Tunk!" she screamed and brought her heel down again, focusing everything she had left into the strike. The floor gave way like the lid of a tin can, and Gus plunged into the dark, yawning elevator shaft.

The first couple of dozen feet of the fall were rough. Gus bounced back and forth off the black walls before her boot thrusters fired. They slowed her fall, but she still hit the bottom of the shaft with a *crash*. Coughing and wiping grime from her face, she pried open the ground floor doors and fell into the town square.

To her surprise, she found it bathed in celebration. What remained of the townsfolk watched the destruction of *Shenandoah*, and thought the fight won. The survivors danced in the streets and fired triumphant shots into the air as the Stormrider glided past the dome.

Gus hacked and spat. She tried to yell, "It's not over!" but her throat clamped down and she choked on another cough instead. From her knees, and doubled over in another coughing fit, she pointed frantically at the blinking light over the second set of lift doors. Laszlo and his combat-robs were coming.

Moe and Oscar appeared at her sides and pulled her to her feet. Each wore a victorious smile on their face.

She sputtered and tried to clear the dust from her throat. "*No, we've got—*" she started but doubled over in a hacking fit instead. Oscar laughed and clapped her on the back. Bernadette, with Hector at her side, joined them. Unlike her husband and farmhand, she wore a more reserved smile, and her eyes moved nervously around the rejoicing townsfolk.

Gus dragged a deep breath into her lungs, gave one hard cough, and finally cleared her lungs and throat. "Get everybody off the street! *Now!*"

"What?" Moe and Oscar said in unison. Their eyes met over Gus's shoulders with matching confused expressions.

Bernadette pointed to the blinking light above the lift doors. "Hector, get in the Marshal's Office!" she bellowed.

At first, Hector didn't move. His eyes were fixated on his mother in youthful defiance. He opened his mouth but shut it again when his mother's face darkened with fear and fury.

No sooner had Hector run for the jailhouse than Bernadette turned her furious authority on the rest of the town square. She roared instructions and drove as many people as possible back into cover before the lift could reach the esplanade.

The light above the lift doors stopped blinking and turned bright green. The doors slid open, and a wall of laser fire exploded from the lift. The survivors' cheers changed to screams as they fled back into the ruined buildings. Separated from Gus, Oscar, and Moe, Bernadette ducked into the mercantile with a group of stragglers.

"Bernadette!" Oscar shouted and tried to run across the square to her. Gus grabbed him by the back of his shirt and dragged him into what remained of Daniel's med-lab and apothecary.

Gus cursed as all seven of Laszlo's towering combat-robs stepped from the lift. She'd expected to destroy at least one of them with the explosion from her lighter. No such luck. Laszlo followed them into the square, his face ugly and orange with fury. "Where are you, you little bitch?" he thundered. "I'll kill you for this!"

"Where's Aurora?" Gus asked once they took cover behind rows of herbs and drugs.

"They set off for the mining level when *Shenandoah* went down. We told them to wait for you. That there could still be copperheads or bulls down there, but Aurora insisted," Moe said.

Gus's mind raced. She had to get Laszlo away from the townsfolk. The man had lost his rutting mind. He stood in the center of the square, surrounded by his combat-robs, screaming incoherently at the storm above while the robs fired indiscriminately into the buildings.

But maybe she could kill two birdles with one skiff.

Gus stood and made for the door, but a hand reached out and grabbed her wrist. Gloria hid behind a barrel of some sort of fragrant spice. "You can't kill him," she said again with wide, glassy eyes.

"Oh, yes, I can," Gus said, then called over her shoulder, "Stay here until I draw him away from the square. Then get everybody the *tunk* out of this godforsaken town." Without waiting for a reply, she bolted for the doorway and drew Delilah as she stepped into the open.

She squeezed off a shot at one of the damaged combat-robs and took it out before Laszlo spotted her. "I'm right here, you foppish, yellow-bellied gas-huffer," she called.

Laszlo's face turned from orange to purple as he screamed incoherently.

"You want me? You'll have to come and get me." She fired twice more, directly at Laszlo. His shield easily absorbed both beams, but it offered her the opportunity to take off down the alley between the apothecary and the Administration Tower.

Gus raced along the apothecary's outer wall with her head craned back over her shoulder. She needed the head start but also needed Laszlo to follow. She'd only made it to the rear corner of the ruined building when she crashed into Moe.

"What are you doing?" she screamed at the hapless rob as they tried to untangle themselves.

"You can't kill him!"

"Why the hell not?" Gus ducked as a crimson beam struck the alley wall over their heads. She yanked Moe to his feet and the two raced into Las Ráfagas's ruined residential quarter with Laszlo and his combat-robs hot on their heels.

"Where are we going?" Moe shouted.

"Away from the square," she said.

Moe shot her a confused glance.

She shrugged. "Hey, it's all I got so far."

They ran through the remnants of houses and took cover where they could as Gus led them deeper into the debris of homes. When they got closer to what remained of Genie-town, she directed Moe to take cover behind an old building that had crumpled like a paper lantern.

"Alright, spill it. Why can't we kill Laszlo?" She chanced a peek back and ducked quickly when a beam sizzled through the air. She could hear Laszlo's unintelligible yelling as the combat-robs picked their way through the rubble. "Better make it quick."

Moe's face puckered. "Gus says—*Tunk!* Not Gus, Gus—Rutting *tunk!*"

"Gloria?"

"Yes!" He nodded emphatically. "She says the combat-robs are on a dead man's switch. If you kill him before shutting it off, they'll go berserk and blow their power cores. One's enough to scuttle the outpost."

"Where is this dead man's switch? Can we get it off him?"

"She said he forced"—his face twisted—"her husband to build it and"—another grimace —"the medic to implant it. It's connected to his heart. Like a rutting pacemaker. *We can't shut it off.*" A flash flew across Gus's mind: Laszlo's half-naked body, and a faint but distinctive scar running over his heart. *Tunk.* It meant they would have to pick the robs off one at a time and leave Laszlo for last. Not an easy hand to play. They'd need an ace in the hole.

They'd need Aurora.

Another beam flew over their heads leaving a crater in the wall. Laszlo was closing in.

"Six of them against the two of us ain't gonna cut it. You go find Aurora. They'll be on the refining level." She pointed to the mining lift maintenance access hatch in the middle of the road some fifty yards away. Very little cover stood between it and them. "I'll keep Laz occupied."

"You can't take them all on alone."

She smiled at him. "I'm *not* alone, Moe. I've got you and Aurora. I can manage a simple game of hide and seek until you two get back." She thought of Hector climbing through El Dorado's anti-grav foundation and smiled.

Moe nodded reluctantly. Gus turned away and prepped to give him some covering fire, but the rob stopped her and held out his hand. "One more thing," he said and dropped a fresh comms earpiece into her hand.

As she took in that cracked face with its kind, smiling eyes, it struck Gus how odd a pair they made. An escaped cobbler-rob turned farmhand at the ass end of the Arm, guilty of murdering his owner. And the sorry excuse for a beamslinging void-drifter hoping to cash in on his bounty. Now Marshal and faithful Deputy—and potentially Las Ráfagas's last hope of survival. She took the earpiece, shook Moe's hand, and hoped it would not be the last time.

"Ready?" Gus asked. She held Delilah high. Moe's eyes focused on the access hatch. He gripped his stolen sidearm and nodded. "Good luck," she said.

"You, too."

Gus stood and fired three times at the advancing combat-robs and Moe made a break for the hatch like a gazelle. Those long, gangly legs moved like pistons and carried him across the distance with extraordinary speed and grace. Gus threw a few more beams Laszlo's way to keep him and his entourage distracted, and Moe disappeared down the hatch in a flash.

Despite her covering fire, Laszlo caught on. "Where's your murdering rob friend off to, I wonder?" he called to her. "Oh, I know. You've sent him off to free your little spider friends. No matter, I'll get to them soon enough!"

Gus fired. It bounced off Laszlo's shield harmlessly but startled him again. A fresh barrage from the robs forced her back to cover. "You won't get away with this Laszlo!" she shouted over the rain of fire.

"How cliché! And who's going to stop me? *You?*" He laughed manically. "You foolish little girl. Do you think this is the first time I've done this? Once I'm done with you, I'm going to wipe out all your friends, and then those rutting spiders, too. I'll take what I need and exterminate the lot of 'em. I'll be doing the Arm a favor! One less planet full of primitive parasites."

The wrecked wall behind Gus began to disintegrate under the repeated salvoes. She rolled away as it crumbled to dust and, screaming at the top of her lungs, fired twice more from her knees. Both beams struck the lead rob square in the chest and knocked it off balance, but neither penetrated its breastplate armor.

Again, she scrambled for cover behind a pile of debris. She peered around a shattered crib, a once-colorful dresser, and the remnants of a wall painted with clowns and balloons—the ruins of a small child's room. Her eyes narrowed into a scowl. *So many lives ruined.*

Gus loaded a fresh coolant cap into Delilah and checked herself for wounds. In the heat of the firefight, she hadn't noticed she'd been hit—more than once. She bled from a handful of grazes, but the through-and-through on her left thigh concerned her. She was pretty sure it had missed the femoral artery, but it bled like a stuck pig. She had barely enough time to pull a dirty rag from the debris and tie a crude bandage before the laser fire stopped and Laszlo's voice again drifted to her across the flattened neighborhood.

"So, you *do* have a soft spot for the spiders. Junior was right after all." Gus heard the smile in his voice. "You know, I've had a tremendous idea. Why kill you now? It would be so much better to let you watch as I raze this pathetic little town, and everyone in it, to the clouds first. Maybe *then* you'll see you should have taken my deal. You two," Laszlo said to his robs, "get back to the square and see to our dear townsfolk. The rest of you, to the mining lift. We're going below. What will you do, *'Marshal?'* Will you save your new 'family,' or will you protect the innocent little natives?" Laszlo's voice dripped with sarcasm as he and the remaining four combat-robs moved toward the lift.

Gus pressed her back against the clown-printed chunk of wall and squeezed her eyes tight. She didn't know *what* to do. If she ran for the square, she could kill the combat-robs before they did too much damage. But she'd never make it back to the mining levels in time. It would be a slaughter. But if she went to help Moe and Aurora, and something happened to the Vegas ...

To Hector. Or Oscar.

To Bernadette.

She tapped the earpiece. "Moe, I'm sorry. Laszlo's coming your way with murder and mayhem on his mind. He sent two robs back for the families in the square. Hold him off as long as you can! I'll get down there—"

An incoming transmission crackled in her ear and cut her off. "Don't you *dare* leave those people down there to die while you rescue us, Marshal!" Bernadette scolded. "This is our town, too, and we can defend her."

"But—"

"Marshal, you made a promise to Aurora and to those people down there. Ray would want you to keep it. We can handle Laszlo's goons. *Go.*"

Tunk. I don't like it, but she's right.

"Moe, Laszlo's coming for you. I'm right on his heels but keep an eye out. He wants blood. Moe?" The comms unit was quiet. "Moe! *Tunk!*" Gus gritted her teeth against the pain that rippled through her leg, combined with the ache in her calf, and ran up her side and into her left armpit where it mingled with the misery of her shoulder. She pushed through it and ran for the access hatch.

Gus slid to the bottom of the access hatch ladder, careful to land on her uninjured leg. The mining levels were dark, cold, and silent. "Moe? Can you hear me?" she whispered.

Static.

"Laszlo's coming, Moe. I hope you and Aurora are at the holding cells on the refining level, 'cause that's where I'm going. I'll try to head him off at the pass before he gets to you."

Still no response.

Dammit, Moe. Gus limped as quickly as she could through the labyrinth of tunnels and corridors. *You better not be dead.*

Gus tried to retrace her steps from before, praying she'd gotten ahead of Laszlo and his robs. The access hatch ladder was much faster than the lift, but this was Laszlo's outpost—he undoubtedly knew these corridors like the back of his hand. She came to a wide intersection she didn't recognize and stopped. *Tunk. I'm lost.* She stared down dark hallways, her body shaking from adrenaline, agony, and anxiety. *Which way?* As she picked a route at random, the crackle of laser fire echoed toward her from another direction. She hobbled toward the source and found herself on a high platform overlooking the refinery level.

The giant, twin vats of unrefined rubidium and the catwalk that passed between them sat below her. On one side, Laszlo stood, surrounded by his four remaining combat-robs and his twinkling shield. Through the pass and hiding among the machinery, Moe and Aurora cowered with three or four dozen Deiopeans. The flashing lights from the multitude of eyes dazzled Gus's own. Moe's sidearm and Aurora's Hammer were no match for the military-grade firepower raining down on them.

Laszlo pointed the robs toward the narrow pass between the gigantic vats. Two stepped forward toward the gap and the cowering natives. Their barrage never slowed. If Gus didn't do something, Moe and Aurora would be overrun in seconds. But Delilah only had three or four shots in her coolant cap, and Gus had only one full cap left.

Oh, well. At least I'll be going out with friends.

She brought her last cigar to her lips and bit down. Gus yanked on the rag-bandage tied around her thigh and grunted through the fresh jabs of pain as it tightened. *Now or never.* With Delilah in one hand and her last coolant cap in the other, she climbed over the platform's guardrail and leapt to the refining level catwalk below.

Gus discovered too late that her boot thrusters were empty, landing hard on her bad leg. The pain shot up her side like acid in her veins, searing into her armpit. She collapsed to the catwalk and dropped Delilah. The big gun bounced along the grated floor toward the vats, well out of reach.

"Ah. *There* you are, Marshal," Laszlo said. That snake-tooth smile spread across his Sol-tanned features. "Kill her."

Defenseless, Gus watched as the lead rob lowered the barrel of his laser rifle toward her.

A deafening *crack* filled the air, and a deep dent appeared in the rob's bucket-like head. It rocked back on its heels but stayed on its feet. Another *crack* rang out and the dent became a crater. The rob stumbled but caught itself. Finally, a familiar pink beam lit up the dim refining level. It punched through the crater and took the back of the big rob's head clean off.

The combat-rob tumbled backwards like a log. A stunned hush fell over the refining level. Gus turned to find Moe and Aurora in the gap between the raw rubidium vats; Aurora with their complicated rifle held high, Moe clutching Delilah in his sophisticated hands.

For the briefest of moments that stretched on for an eternity, Gus stared up at them—her friends. Not marks. Not partners who'd just as soon stab her in the back. Actual friends.

The moment collapsed under Laszlo's scream. *"I said kill—"* Another *crack* shattered the air, whipping his head back as though he'd been slapped. A cut appeared, like magic, across his temple. Laszlo brought his hand to his head. His rage bubbled at the sight of his red fingertips. *"Kill them all!"*

Gus scrambled against the searing pain that engulfed the entire left side of her body and scooted backwards on her ass toward her friends. Aurora and Moe stood their ground in the pass and fired slugs and beams into the approaching robs, but their advance would not stop. At nearly the same moment Gus reached the gap, Aurora was hit. The Deiopean's eyes flashed in surprise and pain as The Hammer, along with a pair of Aurora's arachnid-like arms, fell to the catwalk. Gus grabbed the rifle and dragged herself to her feet. Moe grabbed Aurora by the back of their robe, and the trio dropped back through the pass and into cover behind the vats.

Gus pressed her back against one vat and looked across the catwalk to Moe. Aurora sat at his feet. The hunter's eyes flashed dimly, but Gus didn't understand. "Where's your sidearm?" she yelled.

"It's out of caps. You got any?"

"Just one," Gus said. She turned her eyes to the refining level. Dozens of Deiopeans huddled there together, hiding where they could; their eyes threw ominous shadows in every direction.

"What do we do?" Moe's eyes pleaded with Gus to tell him she had a plan.

Gus studied the unfamiliar rifle in her hand. "Can you shoot this?"

"Normally, yes, but—"

"Can you, or can't you?"

"Not with the damage to my tool changer!" He held up his right arm. Try as he might, his hand wouldn't split as it did the day they'd all met.

Aurora's eyes flashed weakly from Moe's feet. Moe's face flashed in return.

The robs continued to fire and advance.

"What is it?" Gus shouted.

Moe stooped, and Aurora climbed up into the crook of his right arm, clinging to his metal body with their third arm—the only one remaining on Aurora's left side. Together, the two of them had the proper number of limbs in the right places. Gus nodded. Now, they just needed an opening.

The stream of laser fire abruptly stopped, like someone turned off a faucet.

"What's going on, Laz?" Gus called out. "You ready to throw in the towel?"

"I thought I would give you one last chance, Marshal. Give yourselves up."

"And what? You'll let us live while you get fatter and richer off the backs of these people?" Low, nearly under her breath, she said to Moe, "The belt buckle." Moe took a moment to process, then smiled. He nodded. *Good.* As usual, they would get one shot.

Despite his rage, Laszlo chuckled. "Oh, no. I'm not letting anybody leave this town alive. I told you, this isn't my first rodeo. And now that I know how the spiders' tech works, all I need to start somewhere else is enough of 'em to breed my own.

"No. I was going to say, give yourselves up, and maybe I won't have a little fun with Bernadette Vega and that snot-nosed brat of hers before I burn this place to its foundations," he snarled.

"Now!" Gus roared. She tossed The Hammer across the gap between vats. Moe, in turn, tossed Delilah across to her. As the weapons passed each other, Moe's long left hand divided between his middle fingers. The mechanics in his forearms split apart from hand to elbow and he caught the rifle in his two left hands. He brought the stock to Aurora's right shoulder, spun into the gap, and crouched into a firing position. At the same time, Gus caught Delilah, slapped her last cap into place, and stepped into the pass behind the farmhand and the hunter.

As Moe held The Hammer steady, Aurora aimed and fired.

Boom!

The sound echoed across the refining level. Like lightning in reverse, Delilah's pink flash followed on the heels of the slug's thunderclap.

Sparks flew from Laszlo's belt buckle. Aurora's slug proved slow enough to pass through Laszlo's shield and had smashed into the buckle's shield control mechanism. Laszlo fell to his knees and gurgled wordlessly. He patted his chest, then stared quizzically at the red dripping from his hands. A gaping hole had appeared where his heart should have been. Gus's aim had also been true, and with his shields down, her beam vaporized his chest—and the dead man's switch along with it. The combat-robs, no longer receiving a signal, snapped to attention with their rifles slung up over one shoulder.

Laszlo's face contorted grotesquely. "You can't ... I can't ... I'm too ..." He staggered toward them, each step less sturdy than the last. He stumbled the final few feet and collapsed to his knees. Laszlo stared at Gus with eyes sunken into a gray, drooping face. His chest heaved as he tried to draw air into his perforated lungs. The crater in his chest wheezed and bubbled with every gasp. He reached out, grasping for Gus with scarlet fingers. "You worthless, little ..."

He fell face-first to the catwalk grating before he could finish his final thought.

Gus lit her final cigar, still clenched between her teeth, and knelt next to Laszlo's body. She took a long drag, held it, then blew it out over the corpse.

"I rutting hate bullies."

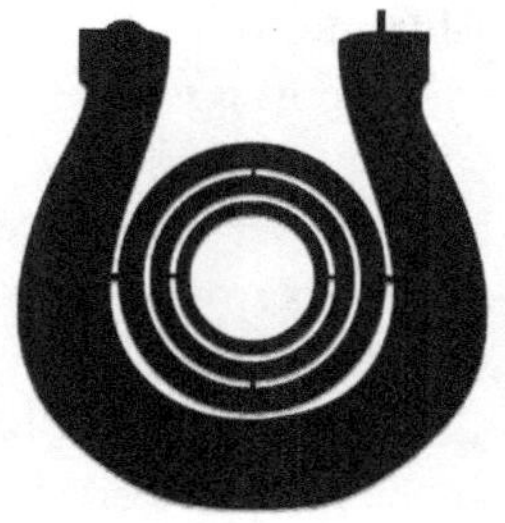

STARS OVER AEOLUS

Nearly a month had passed since what the townsfolk called the "Battle of Las Ráfagas," and word around town was the UCET 7th Army would be arriving that very day. The general attitude seemed to be "better late than never," but Gus thought most of the remaining population would be happy to see the supply wagons drop through Aeolus's atmosphere.

After the initial shock of the fighting wore off, the last few weeks had been spent rebuilding Las Ráfagas and burying their dead among the shelves behind Santa Barbara. All, that is, except for Laszlo and his sons, whose bodies were jettisoned into the void. Of Mackenzie Leconte, they found no sign. With several of the Company Bull ponies missing, it was assumed she fled. Gus had a feeling Las Ráfagas would see her again.

The Deiopeans had been more than generous and offered aid in the form of medics, laborers, and nearly all the resources needed to rebuild. Gus stayed, both because she now felt a connection to these people, and because she had no means to go. With *Tilly* lost to the gas giant, Gus was stuck. But now, with Las Ráfagas rising from the grave and the 7th Army on its way—likely with a warrant for her arrest—she itched to get back to the void.

Gus stepped from the bright, sunny day into the comfortably dim environment of the freshly reconstructed Cirrus House. The gaming tables stood empty, but come nightfall, the floor would be crowded with the remaining townsfolk, eager to continue celebrating their survival and victory. Not to mention reward their labor.

She slid onto a makeshift barstool fashioned from a shipping crate, and for the umpteenth time, pulled her tobacco tin from her pocket. Without thinking, the powerful habit guided her hands until she opened it and found it empty. The lingering aroma teased her.

Right. Dry.

As she sighed, a shadow fell over her. Walter stood behind the bar wearing a ribbon tie, sleeve garters around each of his many arms, and a bittersweet smile on his melted face. Since rebuilding, Walter had become the sole owner and proprietor of Cirrus Hotel, Bar, & Gambling House.

"What'll it be, Marshal?" he asked. He gazed lazily over Gus's shoulder toward the batwing doors.

"Pair of overalls, Walt," a gruff voice replied.

Gus swiveled on her crate. Ray sauntered into the casino and dusted off his big, stupid hat inside the swinging doors.

"What are you doing up?" Gus said with a chuckle. "Aurora'll have both our hides if I don't get you back to bed."

The old marshal smiled as he limped to the bar. "I'm free on doctor's orders. Somethin' about movin' around helping the circulation, or some such." Ray unbuttoned the top three buttons of his shirt and pulled it open to examine the Deiopean bandages on his chest.

"Ya know," he said, poking at the edges of the wound, "I haven't ever said this before, but I thought we were gonners when they turned that repeater on us. But Walt, 'ere,"—he smiled at the genie across the bar—"he saw it comin' and got me out o' the way. Of the damn beams, anyway." He winked at the bartender.

Gus squinted at the bandage. "Then what got you?"

"Splinters from a ruttin' rent-rob headboard! Can you believe it?"

"Splinters!" Walter scoffed. "They were as long as your arm!"

Ray chuckled. "True enough. But thanks to Aurora's administrations, I think I'll be right as rain in no time." He sat down on a crate barstool next to Gus and Walter poured their whiskey.

"Still," Gus said and gave the old man a smirk, "I doubt drinkin's part of your recovery routine."

"Well." Ray tossed the whiskey back in one gulp. "I've recently learned sometimes you gotta do what feels *right.*"

Gus snorted and drank her own.

A smallish rob, with dozens of arms—just like Walter—a spherical central brain box stamped with the LCR logo and six little blue lights that stood in for a face, zipped out of the counting room. It ran laps around the razz tables and giggled playfully. Walter's eyes followed the little rob around the room and a melancholic smile played across his features.

"Who do we have here?" Ray asked with a broad grin under his bushy moustache.

Walter's smile widened to match the marshal's. "Augustine!" he called. "There's someone special here I want you to meet." Ray's eyebrows rose at the name as the child-rob zipped to the bar. "This is Marshal Gascon, he was a dear friend of your mother's."

"Well, hello, Augustine," Ray said, taking one of her hands in his. "It's very nice to meet you."

"Nice to meet you, too!" her voice was high and light, like her mother's. "Daddy, can I play out on the porch?"

Walter beamed down on her. "Sure, Auggie. But mind the workers. Stay out from underfoot."

"Yes, Daddy!" she cried, already on her way toward the batwing doors.

Ray's eyebrows climbed higher on his forehead as he twisted back to Gus. "Augustine?"

Gus twirled the last of the amber liquid in the bottom of her glass. "Hey, it wasn't my idea." She threw Walter a wry look.

"*There* you are. I've been looking all over town for the two of you," Moe said as he stepped into the cool casino. The star-shaped badge pinned to his cloth chest glinted in what little sunlight crept in through the shuttered windows.

"What is it, Deputy Maurice?" Ray asked good naturedly. He pointed to their empty glasses and Walter poured.

"It's the mayor. He wants to see us."

Gus, Ray, and Moe stood in silence as they rode the lift to the top of the Administration Tower.

Until I got to Las Ráfagas, Moe lived in anonymity. But now it's only a matter of time before another bounty hunter shows up to claim the price on his head. Worse still, as marshal, Ray's still obligated to help any that come calling. As for me, Tuco may be dead, but the UCET'll still want somebody to blame for that coach robbery back on San Juan-Paul Station. Not to mention the deaths of three UCET officers. The new mayor promised to smooth things over with the bluebells, but how much influence could Las Ráfagas have?

The lift *dinged* cheerfully, and the doors slid open with a *swoosh*. The room at the top had completely changed. Where once every surface was covered in gold and other useless symbols of wealth, a more egalitarian reception area now stood. The Sol-simulation lamps, along with Laszlo's med-pod, had been redistributed to the medical lab to help the injured and sick recover—including a certain daughter of the Stonewall family. Leconte family portraits and busts were gone and in the process of being replaced with framed photos of the town and its people.

"Anybody know why we're here?" Gus said as they stepped off the lift.

Before either of her companions could respond, however, the mayor appeared, limping into the room.

"Ah! There you are," Oscar said with a smile.

"Mayor," Ray said with a smirk and a tip of his hat.

"What's this all about?" Moe asked.

Ray turned his smile toward his deputies. "Me 'n the mayor here, we've been chattin' with UCS *Cairo*. They're the 7th Army's advance reconnaissance wagon—the rest of 'em will be arriving this afternoon. *Cairo's* been in orbit for a couple of days now. Seems they've got some news the two of you might find interesting."

"It appears that while we had our hands busy here, the president went and made some speech they're callin' the 'Liberation Declaration,'" Oscar continued.

"Meaning what?" Moe asked.

"The president set all the robs free, even those still in the CCO! And pardoned any that escaped! Your bounty's been voided! If your freedom was ever in doubt, it ain't any longer, *mi amigo!*" Oscar said.

Moe stopped dead still, like he had a processing error. Gus smiled and put her hand on his shoulder. "It's over. Nobody's gonna come looking for you now."

The rob's smile grew slowly as the truth dawned on him. But then it vanished in a flash. "What about Gus?"

"Well," Ray said. He took his hat off and fiddled with the brim. "In Gus's case, there's a lot to answer for."

Tunk. Still, no surprise there. Everyone had to pay for their actions, eventually. Laszlo taught her that.

"But," the marshal continued, "thanks to security feeds showing you had nothing to do with the coach robbery, and in light of the fact that those UCET officers took Tuco against orders and regulations for their own personal gain ... *and* since the bluebells want to sign a trade treaty with the Deiopeans—who are pretty big fans o' yours—to supply the Cygnus Trail waystations with their refined rubidium, they're willing to drop all the charges and wipe your record clean."

The room fell silent as her friends watched her. Her eyebrows knitted as she processed the news. *Wiped clean.*

"*What?*"

Oscar and Ray beamed matching smiles, and the marshal clapped her on the shoulder. "That's right. Yer a free woman."

"I—" she stammered, her eyes shifting from Ray to Oscar and back again. "Thank you."

"It's the least we could do," Oscar replied.

Moe grinned. "It really is over."

"Not quite," Oscar said, and beckoned them to follow him back onto the lift.

The trip down was as silent as the ride up had been. The new mayor rubbed his calloused hands together and grinned enthusiastically. When they reached the esplanade, the lift doors opened on the town square; all of Las Ráfagas's survivors had gathered in a rough circle. Walter and Augustine, the Mwangis, Mrs. Wagner and her son. More she had only met in passing. There were too few of them left, yet here they all were, together.

When she stepped off the lift, the small crowd burst into spontaneous applause which rose to a cheer before the circle collapsed in on them. Gus was surrounded by a multitude of hands, all trying to shake hers or pat her on the back.

"What's going on? What is all this?" Gus asked.

Hector and Bernadette materialized from the throng. "We know staying here for this long has been difficult for you," Bernadette said. "And we wanted to say thank you one last time." She leaned in and kissed Gus on the cheek.

"What do you mean, 'one last time?'"

Bernadette smiled as Oscar put his arm around her.

"Promise you'll come back and visit?" Hector asked with tears in his eyes.

"I don't—" Gus said. Her eyes darted from face to face, taking in the bittersweet happiness they each exuded. "I don't understand."

Aurora emerged from the crowd. The hunter's left arms were already growing back. Aurora's eyes flashed a complex pattern of colors, and the new translator clipped to their robe interpreted in a squawking electronic voice. "After the Stormrider passed, my people found something in the lower atmosphere that may be of great interest. Come with me, please."

Gus, Ray, Moe, and the Vegas followed Aurora through the square, leaving the townsfolk behind. At the engineering corral, Gloria stood outside her new office, dressed in her late husband's singed leather apron. She smiled when the group approached and embraced Gus in a tight hug.

"Thank you," Gloria said hoarsely. "If you ever need anything, you know where to find me." Gus returned the hug. Her heart rate rose in anticipation. *It couldn't be. Could it?* Gloria released her, smiled again, and led the group deep into the shadows of the corral.

They came to a section of the corral temporarily taken over by debris salvaged from the wreckage of *Shenandoah* for Las Ráfagas's rebuilding efforts. Gus's heart sank. What could be so damn exciting among this wreckage?

"Boys?" Gloria called out into the dimly lit bay. "Now, if you please."

The bay's darkest corner lit up, revealing a large canvas tarp draped over a bulky, almost familiar shape. Two of Gloria's engineering team stood on opposite sides of the tarp and yanked a pair of ropes at her signal. The canvas slowly rippled to the floor, gaining speed until at last, it revealed the old, horseshoe-shaped mount.

Gus's heart leapt in her chest. *"Tilly!"* Tears threatened to spill from the corners of her eyes as she laid them on her oldest friend. *It's impossible.* She let her gaze slowly roll over every curve, every corner, every edge. Impossible or not, it was *Tilly.*

"How did you—? Where—?"

"We found her floating between atmospheric layers," Aurora replied. "That's an impressive vessel."

"You're damn right she is." Grinning from ear to ear, Gus grabbed Gloria in another bear hug. "Thank you."

"Even though the UCET agreed to drop all their charges, we figured you'd prefer to be gone before they got here," Oscar said.

"But we do hope that you'll think of Las Ráfagas as home. As family," Bernadette added.

Gus nodded. "I can't think of a better place to put my spurs up when the void gets too big."

"Does that mean you'll be back to visit?" Hector piped up.

"It does, little man."

"Hooray!" he cheered and hugged her.

Although Moe didn't have tear ducts, his simulated eyes overflowed all the same. He grabbed her in a pointy, mechanical hug. "Don't stay out there too long, ya hear?"

"I hear, partner," she said and wiped a tear from her own eye.

That left Ray. When the big man held out his hand, Gus put her deputy badge into it. His eyes widened at the sight of it.

"I told you," she said and chuckled, "I'm no lawman. Besides, you've got yourself one hell of a deputy there." Moe blushed. "Just let him bend a rule or two once in a while, alright?"

Ray shook his head and handed the six-pointed star back. "Keep it. You can think of it as a souvenir if you like, but as far as I and everyone else in this town are concerned, you'll always be a Las Ráfagas Marshal's Deputy."

Tilly's systems sprung to life the moment the drifter stepped aboard, and the pony greeted her with that same old nicker through the environmental systems.

I missed you, too, girl. It's good to be back.

She sat comfortably in the saddle and guided *Tilly* out of the corral with a final wave to the Vegas below. Within twenty minutes, they broke free of Aeolus's gravity and slid through the dark, past the brightly lit cities of Deiopea.

The Arm called, and she was eager to drift. She wasn't sure where she would go, but Holliday station seemed like a fine jumping off point. She keyed in the waystation's coordinates and prepared *Tilly* for an FTL sprint.

A small warning light lit up on her console. *"Calculations invalid due to incorrect mass estimates"* blinked on the screen.

What the tunk?

The drifter swung her leg over the saddle and stepped into the engine room. Everything looked normal and in its place. She continued to *Tilly's* rear and poked her head into the living quarters. What few possessions survived the atmo-fall were neatly arranged on the small room's shelves. Nothing was out of the ordinary. That left the cargo hold. She stepped into *Tilly's* small hold. Empty, as expected.

What the ...

The small flowerbed's familiar scent brought her attention to the only place left: her contraband hole. She wedged her fingers into the panel behind the flower bed and yanked. It held firm, but something hidden behind it glinted in the brief light. Her heart skipped a beat, then raced. She dug her fingers in deeper, braced a boot against the wall, and heaved. It gave way.

With the panel still in her hands, she tumbled back. Slowly, she set it down on the floor and peered into the wall. The space behind the panel that usually held her beehive, drugs, and other smuggle-worthy products, was filled with row upon row of gold bars.

The drifter laughed frantically and ripped panels off the cargo hold walls, revealing stacks of CCO gold behind each.

She found a single, small scrap of paper laid with care among the bars. In a fancy, looping script that could only have been written with Bernadette's hand, she read two simple words:

"Thank you."

Tilly's tri-axis engine gimbal unlocked and spun smoothly. The three tumbling rings built up speed until they were a blur. With a brilliant flash of pure white light, and the sweet, rolling laughter of the drifter, *Matilda* vanished into the interstellar void.

ACKNOWLEDGEMENTS

I would like to start by expressing my deepest gratitude and all my love to my wife, Jessamine, without whom none of this would exist. Thank you for not only putting your faith in this and in me, but listening tirelessly to every complaint, plot hole, and wild inspiration along the way.

Thank you, Heather, my book-dragon mother-in-law, who printed the manuscript out, put it in a 3-ring binder, and with her trusty pen, became my first real developmental editor.

Thank you to all my friends who encouraged me along the way as beta readers, sounding boards, and cheerleaders—Matt and Crystal, Sam, Roz and Curtis, Emily, and Gary. Congratulations, guys! Now you get to hear about every cockamamie story idea that pops into my head for the next several decades. Hope you're ready for what you signed up for!

Thanks to everyone at Alex Parker Publishing for taking a chance on this crazy, genre mashup debut novel. Thank you, Stephanie, for guiding me through this entire process as well as all your hard work on the developmental edits. And thank you, Julia, for helping me fine-tune the language and answering all my copy-editing questions.

Special thanks to Rafael Andres Pio and Saumya, who created the cover and maps, respectively. I never had the faintest idea what the cover should look like, but Rafael figured it out and I couldn't be happier. I *did* know what I wanted the maps to look like, and Saumya took that idea and made it not only real, but far better than I ever imagined.

And finally, thank you, reader. Thank you for picking up this novel. Thank you for giving a debut author your time. Thank you for making it this far.

I hope to see you back this way again.

ABOUT THE AUTHOR

E.S Raye is a dual citizen of the United States and Canada, he has a B.A. in Psychology from Carleton University, and a diploma in Creative Advertising from Seneca College. This study of human behavior helps him write complex characters with meaningful motivations. He writes horror and science fiction short stories, novels, and screenplays and is editor-in-chief of Perseid Prophecies: Weird Fiction, Science Fiction, Fantasy & Fact. E.S. lives in southern Ontario, Canada with his incredibly patient wife Jessie, the quintessential orange cat, a stubborn French bulldog, and a happy-go-lucky mutt from Greece. When he isn't writing, reading, or editing, he lets people shoot pucks at him for fun three nights a week.

https://esraye.com